THE SNARE OF THE HUNTER

When Irina crosses through the wire from Czechoslovakia into Austria, she leaves her recently divorced husband —a high-ranking officer in the political police—and looks forward to joining her father, a world-famous author who has found secret sanctuary somewhere in the West. But even as the first friends help her towards her unknown destination, death strikes, and suspicion becomes her regular companion: is she now bait to snare her father, or a pawn in a game for even higher stakes? Thus there begins a chase through the deceptively picturesque Austrian countryside, with its castles and inns, peaceful meadows, white church towers, bustling towns and winding mountain roads. For survival and escape, Irina relies on a small group of men and women—among them David Mennery, whom she once loved and who is now willing to risk his life to save hers. Gradually it dawns on them that at least one of their number must be a traitor. The menace of violence is constant and real, the pace of the hunt is relentless and the climax is a *tour de force* of tension and the unexpected.

Also by
HELEN MacINNES

★

ABOVE SUSPICION
ASSIGNMENT IN BRITTANY
NEITHER FIVE NOR THREE
I AND MY TRUE LOVE
PRAY FOR A BRAVE HEART
NORTH FROM ROME
DECISION AT DELPHI
THE VENETIAN AFFAIR
THE DOUBLE IMAGE
THE SALZBURG CONNECTION
MESSAGE FROM MALAGA

THE SNARE
OF THE HUNTER

*

HELEN MacINNES

THE
COMPANION BOOK CLUB
LONDON AND SYDNEY

THE COMPANION BOOK CLUB

The Club is not a library; all books are the
property of members. There is no entrance fee
or any payment beyond the low Club price of
each book. Details of membership will gladly
be sent on request.

Write to:
The Companion Book Club,
Odhams Books, Rushden, Northants.

Or, in Australia, write to:
The Companion Book Club,
C/- Hamlyn House Books, P.O. Box 252,
Dee Why, N.S.W. 2099

*Made and printed in Great Britain
for the Companion Book Club
by Odhams (Watford) Ltd.*
600871916
8.75/291

For Gilbert,
with the sweet memory
of my good fortune

For he shall deliver thee from the snare of the hunter.

PSALM 91:3
The Book of Common Prayer

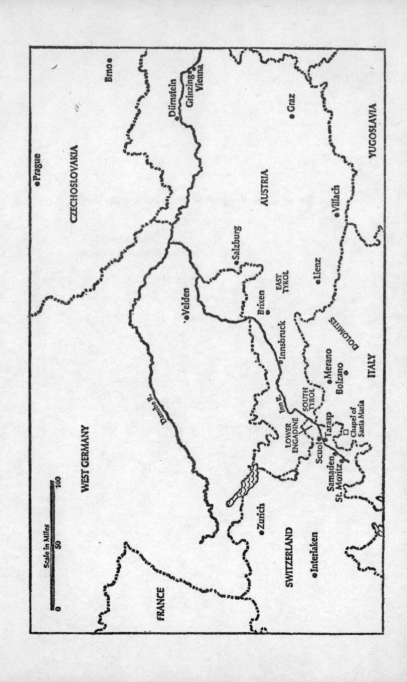

Chapter One

A FEELING OF LAZINESS, of a gentle slipping into sleep, spread over the fields as the July sun moved slowly downwards, deepening in colour, yet losing intensity. Here, at the edge of the trees, the cool shadows of late afternoon turned into evening cold.

Irina Kusak drew the cheap raincoat, dingy brown and as unobtrusive as her grey skirt and blouse, more tightly around her. The dark headscarf, which had hidden her fair hair all through the long day's journey south, was now loose over her shoulders. She pulled it closely around her neck, shivering not so much from the deepening shadows of the wood as from her mounting anxiety and fear as she stared down over the long naked slope of grass to the barbed-wire fence. The boundary. And across it, on the other side, in another country, was a stretch of quiet narrow road, sandwiched between the barbed wire of Czechoslovakia and the hills of Austria.

Josef, lying close to where she sat, propped on his elbows, his eyes watching now the road, now the wide slope of grass in front, now the trees protecting them, had felt her tension.

'Relax.' His voice was low, almost a hoarse whisper, but not unkind. He even gave her a smile of encouragement. An improvement, she thought, on his sullen silence all through their journey. 'Not so long now. Another forty minutes. Then we should see the car, a light-coloured Volkswagen, begin to drive along that road. They'll be coming from the west. The sun will have set, but it won't be completely dark. Don't worry. They'll see us, all right.'

'Anyone could see us.' She looked at the open field in front of them.

It was vulnerable, stripped bare, a bleak contrast to the rich farm lands and confusion of streams, paths and country roads

9

through which she had travelled. Here, all trees and undergrowth had been cleared right back to the edge of this high wood.

She wondered if her feet, tired and blistered after the three hours of rough walking which had brought her to the last stage of her journey, could move quickly enough to carry her down to the fence. The last stage? It was the beginning of another journey, another life. That was what made her fearful. The anxiety came from the field in front of her, stark and threatening, and the barbed-wire fence. It tore at her heart.

'Anyone could see us,' Josef agreed. At last he was becoming talkative, even friendly. 'That's why the patrols only come along every two hours. They were here at six. But before eight, just as dusk begins, the car will appear on the Austrian side. And if there are some farmers driving their carts along that road'—he pointed to it as a cart did trundle along, heavily piled with hay—'well, we don't have to worry about Austrians. They won't report us at the nearest police station.' He almost laughed. 'Strange, isn't it? My grandfather used to curse the Austrians for taking over the Czechs. My father cursed the Nazis. My brother and I curse the Russians.' Suddenly his voice was bitter. 'Is that all we can ever do? Curse the invaders? Form small patches of underground resistance?' He eased up, but still kept on talking in his hushed voice, as if he felt that words could bring her back to normal. 'My brother— do you remember him? Alois?'

She searched her memory. She was honest enough to shake her head.

'He wrote for the *Chronicle* before it was closed down. But I don't suppose your husband ever allowed you to see an underground newspaper.'

'I separated from my husband.' Her voice was as cold as her chilled legs. She rubbed them, and wished the lost warmth in her feelings could be as easily restored. 'He divorced me last month.'

'Too much of a handicap for him? Even the daughter of the great Jaromir Kusak, our internationally acclaimed cultural hero, was of no more use to him?'

'Please——' She bit her lip.

He was silent, but he didn't apologize. Didn't she know he was guiding her to safety because she was Kusak's daughter?

Not because she had once been the wife of Jiri Hrádek. She had seen through that son of a bitch eventually; perhaps had never known how important he was in the security police. She's had troubles enough, he decided. And once, long ago, she had been his friend. 'It has been many years,' he said, his voice losing its harsh edge. A bunch of students gathered round a café table in Prague, talking about music, whispering about politics and the Hungarian revolt, waiting—Well, we waited too long. 'I still remember you, though, as the prettiest girl in Prague. How old were you then?'

'Seventeen.' She kept stretching her legs and feet, her shoulders and back. She mustn't freeze up. She must be able to move, and move quickly.

'Fresh from the country, filled with enthusiasm. You had the merriest laugh, Irina. Yes, I used to remember it when I'd hear your name every now and again.'

She tried to laugh now, only managed an uncertain smile. 'Was that why you volunteered to get me safely into Austria?'

'Put it down to curiosity. I wondered whether you were still your father's daughter; or had your mother won in the end?'

'I never became a party member.' Her voice was scarcely audible.

'Well, I guess your mother was Communist enough for both you and your father. I must say——' But he didn't. Tactless, he warned himself, it would sound too much like gloating. Hedwiga Kusak, the devoted party member who had been jailed as a deviationist back in the early sixties by her own comrades. She had had a taste of what she had dished out to others. 'Politics really screws a family up, doesn't it? So now you are going to join your father. Why didn't you leave with him when the Russian tanks came in four years ago?' Yes, almost four years ago, he thought grimly: August 1968. Today was July 24 1972. Four years and the trials still going on.

There was a long silence.

'I had two children then.'

He swore to himself. He had forgotten the tragedy of the children. Too busy having his own personal triumph over Hedwiga Kusak. (She had destroyed his father's career, had him banned from teaching, lecturing, publishing.) 'I am sorry, Irina,' he said.

She touched his hand briefly. 'I think you are still my friend in

11

spite of what you heard about my name. Even now and again.' She managed a firmer smile this time. 'Today, you were so silent most of the journey. I began to think—ah, well——' She sighed, looked at the western sky. Clouds were streaked with gold, tinged with vermilion. Would she ever see another sunset from her own land? 'Thank you for bringing me safely here.'

'I was given the assignment. It's my job.' He was brusque, but pleased.

'You are good at it.'

He shrugged that off.

'Who gave you this assignment?' She was tense again. She could see the strong handsome face of the man who had once been her husband looking at her intently, speaking with sincerity. Jiri's words were as clear in her ear now as if he were doing the talking, and not Josef. *You'll be safe. I have arranged it. No trouble.* It could all have been a trick, another lie. Perhaps Josef and she were to be trapped at the border. Then Jiri could have her legally imprisoned, using that as the blackmail to bring her father back from exile. Yet Jiri's voice had been sincere. She could sense by this time when he was lying. And in any case, this was her only chance to leave. Until those last few weeks, she had been closely watched, constantly under surveillance. In the last month she had been freed from all that. It was part of the deal that Jiri had made with her.

'Sorry,' she told Josef. 'You were saying?'

'I was saying I couldn't tell you who gave me the assignment. The less you know, the safer for all of us. But you're in good hands once you get through the fence. Ludvik Meznik will be in the car along with my brother.' He glanced at her startled face. 'What's wrong?'

'Ludvik Meznik—is he one of your group?'

'I didn't know you had met him.'

'Only vaguely.' She nearly blurted out that she had seen him visiting Jiri: quiet visits. But that had been three years ago. And she told herself that Ludvik must have changed his politics—many were doing just that—or more likely, as a secret member of the resistance, he had been assigned to infiltrating Jiri's staff. She had lived too much with suspicions, she thought: they twisted her judgment. She could scarcely tell truth from untruth any more, or friend from enemy.

'Ludvik is all right,' Josef told her. 'He did some good work for us in Prague. He has brains and he has courage. Doesn't give a damn for danger.' He glanced at his watch. 'Almost time.' Dusk was beginning to dim the fields and hills. 'Enough light to see, not enough to be seen too clearly.' From one deep pocket inside his scruffy leather jacket he took out a pair of wire cutters, small but strong. From another pocket came heavy rubber gloves. He was wearing thickly soled shoes, again of rubber. He noticed her curious glance. 'Cautious, that's me. They may have some current turned on along that fence. I'll go first. You count off ten seconds, then follow. But don't touch any wire. I'll see you through. Then I run like hell, just in case we've set off an alarm. The nearest border crossing is well guarded, but it is six kilometres to the east.'

'They could have searchlights mounted in jeeps,' she said as she rose.

She pulled her scarf over her head, fastened it tightly around her chin. Barbed wire, she warned herself, and repressed a shudder. She picked up the canvas bag which had lain against the tree that had sheltered them.

'It won't be dark enough for searchlights to be really effective.' Not altogether true, but he wanted to reassure her. She would have no need for extra worries in the next five minutes. 'Besides, they'd have to bump along six kilometres of rough grass. The road is on the Austrian side, remember?' He smiled widely, a gaunt-faced man of thirty-three with sharp brown eyes that now softened as he studied her face. 'You're all right, too, Irina. Now, are we ready?' He pointed down towards the small ribbon of road.

The Volkswagen had just come into view, travelling slowly without lights.

'Don't come back this way, Josef,' she said quickly. 'Don't even collect your motor cycle where you left it. Go in another direction altogether.' She was thinking of Jiri.

He paused for one brief moment, stared at her in surprise. 'Don't worry, Irina. I'm an old hand at this game.' He shouldered her bag and left, running swiftly. She made sure that the knot on her scarf was tight, ended a spaced count of ten, and stepped out of the trees. She raced after him, stumbled twice on the rough ground, but kept on running. He had reached the fence before she was halfway there, had started

13

cutting the wire expertly. The car was still some distance off. Thank God, she was thinking as she reached the cruel tangle of barbs, thank God Jiri had kept his promise: no patrols crashing out from the shelter of the trees behind her, no sudden burst of machine-gun fire raking the field, no searchlights. There was just the grey veil of dusk falling more thickly over the wooded hills, shrouding colours, deepening the silence. She knelt down, touched the earth with her hand outstretched.

'Now!' Josef told her. He had dropped the wire cutters. He anchored the lower strands with his feet at one side of the gash he had made. The middle strands were forced aside, held with an effort.

She crouched low, kept her arms close to her body, passed safely through with only one small rip on the sleeve of her raincoat.

'Step clear,' he warned her as she turned to look at him. He stepped back himself as he let the wires go. He picked up her bag, tossed it high over the fence towards her. She couldn't speak.

She stood there looking at him.

Behind her, the car had stopped. A man jumped out, came running over the narrow strip of grass that separated the road from the boundary fence. He grasped her arm—it was Ludvik Meznik—and swung her round towards the car. 'Get in!' he told her as he pushed past her to reach the fence. 'Okay, Josef? No alarms?'

'All okay.' Josef was picking up the wire cutters, stowing them into his pocket.

And at that moment there was a shot. One bullet only, neatly cracking the deep silence, sending a swarm of ravens out from the treetops. Their hoarse cries echoed across the shallow valley.

Irina, almost at the car, turned swiftly. At first she could only see Ludvik's thickset body backing away from the fence. 'Get in, get in!' he yelled at her, catching her arm. 'They'll shoot us all!'

She pulled herself free, stood looking at the cut fence. Josef was lying quite still. She started forward. Ludvik took a firmer hold on her arm, dragged her back to the car. The driver had left it. Ludvik caught hold of him too.

'Get in, you damned fools,' he said. 'We can't help him. He's

14

dead. Get in, damn you, or they'll get us all.' He thrust them ahead of him.

'We can't leave him there,' Irina was screaming.

'He's my brother——' Alois shouted.

Then all protest, all argument was over as a searchlight beamed across the sky and the distant sound of a powerful engine came closer, closer.

'I'll drive,' Ludvik said.

He drove furiously over the cart-tracks and bumps, grim-faced, silent.

Alois said nothing at all. He was still in shock.

Irina was weeping. When she had enough control over her voice, she said, 'But where did the shot come from?'

Ludvik was intent on the road they had entered, a broader road, well marked. He had turned on the car lights, kept a saner pace through a straggle of traffic. 'We've just turned south from the border crossing. See the guardhouse back there? Symbolic last view of Czechoslovakia, Irina. Look well!'

She didn't turn her head to look. She repeated her question. 'Where did the shot——'

'From the wood, I thought.'

'No, no. We were hiding there. Josef had scouted it. He said it was safe.'

'Then from the trees farther east. That's where those damn birds were nesting.'

She shook her head, unconvinced. 'But the light was so poor. How could anyone shoot——'

'They've got all the gadgets, infra-red tricks. Don't ask me. I'm not a small-arms expert. Or perhaps it was just a lucky shot from one of their special snipers. There was no wind, not even a breeze tonight. That's what they like: no variables. A lucky shot, though. The first one came nowhere close.'

'Two? I only heard one.'

'The first that missed both of us. And just as Josef turned to run, and the birds loosed all hell on us, the second shot came. That's when he fell.'

Yes, Irina could agree, she had heard nothing above the wild clamour of the ravens. She fell silent. Beside her, Alois was sitting stiffly, his hands clenched, his eyes closed.

Ludvik told her, 'We are on Highway 2. We'll have you safe in Vienna in a couple of hours.'

15

Safe. She thought of Josef's still body. She began to weep again, but this time quietly.

Ludvik's voice was angry. 'Someone had to keep his head tonight. And what could we have done, anyway?'

Then they were all silent.

Chapter Two

DAVID MENNERY kept trying to concentrate on his desk. There was plenty of work to finish there before he drove back to New York tomorrow morning. This weekend he had written a fairly good article, in spite of distractions from the weather (Saturday and Sunday had been perfect for swimming and lazing), but it needed editing, tightening up. As always, before writing a piece, he'd spent days worrying that he hadn't enough material; and then, once he started, he would find he had far too much. So he re-read his typescript with a hard critical eye, began sharpening a batch of pencils, and made an effort to ignore the rhythms of the Atlantic breaking over firm white sand, or the afternoon sun baking down on the high dunes outside the beach cottage.

Its windows, recessed under the roof's deep overhang, were opened wide, shutters folded back, letting the south-west breeze play through the free arrangement of rooms. (But not near this alcove, where loose papers and notes and concert programmes were scattered around to suit his reach.) The lighting, from a plexiglass skylight overhead, was efficient and tilted towards the north. He was almost cool, even with the temperature on his front porch hovering around ninety-four degrees. No complaint there. Since Caroline and he had split up—four years ago, my God, could it be really four?—he had made sure his working conditions were good, simple but satisfying. Out had gone Caroline's tripping rugs, draperies, cushions piled on unsittable couches, baroque-framed mirrors and Venetian sconces, however charming; in had come bookshelves and stereo and hi-fi speakers, a few comfortable armchairs on a wooden floor, lamps to read with, and a telescope for the stars over the ocean. He could accomplish more here than he did in the city, even allowing for a morning round of golf or a walk along the beach, or an afternoon spent soaking in the sun, or a dinner in the evening with one of the charmers who spent their summers perfecting their tans: pretty girls bloomed as rampant as roses in this stretch of Long Island. Four years had slipped easily away.

The city, of course, was his necessity, his base of operations as a music critic for *The Recorder*, a monthly magazine with an appreciation of sound whether it was classical or contemporary, jazz or rock, lieder or country-and-western, opera or symphony. David Mennery was one of *The Recorder*'s permanent stable of writers, with a couple of pages of general criticism in each issue. In addition to that, he headed a specialized department of his own, which he had more or less invented by virtue of having written a book dealing with music festivals. He had combined two of his chief enthusiasms, travel and music, and discovered that thousands of Americans who loved music were also travel-prone. *A Place for Music* established him as a foot-loose critic with wide-ranging tastes. Just as importantly, it had provided for his travels as well as for such necessities as butcher's bills and house repairs. He had never quite fathomed how a book he had so much enjoyed writing should have earned him money and won him an opening into a steady career. The freelance criticism which he had done, previous to the book, was all right for the feast-or-famine years when he had been in his twenties and was still searching. Now, at thirty-nine, he knew what he could do and couldn't do; and at least he could feel he had a definite idea of where he was going. He would settle for that and count himself lucky. (He need not have been so modest. He wrote well, with a good critical bite. He had standards and wasn't afraid to judge by them. He knew a lot about music, about the composers, about the people who conducted or performed it. He belonged to no clique, followed no fashion. He was very much his own man.)

He had sharpened his last pencil, poured himself some cold beer, and could find no more excuses to postpone the compulsory, always painful, self-amputation. He began crossing out the unnecessary sentences, obliterating phrases, making rewrite notes in the margins. A passage he had somehow imagined last night to be tactfully diplomatic was a fuzzy mess to today's colder eye: a spiritual wallow in intellectual ooze. There was just no way to handle a modern composer gently when his jangle of sounds was basically thin and tedious. Just no way. The kindest criticism you could give such a man was to tell him to stop wandering down a path to nowhere, avoid the cute tricks, and get back on to a road which could lead him to something with real promise. Music was more than a collection of sounds.

He worked on, forgot about the sea and the sun outside, forgot about time. He rewrote the whole article, got it into proper shape at last, and began to type it out into good clean copy. He wanted it ready for delivery tomorrow before he took off for the Salzburg Festival. It was then that the telephone rang.

As he rose to answer it, he noticed the clock at the side of his desk and was startled to see that it was almost six. He picked up the receiver. Cocktail time, he was thinking, and the usual casual summer invitation. He was preparing a gentle refusal, but he never had to use it. The call was from New York.

At first he didn't recognize Mark Bohn's voice, simply because he hadn't expected it. Bohn was a journalist who now lived mostly in Washington, specialized in foreign affairs, travelled around. He was an old friend, but sporadic in his appearances: it must have been almost four years since he had last surfaced. And here was his voice, as quick and businesslike as ever, telling Dave he was one hell of a fellow to track down. Bohn had called David's apartment in New York several times, had eventually telephoned the superintendent and extracted—with difficulty—David's unlisted East Hampton number. 'And,' said Bohn reprovingly, 'I only got it out of him by telling him your brother had had an accident and I was the family physician.'

'Brother James won't be amused. What kind of accident?'

'Automobile accident. If he's anything like you, he's car-crazy, isn't he?'

Which was Bohn's way of saying that David enjoyed driving and Bohn did not. David said nothing. He was now past the surprise of hearing Bohn's voice. He began to speculate on the reason for the call: Bohn in New York, finding the heat and humidity as bad as Washington, thinking of borrowing a cottage beside a cool ocean for a few days.

Bohn was rattling on. 'I want to see you, Dave. Urgent. When are you coming to town?'

'Tomorrow around noon.'

19

'I'll drop in at the apartment. Twelve o'clock?'

'Not possible. I'll be clearing up some things at *The Recorder*.'

'Then after lunch. Two o'clock—or three?'

'Packing. I'm flying out early tomorrow evening. I'm heading for Salzburg.'

'I know. I know.' Bohn sounded sharp, as if he were worried or annoyed. 'You're going to the festival.'

'How did you know?'

'I read *The Recorder* and listen to your friends' chatter. But I thought the festival was in August?'

'It begins the last week of July. This Wednesday, I'll be at the opening night, seven o'clock sharp.'

'What's playing?'

'*The Marriage of Figaro*.'

'Couldn't you skip it? Hear it the next time round? You must have listened to it twenty times.'

'But not with Karajan and the Vienna Philharmonic.' David's voice was cool. Bohn was a highly knowledgeable man, but he was damned ignorant about some things. 'And I can't hear it next time round, because on that night I'll be listening to Geza Anda, just one of the top pianists in this whole wide world. What's more, you just don't switch tickets around at this date. I booked last January, like thousands of others. Sorry, Mark. Can't see you tomorrow. We'll have to wait until I get back at the end of August. I thought I'd fit in a quick visit to Bayreuth after a week in Salzburg, and then breeze on to Switzerland for Lucerne, and then to Scotland for Edinburgh.'

That silenced Bohn, or perhaps he was making other calculations. Or was he consulting with someone else? At last he said, 'Could you possibly cancel any engagement for fun and games tonight?'

'I've no engagements, except for some work to be finished.' David hoped the hint was strong enough. It wasn't.

'An hour will do us, not much more. Are you alone down there? No weekend guest helping you with the typing?'

'I'm alone.'

'Good.' There was another pause. (He *is* consulting with someone else, thought David.) 'I'll see you about eight o'clock.'

'You're driving a hundred and ten miles in two hours?' That wasn't Bohn's style. 'You know,' David added, 'there *are* other cars—not to mention trucks—on the highway. I think you've a fixation on accidents today.' And what's so urgent that he'd even suggest this idea? 'What's it all about?'

'I'll see you around eight, perhaps half-past. I'd like to find your cottage before it's too dark to judge what turn I make at the potato fields. Last time I visited you, I came down the Montauk Highway, made a sharp left at the pond, passed the village green, kept on going along Main Street—old houses and big trees, then some shops, et cetera, and then a windmill. And then what?'

'Bear right and take the next turn on your right. Follow that until you reach the golf course. Then turn left, keep on going for half a mile.'

'And then the potato fields. Are they still there?'

'Mostly. Take the second lane on your right. Towards the ocean.'

'And there you'll be, among the honeysuckle, thornbushes, and dunes. See you.'

David was left staring at a dead receiver. He replaced it thoughtfully. Mark Bohn's telephone calls were usually brief. Bohn liked his comforts, and five hours of driving (here and back to New York) wasn't his idea of bliss. Bohn never did anything without a purpose. So what was bringing him out all the way here? Urgent, he had said. It must be damn urgent.

David put one of his long-playing tapes into the machine, adjusted the volume and tone, went back to his typewriter. He had the work completed by half-past seven, with a varied selection of Vivaldi and Albinoni keeping him cheerful company. The special thing about that kind of music, he thought as he changed into his swimming trunks, was that it didn't add to your aggravations and annoyances. It didn't jar your spine, set your teeth on edge. And the miracle was that it didn't cloy either. Small wonder that people were still listening to those clever old Venetians after two hundred and fifty years.

He went into the porch, waited for the last movement of an Albinoni concerto to end. You couldn't walk away from that interweave of strings with the trumpet dominating the intricate background. Just the finest trumpeter in the world he thought, as Maurice André let his last notes ripple and soar. Soar as high as these white clouds, tingeing now with gold, over the immense sea. Then there was only silence and the steady beat of breaking waves.

21

He walked over the short stretch of rough grass, followed the path between beach-plum bushes and dog roses, came to the big dunes that blocked his cottage from winter storms. The path went round one side of them—Long Islanders didn't approve of breaking down dunes by trampling over them—but tonight David went straight over, running now as he jumped on to the deep soft sand. His pace increased as he reached the harder stuff, packed and smoothed by the tide's reach. He let out a long war whoop as he raced for the edge, running slow-motion until the water was waist-high. Then came the big ones rolling in from the Atlantic. He dived at the base of an upcurl-ing wave, got safely through before it smashed downward. Another dive and he was beyond this line of surf and swim-ming strongly. It was almost calm tonight, by Atlantic stan-dards, but it was wiser to turn back before he reached the second line of breakers which rose and fell over some unseen reef or sand bar. This was far enough from the shore: he might enjoy taking a risk, but he was not foolhardy. The return was easy, with the ocean helping him tonight: the spasms of the hidden waves floated him in. Some days, he almost had to fight his way back; other days, he wouldn't put an ankle into this water.

He flopped down on the empty beach, rested in its peace. There wasn't a fishing boat in sight. Some gulls. Some sand-pipers, scuttling along the frothing edge of the waves, their sharp bills busy searching for food before the brilliant sunset ebbed away. At last he picked himself up and began walking to the cottage. He was beginning to feel cold, but pleasantly: it was the first time he had been really cool today. He wondered, still listening to the perpetual waves, how the whalers in the old days managed to get their boats launched through that surf. They did, too. Now that was real toughness for you, he told himself, as he broke into a jogging run.

A Buick was standing in the driveway beside the cottage. Two men were waiting on the darkening porch.

'Eight-fifteen,' Mark Bohn called out. 'I told you we'd manage it. And I brought a good driver along with me, just to make sure. Hugh McCulloch.' He nodded to a tall man beside him.

Hugh McCulloch? David studied the stranger briefly. Am I supposed to know him? he wondered. 'Let's move inside,' he suggested. He shook hands and led the way, switching on the lights. 'Pour yourselves a drink. I'll find some clothes. You both look so damn formal.' Hugh McCulloch was carrying a brief-case, looking round uncertainly for a place to drop it. David moved into the bathroom for a quick shower to free the sand from his hair and skin. Dressing took a couple of minutes: chino pants, short-sleeved shirt, feet shoved into loafers. Outside in the living-room he could hear Mark fixing the drinks and doing all the talking. It struck David suddenly that all three of them were embarrassed by this meeting, each in his own way. It was an intrusion on him, certainly. ('Look at this,' Bohn was saying near the desk, 'he really has been doing some work!' It obviously surprised him.) On the other hand, it had certainly been one hell of a nuisance for these two men to come chasing down all this distance. Bohn would go anywhere in search of a story. But McCulloch did not look the type to make unneces-sary journeys.

Chapter Three

'WELL,' DAVID MENNERY SAID briskly as he returned to
the living-room, 'do we eat now or later? There isn't much to
offer you, I'm afraid. Closing up house, you know.'

'Wouldn't trouble you,' McCulloch said. 'We can stop for
some food on the way back to New York.' He left the book-
cases, where he had been studying the titles. He had a pleasant
voice, quiet and gentle like his manner, yet firm. He stood at
least six feet, a couple of inches above David and four inches
more than Mark Bohn. His hair had been reddish blond: it was
now well mixed with white, and thinning. It was conservatively
cut, giving him a neat, smooth look. So were his clothes, a
lightweight grey suit, a white shirt, a navy tie. Observant
brown eyes; pale complexion as if he spent a lot of time indoors.
A man in his mid-forties? Not much more. No, thought David,
I don't remember this McCulloch at all, yet there's a friendly
look about him as if he recognized me.

'No trouble,' David lied cheerfully. Too bad about that
steak he had hoped to broil tonight. Divided three ways, it
would supply a couple of mouthfuls apiece. 'There's cheese and
some ham. And,' he added with a grin, as he caught sight of
Bohn's face, Mark the well-travelled epicure, Mark the con-
noisseur of wines, 'we can always fill up the corners by opening
a can of beans.'

'I think we should talk first,' Bohn said.

'Fine,' David agreed, and took the Scotch Bohn handed him.
Bohn was trying to appear at ease, but he was definitely nervous. Physically, he looked much the same as always: thin-
faced, hawk-featured, with amused grey eyes behind round
wise-looking glasses. He had dark hair, straight but now
long-stranded with limp locks straggling over his collar. By
startling contrast, there was a fuzz of sideburns, thick and grey,

24

bulging from his cheeks. If Bohn had grown all that hair in the hope of looking younger, he had achieved the opposite effect. He looked a tired fifty, with all the weight of the world on his narrow shoulders. Actually, he was two years younger than David, making him thirty-seven. David resolved to have a good haircut tomorrow, not short, but not below the collar line either.

'Well, what's all this about?' And what, he was wondering again, could bring three men like us together?

McCulloch had taken a chair, his brief-case lying neatly and not too obviously alongside. He was going to leave the talking to Bohn. A very diplomatic type, thought David, sitting opposite him: he looked as cool and crisp as if he hadn't travelled almost the length of Long Island on a hot and sticky evening. Bohn, by contrast, was feeling the humidity, although the chill sea air was circulating through the room. He pulled his wide Italian silk tie loose, opened his striped English shirt, then went the whole way and took off the creased jacket of his light gaberdine suit. He threw it aside, took another drink, ran his hand through his hair. Yes, thought David, definitely nervous. Of me? That's unlikely. Of McCulloch, who looked like a good-tempered kind of man? Then Bohn's hesitations dropped away from him. He became his old businesslike self: very capable, quick-talking, thoughts arranged in neat patterns. He went straight to the matter. 'Jaromir Kusak's daughter wants to get out of Czechoslovakia.'

David felt all expression drain from his face. 'Irina?'

'Irina. And she needs help.'

David made no reply. The door to one of the rooms in his past life had been wrenched open. He had closed it, locked it, eventually thrown its key away, and here it was, forced ajar and gaping. At least, he thought, he could now bring himself to look inside, see it all as a small museum. Sixteen years was a long time in emotional drainage. He had no feelings left about Irina. Now he could even let himself remember her, remember Prague in the autumn of 1956. A girl he had met on his first day there. By accident. The totally unexpected. And himself when young, almost twenty-four, just out of the army, with enough money saved to let him wander through Europe for a couple of months. It might be a while before he'd ever be able to travel there again; it would give him time to decide whether

25

or not he was going back to college. He had enlisted voluntarily at the end of his sophomore year at Yale, in the middle of the Korean War, when the draft had been stepped up. Partly because an enlisted man had some choice in his branch of the service. Partly—to be brutally truthful—because the group around him talking of draft evasion (and let the other guys do it) had given him a smart pain at the base of the spine. What other guys? Anyone except me, me, me? Of course, no one put it as bluntly as that: rationalizations were neat as always, and even dear old morality got dragged in by the hair of its head. The comic thing was, he had enlisted in a state of depressed anger, and then he hadn't been sent to Korea to get his tail shot off. Instead, he had been assigned to West Germany. And when he was free, he had headed for Vienna because the action was there, music and international politics, his two developing interests. (The German experience hadn't been all sausage and sauerkraut.)

Eastern Europe in that autumn had been simmering with revolt. The first Polish riots had taken place in July, and failed, with fifty killed and hundreds wounded. By September, there were still dangerous tremors in Warsaw. So he left Vienna for Prague, thinking that he might reach Poland by way of Czechoslovakia; or if that failed then he'd try for Hungary, where—the talk in Vienna had it—there could be some trouble too. Just the brash bright young observer, about to produce some inspired reporting, definitely a find for the *New York Times* and a future winner of the Pulitzer Prize. Yes, he thought now, I was very young.

And on his first day in Prague he met Irina. He forgot everything else. It was Irina, Irina. . . . Three weeks of laughter and music and love. He had never felt that way before, never since. A mad and wonderful kind of happiness, a joy that floated you over the solid grey buildings, set your heart dancing in prosaic city streets. Yes, it was love in all its first tenderness and delight, world without end. Except that it was ended for them. Power politics took over. Irina was locked in. He was locked out, sent back to Vienna scarcely knowing how it had all been done so adeptly. But that was what happened to you when you fell in love with a girl whose mother was a Communist party official and whose father was far from Prague, unable to help anyone. He was a prisoner confined to the limits of his house and garden. And that was what could happen even to a major **novelis**t, a Nobel Prize nominee, if he was too admired among his own people, too famous abroad to be jailed without international protests.

'Dave,' Mark Bohn's voice said with marked patience, 'Dave —didn't you hear me? Jaromir Kusak managed to get out of Czechoslovakia four years ago. He's living in exile. Irina wants to join him. She needs help.'

'Then give it to her,' David answered sharply. He got control of himself, and added in a quiet unemotional tone, 'You have connections in Washington who would know how to help. Get your friends in the CIA to take on the job.'

'They won't touch it.'

'What?'

'Neither will the British: MI6 has backed off too.'

'Aren't they interested?' David was incredulous.

'Definitely. Most sympathetic. They wish Irina all the luck in the world, but they won't become involved.'

'Why not?'

McCulloch broke the long silence. He said to Bohn, 'I think we are getting a little ahead of ourselves. Why don't you start your story from the beginning, and give Mr Mennery a better idea of the whole problem?'

David cut in, getting well ahead of both of them. 'If you've come here thinking I can be of any use, forget it.'

'Why?'

'I'm not trained for this kind of job. I'm no escape expert. I'd be no help at all. I couldn't get into Czechoslovakia in the first place. Not legally. I was thrown out of there pretty damn quick in 1956.'

'That was quietly done, all *sub rosa*. No official record was made. Irina's mother saw to that. She had the power at that time, and she used it.'

'All for the sake of her husband,' David said bitterly. That was the reason she had given him before she had him deported. If he stayed, if he insisted on seeing her daughter, she would be powerless against her husband's enemies. They'd say that his daughter was being used to reach him. A Western militarist (wasn't David barely out of the army?), certainly a capitalist and an anti-Communist, possibly an agent of the CIA (proof wasn't necessary, only an official statement)—yes, there was enough there to have her husband arrested on conspiracy charges. Neither his reputation nor his name could save him then. A serious charge, always: a deadly charge at this moment, when a revolt had just started in Poland in spite of the magnanimous handling of the July riots. Even now, David could hear the rat-a-tat of her angry words, streaming at him like machine-gun fire. 'And for her own sake too, I guess.'

'There's always that,' McCulloch agreed. 'But she did protect her husband, even when they were miles apart, both ideologically and physically. And what would have happened to her, do you think, if her daughter had left, without permission, for America? She would have been held accountable. They take that kind of thing rather poorly in Communist countries.'

'Well, even if I'm not on any official blacklist, I still haven't been trained for the job of getting Irina out. Safely. And it's her safety that matters.'

'We don't want a man with special training. We need a man who can identify Irina. We need a man who is a capable driver and can bring her out of Vienna.'

'We?' There was challenge and wariness in David's eyes.

McCulloch repressed a small sigh. 'I am not connected with the CIA, or any other branch of United States Intelligence.' And why should any of us have to apologize like this? he wondered. If we had no intelligence agencies we'd be back to the stupidities of Pearl Harbor. 'I am a lawyer, working mainly in Washington, who was once with the State Department. My firm specializes in legal work for American businesses investing abroad, and for foreign firms who are setting up branches here. We have offices in Paris and Geneva. That is as far as my international involvements extend.'

Once with the State Department? David said, 'I keep thinking I ought to remember you somehow. Should I?' He looked at McCulloch long and carefully. 'Vienna?' he tried.

'Yes. October 1956, although I don't suppose there was any reason for you to remember me: I was one of the junior officers and no help to you at all.'

That was when I haunted the consulate and the embassy, pleading with them to get Irina Kusak out of Czechoslovakia so I could marry her. 'And I was another citizen making a nuisance of myself. My God, I *was* young, wasn't I?' he added, and he could smile at himself. 'But how the hell could you remember me? You had hundreds of complaints and demands.'

'Mostly forgotten. But I noted you. The name of Jaromir Kusak rang all the bells. I was one of his enthusiasts. I still am. A very great writer, a very great man.'

Bohn, who felt he had taken a back seat long enough, broke into the conversation. 'It was Hugh here who suggested you as the best candidate for this job. I made out a list of five Americans who had known Irina personally. One is a symphony conductor, now on a world tour. Another is a geologist, testing for oil somewhere in the wilds of Alaska, not available at such short notice. The third is with a branch of national security. The fourth is running for Congress. I still think we should have twisted an arm or two in the CIA, and got them to take action. However, time is short, I just had to settle for you.'

'How about an Englishman? Jaromir Kusak has friends in London—the publisher who brought out a collected edition of his early works last year.'

'George Sylvester? Yes, he's an old friend. It was through him I tried to get British Intelligence interested. No go. And as for two Englishmen who met Irina when they were in Czechoslovakia some years ago—well, one of them is now with NATO and the other works for the British Government.'

David made one last try. 'I only had a few phrases of Czech. I can't even speak it now.'

'You aren't going into Czechoslovakia. You are going to Vienna. You speak German well. You can handle a car. You know the Austrian roads—you've driven there, haven't you?'

'Only in certain areas.'

'And you've driven through northern Italy, Switzerland, Germany.'

'Only certain areas,' David insisted. And I've told you too damn much about my life, he thought as he eyed Bohn.

'You're a natural,' Bohn said with a wide grin. 'You have a good reason for being in Austria for the next couple of weeks.'

'For one week.'

'You could stretch it.'

Yes, I could stretch it. But do I want to stretch it? It could be too painful. And what about Irina? Would she want to see me again?

29

'No one, not even the Czech state security boys,' Bohn was saying, 'could possibly guess that you were going to be involved. You're in Salzburg, right? Black tie and dinner jacket, doing your thing. All arranged months ago, long before I got a letter from Irina. You're perfect.'

'I thought I was your last choice,' David said dryly, and rose to pour himself another drink.

Here filled McCulloch's glass too. Bohn was already at his third.

'Not among the amateurs,' Bohn said.

'What about that letter?' David asked suddenly.

'What about some food?' countered Bohn. He led the way to the kitchen. The late Caroline had left some improvements here, he thought, as he headed for the refrigerator. Did Dave know she was divorcing her second husband, and had already staked out her third? No, better not mention it tonight, Dave had to be kept in a serious mood, and Caroline was a comic character.

They ate a quick meal, and Bohn began talking as they finished their coffee around the heavy wooden table at one end of the kitchen.

Late in June a letter had reached Bohn in Washington. It was mailed in Vienna and it came from Irina. It had been written in Czechoslovakia and—this was Bohn's fairly obvious assumption—smuggled out of that country by one of Irina's friends in some resistance group. The letter stated that her mother was dead, her two children were dead, she had left her husband who was now divorcing her, and she had contacted some friends who were willing to help her leave the country. They could take her as far as Vienna. From there she needed help to reach her father, wherever he was. She was enclosing a note for Bohn to forward 'to anyone who can reach my father.' The note was brief. *Please let me see you. I need you.* She gave a Vienna telephone number which Bohn could use to make contact with her. Any message sent there, using the name Janocek for identification, would be passed on to her. She begged him to let her know if he was willing to help her. If so, she could leave in a matter of weeks.

'Everything stated clearly and simply,' Bohn said. 'And that telephone number was real.'

'You telephoned?' David asked.

'Why not? I wanted to test that letter. The Janocek dodge worked. And I also learned that they plan to get Irina out of Czechoslovakia by early August. So that's our target date: the first week of August. My guess is that she will be hidden in a safe house in Vienna by her Czech friends until we can pick her up.' He noticed David's frown. 'No compliments on my efficiency? Come on, Dave, what's bugging you?'

'You actually telephoned you were going to help her? Even before you had anything lined up?'

'What would *you* have done—left her unanswered?'

'No. I'd have said I was trying. I'd have said I had got the letter, and I'd let her know if I could get something worked out.'

'But I *was* working on it,' Bohn said with some annoyance. 'I began that very day. I went out to Langley and saw one of my CIA pals. The letter was passed on to someone else out there, presumably higher up. I heard that other agencies were consulted too. Big huddle. But Jaromir Kusak is a big name, and now more than ever.'

As Bohn paused to pour himself some brandy, McCulloch leaned over to David and said quietly, 'I can fill you in on the increasing importance of the name. Later. Along with any other points you may want developed.' He went back to drinking his coffee.

Bohn again took centre stage. 'I was pretty sure that one of our intelligence outfits would come to the rescue. I was wrong. I was even told that they didn't know where Kusak was. So I called George Sylvester on the phone—that's the London publisher who *must* be in contact with Kusak, or else how could Kusak's manuscripts reach him? I told him I had a note from Irina for her father, and I had just mailed it to him; he'd better make sure he was the only one to open it. I asked him to call me back when he had received it, and let me know how he could help. I thought his friends in Whitehall might be interested and could arrange for everything to be handled efficiently. I also said I was ready to fly to London as soon as he had something definite to suggest, have a private discussion, and show him a letter I myself had received from Irina.' Bohn drew a deep breath. 'Yes, I think you can say I did go to work on it.' He looked pointedly at David. 'Then I called on Hugh

31

and enlisted him for the battle. He has connections, knows ways and means.'

'You were really desperate,' McCulloch said, smiling.

'No results with George Sylvester?' David asked.

'Yes and no. He had sent Irina's note to Kusak, but he wouldn't give me Kusak's address. Said he didn't know it: he only knew the first step in a series of contacts that led to Kusak. And there had been a lot of interest among Sylvester's friends in the intelligence field, but they suggested I should do the job myself. Funny fellows. The last time I was in Czechoslovakia, I left with rumours chasing me out. I'm definitely on the Czech blacklist. Of course I had no actual connection with any intelligence agency, but the Czechs were paranoiac about that.'

'And still are,' murmured McCulloch.

'Anyway,' said Bohn, walking up and down the kitchen, getting into full stride as it were, 'Sylvester was helpful on three points. One: Kusak wanted to see his daughter—her note was authentic, all right: he had identified her handwriting. Two: if I could arrange Irina's escape beyond Vienna, Sylvester would arrange Kusak's appearance. And three: Kusak authorized him to pay expenses, drawing on Kusak's royalties.'

'Expenses will be kept down,' McCulloch said. 'I'm going on business to Geneva anyway. And Jo Corelli also is on a business trip—to Vienna. And Walter Krieger is about to return to Austria, which he visits frequently. So we pay most of our own way. The extra costs will come from a car, or travel expenditures by Irina and Mr Mennery. That is, if Mr Mennery is going?'

David said, 'Who are Jo Corelli and Walter Krieger?'

'We are all friends of Jaromir Kusak. It is as simple as that.'

'They all know their way around,' Bohn assured David. 'They know the score.'

David drew a deep breath.

'What do you want me to do?'

'Well, well,' said Bohn. 'Let's all drink to that.' He went over to the Welsh dresser for two more brandy snifters.

'I'll give you the details on the plane tomorrow,' McCulloch told David. 'What's your flight, by the way? Got the particulars?' He took out a small diary and pencil from his inner pocket. 'I suppose you're taking the direct route to Vienna, touching down at Amsterdam?'

David looked startled. He nodded, gave time of departure, flight number, and space. These were details he always memorized, just in case of a misplaced ticket. 'But isn't that a risk—I mean, if you and I take the same flight and are seen talking——?' He foundered slightly.

'Why shouldn't I take that flight? Or Jo? Or Krieger? We're pressed for time, and you've got to be able to know them again. What is a quicker way? I'll talk with you. I'll point them out. That's all. Don't worry. Not even one of Jiri Hrádek's agents could possibly tie us together, not at this stage.'

'Jiri Hrádek?'

'Chief aide to the head of state security in Czechoslovakia. That means secret police. Gestapo powers.' McCulloch hesitated. 'He was Irina's husband.'

There was a brief silence. 'Irina's mother could certainly pick them, couldn't she?' Bohn remarked. 'Hrádek is in line for the top spot in security.' He studied David with a touch of amusement. 'Want to back out?'

McCulloch was annoyed, and let it show. 'Stop fooling, Mark. Or else we'll forget some important point.' He turned to David.

'When can you be in Vienna?'

'By the second of August.'

'No sooner?'

'No.'

'And how long could you stay there? There may be delays.'

'Until the twentieth.' And goodbye to Bayreuth, Lucerne, and Edinburgh.

'All right. I'll pass your dates on to Krieger, let him play around with them. He's making the Vienna arrangements.'

'When do you want me there?' Bohn asked.

'Krieger will let you know if that's necessary.'

'Of course it's necessary,' Bohn said good-naturedly. 'You aren't going to cheat me out of a story, are you?'

'I think you'd better clear that with Jaromir Kusak. If he doesn't want any publicity about his daughter joining him in exile, he doesn't get it. Understood?'

'Understood.' Bohn was smiling. 'I'll outlive the old boy. The story can be told someday, and I'll be the only one who can do it. Say—look at the hour! Better get back into town, Hugh. I want to call Vienna as early as possible tomorrow morning, let them know we're all set. That should give them enough time to bring Irina safely out of Czechoslovakia by the beginning of August.'

McCulloch nodded. He was watching David. 'Something wrong?'

'No,' David said. 'Just puzzled.'

'By what?'

'Jaromir Kusak. Is the place where he is living in exile so well hidden that no one knows where it is? Not even his publisher?'

'It's the best-kept secret since the atom bomb,' said Bohn.

'He has his reasons,' McCulloch said very quietly. He hadn't touched his brandy. 'I'm driving,' he explained with a grin, and finished his third cup of black coffee. 'I'll see you tomorrow, Dave.' The slip-over to a first name was unobtrusive.

David nodded, walked with him into the living-room. Bohn was already on the front porch, pulling on his jacket.

McCulloch lifted his brief-case from the side of the armchair, opened it. He took out two or three sheets of paper, typed clearly, lines well spaced, easy reading. 'If you have time tonight, you could glance over these notes. And burn them once you've read them.'

'Top-secret?' David asked with a smile.

'My own special brand. Let's say they are a greater risk, if anyone left them lying around, than you and I accidentally meeting on a plane tomorrow. By the way, I'll take the liberty of changing your space from economy to first class. That's much quieter at this time of year. Any objections?'

David had none.

There was a general handshaking but no talk on the dark porch. McCulloch produced a pocket flashlight: Bohn and he made their way easily to the car. A last wave from Bohn, and they were off.

David stood for some moments, listening to the sea, looking at the sky. A clear and beautiful night. A strange and fantastic night.

He came back into the house, sat down at his desk, pushing his manuscript aside, placing McCulloch's pages in front of him.

They consisted of three crisply written but fairly detailed biographies: Jaromir Kusak; his wife, Hedwiga Kusak; Jiri

34

Hrádek, Irina's husband. When he finished reading, he burned them in the fireplace and stirred up the black ashes with a poker until they were crumbled into powder. Now he knew some of the background to Irina's life in those last sixteen years. Sadly, he shook his head, gathered up his own papers, and began packing them for New York.

Chapter Four

DAVID SETTLED HIMSELF comfortably in his new location. Hugh McCulloch had managed the change-over to first class on the flight to Amsterdam-Vienna. It wasn't that McCulloch was a sybarite or a wild spender. It turned out that his under-statements had double meanings. 'Quieter', he had said yesterday, which meant simply a better chance of finding last-minute space for himself and his travelling companions. McCulloch was a planner, no doubt about that. He had even got the seat next to David.

McCulloch gave a casual but friendly nod as he took his place. Just one stranger briefly summing up another who would share close quarters with him on a long journey. David took his cue, nodded back. Where were Jo Corelli and Walter Krieger? he wondered. He had made several amused guesses while waiting at Kennedy for the usual business, nowadays, of getting on board: individual searches—this airline was really careful, thank God—for concealed weapons on possible hijackers. And anyone who looked Neanderthal, or muttered to himself, or talked aggressively, or shifted his eyes like a spooked horse, or glowered with general hate at the world around him, might find a coldly appraising psychoanalyst studying him with growing interest.

Now it was time for seat-belts and nervous silence. The plane lifted off, gained altitude, stayed there. Everyone could unfasten and relax.

'Cuba next stop?' David asked.

'As long as we don't have a prolonged visit——' McCulloch shrugged his shoulders to end the sentence. The airline hostess, waiting for their orders, wasn't amused. Funny way some people had of breaking the ice, she thought, but she smiled her warm, enveloping smile and talked of dinner in half an hour.

'Or a little later,' McCulloch guessed. 'Anyway, time for a double Martini.'

'Scotch on the rocks, water added,' David told her. 'Make that two, please.' It would save any gap in service: the girl would have enough to do with the batch of women on the aisle opposite, not to mention the child behind him.

She left, neat and demure in her crisp suit, pretty face still carrying the beautiful smile. No trouble with these two, she thought. (There would be plenty with the small boy and his mother one seat back; or with the group of women, elderly and still nervous, who were making their first flight over the Atlantic to see bulb farms in Holland, lace shops in Brussels, and châteaux on the Loire.) What were they, anyway? The older one looked like a professional man—he had kept his thin brief-case beside him, saying he had some work to finish. Lawyers were always doing that, never seemed to get rid of their offices. The other had magazines with him—no bright front covers, all serious-looking—and a couple of paperbacks. A reader, obviously. Someone in teaching, or in publishing, or a young executive? They were all mixed up nowadays: you couldn't tell much from their clothes any more. Not stage or movies—his hair wasn't wild enough, and he wore a tie. Not a talent scout, either: he hadn't that wandering, how-do-you-look-stripped gaze. Light brown hair, dark eyes—a neat combination with a healthy tan. Veree attractive. *Molto simpatico.* The only thing she hadn't liked about him was his sense of humour. Cuba, indeed. . . . When she brought back a tray of various orders, she noticed that they were introducing themselves but hadn't reached the stage of talking freely. Must be the reserved type, both of them. Well, that never caused any bother. No complaints from her on that score. She bustled away, happily. Plenty to do elsewhere.

David studied his double Scotch in a single glass, soda added, and shook his head. No one really listened, it seemed. He hoped that this would also hold for his fellow passengers—he was still worrying about the risk of any talk with McCulloch being overheard. He assessed the immediate field.

Across the aisle, the women had rediscovered their voices. In pairs, they were discussing future plans over their champagne cocktails, and dropping heady names with abandon—Chaumont, Chambord, Chenonceaux, Cheverny. And to hell with exact pronunciation, thought David, enthusiasm was the thing. But where were the husbands? In flight from culture? Gone fishing? Anyway, he could relax about the Ladies' Self-Improvement Society: it was too absorbed in its own projects to overhear McCulloch's.

Behind David, the small boy was raising his own barrage. He blotted out any voices within a six-foot radius with his constant argument. His mother sounded young and harassed, when she could be heard, and then only by raising her voice. She'd pay no attention to anything except the battle on hand.

And in front of him there was the only risk to privacy. It came in the nicest possible form, too. A girl travelling alone, sitting by herself, who had boarded the plane just ahead of him. Dark hair, smooth and shining, carefully shaped. That was all he had seen, except for the way she carried her head. A slender, erect figure dressed in a smartly cut trouser suit that may have hidden her legs but certainly emphasized trim hips and waist.

McCulloch took off his eyeglasses, folded back the newspaper he was reading, dropped it on his lap. He had been judging their surroundings too. 'We can talk,' he said quietly, and tucked his glasses into his breast pocket.

David made a small gesture to the seat in front.

'That's Jo.'

For several moments David was wordless. Jo Corelli. Well, well, well. Neatly positioned too. He looked at McCulloch. 'I wouldn't like to play you at chess.' Then he had a reservation about Jo. 'Is she up to this job?'

McCulloch's serious face rounded into his genial smile. He dealt with that question by leaving it unanswered. Dave would find out soon enough. 'She's leaving this flight at Amsterdam, along with me. Before then you'll have a chance to see her and hear her. Listen to her voice carefully: make sure you can recognize it over a telephone. Memorize her face too. The same goes for Walter Krieger. When he walks past on his way to the lounge, I'll tip you off. You can follow him five minutes or so later. See him and hear him, that's all.'

'And where's Bohn? I thought he'd be hanging in.'

'He's done his part of the job. No need to have him around.'

'He'll be in at the finish, though. You can't keep him away from a good story.'

38

'No doubt.'

'So this is all of us?' Jo Corelli, Krieger, McCulloch and myself.

'That's it. I'll be in the background, in contact with all of you. Krieger will keep within reach, if you need him. Jo will be with you most of the time.'

'I don't know if I like the sound of that.'

'Jo is capable.'

'I wasn't thinking of Jo. I was wondering who is in charge?' I don't want any arguments on that trip west, he told himself.

'You. You have to make the decisions, choose the safest routes. And you'll be there, all the time, until you make our— our special delivery into the right hands.'

'Where?'

'To be arranged. You'll learn your destination as soon as I do. And on that journey, let me know your progress; or tell Jo. She'll keep me informed if you can't. Here's my number'—he slipped a card into David's hand along with an envelope of cash—'and that's your expense account. Keep in touch with me. There will be someone by that telephone day or night. And why Geneva?' he asked, forestalling another question. 'It's central. Good telephone service, good airport, roads and trains. And I have two members of my staff there, who are completely discreet and absolutely honest.'

David resisted looking at either the card or the envelope, stashed them safely in a deep pocket, and brought out his cigarettes as an excuse for reaching into his jacket. 'Can you give me a rough idea how long we have to wait before I start making the delivery?' That would be the worrying time, just dawdling around Vienna, waiting in uncertainty.

'That depends on your last concert in Salzburg.'

'A week from tomorrow—Wednesday. Eight o'clock that evening.'

'Where is it being held?'

'The Grosses Festspielhaus.'

'Ah, the big theatre. Black tie? And supper to follow, no doubt?'

'Yes, I've arranged to meet some friends——'

'Then we'll skip my idea and you can leave Salzburg in the morning.'

'I could cancel the supper date.'

'No, no. Keep everything as it is, and raise no one's curiosity. But next morning, take only necessary clothes—travel light—and leave the rest in Salzburg for later pickup. Or have them sent to London or Paris, or wherever suits you. You'd better hire a car in Salzburg for a week; and once you reach Vienna, stay at the Sacher. We'll have a room reserved in advance. In your name. Then Jo will know where to find you. She'll be able to give you more details on the arrangements we've managed to make. We'll have quite a week, getting it all squared away.' McCulloch gave that surprising smile of his, and his eyes sparkled at the prospect. Then he was back to his businesslike self. 'You'll have one night at the Sacher. Get set to leave by next morning.'

So soon? 'Can you be sure of that?' David asked. If McCulloch had only eight days to make all his plans, the resistance group helping Irina to reach Vienna would certainly need more time than that. Escapes took preparation. There would be delays, postponements.

'She is already out,' McCulloch said very quietly.

Irina? Out of Czechoslovakia? David stared at him briefly, recovered. 'When?'

'Yesterday.'

'Good God,' said David under his breath.

'She is safe. And waiting.'

'Look, I can't cancel any of this coming week. I've *got* to be in Salzburg.' David was low-voiced but angry.

'I didn't ask you to cancel anything.'

'I just don't like the idea of her hanging around Vienna for more than a week.'

'She won't be doing that. She'll be kept out of sight—indoors. Stop worrying about something we can't change. We'll stick to our schedule.' McCulloch's mouth was definitely tight-lipped.

David said bitterly, 'Jumped the gun, didn't they?'

'Someone did. Bohn was given the news this morning when he telephoned our okay to them.'

'I bet it gave him a bit of a shock.'

'Damaged his ego slightly. But he soon recovered. He's a resilient man.'

David was suddenly off on another tack. Irina's friends must have been pretty sure we'd come through. What had led them on? Bohn's initial approach, no doubt; optimistic and confident, that was Bohn. 'Good God,' he said again, realizing the full force of this latest piece of news. 'What if I had refused last night?'

'We'd have been searching wildly for a replacement. And by the end of this week I'd have been on my hands and knees pleading with the pros to lend me one of their bright young men.' McCulloch shook his head over the likely reply to that request.

'They'd have still refused?' What has turned Washington into a bag of jelly beans? David asked himself and glared at McCulloch, who merely lifted his newspaper, held it out, pointing to a long report with a circle pencilled lightly around one paragraph.

David took the newspaper and looked at a Reuter's dispatch from Prague, dated yesterday. The headline was TWO MORE SUBVERSION TRIALS BEGIN IN CZECHOSLOVAKIA. He started to read, got only as far as the first sentence. The dinner trolley was arriving.

'Keep it for your coffee,' McCulloch suggested. 'Read it carefully. It may clarify some things. And anyway, cold steak isn't worth eating.'

The hostess was apologetic. 'I'm sorry it was a long half-hour.'

Not long enough, thought David, as he laid aside the newspaper unwillingly.

'Scarcely noticed it at all,' said McCulloch, the ex-diplomat. 'I think this gentleman and I might share a bottle of Bordeaux.' He turned to David with grave politeness. 'You will join me?'

David reflected, as the dishes were cleared away, that McCulloch had scored again: their close conversation had been well timed, for now—with food served and eaten—there was a satisfied silence around them, a general drift towards settling in for the rest of the evening, and no more busy interplay of voices and laughter. Even the small boy, after some last protests, had subsided into sleep.

David adjusted the reading light over him, picked up the newspaper. But from the seat in front, the girl spoke to the hostess as she passed down the aisle after a quick visit to the pilots. 'Are we on time? That's splendid. Then we'll arrive on schedule.' She was rising now, still talking with the hostess.

'How are the weather reports?' The hostess assured her they seemed fine.

'Wonderful,' said the girl, leaving her seat, turning towards the rear of the plane, letting David have a clear view of her face. 'All disturbances are over, I think.' She glanced in the direction of the sleeping child and the hostess joined her in a bright smile. Then Jo was on her way to the washroom.

Girl? If she were Women's Lib and insisted on being addressed as Ms, she'd be annoyed with that description. But, thought David as male chauvinist, she might be a grown woman in her late twenties, and she might be brighter and more intelligent than he was (McCulloch, that careful codger, wouldn't pick a fly-brained cutie for this job), yet she was still a charmer, and definitely of the purely feminine gender. An oval face with smooth pale skin and good bone structure. (The profile view had been clear and well defined.) Large eyes, dark eyelashes, carefully marked eyebrows, all very pleasing below the gleaming dark hair. He wouldn't forget that face. Nor the voice: well modulated, nothing hoarse or raucous; middle register, with a hint of something else than purely American. English? Just a slight influence in the vowels, he thought, with Italian (her name pointed to that) in the softness of some syllables. At least, if she started giving him orders, her voice wouldn't add to his annoyance. Let's hope she doesn't, he decided; let's hope we both keep the level of command at fifty-fifty. He had his doubts. Jo seemed to be a capable woman, all right. The way she had handled herself there was damned neat.

He returned to his newspaper. McCulloch had taken out some legal-sized sheets from his brief-case, put on his glasses, uncapped a ball-point pen, and was apparently absorbed. David began reading. It didn't take him long to finish the Reuter's dispatch—its four columns covered about a quarter of the full-sized page of the newspaper. Its headline had been misleading. 'Two More Subversion Trials' meant, in fact, two places—Prague itself and the town of Brno—where a number of trials, each involving groups of the more liberal Communists, had been going on for the last week and were still continuing. The defendants were all educated men and women: doctors, historians, a philosopher, two engineers, a clergyman, lawyers. They had been arrested last November, before the

42

Czech elections, for handing out leaflets which reminded citizens of their constitutional rights in voting. Some, too, had given interviews to Western newsmen. They could get as much as ten years in prison. It was, so the paragraph lightly circled by McCulloch's pencil told David, an attempt 'to eliminate any remaining active political opposition once and for all. That this is evidently declining is indicated by the fact that in the months before the trials began Western correspondents heard less than usual from the underground opposition movement.' And there was another eye-catching detail: the present Communist party leader, now in control of the government, was trying to keep the trials in low profile, not disturb the general calm of the country, and give no opportunity to hard-liners 'to step in with tougher measures.'

There's a clue there, thought David, to the way our intelligence agencies are acting, and I can't quite find it. He re-read the dispatch. The clue was there, still evading him. But he had learned something. There were four political groupings in Czechoslovakia. First was the minority who now held power; they were middle-of-the-road, trying to show Russia they were all good Communists too—see how we can keep discipline? Secondly, there was a majority, now out of power, as liberal but not quite as daring as Dubcek in the Prague Spring of 1968, who were being disciplined to encourage them to hold their heads down. Thirdly, there was the group in the background, the hard-liners, the new Stalinists, ready 'to take tougher measures'—which meant the seizure of power and shock tactics. They'd hold bigger and better trials: staged shows with charges of treason, just like the old days. And fourthly, there were the non-Communists and ex-Communists, possibly the smallest group of all, now relegated to silence—at least they had been brushed aside in the Reuter's account: *in the months before the trials began, Western correspondents heard less than usual from the underground opposition movement.*

David folded up the paper, placed it beside McCulloch. He closed his eyes, searched for the key to the riddle. The underground was not dead, or else Irina would not now be safe in Vienna. But it was obviously cautious, avoiding any open publicity. And the American intelligence agencies, the British too, were keeping well away from the Czech opposition movement. Was that the key? No link-up of any kind between

43

Western governments and the Czech underground? No chance of handing the hard-line Communists an excuse for show trials, and for a takeover of power to ensure full discipline? Certainly, bigger and better trials needed sensational evidence, something to keep the world startled and silence its objections. 'Sure,' people must be persuaded to say, 'sure they're guilty, look how the CIA is behind it all: damn shame the way they stir up trouble and leave these poor fools to pay the bill.' All they'd see would be the results of the agony: arrests, wholesale purges, sentences that brought a lifetime's hard labour if not execution. They'd never know the real cause of it: that would be buried under a massive mudslide of propaganda. Which, of course, was exactly what the hard-line Communists wanted. It made their power-plays that much easier.

Well, this time, he thought grimly, we're not obliging the propaganda planners. We're a purely civilian outfit. He looked at McCulloch, who was glancing at the aisle, almost said aloud, 'I take it all back. I'm clued in. Washington is best kept out of all this.' But he restrained himself. You may be an amateur, he told himself, but at least you can try to seem professional. And just then he felt McCulloch's elbow dig quickly into his side.

A man, thickset, healthy colour in his cheeks, was passing down the aisle. David noted a shock of grey hair, a heavy moustache, strong eyebrows, and a lightweight tweed jacket, neutral in colour. So this was Walter Krieger. He carried a pipe in his hand and a book under his arm. He looked neither right nor left.

Five minutes to wait. At the end of them David said, 'Think I'll stretch my legs,' and made his way over McCulloch's feet. Jo was coming back to her seat. He stepped aside to let her pass, acknowledged her 'thank you' and was on his way.

In the lounge, definitely close quarters, there were five men and three women and a general eyeing of every newcomer. David took a seat, smiled around, and ordered a Scotch. 'No,' Walter Krieger was replying to a man who had sat down beside him, 'I don't live in New York any more. Just visit it.'

'I'm from the Midwest myself. Plastics. Better than glass and china. There's a big market for them in Europe. New. That's what they like: something new. We can't keep up with the orders.'

'That's fine,' said Krieger. He had a deep rich voice, full of resonance. If he ever turned it on full power, David thought, he could blow out the side of the plane. A physically strong man who might be pushing fifty, but could possibly outfight the rest of us in this room. Not tall. Less than medium height, but well muscled and taut. He had a magnificent head—perhaps it looked imposing because he was short in stature. Beg pardon, David told Krieger silently, you aren't short, just five feet six, with a chest development that puts the plastics guy to shame. Most of Plastics' girth had settled around his waist. A nice guy, though: baby-faced and openhearted.

'Yes,' he was saying, 'there's a great future in synthetics. The world's before us. All we need is peace. Right? But it's coming, it's coming.'

'That's good,' Krieger said.

'I'm on my way to Vienna. Then to Czechoslovakia, if all the arrangements hold up. You never can tell. Still, they're a booming market. We can use their stuff——'

'Such as glass?'

'Well—that, and other things. And they can use ours. I hear they're filling the shelves in the grocery stores now. No scarcities. Keeps people happy.'

'A good market, obviously.'

'The life of trade. What's your line of business?'

'Chocolate.'

'Oh? You're with a foreign firm? Or is it domestic?'

'We amalgamated some years ago.'

'So you're the European representative?'

'If that isn't too ambitious a description.'

'Where's your head office?'

'Vevey.'

'Switzerland? What takes you to Vienna? You said you were going there—or did I get that wrong?'

'No,' said Krieger. 'That's where I go. Several times a year. Austria makes good chocolate too.'

'You don't say. By the way, what do you think of McGovern's chances? Or are you for Nixon? You vote from Switzerland, I suppose. Absentee ballot or something?'

'I manage to get back around election time.'

'If you ask me——' Krieger hadn't, but the businessman from the Midwest went on talking. Not one of our silent majority, David thought as he finished his drink. Travel loosened a lot of tongues. He listened to the mixture. (My dear, you *wouldn't* recognize Acapulco. . . . I wonder what St Laurent is cooking up this season. . . . Personally, I always liked Jamaica. . . . And the Dow Jones average. . . . Munich has really put money on the line for the Olympics. . . . Two-fifty a seat, five dollars for the two of us, and we just keep walking out! Whatever happened to . . . ?) Then he slipped away before he could be drawn in. But Walter Krieger was now more than a name.

McCulloch had finished his work. The brief-case was closed. The newspaper had disappeared, along with the legal documents. He was fast asleep. It seemed as if Jo was asleep too, like the châteaux ladies and the small boy. Some others were watching the movie, earphones adjusted. It was one he had seen at a special preview in New York two weeks ago, and even if he hadn't paid two-fifty for his seat, he had walked out. Yes, whatever happened to?

He didn't feel like reading either. He was restless in his mind. He closed his eyes, wondered what part of the Atlantic they were over now, envied McCulloch his unflappable calm, let his thoughts run jumbled through his head until, without realizing what was happening, he dozed off.

When he awoke, it was time to fasten seat-belts for Amsterdam.

Chapter Five

DAVID ARRIVED IN SALZBURG with his thoughts still restless and his emotions divided. He fought himself for the first three hours there, and then—as he was shaving before he got dressed for the opening performance of *Figaro*—he made the decision. He was facing two jobs: one for *The Recorder*; one for Irina: each quite separate. So he'd keep his mind separated too. He would be absorbed in music for the next eight days; and once that was over, he would concentrate on the journey west. Because if he didn't, if he kept worrying about one and then the other, as he had been doing for the last twenty-four hours, he wouldn't write a critical piece worth a damn and he'd end up in Vienna frustrated and angry—no way to take on any emergency.

And that journey was going to have its problems. Of that he was sure. Irina's husband wasn't going to let them drive out of Vienna, free and easy. He would take a personal satisfaction, call it masculine ego, in hauling Irina back to Czechoslovakia. Jiri Hrádek might have disowned her publicly for his own personal—or political—reasons, but he'd never forgive her for the last insult of escaping from his security agents. These were tough guys, disciplined and dedicated, and as devious as any secret police. How in hell had Irina managed it? David wondered for the hundredth time. Now that's enough, he told himself sharply: you made your decision, so stick with it. Keep your mind off Irina, or else you're going to cut yourself with this new blade and you'll arrive at the Grosses Festspielhaus dripping all over your shirt front.

She's safe, isn't she? She's safely hidden, and possibly in less danger now than when she steps into your car.

He finished shaving, started dressing and reading the programme notes for tonight, a combined operation as usual.

47

Standard routine was a pacifier. He was in control, no more self-argument, by the time he stepped into the busy street outside the hotel and joined the steady procession of people, couples, singles, small groups, making their way across the bridge to the Old Town. A quiet crowd, young as well as middle-aged with a sprinkling of elderly veterans, low-voiced and smiling, the women in their prettiest late-evening dresses with the breeze from the river fluttering long skirts around satin slippers, lending a raffish note to broad daylight. But there was more than handsome clothes. These people knew their music: they had travelled a long way to hear it. There was nothing bored about them, either. There was a feeling of expectancy in the voices, of excitement in the air, as the looming domes and towers of Salzburg welcomed the pilgrims into its narrow twisting streets. Here, thought David, is another world. Unreal? Scarcely. It had had its centuries of danger and desperation; even—only thirty years ago—its bomb craters and flames, piles of rubble and cold ashes: reality enough for anyone. Suddenly he thought back to one of his antagonists on the staff of *The Recorder*, a recent addition who was devoted to hard-rock festivals. (He'd have trouble with that guy: he was out for David's job.) Well, Woody, he told him now, you can have all the subcultures you can swallow. I'll take civilization.

And with that he entered the vast hall, pressed through the gathering crowds, and saw two friends waiting at the foot of the staircase. He waved to them, caught their attention. Honest smiles and a warm welcome. He was not only under control now; he was back to normal.

The eight days were over. The last reports he had made were already in the mail for *The Recorder*'s copy editor. The hired car was being delivered to the hotel door. The hotel bill was being added up at the desk. He had packed, leaving a suitcase with the porter, jamming the more workaday clothes into a bag which could easily be hauled around. He had the road maps, which he had picked up at the automobile agency yesterday, spread out on his bed along with his own guide to Austria— there was an adequate plan of Vienna at the back of the little book—and these he studied attentively as he waited for the desk to call.

The telephone rang. 'Yes?' he asked, his mind still calculating kilometres: about a hundred and seventy miles on the big new throughway to the outskirts of Vienna. It avoided all towns and villages. So it would take three hours, perhaps less, if he travelled when most others had stopped for lunch. Allow about half an hour, at least, to get through twelve miles of suburbs and streets, until he could arrive in the heart of the inner city. 'Yes?' he said again, realizing it wasn't the desk phoning about the car. 'Mennery here.'

'And how nice!' said a woman's voice. 'Did I wake you?'

'No, I am just about to take off.'

'I thought everyone slept till eleven in Salzburg after a heavy night. Lucky I did call early. There's a slight change in plans.'

It was Jo Corelli, no doubt about that. He switched from surprise to worry. 'Oh?'

'Nothing to trouble you. Very slight. You'll be driving in from the west, so once the expressway ends you might go through the Wienerwald. I could meet you somewhere there. You name a place.'

'Why not Grinzing?' He had intended it as a small joke. It was a once-upon-a-time village, now swallowed up in the sprawl of Vienna suburbs: a tourist lure with conscious local colour.

But she took him up on that, and very quickly. 'Wonderful,' she said. 'Couldn't be better for me.'

'A mob scene like that?' Hardly her style, he thought.

'By the time you get there, most of the crowd will have eaten and left. All we'll find is a few tired waitresses and some beer coasters on the tables. There's a quaint little place right on the trolley-car lines. Green shutters, red geraniums—Yes, I think that's right. It's got a name like the Jolly Peasant, something pretty close to that. You can't miss it: there's a streetcar stop outside its front door, and a parking area at its side. Simple. You'll get there around two, and——'

'Give or take half an hour,' he cut in. She was full of instructions, this girl.

'I'll be winetasting under the vines in the back garden. It's heady stuff, so don't be late.'

'No, ma'am,' he managed to insert before she hung up quickly.

'Goddammit,' he said as he gathered up the maps and guide-book, locked his bag. The telephone was ringing again, but this

49

time with a brief call from the desk. 'I'll be down,' he told the porter. He made one last hasty check around the room—incredible how well you could tuck yourself into a place in eight short days—and then he was on his way.

The steady drive to the outskirts of Vienna had been easy; the small detour to Grinzing a little more complicated. David felt some satisfaction when he managed to arrive at five minutes past two. He parked the car, freshened up in a washroom littered with the debris of departing tourists, and found his way to the garden behind the inn. Jo was there, as promised, looking fresh and untroubled in a simple white dress. Strangely, she didn't seem out of place either, sitting in a vine-covered alcove with the sunlight playing gently through the leaves overhead. The garden was large, filled with close-packed tables and benches: only half of them were now occupied, none near her. In front of her was a thick goblet half-empty, and a carafe of white wine misted over with the warmth of the day. It was almost full, he noted as he reached her. Well, he thought with relief, no apologies necessary: she can't have been here for long. 'Well timed,' he said, putting out his hand for a quick, polite shake. 'And congratulations on the table.' Then his smile turned to a look of surprise. She was still holding his hand.

'I think this is necessary,' she said. 'The waitress would never forgive you if you weren't demonstrative. She helped me get this alcove. She was beginning to worry about me—a romantic soul.'

'And what did you tell her to get this table?' He tightened his grip. If anyone was going to hold hands, he'd do it, thank you. He slid on to the bench beside her. 'Let me know when you get a cramp.'

'I've got to eat,' she said as she pulled her hand loose. And the food was already arriving on an enormous tray, balanced on the shoulder of a middle-aged and ample blonde in a dirndl costume.

'So soon?'

'I took the liberty of ordering,' Jo said. 'I told her you'd be hungry. Besides, there wasn't much choice left. Pork or veal. I chose veal. Okay? Just as well to get all the service over, and then we can really talk. How was the journey?'

50

'Fine.' A hot-plate, with its warming candle lit, was being set before him.

'And how was the music? Up to standard?' Down went the large platter, piled with schnitzel, on the hot-plate.

'Definitely.' At this moment Salzburg seemed very far away. A deep plate of sliced cucumbers afloat in marinating liquid was expertly placed. Slices of black bread. Another heavy goblet along with another carafe.

'Darling,' said Jo, 'it really is so *wonderful* to see you!' If she had wanted to get his attention away from the speed of the service, she certainly managed it. He smiled appropriately, kept his eyes fixed on her face, and hoped the waitress would think it devotion. A clatter of heavy plates, a rattle of knives and forks, the slap of two small checked napkins on the wooden table, and—with one last understanding beam from the waitress and a parting good wish for their appetites—they were left to themselves.

'What *did* you tell her about us?' he insisted. 'Am I supposed to be stealing you away from a jealous husband?' That would be in the best light-opera tradition, and all Vienna loved its Strauss.

'I didn't have to say much.' Jo was unexpectedly embarrassed. 'I just lowered my eyes and blushed a little.'

He had a sudden suspicion. 'How long were you waiting for me?'

'Well—I wanted to be sure of this table, and there was still a crowd to cope with.'

'How long?' he repeated.

'Oh, about half an hour. Perhaps a little more. You see, I couldn't time my arrival very well. So——' She shrugged her shoulders.

If so, that was the only thing she couldn't do well. 'Look,' he said with some asperity, 'I can serve myself. Heap your own plate first.'

'Mr Mennery, we are in the land of dutiful women. Relax and enjoy it while it lasts.'

He took a long drink of wine. A little sweet, but light and pleasant.

'It slips up on you,' she warned him. 'Strange how a young wine—it's practically straight from the press—can pack a stronger punch than a vintage year.'

'You seem to be holding up well. Not a consonant slurred.'

She bridled at last. 'I have drunk exactly half a glass.'

In spite of himself, he was amused. 'Then you're a magician to hold this table for three-quarters of an hour at the price of one small carafe of wine.'

'That's my second. I emptied the other out behind me. It's all right. No one saw. Besides, it wouldn't harm the vine roots.'

He laughed outright. 'No damage done. It will probably strengthen the flavour of the next batch of grapes.'

'Our waitress is delighted,' she reported. 'She now thinks I've quite forgiven you for almost standing me up.'

'Is she so important?' he asked, still amused.

'Everyone is important. And even more so in this little game we are now playing.'

A game? Was that what it was to her? Something to break the monotony of her social rounds? Something new, something different? He concentrated on the paper-thin veal cutlet encrusted in egg and bread crumbs. It was always palatable in Austria, even digestible.

She was studying him. 'Sorry there are no anchovies on top: I guess they've run out of them. But cheer up—the zither music doesn't start till the evening.'

'I like zither music in its home base.'

'So do I,' she agreed. 'I love all of this. But just now and again,' she added quickly, 'not as a permanent diet.'

Like the game we are now playing, he thought. 'Breaks the monotony?'

She had sensed something in his voice. She frowned, helped him to the cucumber salad, didn't splash any of the liquid dressing over him. 'One of the reasons we met here was an idea I had. I thought it would be useful if we could get to know a little about each other before we started work tomorrow.'

It wasn't a bad idea at all, he admitted to himself. 'What are the other reasons?'

She dropped her voice. 'We had to make a change in plans. Krieger is being followed.'

He looked at her quickly.

She went on, low-voiced, calm and businesslike. 'So he has pulled out of the Sacher, and I've been told not to contact you there, and we can't have that little meeting in your room tonight, as he had planned. He's still in Vienna, of course, keeping an eye on things, but he's lying low. He even called Bohn to Vienna.'

'Bohn here too?'

'This morning. And delighted to be of help. He was in London last weekend, trying to persuade Uncle George and Hugh McCulloch to let him accompany them to the happy reunion of Jaromir Kusak and his daughter. Big story, and Mark Bohn is going to get it.' She laughed softly. 'Can't keep a sharp journalist down: he'll bounce up every time.'

'What's Bohn going to do here? Travel with us?'

She shook her head. 'Krieger needed him to make two telephone calls for him. To the number that Irina gave Bohn in her letter to him. Remember?'

As if I'd ever forget, he thought. 'The Janocek identification routine?'

'Right.'

'Why *two* calls?'

'Krieger is cautious. The first one is to warn Irina to get ready to leave. And also to find out just how much time her friends will need to drive her by car from the place where she has been hiding to the Opera House.'

The Opera House was a central location, with plenty of traffic around it and busy streets leading to it. And the Sacher was close by—just at the back of it, actually. That makes things simple for me, thought David: no chance of losing myself in Vienna streets on my way to pick up Irina.

'You see,' Jo was explaining, 'we have no idea of where Irina actually is, whether outside the city or within it. So the only way——'

'I've got that. Their estimated time will give us a basis for our own calculations, and we can arrive on the spot—with luck—almost simultaneously. And I suppose Bohn's second call is to give Irina the exact time to leave for the Opera House?'

'He'll make the call tomorrow morning, give her five minutes to leave. But her friends won't bring her to the Sacher. That's too noticeable. They'll be told to drop her at the Opera House, and it's only a short block to——'

'——the hotel? She's walking there to meet us? That's insane, absolutely insane.'

She said coldly. 'Far from it. She won't enter the hotel. She'll walk into the café from its street entrance. And that's where you'll see her.'

'Look—it would be safer and simpler if I just parked tomorrow near the front of the Opera House, waited until I saw her being dropped from her friends' car at the corner, cruised along, and then——'

'Can you be sure of identifying her at a distance? She won't be dressed the way you remember her.'

He hesitated. 'Have Bohn give exact instructions about where they are to let her out of the car. I'll be at that very spot.' He drew a deep breath. 'And I can recognize her if I'm near enough to see her face.'

'You'll do that in the café.'

'Why there?' he asked angrily.

'Because you've got to make sure that she *is* Irina, and not a substitution. Not some girl from the Czech secret police who's a good imitation of Irina's last photograph. I've seen it —Krieger has a copy—but I couldn't really know if she was authentic. And you will know, won't you?'

'Yes,' he said at last. 'I'll know.' There was another pause. 'And if she's not Irina—what then?'

'Dump her. Leave her sitting at a café table. We want no part of this escape attempt unless it's for real.'

'I just rise and walk out?' he asked unbelievingly. 'Or I could say, "Hell, no, you're a damn fake. Find your own way back across the frontier!" '

'You don't rise, because you won't be sitting down. Let me explain——' She paused as she noticed the waitress coming their way. 'Later. I've also got some other instructions for you.'

I bet you have, he thought.

'From Hugh McCulloch this time,' she said, and her dark-blue eyes smiled. 'Let's skip the strudel and have a gallon of coffee. Okay with you?'

'Of course,' he said. Was there any other choice? But he did notice that she let him do the ordering. 'Didn't you say McCulloch was in London last weekend?' he asked, once the food had been cleared away. The waitress was shaking her tight blonde curls at their small appetites. He hoped she would blame that on unrequited love (Act II, Scene 3).

54

'Yes. All arrangements are completed with Uncle George. Hugh is in Geneva now.'

'Is that where we are heading once we leave Vienna?' Central, Hugh McCulloch had called it. But would Kusak have chosen Geneva for his hiding place? Too many exiles were there already.

'I don't know.'

'We still don't know?'

'You and I don't. Safety precaution. Uncle George is strong on security.'

'Uncle George—you mean Sylvester? Kusak's publisher?'

'Yes. And he *is* my uncle.'

That was a mild surprise. 'So that's how you got enlisted. I wondered.' We are all friends of Jaromir Kusak, McCulloch had said. 'Do you know Kusak?'

'Yes.'

'You've actually met him?'

'In London, when he was staying with Uncle George almost four years ago. But that's the kind of story we can keep for later. Now, I'd better remember all Hugh's instructions. In the right order, too.' She stirred her coffee, allowed one spoonful of whipped cream. 'Now, where was I? Really, you can be disconcerting.'

That makes two of us. He said. 'We were driving to some place called Nowhere.'

'West will be our general direction, if that's any help.'

'I didn't think we'd be driving south to Yugoslavia.'

'Hugh wants you to head for Switzerland.'

'Because it's so central?'

'Well it is! And it has a choice of good airports in various places too. We won't be driving all the way to—well—wherever it is. It could be Paris or Rome. I imagine, and this is only my hunch, that we get to Switzerland first and then we'll be told what airport to reach, and after that we fly out. It's simple enough: we keep on going until we get Hugh's final instructions from Geneva.'

'I could suggest even a simpler plan: pick Irina up and drive straight to the Vienna airport. It's new, and big, one of the best in Europe.'

'And it is being watched. You can bet on that. As the railroad stations in Vienna are being watched. Perhaps even the

55

Danube boats too. No, you see, the point is that the greatest danger for Irina is anywhere near Czechoslovakia, and Vienna is only about thirty miles away. Not much more. The farther west we get, the looser the net will be. The sooner we reach Switzerland, the safer.' She took a deep breath. 'That is Hugh's judgment, and Krieger agrees.'

'They're possibly right,' he admitted as he thought it over. 'Any special instructions on our route?'

'Krieger is working out our first stop now. After that, you will have to choose the best roads. I think we'd better avoid the logical way through Innsbruck.'

'Too simple?' he suggested with a smile.

'Too clogged. At this time of year everyone is travelling in their pretty new automobiles. There were traffic jams yesterday, as long as three hours at a time, all through that valley. And if you're thinking of detouring through southern Germany and coming down into Switzerland from the north—well, only two days ago I was in a line of cars seven miles long at the German-Austrian frontier.'

'Sounds as though I were back on the Long Island Expressway.' Seriously though, bumper-to-bumper traffic was always a strain, and with Irina in the car it would be worse than that. Her nerves wouldn't be too good, these days.

Jo had opened her bag, a nice capacious travelling pouch in the smartest black Gucci leather. 'Which reminds me, you'll need a map.'

'I have several, thank you.' Not very adequate. He hadn't had time to shop in Salzburg for the map he wanted. He'd find it in Vienna.

'Have you this one?' She drew out a Freytag-Berndt map of Austria. 'In four languages. It counts the kilometres for you too.

She placed it on the bench beside his thigh. He took it without any more argument, without even the comment that he had been going to search for it this afternoon.

'Have you got a red tie?' she asked next.

'How's that?'

'Red.'

'Yes, but it's packed in my suitcase in Salzburg.'

'Then take this.' She passed him a folded tie of a strong dark red. He began to laugh. 'You'll need it for tomorrow,' she told him, and the laugh was cut short. 'What suit are you wearing?'

'This jacket and flannels.'

'Tweed,' she said reflectively. It was lightweight, greyish green. She memorized its colour. 'Then a flower in the button-hole is definitely out. Perhaps the tie will be enough. Have you a raincoat?'

'Everyone travelling in Austria has a raincoat.'

'Could you carry it slung over your shoulder?'

'Limey fashion?'

She smiled and nodded. 'And you'll carry a French news-paper, folded so that its title is noticeable. Also a copy of *Oggi* under your arm. It will be glaring enough. You can get these——'

'Yes, I know exactly where to get these in Kärtner Street. But there's one thing I won't do, and that is carry a raincoat slung over my shoulder into any Viennese coffeehouse. Definitely no.'

'Then carry it folded over your arm. I think that's all. . . . Have you got the idea?'

'How I'll look tomorrow morning when I step into the Sacher café? Yes, I've got the picture.' To please her, he ran over the details.

'I know you think this is all comic, and we may as well have our laugh today. Because tomorrow I don't think we're going to be laughing at all.'

'Tomorrow,' he said, 'what do I actually do? Apart from the fancy-dress routine? You were going to tell me the details over our last cup of coffee.'

'This is what Krieger has planned,' she began, and she gave him more instructions, clear and definite. 'So now you know all that I know.' She finished her coffee. 'I'll telephone you tonight around eleven. Very briefly, giving you the exact time when we start moving out in the morning. Now I think I'd better get back to town. I have some shopping ahead of me. For Irina. What type was she—thin, medium, or pleasantly rounded?'

'Medium slender,' he said curtly. 'And not so tall as you. About two inches less.' He signalled to the waitress across the garden.

That makes Irina five feet five in her bare feet, Jo thought. The height was useful: it didn't change as much as medium slender in sixteen years. Had there been addition or subtraction? I'll play it safe, she decided: choose something knitted that can stretch with the curves if necessary, and add a belt in case it floats around her like a tent.

'She's bound to have some clothes of her own,' David said impatiently.

'Not the way Krieger is arranging it.' She glanced at her watch. 'I'll really have to hurry. Can you give me a lift? I came here by trolley car.'

'That's a new twist.' She had to be kidding.

'I thought so. The last place the man expected to find me was on a trolley car.'

'What man?'

'The one who tried to follow me this morning.'

'You were followed?'

'Don't worry,' she told him. 'There's no damage done. I lost him, way back in Vienna.'

'You're sure of that?'

'Quite sure. No one followed me once I had left the second taxi.' David was staring at her with some bewilderment. 'Oh, now, do you think I'd have come here if I wasn't sure?'

'No.' That he could believe. But had she actually been tailed? Or was she expecting something like that and imagination had done the rest? She certainly was enjoying this little triumph, real or not. 'I'll say this for you,' he said lightly, 'you're one girl who can ride in a trolley car and not even muss up her dress.'

'But it's noncrushable——' she began indignantly, and then saw his amusement.

'Of course, you're the travel expert,' he said as if he had just remembered it. 'Now, about this character who tried to follow you——'

'You don't believe it?'

'Well, it might have been for pleasure.' He could imagine plenty of guys who would spend a happy morning following this cutie-pie around.

'Oh, really——' she said, and shook her head. Strange, she thought, how men never took her seriously, except the older ones like McCulloch and Krieger. Perhaps the man who had tried to follow her this morning hadn't taken her seriously either—until she had vanished. 'Well,' she said, cool and detached once more, 'I've given you a warning.'

'And I'll take it,' he promised, and signalled to the waitress. 'I'll walk around Vienna with my radar working.'

At least, she thought, Krieger would find nothing comic in her story. He would be pleased with her progress: she was learning fast. She felt very good indeed as she remembered the man who had kept close on her heels, even managing to follow after she had changed taxis, and then—as she slipped out of the second cab and bolted through a crowd to disappear behind the trolley car's closing door—had stood glaring in the wrong direction.

She glanced at David, now waiting for the bill. He would soon learn all these little dodges, and not even laugh at himself. Here we are, she thought, without a weapon or listening device or an electronic gadget between us. Two very with-it agents, if we are to be judged by current trends in thought: no violence, no ideology, no cold-war mentality. We're just giving a helping hand to some victims of the cold peace. Aren't we the sweet obliging idiots?

Still, it would be worth it, she admitted more seriously. It was a job that someone must do. Using what? Brains and common sense, Walter Krieger had said. These were what mattered in any emergencies. And he ought to know. He had spent four years right in the middle of Europe when the Nazis were all over the place. The less you depended on gadgets, he said, the more you were forced back on your own ingenuity. You'd be twice as cautious if you didn't carry a two-way transmitter disguised as a cigarette lighter, if you hadn't the feeling you could always call on others to help you out of a mess. The important thing was to rely on yourself, and know your limits. That way, no mess. But thank God, she thought, that old hand Krieger was in the background calling the shots.

David added a large tip to the total, and they left the table with a small chorus of *auf Wiedersehen* echoing behind them. (Act III, final scene. Village women sing a farewell song. All ends happily on ascending major chords.) 'I rather liked it here,' David said. Sunlight through vine leaves. 'Pity we didn't have the time after all.'

'Time for what?' She looked at him sharply.

'For getting to know a little about each other,' he quoted back to her.

'Didn't we?' she asked, and smiled.

59

He changed over to safer talk. 'How did you hear about this place?'

'I came here last year with an Austrian friend. I wanted to see some local colour, tourist-packed or not: zither playing, singing, the whole *Gemütlichkeit* bit. He was amused by the way I liked it. But sort of pleased, too.' She was thinking over that evening. 'Oh,' she said, 'it's good to stop being sophisticated every single waking hour. Isn't it?'

He nodded. A strange mixture, this girl: she confounded first impressions. Make a note of that, he told himself, and stop stiffening your jaw every time she takes charge. If she hadn't been passing out instructions today, where would you be? Wandering into Vienna, blind. 'There's more to Krieger than chocolate,' he said. 'What's his real business?'

'Chocolate.' She frowned, trying to find a reason behind his question. This man might be difficult at times, but he was not a fool. Her brow smoothed out. 'Oh, he was in the OSS.'

'That takes us way back. No intelligence work since then?'

'No. But some of his best friends are with the CIA or MI6. Does that damn him?'

'Not enough to matter,' he said, remembering the Reuter's dispatch from Prague. (And there had been more reports in the Salzburg papers, backing up his theory.) Then he grinned, turned the whole thing into a joke, had her smiling too.

The light mood was kept as they drove in his rented Mercedes, a compact four-door in unobtrusive dark green, into the centre of Vienna. It ended abruptly when she said, 'You can't park for more than ninety minutes at a stretch.'

Taking charge again, was she? 'Then I'll try a garage near the hotel. I'll drop you there first.'

'I'll come to the garage with you. There's a big one near the Neuer Markt.'

'Now, is there? And you just happen to know it?'

'Well, I had an idea——'

'I bet you had.'

'I just thought—for tomorrow morning—that I ought to be able to pick up the car for you. It would fit in with your plans.'

'Nicely. But *my* plans?'

'Krieger's.' She spoke with a nervous smile in her dark-blue eyes, quickly covered by the lowering of long lashes.

'It was well named the Office of Strategic Services.' He

shook his head. But he was pleased somehow that this girl was not much of a liar.

'You know,' she said as they approached the Neuer Markt through heavy traffic, 'it might be easier if we each had a name —just to tag on to the end of a sentence or something. Mine is Jo, short for Joanna. And you are Dave, or is it David?'

'Dave. That's what they call me.' Except Irina. . . . Was that why he used David in his own mind? He turned the car abruptly into a quieter street, halted it by the curb. He took out his bag and raincoat, and said, 'Okay, Jo, it's all yours. Don't forget the keys.' He was crossing the narrow street, walking smartly in the direction of the Sacher, before she slipped over into the driver's seat.

Jo telephoned at eleven o'clock.

'How are you?' she asked, letting him identify her voice.

'Just fine. And how are you?'

'A quiet evening, writing postcards. Ten, to be exact.'

'Ten?' he repeated as a check.

'That's right. And now to bed. I'd better catch up on my sleep. Be seeing you.' She rang off.

Ten. The time had been set. Ten tomorrow morning exactly, and Irina would be sitting at the café table. He folded up the map—Jo's map, which he had been studying since he had come back to his room from an excellent but lonely dinner. He put it into the deep pocket of his raincoat, made sure it wouldn't slip out. Unlike the other maps he had, it didn't end at the borders of Austria, but covered a good part of the neighbouring countries beyond the actual frontiers. Then he packed away his guidebook and the yellow turtle-neck he had worn today, discarded the magazines and paperbacks that cluttered up his bag. He didn't think he'd have much time for reading in the next couple of days.

Couple of days? He couldn't tell at this stage. He wasn't even sure where they'd make the first stop in the journey. Krieger was arranging that, Jo had said.

He went over the details he did know, once more. He tried not to think of Irina, and failed. He was nervous, and he could admit it, alone in this gold-and-red bedroom, too many small tables and fat chairs so that he couldn't even pace around and relax some of his tensions. For half an hour he stood at the long

61

window, stared out at the neon signs and the closed shops of the Kärntnerstrasse. Sixteen years was a long stretch. She has probably forgotten me, he thought. And perhaps it won't be Irina I'll see. A fake, a substitute. In that case, Irina could be dead. She could have been forced to write to her father, and then—afterwards——

He got a grip on himself. He telephoned downstairs and put in an order for breakfast at seven here in his room. There was some small difficulty at first—he ought to have ordered earlier, or written it out for the floor waiter, or something—but he managed to get his way by means of some fluent German. A useful language for giving commands. He ought to try it on Jo sometime.

Then there was nothing else to do but get to bed. Tomorrow . . .

Chapter Six

IRINA HAD LOST COUNT of the days of waiting. They were all alike, running one into another in the sameness of routine in Ludvik's flat. Only Sunday had been made noticeable by the tolling of so many church bells. On Monday it was once more the sound of distant traffic, of children shouting in the street four floors below. All she could see outside the windows was warm sunlight streaming down on the rooftops and attics opposite. She had been told by Ludvik not to go near either of the two front windows. She had to stay well out of sight, not play the radio, never answer the door but retreat into the small bedroom and lock herself in; and, if anyone did enter the flat, she was to keep absolutely quiet.

The top-floor flat was small, poorly furnished, and hot in this weather. Alois shared its expenses, but it was Ludvik who had rented it three months ago. Soon they would be leaving again—she had gathered from their talk that they kept moving three or four times a year. Even their jobs were makeshift, perhaps to shield their true identities. Alois, once a journalist in Brno, was now employed in nightwork at a garage. Ludvik, who had been an accountant back in Prague, had a job as a part-time waiter in a restaurant.

This arrangement always left one of them in the flat, possibly to have a ready answering service for their telephone. Perhaps, too, it made sure that no one searched their place. Visitors were few, and stayed only briefly. The friendly but curious caretaker hadn't even got inside the door. She lived on the ground floor, an elderly woman. Not to worry about her, Ludvik had told Irina, he could jolly the old girl along. Just keep out of sight.

Irina's anxiety about the caretaker didn't quite leave her. It could have been possible, when the two men had brought her here, that the old woman had seen them smuggle her quietly up the long dark staircase. The treads were of stone, she remembered. She had tried to move silently, but she had been exhausted. Had the caretaker heard her heels on the first landing? Her own heart had leapt at the sound, small, but loud against the silence.

'Nonsense,' Ludvik had said. 'She would have been upstairs next morning demanding additional rent. She's more interested in money than politics. She's my friend, didn't you know? I got this flat through her.'

Alois had said nothing. But he seldom spoke. He would leave around ten in the evening, return by eight in the morning, eat the food she had prepared for him, say little more than his thanks, and go to bed. When he rose, at four in the afternoon, he ate breakfast and searched through the newspapers, and then—when she cleared away his dishes—he spread papers and notes on the table and began working on the pamphlets he was preparing for delivery across the frontier. He never mentioned his brother, just watched her with sad eyes when she tried to talk a little, said only a few words in reply, an occasional phrase.

He blames me for his brother's death, Irina kept thinking. If I hadn't tried to cross the frontier, Josef wouldn't have been left dead beside a barbed-wire fence.

And yet Alois had been the one to give up his small bedroom so that she could sleep comfortably. It had a high window which let her breathe in these warm nights. He had moved into a little dark cubbyhole, a storeroom possibly, with only a ventilator shaft for air.

On that first night she had been too distraught to notice what he had done; next day her protests were only met with a stubborn refusal. Ludvik, who slept in an alcove separated from the living-room by a faded green curtain, was amused. 'Alois must think you're something special,' he told her. 'He doesn't give up his bed to other guests. Oh, yes, we have them. Occasionally. And the caretaker has never tumbled to any of you yet.' Ludvik was the one who did most of the talking. He was making a considerable effort to keep her cheerful and confident. She ought to be grateful, but she still didn't really like him. He tries too hard, she kept thinking. He is kind and he is competent, and I am stupid. It's this room. It's this waiting.

Tonight she sat down at the table opposite Alois. It was five o'clock and he was absorbed in wording a new diatribe. He looked up in surprise. Usually she kept in the background, read old magazines, avoided the current papers as if she had come to expect nothing but bad news from them. The brief reports for this last week had been about the trials: familiar names were being listed; the more liberal Communists were being sentenced. The long pamphlet he had been writing gave fuller details and would let the people back in Prague know more than they would read in *Rude Pravo*.

Irina looked at him, her large eyes pleading. For a moment both were silent. She's too pale, he thought; too tense. 'Is this Wednesday?' she asked.

'Thursday.'

'Whatever happened to Wednesday? And how long is it now, Alois? My eleventh night here? Oh, it can't be!'

He nodded. 'Sometimes we have to wait. Don't worry. You are safe.'

'I know.'

He laid down his pen, studied her face. 'You need fresh air. You need to walk in the sun. But you'll soon have all that.'

'Don't *you* ever get out for exercise? Can't you ever go to a theatre, or see your friends?'

'Oh, I'll meet my friends and spend some days with them when——' He hesitated.

'When I'm off your hands.' She stared at the gaunt face which reminded her so much of Josef: an older Josef, less tanned, thinner, less strong in his body, but with the same intelligent eyes. 'Oh, what have I brought on you all?' she cried in agony. She rose, ran to her room.

Alois followed her but she closed the door. He could hear her sobbing. Something is troubling her deeply, he thought as he went back to the table. It isn't the waiting. That is only an added strain. What is it that is troubling her? Josef? He sat down, began writing. Work was his way of forgetting. And now, with Josef's death, with Josef's way of dying, the words that flowed from his pen had even more importance.

Scarcely ten minutes later the telephone rang. As he crossed to the wall beside the stove and unhooked the receiver, he saw Irina standing by the bedroom door. She was always hoping, Alois thought.

He answered, then listened, then spoke in English. With his free hand he beckoned Irina excitedly. He was smiling.

She came over to him, stood hesitant and uncertain, her eyes watching him anxiously. He nodded to her, but put up a hand to keep excited questions from rushing out.

Into the phone he said, 'About half an hour. It depends on the time of day. We can get to the Opera House easily in half an hour when the traffic isn't bad. She will be ready. We await your instructions.'

As he hooked the receiver back in place, he turned to her in triumph. The change in his face, in his manner, was so amazing that she could only stare at him. Then she threw her arms around his neck. So Alois also had been worrying that the call would never come.

He led her over to the table. 'They are ready. They will telephone again tomorrow and let us know the exact time. The place for the meeting must be somewhere near the Opera House. They will tell us tomorrow. They are being very cautious, and that is good. They did give me a description of the man who will contact you—his clothes, what he will carry, so that you can be sure of him. But first—have you a handbag? You mustn't take any luggage, they said. Only a handbag.'

'I have a purse. It isn't big enough to carry——' She hesitated. 'To carry two notebooks I have brought for my father. They were his notebooks—he had to leave them behind, and I found them before the police came searching and——'

'Yes, yes. How do we get you a handbag? If I can find a leather shop open—there's one on the next street——'

'But I shall need some of my clothes.'

'No luggage,' he reminded her. 'I wonder why? They cannot be meeting you at a street corner, anywhere in the open. It must be some place where baggage would look ridiculous.'

She looked at him in amazement. She never could have guessed all that.

'And they'll want you to look different too,' he rushed on. He pulled out his thin wallet. Not much there. The rent had been paid on Tuesday.

'Wait!' Irina ran to the bedroom, came back with her purse. She emptied out the money on the table. 'Take it. Can you find a shop where they'll change Czech currency?'

'I know a place.' But the bag would cost more there. He

66

lifted the folded notes. He couldn't guess how much he'd need. 'You lock the door, and place a chair against it. Don't open for anyone except Ludvik or me. No messenger, no one! Remember?'

'And get a bag that is large enough but not too noticeable. A shoulder-strap is smart.'

He had to smile at that. He closed the door behind him and went running lightly down the flights of steps. Then his pace slowed as he reached the street and walked normally. His excuse would be that he had forgotten his girl's birthday until this last moment. He'd speak with a strong Czech accent to explain the money. Austrians were used to refugees.

Within forty minutes he was back. The handbag was the best he could find in a small neighbourhood store—brown leather, large enough without being comic, shoulder-strap and all. 'And here's the change.' He placed the money carefully on the table.

'That's *very* nice,' she told him as she examined the bag. It wasn't her taste at all. But then her clothes weren't much either: they were the kind of thing that Irina Kusak wouldn't be expected to wear. 'Thank you, Alois.' She gave one of her old smiles. 'I've made some coffee. Now tell me all about the phone call.'

They sat down, elbows on table, facing each other, talking easily. Irina's excitement was infectious. Alois was no longer distant, hesitating. In fact, it was he who brought up Josef's name.

'Josef would be glad for you,' he said. 'I think these Americans have planned very carefully. I feel better now.' He paused. 'That was a bad beginning.'

'And I still don't know how it happened.'

'You've been thinking about it?'

'Constantly.'

'So have I.' He looked into her eyes. She didn't avoid his. 'You saw nothing? No one moving, no one firing from the trees?'

'No one. Nothing. It was peaceful. So quiet.'

'And then the shot. You said you heard only one shot——'

'Only one.'

He was silent.

'I could have been wrong,' she said. 'Ludvik was blocking my view. I couldn't see where the first shot hit.'

'It was growing dark, of course,' Alois said, almost to himself.

'It must have struck close to us.' Unless it was a wild shot. Would a trained marksman fire wildly? Once more, she saw that last brief scene in the wide slope of field. It was becoming shadowed, vague, with only Josef's outline clear-cut. He was stooping to pick up the wire cutters, and she had lost him from view as Ludvik's broad back blotted him out. 'One shot,' she said. 'That was all I heard.' And Josef fell. Then she could see him again, briefly, before she was pulled towards the car. He had lain as if he were asleep, stretched out on the grass, his face turned up to the sky.

Alois sensed the emotion that gripped her and put an arm around her shoulder. It seemed as if the living must always ask questions, even seek blame for a death. What did it matter now? he thought wearily. Josef was gone. Buried by strangers and enemies.

'Perhaps Ludvik had a moment of panic,' Irina said. She was still trying to find an answer. 'That is when one can make a mistake.' I know, she thought; I know that only too well. 'Or am I the one who is wrong? Didn't you hear——'

'Yes,' he said. 'I heard only that one shot. Ludvik made the mistake.' But Ludvik would never admit that. And what did it matter now? Alois asked himself again.

He glanced at the door, and dropped his arm as he saw Ludvik enter.

Ludvik didn't seem to notice the look of embarrassment on Alois's face, or the worry on Irina's. He was genial, and quite in control.

'Well, aren't you two chumming up!' he said. 'That's an improvement.' So they had got round to talking about Josef. *Yes, I heard only that one shot. Ludvik made the mistake.* It was to be expected, of course; but he had hoped it wouldn't happen. Ludvik's smile was broad, his pale eyes expressionless. He made a pretence of searching for a bottle of beer. He had made the mistake, had he? It wouldn't be long before Alois's quick mind took one further step. And then—well, he had better not wait for that moment. 'Any secrets to share?' he asked lightly. His thoughts were harsh and cold.

'The telephone call. It came,' said Irina. 'Alois and I were just discussing it, and——'

'It came? When?' His voice was sharp.

'A little while ago. I must be ready to leave as soon as they call again.'

'Come on, Alois,' Ludvik said, ignoring Irina, 'give me the details. From the beginning.' And when Alois had finished, he said impatiently, 'For Christ's sake, why didn't they tell us the place right away? And settle on a fixed time? We could have worked the rest out by ourselves. The Americans must think they're dealing with a bunch of boobs.'

'A matter of security, I suppose,' said Alois stiffly. 'I like their caution.' He glanced at Irina. 'She'll be safe.'

'I wouldn't say we'd been endangering her. Well, well, our little Irina is on her way. Almost. When does that second call come tomorrow?'

'They didn't say.'

'Cagey bastards.'

'And why not? They don't know us.'

'And we don't know them. So it's even.' He swallowed some beer. 'Did I have a thirst! Walked all the way to Georg's house. He's expecting your pamphlets tomorrow, by the way. How many have you got ready for him?'

'Three. Possibly four if I stay here and work tonight.' Alois rose and went to the telephone. 'I'll let them know at the garage not to expect me.'

'Are you sure it's your editorializing that is keeping you here?' Ludvik asked with a wide grin that rounded his broad square-shaped face. 'You know, there's no need for both of us to be waiting near that telephone tomorrow. I can handle it and get Irina to the meeting place.'

'What about your work?'

'You know damn well I can come and go. There's nothing definite about that job. They don't pay enough.' He laughed, raised his glass of beer in Irina's direction. 'They'll never miss me for one day.'

'I'd like to be here when the call comes; and it may come early,' Alois said. 'I just want to be sure—that's all.' He dialled the garage. (Its owner was a Czech who had been here in Vienna since 1948. He knew enough not to ask questions. Besides, workers who made up for any absence without demanding overtime wages were hard to find these days.)

Ludvik got to his feet, drained his glass, carried it over to the small sink. 'Early, you think? Then I had better get the car and garage it in Anton's place round the corner. Have it ready. Just in case you're leaving at six in the morning ' he told Irina.

'At six?'

'All asleep by ten o'clock!' Ludvik warned her. He was in high spirits. 'And you'd better get these pamphlets finished,' he told Alois as he crossed over to the door. 'Georg said something about sending over for them tomorrow morning.' He left before Alois could answer.

'Who is Georg?'

'A friend. He takes the pamphlets with him when he visits Prague.'

Irina picked up her new handbag. She left the money on the table. 'I won't need it now. And I'd like to think I was subsidizing some of your work.'

Alois shook his head, smiling, gathering up the notes and silver. He put them in her hand. 'Never travel without money, not even when you are with friends.' She is too trusting, he thought. How can a woman who has suffered, as she must have suffered, still have any trust left? Was that what had blinded her to Jiri Hrádek? Was it trust, or misplaced faith, or the stupidity of love? Someday, if we meet again, I may find out. That's one riddle I would like to solve.

'I'll repack,' Irina called to him from the bedroom door. 'And after that I'll get supper.'

'No hurry,' he called back, settling himself once more to work.

The second call came next morning at twenty minutes past nine. Alois, by chance, was nearest the telephone.

As he unhooked the receiver he signalled to Irina, who came running across the room and reached him before Ludvik came out of the bathroom. Alois pulled her close, so that she too could listen.

Ludvik finished drying his hands, threw the scrap of towel on a chair, tried to edge in, gave up. At first he waited impatiently, until he heard Alois say, 'Yes, this is Janocek.' Then he went over to a window, opened it wide, lit a cigarette, looked down at the street. Nothing extraordinary there: safe. He looked now at the small bakery shop opposite, leaning on his elbows, head out of the window to enjoy the morning air.

'All set?' he asked as Alois replaced the receiver.

'We're off—in five minutes. Identifications all arranged.' Alois sounded relieved and happy.

'A brown coat and a blue scarf,' Irina said as she went towards the bedroom, leaving the rest of the explanations to Alois. She was ready. She had only the raincoat and her bulging handbag to pick up. And the scarf. She paused to look at the old discarded canvas bag. The last of her possessions, she thought. But she was taking what mattered: her passport, her papers, some money, the two small notebooks that her father had left behind in his own rush to leave. And there were the little things like powder and lipstick and comb. And the silk scarf, a pretty pale-blue one, which she folded into a cravat, making the brown raincoat look slightly better. She examined the mended tear, where the barbed wire had ripped the fabric. Her stitches were neat: they didn't show too badly. With the belt pulled tight and the handbag's strap hoisted over her shoulder, and the excitement in her eyes, she looked almost jaunty.

She glanced at her watch as she came back into the living-room. Two minutes over; three to go. Excitement ebbed. Anxiety set in.

Alois had finished giving Ludvik the details of the phone call. He was now searching for his shoes. 'Where are they, damn them?' he asked, padding around the room in his old slippers. 'They were under that chair. I know it.'

'I'll get the car. You follow in two minutes,' Ludvik told Irina. 'Turn left when you reach the street. I'll meet you at the corner. And don't worry.' He nodded towards Alois. 'He will find his shoes. He's always mislaying things. I'll get you safely to the Opera House.' Ludvik was out of the door, leaving it wide open in his haste.

Irina kept her eyes fixed on her watch. Her lips felt dry. The two minutes were almost up.

'Got them!' Alois said in triumph. 'Who the hell put them under the dresser? Go on, Irina! Hurry! I'll be with you before you reach the hall.'

She left him jamming a foot into a shoe, and began running lightly down the flight of stairs to the next landing. She was almost at the second floor when two men came climbing up towards her. She pulled herself against the wall, fear gripping her heart. But they passed her in single file, not even bothering to look at her.

She drew a long breath, and ran on.

The entry hall on the ground floor was a dank and dismal place smelling of cats and red cabbage. The caretaker lived there. Irina listened, heard nothing except the cries of a baby behind a closed door.

Quietly she made her way round a battered toy bicycle, a baby carriage, two garbage cans. Then she stepped into the daylight and turned left. Three women with baskets were grouped outside the entrance to the tenement, talking busily. Across the narrow street she saw a scattering of shops. Now she could smell new bread and hot coffee, mingling nicely, coming from a small bakery that also claimed to be a café. She reached the corner. And there was the car, its motor idling, and Ludvik at the wheel.

She slipped in beside him. Almost five minutes since the telephone call had ended. Ludvik went from neutral into first, and they were moving. 'But Alois——' she began.

'He won't make it, I'm afraid. Didn't you meet Georg on the staircase? He was on his way to pick up the pamphlets.'

'I saw two men.'

'Georg with a friend. They'll be leaving for the frontier within an hour. Each will smuggle across two of Alois's editorials and get them printed in a small town south of Prague. And Alois's fine phrases will be circulating in the city streets by tomorrow night. Now, is that service?'

'But Alois wanted to come with us. He——'

'Alois will be too busy giving them final instructions about the way he wants the pamphlets set up. He's an old pro, is Alois. Did you ever read any of his stuff?'

'I suppose I must have.' She had seen several of the single sheets of newsprint that were constantly circulated in Czechoslovakia. But the articles were never signed. She had no way of telling whether she had read Alois or not.

'The clandestine press,' said Ludvik with a wide smile. 'It may not seem very much to you, but it worries the hell out of the security men.'

'How often does Georg make this kind of trip?'

'Now, that's giving away trade secrets, isn't it?' he teased her. 'Let's say he goes when he can, and gets back if he's lucky.'

They were coming into busier streets, and Ludvik concentrated on the traffic. 'You're looking fine,' he said. 'Better than when I first saw you. It must have been dull for you in that flat. Not what you were once used to, was it? But at least you got a rest. How far are you travelling?'

'I don't know.'

'Well, where's your father? You don't have to give me his street number. The name of a country will do.'

'I don't know even that.'

'Then your American friends must know. Just leave it to them. It's the CIA that is stepping in, isn't it?'

'I have no idea.'

'It's bound to be. Can't pass up a good chance.'

'Chance of what?'

'To get you and your father to America. Think of the propaganda blast that would make!'

She tried to turn the conversation. 'Will we get to the Opera House soon?' She was to leave the car at the front entrance and then walk, by herself, to the Sacher café at the back of the Opera House. Those had been the instructions.

'Yes. Traffic could be worse. I suppose that's why they chose this time of day. Who are you meeting? Alois didn't get around to telling me that. Or he forgot.'

'A man.' She stared out at the broadening streets. She could see green trees, masses of flower-beds, a wide park.

'Wearing what? You have to be able to identify him quickly, you know. I'm worried about you, Irina.'

'He's carrying papers and a coat.'

'That's all?' he asked sharply.

If Alois didn't tell him the details, she thought, I certainly won't. 'We stop in front of the Opera House,' she reminded him.

'I'll save you a walk. I'll take you to the corner, just behind the Opera House.'

'No.'

'Why not?'

She didn't answer, pretending to be absorbed in the buildings. They were big and handsome, solid, spaced with wide squares. And trees. Trees everywhere.

Quietly, he said, 'I'd like to come into the café with you. They'd never know. I'd keep at a distance.'

73

'No,' she said again.

'I've got to be sure that you are all right. In fact, I'd like to keep an eye on you all this first day.'

'You will not follow me!'

'But they are strangers.'

'So were you and Alois.' Pointedly, she looked at her watch.

'You know, Irina, you are a big responsibility.' His voice was both worried and friendly. 'I just don't want anything to go wrong. Not now.' He lapsed into silence.

Why do I always feel I am being ungrateful to Ludvik? she wondered. He's trying to help me, and he has risked a lot for me, and all I do is snub him. I'm uneasy with him, and I don't know why. I haven't any real reason at all.

'Here we are,' he said as he pulled up at the corner of a massive building. He had brought her to the rear of the Opera House after all. 'I'll wait here,' he told her, 'until I see you enter the café. Are you sure you don't want me to park the car and join you? At a distance,' he added hastily.

This time she smiled when she said no. She gave him her hand. 'Don't worry,' she told him. 'I'll be all right. And thank you. Thank Alois for me too. Tell him I'm sorry I couldn't say goodbye.'

'The café is at the side of the hotel. See it?' He pointed across the street, towards the left.

Briskly she got out of the car. It didn't move away. He is doing more than he was asked to do, she thought uneasily. When she reached the terrace outside the café she gave a brief glance over her shoulder at the corner of the street. Ludvik was leaving now. But what had kept him there? Curiosity, caution, or distrust of the Americans?

As she crossed over the terrace, her confidence completely vanished. There were people having late breakfasts: a *croissant*, a cup of coffee. She was aware of them, and yet she didn't see them, couldn't even have described their faces or clothes. Nervousness increased to fear as she stepped into the room. What if no one met her? What if she waited, and waited, and no one came? At this moment she could almost wish that Ludvik was following her, watching, making sure.

Walter Krieger had arrived in good time to observe that everything went smoothly. In fifteen minutes Irina should be coming

74

out of the tenement opposite to where he sat, enjoying morning coffee and crisp rolls in the bakery. There were four small tables at its window, and he had one of them. The only other customers for coffee were two men, young husky types, more interested in the street than in the people behind them in the shop, who were buying bread and cake and having a neighbourly gossip. After one sharp glance in his direction, they had turned their backs on him. Which suited Krieger. He wasn't here for friendly conversation.

Yesterday he had strolled through this neighbourhood, to check the address that belonged to the Janocek number. (In six minutes by his watch, Mark Bohn would be telephoning for the last time.) He had noticed the bakery and decided that was where he would station himself and have a clear view, in comfort, of Irina's safe departure. The address hadn't been too difficult to track down. One of his old OSS contacts in Vienna was also a true friend, and now an inspector of police—a useful combination. There had been a possibility, of course, that Irina might not be staying at that address, but Bohn from his first telephone calls had been positive that 'Janocek' was not an answering service: the response was too quick—the man who spoke with Bohn was one who could make decisions without referring his query to someone else in another place. And the fact that Bohn's instructions last night were accepted without any argument, that Janocek saw no difficulty in having Irina leave as soon as the final call came, strengthened Krieger's belief that this was Irina's hiding-place. Of course (Krieger admitted to himself) he could have made a false deduction. But that was all he had to go on. Better that, even if wrong, than nothing at all. And the coffee was excellent.

He kept an eye on his watch, seemed absorbed in his newspaper. At twenty minutes past nine he laid the paper aside, poured himself another cup. He looked at the building opposite, wondering which of its small apartments was now answering the telephone.

How very satisfactory, he thought, to sit and watch something happen when you had done most of the planning. Then his attention suddenly focused on the two men who sat at the next table. What the hell were they watching, to make them so intent?

Two bird dogs, he thought, and picked up his paper again to

disguise his curiosity. Yes, they were looking at one window on the fourth floor of that tenement over there. A man had opened it wide. He was standing in plain view, lighting a cigarette, looking down at the street. Then he leaned his elbows on the sill, stuck his head out as if to enjoy the summer morning. Light hair, noted Krieger, broad shoulders, and a blue shirt. And, damn it, he was looking right here with a smile on his face. Then suddenly he withdrew his head, retreated into his room, leaving the window open.

The two men were on their feet, paying for their coffee. They left directly, headed across the street and entered the building. Now, thought Krieger, this is really interesting. And worrying. He put his paper down, filled his pipe, and watched.

Someone was coming out of the building: the light-haired man, wearing a grey jacket over his blue shirt. He was tall, well exercised too. He disappeared round the street corner, twenty yards away, in a couple of seconds.

Krieger raised an eyebrow. He glanced at his watch. Two minutes later a girl appeared at the doorway of the building. Brown belted coat, blue scarf, blonde hair. She carried a handbag over her shoulder. She wasted no time either. She headed straight for the corner, reached a grey Fiat that had paused there, and within another few seconds she was in the car and it was moving away.

Krieger looked at his watch again. It was twenty-seven minutes past nine. That was Irina. And she was en route. A very satisfactory morning, Krieger decided, except that his pipe had gone out. He relit it, and prepared to leave, money in his hand ready for the cash register.

The baker's buxom wife was ringing up his change when suddenly, cutting right across her pleasant remarks, there was a woman's piercing shriek. He turned to the door, saw something hit the street in front of the building opposite. It was a body. The body of a man. The screaming woman was only a few yards away from it. And now the women beside her were screaming too. A man shouted and ran. More shouts, more people running.

Krieger didn't join the gathering crowd. There was nothing that could be done. The baker's wife had rushed to see, but soon returned—remembering the open till, or perhaps her curiosity was satisfied.

'Poor man!' she told Krieger as he stood by the shop door. 'He was so quiet. Very pleasant. Always polite.'

'Oh?'

'Who would have thought he would jump out of a window? Nearly killed those women too. He came all the way down from that fourth floor. No warning. Terrible, isn't it?'

'Who was he?' Krieger asked. He was watching two men who had come out of the tenement's entrance to move round the edge of the crowd, the same two who had sat at the next table and scanned the street. They began walking towards the corner where Irina had met the car.

'One of those Czech refugees.' She might have said more, but someone called to her from the shop and she hurried inside.

There was a vague disquiet in Krieger's mind. He left without any more delay, following the direction the two men had taken. They had already reached the corner of the street, and turned it. Krieger quickened his pace, glimpsed them entering a small garage. What did he do now? Wait? The last thing he wanted to do was to draw any attention to himself. Even as he hesitated, a small Volkswagen shot out of the garage. The two men hadn't wasted a moment. He made a pretence of studying the nearest shop window, but he had identified them clearly as they drove past.

They were well away before the first police car arrived.

Krieger walked on. The disquiet in his mind was no longer vague. A talk with his friend in the police department was the proper idea. Except that he had little time left in Vienna. Better make time, he told himself sharply. That Czech refugee hadn't fallen or jumped from the fourth-floor window: he had landed well beyond the sidewalk, on the street itself.

Chapter Seven

ON FRIDAY MORNING, David Mennery came down into the hotel lobby with half an hour to spare. He had paid the bill and tipped every uniform nearby, making sure he wasn't leaving the Sacher with any unfinished business behind him. That way, he'd be quickly forgotten. He dropped his bag as near the front door as possible. 'Waiting for a friend,' he told the bellboys on duty there. 'No taxi needed.' And now, at six minutes before ten, he began studying the playbills, notices of concerts, lists of exhibitions, which cluttered the notice-board near the porter's main desk. He was dressed in his light tweed jacket, a grey striped shirt that travelled well, and the red tie. His raincoat was folded over his left arm; partly under the other, held securely by his hand, were his copies of *Oggi* and *Le Monde*. At two minutes to ten he checked the lobby clock. It agreed with his watch. Two minutes before the hour. Irina should be reaching the café.

It lay to his right as he faced the front entrance, near the lobby but separate, with a short passageway leading to a door which made entry convenient for hotel guests. He went back to studying the programme of an open-air concert at Schönbrunn. I'll give Irina a few minutes to find a table and sit down, he decided. She's bound to find one free inside the café on a summer morning: most people will be sitting outside. She'll be somewhere at the back of the room, he reminded himself again: a brown coat and a blue scarf. That should let his eye pick her out quickly, even if by some chance the inside tables were well filled. He knew the routine, but he was nervous. He lit a cigarette, dropped it a minute later into an ashtray. Once more, for the last time, he went over his own movements. He'd possibly have to change some details, improvise when necessary. You always had to be ready for that.

78

At five minutes past ten he walked towards the café, a man who looked—at least he hoped so—as though he had decided to see if his friend had got their meeting place slightly mixed. The bellboy, still lingering beside David's bag, probably thought so. He traded the idea of a tip from David for a more certain prospect now arriving with three suitcases.

David paused at the café door, then entered slowly. More tables were filled than he had expected. He had a chilling shock to see, right in the centre of the room, a figure in brown with brassy blonde hair, delving into a thick slice of *Gugelhupf*. A mountain of *Schlagobers* was rising above her coffee cup. Irina? But there was no blue scarf. Thankfully, he halted just a few steps inside the doorway, his eyes searching the room. A waitress stopped at his elbow to ask, 'Would you like a table, sir? There's a nice one over there by the window.'

He shook his head, saying, 'I was hoping to join a friend. A man with long dark hair and a beard.' Even as he spoke, he glimpsed the brown coat and the blue scarf in the corner just behind him. But at this moment he dared not look more closely.

'Haven't seen him,' the waitress said, all interest lost.

And now he could look. Casually. The woman in the brown coat was sitting very still, her eyes looking straight ahead and unseeing. Her order had not yet been taken, and her hands rested on the table before her. They were tightly folded. It was Irina. No impostor. Definitely Irina.

For a moment David was as paralysed as she was. Then he moved.

He turned, knocked against the table next to Irina's, let the papers fall. She glanced at him nervously, but not at his face: she was seeing the French newspaper and Italian magazine which he picked up from the tabletop. Her eyes went to his tie, to his jacket, to the folded raincoat. And he saw the surge of relief, the easing of her lips. She was gathering up her handbag, as if she was tired of waiting for her order to be taken. She still hadn't looked at his face.

He left at once, pace normal, heading back for the lobby. There he picked up his bag, went out into the sunshine. The back of the Opera House faced him impassively. For a split second he imagined what it must have looked like, bombed out, gutted by fire, another total ruin of war. Then he saw only the peaceful street and the massive building that looked as if it had

79

been there for ever, and the green car swinging out from its shadows to reach him. He took a few steps away from the hotel door, towards the café: that would let the car stop out of sight from the lobby, and it would be easier for Irina too. In a few seconds the Mercedes drew smoothly up beside him.

'Hi, there!' said Jo. 'All well?'

'She's for real.' He opened the front door, saw two small suitcases filling the seat beside Jo. So he jammed his bag down on the floor, dropped papers and raincoat on top of it. 'Move back. I'll take the wheel.'

'You'd better concentrate on her.'

That was the last thing he wanted to do at this moment.

Jo caught sight of a blue scarf. 'And here she comes!' Which settled all arguments.

David had the rear door open, his hand extended to catch Irina's elbow and steer her into the car. She looked at his face as she stepped inside; looked again. He heard her gasp. He urged her on with a firm grip and cut short any hesitation. Still speechless, Irina slid over the seat to make room for him. He followed, closing the door as the car began to move. He glanced at the café as they passed by: no one there was paying the least attention; no one was hurrying out or rising from a table. Then he looked back over his shoulder. The hotel entrance was equally peaceful.

'I think we made it,' he said.

Jo didn't speak. She had been watching her side mirror with a frown, and was now concentrating alternately on the rearview mirror and on the traffic in the square ahead. Six streets converged there, not all at once, but closely enough to bewilder a stranger. She was still frowning.

David said, 'There's a quiet spot—just over there. Pull up and I'll take over.'

'Not now!' Her voice was sharp with anxiety. Yet she was manœuvring the Mercedes neatly. Like most efficient drivers, David was uneasy when anyone else was at the wheel, but he began to relax a little as he marked the way she handled the car. She was good: no violent spurts, no afterthoughts that took corners wildly, no weaving in and out. So what worried her? He looked once more over his shoulder. Something in that traffic bothered her, but he couldn't tell what it was. She made a left turn, headed south; then once she crossed the Ring—the giant

80

boulevard that circled the inner heart of the city—she changed direction again, this time travelling to the east. Again she made a left turn, and headed back to the north; east once more, and finally—after one more foray to the north—she swung the car west.

'That was quite a performance,' David told her.

She flashed a smile, glanced for a split second at Irina, and concentrated on the traffic. David relaxed completely: Jo really kept her eyes on the street both ahead and behind her; no problem there.

He settled back into his seat, let himself look at Irina. She was watching him, her blue eyes large and wondering. Her hair was the same light blonde; but it wasn't long any more. It now fell to just below her ears, a little uneven here and there, but still soft and gleaming. She had seemed pale in the café; now there was a touch of colour back in her cheeks, a gentle flush perhaps from the excitement of these last fifteen minutes. Her face was thinner, and sad. She wasn't the young laughing girl he remembered. But she was still Irina.

'Well,' he said, keeping his voice light, 'have you recovered from the shock?'

She shook her head. 'I didn't look at you. I didn't think I'd even know the man. It was only when I was getting into the car——' She looked away from him. 'I ought to have recognized you!' She was upset about that.

'But you found the tie too fascinating?'

'And reassuring. Someone *had* come to meet me after all.'

'Did you doubt that?'

'Yes. Something could have gone wrong. And then—I saw the tie.'

'Well, thank Jo for that. Jo Corelli.' He pointed to the driver's seat. 'She studied psychology at Vassar.'

Jo laughed. 'Don't believe him. I studied as little as possible. The tie was Krieger's idea.'

'In that case I can take it off without hurting your feelings.' He removed it with relief and opened the top button of his shirt. Besides, it was just as well to get rid of anything noticeable.

'Ah,' said Jo, 'the negligent type? I guess it's more suitable now.' She pulled off her hat—a large-brimmed white felt with a rakish air, which had been angled smartly over her left eye—and threw it on top of his raincoat. Then, with a simple straight piece of road ahead of her, she could free one hand to fluff her hair out of its tight brushed-back effect.

'How clever!' Irina said, watching her. 'You look quite different.'

'We'll soon have you different too.' Jo patted the top suitcase. 'This is all yours.'

Now, isn't this the damnedest thing? David was thinking. I'm here, sitting beside Irina, and all I do is make chitchat with Jo, and I can't even bring myself to talk to Irina. Where do I begin, anyway?

Probably it was better like this. It kept everything businesslike; no sentiment allowed. But it wasn't what he had expected. And what was Irina feeling? He glanced at her, and surprised a small smile on her lips as she watched him. She put out her hand and he took it. But still neither of them spoke.

Jo broke the silence. 'Now I can agree with you, Dave. I think we have made it.' She was putting on speed as they left the last of the suburban streets, taking the highway that skirted the southern bank of the Danube at this point.

'What seemed to be the trouble back there?' He hoped he sounded nonchalant, for Irina's sake. Let's play everything low key, he told himself.

'A grey Fiat.'

David felt Irina's hand stiffen. 'How far did it follow us?'

'Quite a way. But we lost him, I think.'

'Where did he pick us up? At the Sacher?'

'He was parked just opposite. Then as we moved away, he swung out and started following.'

'Who the hell could that have been?' David's worry exploded.

'Who the hell could have been trying to follow Walter Krieger all this week? And me, yesterday?' That had jolted David: so he believed her now, did he? '*Somebody* knew we were in Vienna.'

And somebody knows why, thought David. But how? How? He became aware that Irina had slipped her hand out of his. She was sitting with her arms folded around her as though she were cold. 'Are you all right, Irina?' She nodded, but the little worry crease between her dark eyebrows was still there. We frightened her, he thought: all this talk of being followed. Jo's angry; I'm confounded; but Irina is scared. He looked at her, trying to establish contact again, as little as it had been. A mask had slipped over her face, a protection against any mind reading. And once she had hidden nothing. He remembered now her frankness and her laughter: her spontaneity, her scorn of pretence. Changed days, he thought grimly as he blotted that memory from his mind. It was painful to recall.

Irina was telling herself that it was too late to speak up. She had missed the chance. She could have said, perhaps *should* have said—when Jo spoke of a grey Fiat—that there was nothing to worry about: it was only Ludvik Meznik, being too officious. She could easily have explained that. And yet there were some things about Ludvik she couldn't even explain to herself. Ludvik Meznik and Alois Pokorny had no more responsibility for her once the Americans took over. That had been made clear to her by Josef Pokorny before he started his journey with her to the frontier. Josef had only been repeating the instructions from the resistance committee that had arranged their part of her travels: they would take her as far as the meeting point in Vienna: no farther. They were having no direct contact whatsoever with the Americans, and wanted none.

But what really appalled her was that Ludvik had gone beyond his instructions. By attempting to follow her he could endanger his friends back in Prague. Her ex-husband would welcome any chance to link the resistance movement with American Intelligence. Jiri had said as much in his tactful references to 'foreign help' in her escape: he was always so sure that Americans were behind the whole resistance. Was that the real reason why he had let her go? Not to persuade her father to return to Czechoslovakia, just as other exiles were now being coaxed back? (That was the explanation Jiri gave; that was the plea he had made so earnestly, along with a promise to let her father live and write in peace—no harassment, no retribution.) Was the true unspoken reason simply a plan to trap American Intelligence and Czech resistance into some mistake that could be used against them? And here was Ludvik Meznik —stubborn, stupidly clever, overhelpful Ludvik—playing right into Jiri's hands. Ludvik might very well attempt to make contact with the Americans and talk his confident way into joining them—he was just the type who'd like to boast how he had helped bring Irina to meet her father.

83

Irina closed her eyes and tried to sort out her jumbled ideas. She had got some things right, she felt, and some things wrong. But which was which, she didn't know. It all came to this: how much could she believe Jiri Hrádek? Was he really fighting for his own position in the party, as he had said? If so—and how cynical it all was—she could believe him: her father's return to Czechoslovakia would be a personal triumph for Jiri. Yes; that was the only reason that could convince her that Jiri for once had been forced to tell the truth. Dear God, she thought. She opened her eyes, looked at David, and then at Jo. Then, for the first time, she noticed the countryside through which she was travelling.

She could see a curving river, flowing strongly; hills that rose and fell gently, with outcrops of rock on their summits, and vineyards on the lower slopes. Up on the hilltops were perched the ruins of old castles, or the rising towers of medieval abbeys still intact. For a moment, in panic, she thought she was back in Czechoslovakia. 'Where are we?'

'We'll cross the Danube in another fifteen minutes,' Jo told her. 'After that, we are only about three miles from Dürnstein. We'll stop there, and you can change clothes.'

David reached over for his coat, pulled out his map. Dürnstein. 'Why Dürnstein?' he asked. It was only fifty miles or so from Vienna. They had long since left the big highway, but the first-class road they were following along the right bank of the Danube was smooth, if narrow. At the steady rate they had been going, Vienna's suburbs were only an hour away.

'Krieger booked a room in a hotel there for Irina. He hopes to join us for a short visit. Then, refreshed in spirit if not in body, we'll take off in all directions. Have you decided on your first stop after that, Dave?'

'I'll decide in Dürnstein.' I don't like the way we were followed from the Sacher, he thought; and I like even less the idea that someone tried to put Krieger and Jo under surveillance. And least of all I like the way that Irina froze so completely at the mention of a grey Fiat. She spent most of this journey in some other world, and it wasn't a pleasant one.

'We're early,' Jo said, 'in spite of all the time we wasted in twists and turns through Vienna. Krieger suggested he'd meet us around one o'clock. So why don't I pull over at the next *Aussichtspunkt*, and we can get our entrance to the Dürnstein hotel neatly planned? What we do and how we do it—that kind of thing.'

'Save time and confusion,' David agreed. 'Okay, pull over. Now!' The car eased out of the light stream of traffic and on to a small parking area with a gravelled surface and a view of the river, sheltered at the side by trees.

Irina had been listening intently.

'Krieger?' she asked as they got out of the car. 'Is he also with the CIA?'

'Also? What do you mean by *also*?' said David, startled. 'None of us are. We're just a bunch of civilians.'

She stared at him blankly. He wondered for a moment if her English had been so little used recently that she had not caught his meaning. Once she had been fluent, and had read and talked with ease.

'All of you?' she asked. She didn't believe it.

'Just a company of friends,' Jo said brightly. 'There's Walter Krieger, who knew your father in 1943—in Slovakia when they were thinking up ways to make the Nazis hopping mad. Krieger was a liaison man; your father was one of the resistance fighters. Then there's Hugh McCulloch, who was once a diplomat in Vienna, and went into Czechoslovakia to see your father. In 1957, I think. And there's Uncle George, who has been your father's publisher in London since 1935. And I have known Hugh and his wife for years—in Washington, where I run something called a boutique for Maxwell's. That's where all the diplomats' wives buy their clothes, and want things that remind them of Paris and Rome and London and what have you. So I had to be in Paris in July, and I came on to Vienna. I travel a lot. And that's me. As for Dave—he's now a music critic, and he travels sometimes. Oh, and there's Mark Bohn,' Jo added as an afterthought. 'Although, of course, he's really on the sidelines.' She paused. 'Did I speak too quickly? I'm sorry. Shall I go over it more slowly?' Because, Jo decided, all these little facts were important for Irina. They could reassure her that the people around her were her friends.

Irina shook her head, still bewildered. 'I understood most of it. But so much organization—so much——' She halted abruptly. It had been Ludvik, this morning, who had put the idea into her head that the Americans were bound to be professional agents. And before Ludvik, there had been Jiri.

85

He too had assumed that the CIA would be with her. 'Oh, no!' she said, and she began to laugh.

David and Jo exchanged glances.

Irina recovered. But her eyes were still smiling as she said to David, 'What do you want me to do when we reach the hotel?'

With amusement, he nodded at Jo. 'Krieger's little conveyor belt,' he said. 'Ask her. Jo gets all the instructions and she passes them on.' Of that we can be sure. But a fashion buyer? Probably she ran the whole of Maxwell's too. So she had paid a visit to the Paris showings before she came on to Vienna? Her excuse, if needed, for this trip was as question-proof as his own. To Jo he said, 'And what were you buying in Vienna? Dirndls?'

'Alpaca and petit point,' Jo said abruptly. 'Now let's get down to business. Passports, for instance.' She produced a British one from her handbag and passed it to Irina, who was standing with her back to the road. 'You can examine it,' Jo said. No one in a passing car could see what Irina was holding.

'Tesar?—Irina Tesar? But that's using my mother's name.'

'She registered you as that. You were born in London, weren't you?'

David said, 'So she was. March 1939.' That was after Kusak had smuggled his pregnant wife out of Czechoslovakia and returned to join the anti-Nazi underground.

'It's legal enough,' Jo went on. 'The British can claim you as their subject, you know. So go along with them: that's really all you're doing. But why your mother didn't register your birth under the name of Kusak—that's beyond me. Unless she was an advance guard for Women's Lib.'

'She might have wanted to keep Kusak safe,' David suggested. It was the first kindly thought he had ever had for Hedwiga Kusak, née Tesar. But it could be true: if any Nazi agent, back in 1939, had reported that Kusak's wife and daughter were in London, they could have been used—by threats of abduction, or even by some real body snatching—to smoke Kusak out into the open.

'Put the passport in your bag—if it can hold it,' Jo urged. 'You can't stay at any hotel in Austria without producing it when you register. The same goes for——' She bit her tongue: she had nearly let Switzerland slip out there. 'For other countries in Europe. So now you're all set.'

Irina tried to get the passport down the side of her handbag. 'I'll take out the other one,' she decided. 'David, would you carry it for me?'

'You have a Czechoslovak passport?' Jo asked incredulously. 'How on earth did you get it? Or is it an old one faked up?'

It seemed real enough to David as he glanced at it, and brand new too. He hid his surprise. 'I think you should hang on to this yourself. But don't use it meanwhile. Anything else I could carry for you?'

Irina hesitated. Then from the bottom of the handbag she drew out a small automatic.

'Good God,' David said, seizing it—it was so neat that it could be hidden by his hand—and jamming it into his pocket. Jo had said nothing at all: she was staring at the road, perhaps hadn't even seen the exchange. 'Where did you get that, Irina?' he asked quietly.

'It was at the back of my father's desk. I found it before——'

Jo said, aghast, 'It's the same car! He followed us after all!'

'The Fiat?' asked David. 'But that's impossible.'

'It *was* the grey Fiat.'

'There are hundreds of Fiats on the road, and dozens that are grey.'

'But I had this one's number. And a man was driving. Alone.'

'Did he see us?' A damn stupid question, David thought, the moment it was out.

'Couldn't miss us.'

'Then we'll follow him for a change.' And try to solve one puzzle. The Fiat had been at least fifteen minutes behind them. 'Did you see his face?'

'Briefly. He glanced at us as he passed. He seemed startled to find us admiring the view.' Just the same silly stare he wore yesterday after I hopped on to a streetcar, Jo thought. I'm almost sure it's the same man, fair hair ruffled and square face gaping. But I'd better be sure before I blurt it out: Irina had become paralysed enough at the mention of a grey Fiat. 'All right, let's move on,' Jo said, sounding as untroubled as possible. 'I still have some things to tell Irina. Irina! Come along. We'll plan, and let Dave drive.'

'Perhaps,' said David as he eased the car back into the

broken stream of traffic, 'we may have to change our plans. If that character is waiting along the road to see whether we cross the bridge, he'll be with us all the way to Dürnstein.'

'But we have to get there. Krieger——'

'To hell with Krieger, at this moment.'

'No, no! We've got to keep in touch. Or else we're—well ——' Jo didn't finish, as she noticed Irina's taut face.

Irina said slowly, 'I was driven to the Opera House this morning. In a grey Fiat. By one of the men who met me when I crossed the border.' Her voice sank almost to a whisper. 'Ludvik Meznik. He might try to follow us—to see if I were safe.'

'That still doesn't explain how he could be taking this road, so far behind us,' David said. 'And there are plenty of Fiats wandering around. You didn't notice the number of Meznik's car, Irina?'

'No.'

Irina wouldn't. That wasn't the way her mind worked. 'Well, there's nothing waiting for us near the bridge,' David said. There was no Fiat in sight, anywhere. In the back seat he could hear Jo talking, trying to bring Irina back to their arrival at the Dürnstein hotel. He had nothing to do but drive, and keep puzzling this thing out.

First: the man had watched them leave the Sacher, tried to follow, and didn't manage it. (Then how had he reached here a quarter of an hour behind them?)

Second: the man had known all along where they were heading. His attempt to follow them from the Sacher was only a check, to see if his information was correct. (Possible, but unpleasant in its implications.)

Third: the man had given up the attempt to follow and had telephoned—or made contact with—someone who could give him their destination. (Probable, and equally unpleasant to contemplate.)

Let's hope, David thought, as they crossed over a massive iron bridge to reach the left bank of the Danube, that there will be a dearth of Fiats of any colour in Dürnstein.

It was a small but densely packed village, clinging on to the side of a high hill that almost pushed it from its perch above the Danube, into the water below. It had one main street, roughly paralleling the course of the river, with medieval shops and houses on either side, arches and buttresses all restored and painted, and flowers spilling from every window-sill. The street was packed too. The tourists were stopping for lunch. Cars and buses everywhere. He had to drive almost at stalling speed.

'Where?' he asked in desperation. 'Where, Jo, where?'

'There's a baroque church standing high above the river. See its tower?'

'Hard to miss.'

'The hotel is just beyond it—also above the riverbank. Turn left once we reach the end of this street. Krieger said it was almost a U-turn.'

David made it, just in time to let him drive through a wide gateway into a sizeable courtyard. On one side, near the street, it was high-walled, blotting out all sight of traffic or houses; on its other side there was a low parapet edging the top of a plunge of rock to the Danube below. The hotel itself faced the massive gate and almost filled that end of the courtyard. So we must drive out the way we drove in, thought David. He didn't much like the idea: it gave him no choice at all, and he might need it if the Fiat was anywhere among the parked cars. 'Do you see it?' he asked Jo, as he concentrated on choosing a place for the Mercedes. He found one, a tight squeeze, but tucked away in the corner between the giant wall and the hotel. At least he had avoided the more open Danube side of the courtyard.

'Neat,' Jo said. She was still looking around. 'No, I don't see that Fiat, but it has got to be here. Its driver is over by the parapet, watching every car that comes in.'

'Are you sure?'

'I'm sure.' Jo's voice was sharp. 'And you know him, don't you?' she asked Irina. That was obvious. When she had seen the man, Irina had flinched.

'Yes. Ludvik Meznik,' Irina said. 'Oh, the fool!'

'He's more than that. He looks like big trouble to me.'

David cut in, 'I take Irina into the hotel and see her safely into her room. Right?'

'Yes. And wait there. I'll be along soon, with Walter Krieger. I'm going to look for him on the terrace. It's almost one o'clock now.'

'He'll change his mind about meeting us as soon as he hears of Ludvik,' David predicted. 'So tell him I'll be heading out as soon as Irina has changed her clothes.'

'Heading where?'

'To Graz.'

'Graz? Oh, come on, Dave. That's right down in the south-eastern corner of Austria. Twenty miles to your left and you'll be in Hungary; twenty miles farther on and you'll find yourself in Yugoslavia. It's way out of your direction.'

'Graz,' David said firmly. 'And if it seems unlikely to you, then it will seem impossible to Ludvik and his friends. Couldn't you give him a shove over that cliff, or something? Keep him from watching us as we leave?'

'We hold one little ace. Do you see the dark-blue Chrysler over there? Between a Renault and a Cadillac? It's Krieger's. You'll drive it out. We'll give you half an hour's start, and then we'll take the Mercedes on to Salzburg. Where are you stopping in Graz? Any idea?'

'There's a place called the Grand Hotel something or other. It's on the riverbank, near the main bridge.'

'So you know Graz?' That was better. 'Okay. Well, I'll pass the word to Krieger. And after Graz, where?'

'Lienz.'

'Near the Italian border?' She was astounded. 'You certainly are trying to confuse Ludvik.'

'Or whoever replaces him.'

'Yes,' she said slowly, 'there is that to think of too. Well, I'll dump it all in Krieger's lap. He can do the worrying for us. Now, if you and Irina would just distract Ludvik's attention away from me for one small minute—Give me your bag, will you?'

David nodded. He lifted the bag and his coat over the back of the seat with one hand, while with the other he presented Jo with the Mercedes' keys and papers. He picked up Irina's suitcase, and was out of the car in another few seconds. He took Irina's arm, and steadied her.

'Ready?' he asked as she stood beside him.

She nodded, her face pale again but calm, as they began walking towards the hotel entrance. Thank God she could be cool in an emergency, and this was definitely one. He himself was glad that Krieger was around, but he could imagine Krieger's fury: all that neat planning to be discarded, and Graz suddenly thrust into his calculations.

Irina said, 'What will she do with your bag?'

'Take it to the Chrysler.'

'And Ludvik's too busy watching us to notice her?'

'That's the idea.' And it could save time when Irina and he were leaving. They would need every moment. 'We'll manage it,' he told her more confidently than he felt. He even mustered an encouraging smile for her as they entered the hotel.

Chapter Eight

THE TERRACE of Schloss Dürnstein (now a hotel) had been placed with a view in mind. It stretched along the side of the converted castle to overlook a sweeping curve of river. Below it a wall of sheer rock fell to the Danube's edge. The contrast between this northern side of the river and its opposite bank was dramatic: here, a giant bulge of cliffs and crags stood strong as a mailed fist against the fast flow of water; over there, sandy beaches had been pushed by the current into a low shore-line, bordering a far-and-wide vista of gentle fields and undulating hills and scattered villages.

Jo Corelli reached the terrace by the safe route of the hotel's dining-room. (The other approach was down some steps from the courtyard, and completely visible to the man who still waited up there by the parapet.) Bright sun, tables with gay umbrellas, and a host of people combining a midday meal with an admirable panorama. Food for body and soul, she thought as she stood well back against the dining-room wall, keeping out of sight from the courtyard. Among the mixture of tourists, their clothes as bewildering as their languages, she could not see any thatch of grey hair combined with heavy eyebrows, a moustache, and a pipe. No Walter Krieger.

Then she saw Mark Bohn, his long strands of black hair lifted by the slight breeze, grey sideburns fluffed over tanned cheeks. He had a small table to himself, probably because it was jammed close against the hotel wall at the far end of the terrace, with no view except the backs of other guests. He was reading a newspaper and enjoying his second bottle of beer. He didn't even notice Jo until she sat down opposite him.

Bohn said, 'You're punctual. No trouble? How is she?'

'Fine. Where's Walter Krieger?'

'Detained in Vienna.' Bohn grinned as he saw her consternation and, having had his mild joke, added, 'Not to worry. I'm here.' He became serious. 'Krieger had some business to finish—he didn't say what it was when he called me at ten-thirty, but I suppose he didn't feel like talking much over the phone.'

'Did he sound worried?'

'Not at all. Very brisk, very squared away. Asked me to substitute for him. Even sent his car round to my hotel. It was waiting for me ten minutes later. Now, is that co-operation or co-operation?'

'When do we see Krieger?'

'You don't. He will call you from Vienna at one-thirty.'

Jo glanced automatically at her watch. 'Call me where? Irina's room?'

'Yes. It's better than being paged around a hotel lobby.'

Jo nodded. Her stomach muscles untightened. 'Oh, damn Krieger,' she said. 'There we were, chasing up here to be in time, and he was still finishing some deal in Vienna.'

'At police headquarters. The call came from there.'

'How on earth did you find that out?'

'Elementary, my dear Watson. I asked the man who brought the car around to my hotel.'

'Police headquarters?' Then she remembered. 'Not on business, Holmes. A farewell visit with one of his wartime buddies. These old boys really hang on to their friendships, don't they?'

'Knowing Krieger, it was also a useful visit.'

'Could be,' she admitted, and smiled. 'Well, if you're replacing him, you'd better order some lunch, and be ready to move out by——' She tried to calculate. 'Half an hour after Dave and Irina leave. We'll let you know when. You'll stay here?' Mark was a wanderer: curiosity-driven.

He said, 'Where else is there? I don't intend to climb up that mountain behind the village to see the old castle, not even to pay homage to the memory of Richard the Lionheart. As for the cliffs—a nice plunge into the Danube? No, thanks. I'll sit here with pleasure and think of the mobs in the main street.'

'Wish I could sit too. But I'd better pass the news to Dave. He'll be mad. He wanted to leave as soon as I had seen Krieger.'

'Why the rush?'

'There's a man hanging around the courtyard, with an eye

on our Mercedes. Which reminds me'—she held out her hand
—'Dave will need the Chrysler's keys, Mark.'

'Oh? We're switching?'

'Yes. You'll take the Mercedes back to Salzburg: here are its
keys and papers. You can turn it in to the rent-a-car place.'

'Look—I've done enough driving for one day. I'm not a goddamned chauffeur.'

'But I'll probably be with you, sweetie. Think how pleasant
that would make the journey! Besides, it isn't too far, and a
nice easy highway.'

'And then what?'

'You're a free man. I'll be heading for Graz.'

He looked at her in astonishment. 'Where did you get that
cockeyed idea?'

'It's Dave's.'

Bohn laughed and shook his head. 'Where does he think he's
going—Yugoslavia?' Then he asked thoughtfully, 'Or Italy?
Is that where Jaromir Kusak has tucked himself away?'

'I hope so,' Jo said evasively. If Mark hadn't been told about
Switzerland as their target, she wouldn't be the one to tell him.
Not that she disliked Mark. On the contrary, he had brightened
up many a Washington party for her. 'Then I could recuperate
at my parents' house.'

'Where are they living now?' Her father, Bohn remembered,
was a retired Italian diplomat, who had been stationed in
Washington for years.

'Rome.' She rose. Mark's perseverance never failed to amuse
her. Next he'd be asking for their address, and find himself a
pleasant stopover whenever he travelled in Italy.

'No need to hurry away. If Krieger said one-thirty, he meant
one-thirty.'

'I've got to find Irina's room.' And that could take ten
minutes, judging by this labyrinth. She glanced up at the hotel
windows, noticing with dismay how several wings had been
added on. 'See you around two o'clock,' she said, and left.

The hotel clerk's son (one of three small boys anywhere
between the ages of nine and twelve, who were hovering around
the lobby, eager to assist with baggage or questions) guided Jo
along several narrow corridors twisting round an interior
courtyard, until he reached the proper door. As he pointed

to it, the smile of triumph on his face was as beguiling as his helpfulness.

'Thank you. I would have been lost without you,' said Jo in her best German. She slipped him five *Schilling*, which delighted him. 'And if you will please come back here in half an hour, I will give you another five.'

'Here?' He touched the wall beside the door.

'Yes, exactly here. What's your name?'

'Gerhard.'

'In half an hour, Gerhard?' She showed him the time on her watch just to make sure. He nodded solemnly and left. Then she knocked on the door.

'Who's that?' David's voice asked.

'Just your little ray of sunshine.' The door opened and she slipped inside. 'And ten minutes to spare,' she said thankfully.

'Before what?' David's tone was sharp.

'Before Krieger telephones us from Vienna.'

David stared at her.

'Then who brought the Chrysler here?'

'Mark Bohn. He's waiting outside—on the terrace—in a plaid linen jacket. Very with-it. But I wish he'd thin out those sideburns. They——'

'Waiting for what?'

Yes, Jo thought, Dave is having a rough time. 'For me.' She glanced over at Irina, who was standing at the window. The suitcase lay opened on the bed, but Irina was still wearing her old skirt and blouse. Well, it's nice that one of us really has time to admire that view. 'Better change, Irina,' she warned. In a lowered voice, she asked David, 'Difficulties?'

'I don't know. It's as if she's afraid to talk to me.'

'To talk to anybody. I couldn't get through to her at all. Well, let's get on with the job.' Jo turned to the suitcase, picking up a blue dress and a smart chain belt. 'She's thinner than I thought. Lucky I brought something to give some kind of shape at the waist. Irina!'

Irina came slowly over to the bed.

'What's wrong?' Jo asked bluntly.

Irina took the dress, didn't even notice it. 'I am putting you all in danger,' she said, her voice barely audible. 'I should never have come——'

'Nonsense. Let's try these clothes on, shall we? Dave wants

us to be ready to leave as soon as he talks with Walter Krieger. Right, Dave?'

David nodded. He was watching Irina's face. She believes what she says, he decided. She senses danger. She's still the Irina I once knew: she is afraid for us, not for herself. 'Irina——' he began gently, and didn't finish. The telephone was ringing.

Jo picked up the suitcase in her arms. 'Come on, Irina.' She led the way into the bathroom. She called back to David, 'I'd like to talk with him too.'

It was Walter Krieger. His first question was if everything had gone smoothly. Next, had Bohn arrived? And then, was the girl all right? (The name of Irina was obviously not to be mentioned.)

David's replies were equally brief.

Unexpectedly, Kreiger said, 'I've got to see you. Today.'

'Suits me,' David said with relief.

'Where are you heading?'

'Graz. After that, Lienz.'

'Oh?' There was a slight pause. 'Problems?'

'Two, I think.'

'Such as?'

'A man who is too damned interested. He's in the courtyard now. He didn't care if we saw him or not. There could be others around.'

'Can you work something out?'

'I think so.'

'And the other problem?'

'Not so easy to cope with. It's the girl.'

'Is she within earshot?'

'No.'

'Hysterical? Exhausted?'

'No, not that. She's worrying, and she isn't telling us what's wrong.'

'Then get her to tell you,' Krieger said sharply.

'How? She's been keeping too many thoughts to herself in these last years. She's a locked door.'

'Ask her—and this may be important—ask her about Alois Pokorny. Did she know him? If she did, then tell her that he was killed this morning, just a few minutes after she left the building where he lived. The police identified him, and are now investigating. Note her reaction. It could help us all.'

'Where do we meet? I thought we'd stay at——'

Krieger broke in, 'Meet me on the castle hill, under the big clock tower. At six?'

'I'll be there.'

'Is Jo around?'

'I'll get her.'

'No, just tell her to reach Lienz as quickly as she can. Don't worry—she'll figure it out. Early tomorrow I'll call her at Die Forelle, a comfortable little inn. Good luck!' And Krieger ended the call.

Jo was annoyed for almost two minutes. Then she laughed ruefully. 'All right. So I missed Krieger's call. But does he think I have wings? Am I supposed to drive over the Grossglockner by myself? And how else do I get to Lienz from Salzburg? Oh, really!'

'He said you would figure it out.'

'*Early* tomorrow?' Jo's indignation had made her forget her achievement with Irina. But David was admiring enough. The deep-blue dress was simple and well cut: cinched in at the waist, and with a blue-and-green scarf at the neck, it looked dandy. So did the matching coat—useful for cool Austrian evenings. He noted the added colour in Irina's cheeks and lips: not too strong, just the right touch. But most amazing of all was the transformation in her hair. A dark-brown wig, softly curling around temples and ears, changed her completely. It looked natural. She was unrecognizable unless you had studied her closely and could remember the exact lines of her bone structure.

Few would qualify for that.

'Terrific,' David told Jo. Irina was actually smiling as she caught sight of herself in a long mirror.

'I was once driven over the Grossglockner by a Frenchman in his new Ferrari. And I just about froze to death at twelve thousand feet. Between that and twenty-four, or was it twenty-six, hairpin bends, one after another, I thought I'd die.'

'Where are the old clothes?' David asked Irina. 'In the suitcase?' It was bulging slightly, but the locks held firm. As she nodded, he said, 'We can stop well outside Dürnstein and heave them into a wood. We'll also get some food, farther south. Are you hungry?'

'A little.'

That was a good sign. An hour ago she had refused any food
—even a sandwich. 'I'm starved,' he admitted. 'But first we'll
clear out of here. Jo—come on! You're holding us up.'

That fetched her attention.

'This is what we do now,' said David, and he gave them his
plan of escape from the hotel. 'Got that, both of you? It's all
a matter of timing.' He glanced at his watch. 'Ten minutes of
two.'

'Heavens!' said Jo, and wrenched the bedroom door open.
She beckoned to someone outside. A small boy in the nine-year
range, hair brushed, face shining, came in. 'Gerhard,' Jo
announced. 'He will carry the suitcase to the Chrysler for ten
Schilling. I promised him five, but I think our expense account
can stretch to forty cents.'

'Does he know cars?' David was doubtful.

'Try him. He watches them all day long, coming and going.'

In German, David asked, 'Did you see a dark-blue Chrysler
in the courtyard?'

'Chrysler?' Gerhard repeated, and frowned. At least he was
honest.

'It stands next to the big black Cadillac,' David tried slowly.
Gerhard's smile beamed at them. 'I saw the Cadillac.'

'The Chrysler is beside it. It is darker blue than this lady's
dress. Next to the Cadillac. Got it?'

Gerhard nodded, picked up the suitcase.

'One moment,' said David, and gave him the ten *Schilling*.
'Just put the case into the back seat of the car. Then leave.
Okay?'

'And many thanks,' called Jo as Gerhard left at his usual
half lope. 'He'll make a champion long-distance runner some
day.'

'You too,' David told Jo, 'beat it. Vanish.'

'The bill?' she asked.

'Paid. How else did I get the passports back?'

She laughed and was gone.

He glanced at Irina, and hesitated. Had she really understood his plan?

'I shall follow you,' she told him.

'Keep in sight.' And he too left the room.

Irina picked up a *Do Not Disturb* sign and hooked it over the door handle as she heard the lock click shut behind her. Then she was following David along the bewildering maze of passageways.

Jo had reached the terrace. Mark Bohn was still sipping beer. 'Thought we might have lunch together,' he began.

'Later. First—come with me.' She led him along the inside of the terrace, suddenly halted when she could see Ludvik. 'Get up there quickly. Speak to that man: the fair-haired man in the blue shirt, leaning on the parapet. See him?'

'But——' Mark was uncertain, almost tense.

'Speak with him! Say anything, anything at all to distract his attention from the courtyard. You talk to strangers often enough, don't you?' She gave him a nudge that started him towards the steps. He kept on going, and soon he was sauntering beside the parapet until he reached Ludvik Meznik. She saw Mark address the man quite casually. And there was a response. The man seemed startled, but he was answering. Definitely talking. Then Mark was pointing out one of the large Hovercraft, the new type of ferryboat, crisscrossing the Danube. With its muted roar of power it was like a tidal wave rushing towards the cliffs. Everyone on the terrace rose to their feet to get a closer view as the Hovercraft swept below them to its landing place. Ludvik seemed as interested as anyone, for at least one full minute. Then he looked back at the cars in the courtyard, and went on listening to Mark.

Had Dave managed it? Jo wondered. One minute wasn't much. But luck, even measured by the minute, was something to treasure.

Of course, she reflected as she went slowly back to Mark Bohn's table, if there hadn't been the giant Hovercraft to catch Ludvik's attention, Mark would have found something else— such as questions about that far abbey, another fortresslike place standing on its distant hill to the south of the Danube. Or about the vineyards over there on the slopes. Or—she had never known Mark to be at a loss for words. His recent line of writing—'interview in depth' was the fashionable phrase— proved he was as quick-tongued as any in the New Journalism field. It was strange, though, how he had hesitated there for a few moments, almost as if he were suddenly nervous. Mark nervous? Only of driving at night, or on twisting country roads.

He had once made a joke about that. 'Just haven't got your reflexes,' he had said. 'I pass a direction sign before I notice it.'

She glanced at her watch as she picked up a menu. What bliss it would be to relax in a few days' time, never look at a watch, never calculate a minute, never keep travelling, just stay put. Preferably beside a swimming pool with a cold drink in her hand and a handsome man stretched near her. Then, thinking of tanned torsos, she remembered the Frenchman. And his Ferrari. And the Grossglockner's hairpin bends. How am I to get to Lienz? she asked herself again.

David strolled through the small lobby, stood by the side of the hotel door. He couldn't see Gerhard: too many cars overtopped a small boy's head. But he could see Bohn walking beside the small stretch of parapet to reach Ludvik, still stationed at his post. Now? No, not yet. The two men were talking, but Ludvik's attention was not completely absorbed. Then Bohn pointed at the Danube. *Now*, David decided. Irina was just behind him. Would she remember to wait a few seconds, give him time?

He didn't look back at her, but headed for the parked cars. Behind the first row, he felt less exposed. A pity he couldn't be collapsed into Gerhard's size, he thought. He heard a distant muted roar from the Danube, but didn't halt. He reached the Chrysler, ducked down as he yanked the door open, and slid behind the wheel. One glance at the rear seat and he saw Irina's suitcase, and took a deep breath of relief. He couldn't see his own things, though. Where would Jo put them? He groped under the seat, found nothing. He tilted the seat beside him forward. She hadn't forgotten. Bag and raincoat lay on the floor, tucked as far as possible out of sight. He lifted the raincoat, struggled into it. He would swelter, but it disguised the colour of his jacket; and the car's visor, pulled down and swerved round as if to block sunlight through his side window, would hide his hair and most of his face from Ludvik's searching eyes. He only had to put the key in the ignition, check the position of all the gadgets on the strange dashboard, have his map at hand, and wait.

A matter of seconds now.

Irina opened the door and slipped into the seat beside him. He turned on the ignition, went into reverse, and carefully backed out. Then he put the transmission into drive and they were heading for the gate.

'Ludvik saw me,' Irina was saying. 'Ludvik saw me as I came into the courtyard, and then he turned away.' She laughed softly. 'I paid no attention to him, and he turned away.'

Again Irina laughed. It was a good sound. 'He glanced at the car as we left, but he was not interested. He went back to talking with a man. Is that one of his—friends? And at this moment, she thought, I don't care. We can lose them all, every one of them.

'No. That's Mark Bohn.'

Irina said nothing more. She was watching the crowded street, the troubled frown back on her brow and deepening.

'This won't last long,' David reassured her. 'Soon we'll reach the bridge and cross to the right bank of the Danube. The traffic will ease there, and we'll pick up speed.'

She was still silent by the time they had crossed the bridge. David checked behind him several times. Then he could say, 'No Fiat. We got away, Irina.' Pulling up to the side of the road, he took off his coat and jacket before he drove on. 'Now we can really travel. We'll stop for something to eat in half an hour.'

'I'm not hungry, David.'

So we're back to that again. 'We'll pick up sandwiches, and you can eat them whenever you feel like it. Irina—please— better eat something. Will you?'

Irina heard his worried voice. She smiled faintly, nodded, and kept her eyes fixed on field after field of vines.

I'll persuade her to eat first; then we can talk, David decided. 'How?' he had asked Krieger. How? he still kept wondering. He wasn't Krieger, calm and objective about Irina; Krieger had sent the wrong man for this job. One hell of a journey this was going to be. David lapsed into unhappy silence. Nothing was ever what you had expected, he thought. Nothing.

Chapter Nine

THEY WERE IN the hill country now, less than an hour's drive south from the Danube. David risked stopping at a roadside café, one of a patch of eating places that had spread near a ski-lift. The rest of the village sprawled around the highway, which ran along the lower slopes of hills rising into low mountains. In winter the little hotels and weekend cottages would be filled with Viennese and their skis. Now there were only a few stray cars, and a scattering of people enjoying the air while they digested lunch and wondered what to do.

Inside, the café was small, built of new wood varnished to a yellow gloss, one wall spiked with tiny antlers, another displaying a jukebox. Some red-faced men in local costume—green jackets, black trousers, and heavy boots—sat along the bar, their low rumbling voices alternating with bursts of argument. A waitress in a miniskirt was mopping the tables with a grey washcloth. Neither she nor the men paid any attention to the two late-comers. David chose a table that had been cleaned more or less, settled Irina there, and went over to the waitress. 'Kitchen is closed,' she told him without looking up.

Perhaps it was just as well, he thought as he noticed her soiled apron. If he hadn't been pressed for time, he would have walked out after the first glance around him. And the rest of the kitchens in this summer-sad village could also be closed. So he said, his voice friendly, 'We are late, I know. Could you get us some bread? Some cheese? Some tea for the lady and beer for me? We haven't eaten since breakfast, and we must leave soon. I am sorry to give you such trouble, but I would appreciate it. Very much.'

The girl—her make-up was almost expert, her hair high-styled in last year's fashion—stopped work and stared. Then unexpectedly, she smiled. She smacked down the washcloth on the vinyl tabletop, speaking in a dialect so thick that he could hardly understand a word, and hurried away, her thick-heeled sandals clacking on the wooden floor. She was back in ten minutes, with a fresh apron tied round her waist, and the beginnings of a simple meal. It wasn't good, but it was edible, and carefully set out. And Irina, noticing David's dejection, made an effort. She ate enough to please him. 'You were right,' she said. 'I needed some food.'

'How do we get her to turn that noise off?' The jukebox had been switched on the moment they had picked up the thick chunks of stale black bread.

'We don't. She took such care in selecting the tune. What is it?'

'Le jazz hot. European Chicago style. Boogie-woogie with a stomp stomp.'

Irina almost laughed. She controlled it, but brightness was back in her eyes.

That's better, David thought. 'Have some more delectable cheese?'

'It wasn't too bad. And the ham was good. And the bread is —nourishing.'

Neither said anything about the uneaten slices of marbled sausage, left to curl on the platter with a wilting radish, or about the yellow potato salad. The beer had been bottled, and foamed like a bubble bath; the tea was made with warm water out of a faucet. But at least there was no temptation to linger. David doubled the tip, and they hurried out. 'Come back soon,' the waitress called after them. She stood, Brigitte Bardot, at her empty doorway, with a blare of sound pouring over the quiet valley. The hills looked down, imperturbable and silent.

'We can laugh now,' said David as he closed the car windows and put on some speed. 'The funniest thing was me, though. There I was, ordering tea, with a neat little pistol in my jacket pocket, and suddenly remembering it.' He pressed the button to lower the windows, once the Alpine village and tom-tom beat were left behind. The air from the pine trees was scented with resin; and the only background sound was the music of fast-flowing water over rocks and gravel in a mountain stream. 'You noticed?' he asked as he saw the smile in her eyes. 'Was it so obvious?'

'No, no. I was thinking of something else. Of a café table in

103

Prague. My friends were telling you all about New Orleans and Chicago style in jazz. And you were in agony, trying to explain and not having one word understood. They had it all wrong, hadn't they?'

'Well—they knew their Bach better than I did then. It evened out. Did they all stay with their music? I never met so many future composers, conductors, concert violinists, around one small table.'

'No.' She hesitated, frowning. 'One teaches. One has gone political. Some have—other jobs.' Her voice drooped.

'And you?' he asked quickly. 'Did you give any concerts?' She shook her head. 'And you?'

'I write for a music magazine.'

'And why are you in Austria—just at this time?'

'Salzburg.'

'Oh—I always wanted to go to the festival. What is it like?'

That was a safe topic, and he expanded on it for a full five minutes. She had listened, intent, interested. But now, as he waited for her to say something, she seemed withdrawn, more remote than ever.

'Haven't you a wife, David?' she asked.

The question, cool, detached, caught him by surprise. He answered abruptly, 'Once. It lasted four years. No children.'

'I was married—and now divorced. Two children.' There was a long pause. 'They died. In a boating accident on a lake. Three years ago. They would now be nine and eight years old.'

'Look, Irina——'

'No. I *must* tell you—or else you would never understand.'

Understand what? he wondered.

'Where do I begin?' she asked herself aloud, and shook her head.

'Perhaps when I left Prague, and waited for you in Vienna.'

'And I never came.' She watched his eyes. 'I couldn't. David—please believe me! My mother had me taken to the country—to my father's house near Rajhrad. That is south of Brno: far from Prague and my friends. My father wasn't even allowed to walk into the village. And that's the way I lived, closely guarded, until the last of the troubles in Hungary were put down, and my mother felt it was safe to let me return to Prague and meet friends again. Only she chose them this time.'

'Safe for her position in the party?' David asked bitterly.

Irina nodded. 'But that did not last. Five years later——'
She broke off. 'I never got your letters, David.'

'I never got yours either.'

'You knew I was writing to you?'

'I hoped you were.'

She sat very still, completely silent.

'And after five years—what happened, Irina?'

'They arrested my mother. Then, a year after that, they tried her secretly. Sentenced her to prison for ten years.'

'For what?'

'She never knew. None of those who were arrested knew.'

'But she was one of the top executives in——'

'So were they all. She was luckier than some. They had to confess publicly in a show trial. And when they were being transported to prison, eleven of them were taken out of the cars on a lonely road, and shot.'

It was he who was silenced now. He listened, asking no more questions. So, Irina went on, she was alone in Prague. She was not given permission to go to her father. A concert she had been preparing for was cancelled. She and two other music students were assigned to work in a factory. Most of her friends, and all her mother's old friends, avoided her. Except Jiri Hrádek. He had been a history lecturer at the university when she had first met him at her mother's flat; and then he had gone into government service. He never talked about it, even after he had married her, taken her out of the factory, managed to have her mother sent to an easier prison with less hard labour. Now she could see that perhaps Jiri's chief interest was in her father: doing everything to make her father like him, even trust him. But at the time, she only thought of Jiri as a man of great courage, and she had been grateful.

As for Jiri's hope that Jaromir Kusak could be persuaded to write a novel sympathetic to the present regime—it wasn't so wild a hope as it must sound to David. When her mother was released from prison in the spring of 1968 along with several other Communists, she was still a Communist, more intense than ever in her beliefs. Could David explain that? Of course not: no American could understand it. And neither had Irina's father. He was appalled: he was rejoicing in the liberalizing of politics in Prague while her mother was only filled with bitter disapproval; Dubcek had freed her, and she distrusted him;

she welcomed the Russian tanks, to keep the country out of the hands of fascists. Irina's father gave up all hope of ever regaining his wife or of seeing freedom established. It was then that he left the country—an admission of complete despair.

Irina hadn't left with him. She wanted to. She had drifted away from her husband: his secrecy, his long absences, his veiled contempt for Dubcek; all these troubled her, set her apart from him. But there were her sons, still too young to risk on any journey with her father. They could have endangered his escape. So she stayed, waiting for the boys to be old enough, hoping, planning. Then her mother fell ill, was dying. Jiri sent her to be with her mother, and took the two boys on a fishing holiday. His cottage was on a remote lake. But it was more than a fishing expedition. He had visitors there, coming secretly. Old Stalinists, true believers. And on the morning he and three men were talking in a closed room, the boys went down to the lake and pushed off in a boat. That was against the rules, of course, but there was no one near to prevent them. They couldn't handle the oars. They drowned in six feet of water.

David was pulling the car on to the side of the road. 'But I have to tell you,' Irina said, 'I have to——' He tried to wipe away the tears streaming down her face. He took her into his arms. The weeping subsided. He held her firmly, pressed her cheek against his shoulder. 'No,' he said, 'you don't have to tell anything.'

'I must, I must——'

'Later,' he said. 'We can talk——'

'No.' She lifted her head, and he let her go from his arms. 'I must finish this part at least. There isn't much more. I left Jiri and all his politics. He had become very powerful. That secret meeting on the day the boys died—it gave him what he wanted.'

David had edged the car back on the highway, slipping in ahead of a stream of heavy trucks, and increased speed so that they wouldn't be tempted to pass him.

'I asked for a divorce. Jiri wouldn't give it to me.' Irina's voice was now calm, almost detached. 'I got permission to live in my father's house at Rajhrad, and—very slowly, very carefully—I made contact with two of my old friends. They were working in factories in Brno. And at last—they agreed to help me get out of the country.'

The trucks had given up the attempt to get ahead of him, but David still kept a steady seventy. The highway was narrow but well surfaced, with no sharp turns and good visibility. 'I think I know the rest,' he said gently as he noticed her sudden hesitation.

She shook her head, and was about to speak. Then, abruptly, she fell silent and turned her head away. She seemed absorbed in the fields and the forests spreading over the rolling land.

David searched in his mind for some way to bring up Krieger's question. He even wondered if it were needed now: Irina had told him much. And yet this sudden reversion to silence puzzled him. He eased off his speed to fifty, as the traffic coming out of the Graz area thickened. Yes, she had given him many facts, but they all dealt with the past. A preparation for something she might tell him later? *Or else you would never understand.*

Small second-class roads were weaving a web around the highway, bringing more cars and many trucks. His speed went down to forty miles an hour; there were only two lanes on this stretch, and some bad drivers were loose on them. So he kept his eyes on the road as he prepared to ask Krieger's question. He didn't sidle into it: he wasn't going to give Irina a lot of diplomatic double talk. He said, quite simply, 'Did you know Alois Pokorny?'

'Alois?' She came to life again. 'Of course. Do you?'

'No. Krieger was interested. He wanted to know if he was a friend of yours.'

'Yes, he is. But I'm not going to talk about Alois.'

'Why not?'

'It could be dangerous for him. The less his name is mentioned, the better.'

'I don't think so. Not now. He's dead, Irina.'

Her eyes widened, her face went rigid. 'Oh, no! . . . Oh, no!'

'I am sorry,' he said. 'Alois Pokorny died this morning.'

'But I saw him—he was well—he wanted to bring me to the Sacher.'

'Where did you see him?'

'In the flat—his flat—the one he shared with Ludvik. They met me at the frontier and took me there and hid me for eleven nights.' Her words had been racing on, almost a protest of disbelief. Then she said more slowly, 'He couldn't come with me.

Two of his friends arrived to collect—to collect some pamphlets he had been writing. They passed me on the stairs as I was going down to the car where Ludvik was waiting.'

'Did they speak to you?'

'No.'

'Had you ever seen them before?'

'No.'

'Then who told you they were his friends?'

'Ludvik.' She stared at him. 'Why ask these questions?'

'Krieger said Alois was killed just a few minutes after you left the building where he lived.'

'Killed?' Disbelief gave way to pain. She closed her eyes. At last she said in a strangled voice, 'First there was Josef. And now Alois.'

'Josef?'

'Alois's brother. He brought me to the frontier, and then he was——' She broke off. She opened her eyes, fixed them on the road ahead, saw nothing.

They came through the last of the gentle hills invaded by factories. What the Turks could not do to Graz in two hundred and fifty years of repeated attacks, the machines had achieved in less than twenty. When David had last visited Graz he had thought of it as a country town that happened to be the capital of a province famed for hunting. Now the traffic was thick and clotted. All the cars and trucks on the right bank of the river that ran dark and swift through the town were trying to reach the left bank, where just as many cars and trucks had decided to cross to the right bank. It was complicated too by the fact that the left side rose abruptly from a compression of streets to form a considerable hill on which a fortress had once stood. What the Turks didn't manage there, Napoleon had accomplished: everything destroyed except for a truncated tower, now embellished with a giant clock that dominated the city far below. At least, thought David as they travelled over a bridge and saw the hotel's sign, the Grazer will always be punctual. Who would dare be late with that monster of a clock reminding you that everything passed, including precious minutes? He had forty-five of them left before he had to get up that hill and meet Krieger.

The hotel wasn't so grand as it had been fifty years ago or

more, but it was doing its best to keep up with the newer places. Early August was not the season for Graz, apparently: there was no difficulty in getting two rooms, adjoining. Modern and cramped, everything built in so that there could be eight feet of clear floor space. Together, they had probably formed half of one of the old bedrooms. There was something to be said for ampler days.

'Will you be all right?' David asked Irina. She was calm, much to his relief. 'I'm going to see Krieger.'

'Would you ask him what happened to Alois?'

'If you want that, yes. Is it important to you?'

In the same detached voice she said, 'It could be important to all of us.'

'I won't be long.' He tested the bed. It was comfortable. 'You could rest—try to sleep? We'll have dinner downstairs as soon as I get back.'

'Would that be safe?'

'I haven't seen one sign of a grey Fiat,' he said. Then he added quietly, 'Why was Ludvik following you, Irina?'

'I don't know. This morning I thought I had an answer. But now—I just don't know. Since Alois——' She cut off that sentence. 'I'll be all right here.'

David opened the window—it was on the second floor, overlooking a street on the riverbank— to let the sound of rushing water as well as cool air into the room: that would help her fall asleep. All that came in was the shrieks and groans of traffic and the smell of diesel fumes from lumbering trucks. Hastily, he closed the window.

Irina was actually laughing. 'Oh, David—your face!'

'I'm glad something is funny around here.' For a moment he stood looking at her. Then, impulsively, he put his arms around her, hugged her tightly. 'Don't worry, Irina. We'll find the answer to all this. Together.'

He left at once. He had twenty minutes to park the car safely in the garage behind the hotel, call for a taxi, get up to the one-time fortress. Distances were short within the central core of the old town, but the maze of streets on that side of the river was an added trap for the stranger. A cab driver would know the quickest route.

The hotel clerk called for the taxi, while David took the Chrysler round to the garage—he wasn't going to entrust

Krieger's car to the hands of any bellboy (the only one visible was nearly eighty, anyway). By the time he was back at the hotel door, the taxi was waiting. He had twelve minutes to get up that damn hill—why Krieger should choose there as the meeting place was beyond David. The cab made it in just under ten minutes, using a curving driveway that branched away from the city street to climb easily up to the level of the clock tower. And now David was beginning to see Krieger's purpose. The whole place was an enormous public park, with trees and flower-beds disguising the levelled ruins. And it was popular. Here, people walked; here, people met to sit and talk. There was constant movement, and plenty of space for it. In fact, it might be difficult to spot Krieger.

I'll let him find me, David decided: he probably saw me paying off the taxi; he certainly has been watching me walk over to this low wall. It's beside the tower. And it's six o'clock. Now, I'll just look at the view way down there, as fifty others are doing.

Krieger's deep voice said, 'Quite a drop, isn't it?'

Chapter Ten

TO BEGIN WITH, Krieger asked the questions and kept them brief. He listened intently to David's answers and seemed to be trying to fit them into some logical pattern. But he was baffled. 'There is something wrong somewhere.' he said at last. 'Apart from Ludvik, who knew where to find you, apart from the fact that he didn't gave a damn if you saw him, there is something wrong, something phoney about this whole deal.'

'Irina isn't faking anything.'

'No. But she isn't telling everything either.' Krieger glanced at David's taut lips. 'Come on,' he said more easily, 'let's walk up through the trees. This view was worth ten minutes, and we've given it that.'

'Irina,' David said as they began to follow a steep path to another spread of park land, 'isn't sure, herself. When she is sure of what she knows, she will tell us.'

'I hope it won't be too late,' Krieger said grimly.

'For Irina?'

'For Irina and her father. For you too. For anyone who helps in this escape.'

David said, 'That's a comforting idea. Where did you get it? From Alois Pokorny's death?'

'And from his brother's.'

They were entering a long avenue of trees, winding over the hill. There were several couples wandering here, arms around waists, girls' heads on boys' shoulders; a few family groups with children racing around; elderly slow-moving men with hands clasped behind their backs as they paced uphill; students arguing, laughing. And we talk of death, David thought. 'How did Alois die?'

'He was thrown from his window.'

'Thrown?'

'Yes. The police are certain of that. They found evidence of some struggle. And the poor devil had only one shoe lying near him. The other was found beside his slippers up in that room. Does a man commit suicide with one shoe on? Besides, I saw the body land. It didn't hit the pavement. It fell well beyond the kerb.'

David stopped short.

'No, no, let's keep moving. I was in a baker's shop across the street. And the damnable thing is that I sat next to the two men who murdered him. I saw them get a signal from the window of Pokorny's apartment. I saw them go in. I saw the man who gave the signal leave. I saw Irina come out and enter a grey Fiat and it drove off. I even relaxed about those two men: they had made sure Irina got safely downstairs. I was feeling pretty good. That was the damnable thing. I thought the worst was over: from now on—with some care—we had it made. And then the body landed, thirty feet away from where I stood.'

'And the man who gave the signal?'

'The same man who came out just before Irina did. He drove the Fiat, didn't he?'

'Ludvik.' And Ludvik had met Irina when she crossed the frontier. 'How did Alois's brother die?' David asked.

'Josef was shot at the frontier. According to the Austrian translation of a Prague newspaper clipping which I saw this morning when I was visiting a friend of mine—his department is interested in Czech activities: a matter of Austrian security—we're supposed to think Josef was killed by a border guard as he was attempting to escape from Czechoslovakia. Yes, escape. No mention of Irina. Just that "the traitor Josef Pokorny was shot by the frontier patrol while trying to join his accomplices. He had been under observation for some time. It is known that Pokorny was a paid agent of Western imperialists who, from the safety of a neutral country, have been supporting reactionary conspiracies directed against the Republic." Of course,' Krieger added as he ended his quotation, 'it was the mention of a neutral country which drew the Austrians' attention to that piece of bull. Clever, isn't it? On the one hand, Jiri Hrádek reassures his comrades that he's on the ball: no need for them to lie awake nights worrying about fascist subversives conspiring with a foreign government to overthrow the Republic. On the other hand, he has got rid of two members of the resistance: Josef and Alois Pokorny. In a few days I shouldn't be surprised to see another small paragraph in *Rude Pravo*, this time about Alois. Suicide in a state of depression over his brother's death and the failure of their conspiracy: so perish all traitors.'

In silence, they walked on, left the avenue of trees for a path which led them towards a large sunken courtyard and some relics of the destroyed fortress in its broken walls. David halted, looking down at the garden that had been planted to disguise the ruins. *We're supposed to think Josef was killed by a border guard* . . . 'Who shot Josef?' he asked.

'There's only indirect evidence, but it's strong enough. Two Austrians, going off duty from their border post, were cycling home along the road where the car was waiting for Irina. They were some distance away, but they could see the car with a man and a girl close together, while two men talked across the barbed wire. Then they heard a shot, and the man on the Czech side fell backward.'

'Backward?'

Krieger nodded grimly. 'The car drove off. The Austrians reached that section of the fence, and saw it had been cut. The man seemed dead, but one of the Austrians went right up to the wire—it's my guess, he actually broke the rules and stepped through it to see if the man was still alive, but he wouldn't put that in his report. He did state unequivocally that he had a clear view of the man, who had been shot in the chest by someone facing him. The wound could only have been made by a revolver fired at very close range—powder burns were visible. Then the Austrian patrol heard a jeep approaching, so they moved back to the road, picked up their bicycles, and went on home. They made a routine report; and that was the end of it, as far as they were concerned. Then *Rude Pravo* published its version, and the incident on the road became interesting to the Austrians.'

Krieger was taking out his pipe and tobacco pouch, his heavy eyebrows frowning as he carefully packed the bowl. 'So your Ludvik is not to be taken lightly. In the Austrian files there is no record of him as a Czech agent; he is only identified—like Alois Pokorny—as a refugee. Which means he is far from stupid. He has been so well covered that he must be important: one of Jiri Hrádek's hand-picked men.' Krieger lit his pipe, drew on it, got it going to his satisfaction. 'But the two who went into Alois Pokorny's building—they're on file as agents. I picked out their faces at noon today from a small collection of candid-camera shots. I got duplicates made of them—just a little *quid pro quo* for information rendered.' Slipping his tobacco pouch back into his pocket, he took out two snapshots and handed them to David.

'I thought you ought to keep your eyes open for these two mugs.'

David studied them. One photograph had been taken in a beer garden, the other at a street corner. Both were clear shoulder-and-head studies, three-quarter-face. 'How tall?'

'The dark-haired man is your size—about five feet ten, I'd say. The other is six feet. Strongly built. The dark one has a narrow head and dark eyes. The light-haired man—not blond, just light brown—is round-headed and square-faced, with pale eyes. Two distinct types of Czech—one from the east, the other from the west. Both are obedient, that's for damn sure: no questions or quibbles in *their* minds.'

'Any names to these faces?'

'Milan—dark hair. Jan—light hair. No, no,' Krieger said as David handed the photographs back, 'I had these made for you. I'll know them again all right. Besides, show them to Irina. She may have something to say about them.'

'How much shall I tell her?'

'Whatever you feel she can take. The more, the better. Well, have we seen enough of this garden? Let's finish our walk up to the top of the hill. I left a car up there. How's my Chrysler?'

'Safe in the garage behind the hotel.'

'And which is that?'

'The Grand.'

Krieger nodded noncommittally. Possibly he'd have chosen a less central hotel. 'Lienz tomorrow. And then where?'

'I thought I'd cut over into northern Italy and take the road through the Dolomites to the old South Tyrol. Merano seems a good stopping place. Switzerland is just over the mountains to the west.'

'I don't think they'll be watching that route,' said Krieger. 'But you'll land in a remote corner of Switzerland. Still——' He nodded again, this time with approval. 'We might work out something from there. Have you called Hugh McCulloch in Geneva?'

At the gentle reminder, David almost smiled. 'I'll do that this evening. I suppose it's only a routine call?'

'Just say you've been in contact with me, and I'll give him a progress report tonight. He likes to be kept in touch. That's the legal mind for you. Did he tell you we went to law school together? After that, I got stuck with blue-sky work—checking newly launched stock prospectuses against all the states' laws. So I branched off into business; something to let me travel.'

All this pleasant talk, thought David, is only to bring me back to normal again. He must have noticed my face freezing up when he was reconstructing Alois Pokorny's death. David tried to lighten his voice. 'And meet old friends again. Are there any others along the way?'

'Not till we reach Switzerland. Until then, we're on our own. No help from anyone, unless the Austrians find Ludvik. They have some pretty sharp questions to ask him.' Krieger paused at the top of the path, looked back at the ruins in the courtyard. 'Man's bloody-mindedness,' he said, almost to himself. 'Napoleon had this fortress levelled—*after* he signed the peace treaty with the Austrians. Never did manage to take it by assault.'

He resumed his former steady pace, but the pipe no longer gave him much pleasure. He tapped the bowl against his heel, and then pointed its stem at David's pocket. 'Have you started smoking a pipe too?' he asked with a wide grin. It was the first time he had smiled.

David drew out the small automatic, just enough to let Krieger glimpse it. 'Irina's. Her father's, originally. She asked me to carry it. And I'm damned if I know where to leave it,' he said, embarrassed.

'Not in your bag,' Krieger warned him. 'It could be searched —perhaps is being searched right now.'

'Oh, come on——'

'I said "perhaps." It depends on whether Ludvik or his action squad has followed you to Graz. And why not? They knew where to reach you in Dürnstein. Who's been telling them, I wonder?' The words were casual, the voice hard.

'Not Irina! She didn't know she was being taken to Dürnstein.'

'Nor you. Same reason. But I knew, and Jo knew.'

And Mark Bohn.'

'And that was all. Who knew about Graz? You and I, and Jo. And Irina?'

'If she was listening. She had thoughts of her own. And I can't believe that Jo——'

'Nor I,' Krieger said. 'I've known her Uncle George for years. He was in SOE—Special Operations Executive—in the big war. That's English for secret intelligence dirty tricks. I met Jo in London, at Sylvester's flat. She's all right. I'm sure of that. She was a great favourite of Jaromir Kusak. He had just got out of Czechoslovakia—but she'll tell you that story.'

'Is there any word on Kusak? Has George Sylvester produced him yet?'

'So far, Sylvester is only publishing him. There's a new novel scheduled for next spring. Kusak's first in twenty-two years, and Sylvester says it will be a major work. Prague won't like it. It's the opposite of what they'd been trying to persuade him to write while he was still in Czechoslovakia. All he turned out then for publication was a series of short stories about country life: no politics, no propaganda, no whitewash. So this makes one more hazard for all of us, doesn't it? That manuscript must be destroyed, and the man who wrote it too, perhaps. Certainly discredited. Even its very title is something that Jiri Hrádek will never forgive: *The Prague Winter*.'

They were coming out now on to a broad stretch of ground, with an open-air restaurant, a collection of buildings and souvenir shops, and an area for cars. It was crowded in spite of its size, and gave a feeling of safety by its constant movement.

A feeling of safety, David thought bitterly. 'Jiri Hrádek. What kind of bastard is he?'

'Highly intelligent, cold, calculating, thoroughly dedicated. He is also a charming man when necessary, with a sincere smile and a warm handshake. Very ambitious, and almost at the top. He seems completely loyal to the present regime, but he always has been farther to the left than they are. If the old-line Communists, the hard-nosed boys, ever take power again, then Jiri will be right among them. Physically—tall, dark, strong-featured, very attractive to women, I've heard. He's forty-one and——' Krieger glanced at David. 'Had enough?'

'You're convinced that Hrádek is Ludvik's boss?'

'Jiri Hrádek's first job was in the propaganda section of state security. From there he moved into state security police, which has its agents abroad as well as at home. With that background he could be responsible for more than Ludvik.' Krieger halted by some trees, nodded to a row of parked cars in an open space. 'See that green Mercedes? I hired it in Vienna. It's yours. I'll pick up my old crate at the garage. All we have to do is change keys and papers.' They did so. 'I'll meet you—and Irina—in Merano. There's a hotel called the Bristol, big enough to lose ourselves in. See you there. On Sunday.'

The roads would be hell on that day, David thought. Yet he had no other choice. It was just possible that the Sunday drivers would choose easy highways to picnic areas and avoid mountain routes. But after all, that was the least of his troubles.

Krieger noticed his hesitation. 'Any problems?'

'We have enough, haven't we?' he asked with a slight smile.

'Don't worry too much about Ludvik appearing at Dürnstein. It could be that Jo let something slip in Vienna when she was picking up your car at the garage. She might have inquired about the best route to Dürnstein, or wanted a map of the town. If someone came asking questions at the garage—well, that's how information gets leaked quite innocently. Most people talk too much. Including me, these last forty minutes.'

'I'm glad you did.'

'Can't work in the dark,' Krieger agreed with a firm handshake. 'Now I'll take the cog railroad down the cliff to the street. Ever tried that kind of travel?' He was off, making his way round the busy tables of the dining area to reach a neat little station beside a souvenir shop, and was lost in the flow of the crowd.

Chapter Eleven

DAVID REACHED THE HOTEL ten minutes later. The Mercedes handled well, and it was compact enough to manœuvre easily. Its colour was good too: the subdued dark green that he favoured. He left it at the kerb, just beyond the front entrance. (That would cause less speculation than driving into the garage with another car. Besides, he might meet Krieger coming in as he was going out: funny, but stupid.) The street outside the hotel was now quiet, almost deserted: the frenzied traffic of late afternoon had vanished. And the Mercedes did not look lonely, parked beside a couple of other cars. It didn't even look noticeable.

The small lobby was empty: the café beside it had only one table occupied; the dining-room, out of sight, was busy—a clatter of plates, a waft of goulash and paprika came floating around the corner, reminding him that, as far as food was concerned, this was Balkan territory. He glanced at his watch. Almost seven o'clock. People ate early in Graz. David looked again at the café, wondered if he had time for a quick Scotch, and then decided not. He had better get up to Irina; she might have started to be anxious about him, and he was certainly anxious about her.

There was one clerk at the desk (everyone else being still at supper, presumably), now doing double duty at the switchboard. David waited for his room key. Only for a few seconds, surprisingly.

As soon as the clerk saw him, he put down the earphone and came hurrying. 'There was a call for you, sir. I told them you had gone out. Then they asked if they could speak with the lady and give her a message. She is talking with them now. I hope I didn't disturb Fräulein Tesar.'

'A call from where?' Hugh McCulloch? or Jo?

'A local call—from the airport, I think.' The clerk handed over the key at last. 'They said it was important. But perhaps I should not have disturbed——'

David was already on his way into the hall to the rear of the desk, leaving a startled man behind him. The solitary elevator was up at the fourth floor. He didn't wait, but ran up the staircase to the second. The desk clerk's eyes, if they could have seen him, would have popped even more.

David tried the handle of Irina's door—locked, of course—and then knocked. The call might have come from Krieger: some afterthought, or a warning? And yet there hadn't been time for Krieger to get to an airport.

He knocked again, his worry growing.

At last Irina opened the door, white-faced and tense. He glanced at the telephone. The receiver was back in place.

Irina did not look at him. She moved over to the window, opened it, stood watching the dark river.

He closed the door and locked it. 'Did you get any sleep?' he asked. The pillow on one bed was slightly hollowed. The other bed had the opened suitcase and a few clothes scattered over its white eiderdown.

'A little.' She drew a thin dressing-gown more closely around her neck. She had taken off the brunette wig and was back to her own blonde hair.

'I saw Krieger. I'm sorry if I'm late. We didn't really waste any time.'

'How is he?' she asked listlessly.

'Full of information,' he said, keeping his voice light. 'And we've got a new car. I guess he missed his own.'

Talk and keep talking, he told himself. He glanced again at the telephone. She'll tell me, he kept insisting. Why shouldn't she?

'I suppose so,' Irina said.

'We'll have dinner. Then, after we eat, I'll pass on Krieger's news.'

'No,' she said, facing him quickly. 'No! I don't want to hear it.'

He stared at her. 'Not even about Alois?'

She was quite silent, her eyes wide and shadowed.

'Better come away from that window. The air is chillier now. I don't want you coughing and sneezing your way through the mountains.' He had kept his voice normal, but his depression was deepening.

She said nothing. But she did leave the window. She came slowly over to the bed, pretended to be interested in the clothes that were strewn there, picking up a light-green wool dress, dropping it. Then she went over to the dressing-table and lifted the wig.

She stood with it in her hand, looking yet not seeing.

David waited. Still she said nothing. She wasn't going to say anything about that telephone call. Who had made it? The call had never been intended for him: his name had only been used to find out if he were around. As soon as that was established, the caller could speak safely with 'the lady.' Did that mean the man wasn't sure what name Irina was using? Only one thing was certain: Irina should not have received any telephone call whatsoever.

David said, 'I'll order dinner up here. It will be safer—as you said.'

'Safer?' The word whipped across the little room. She threw the wig down. 'Useless—all useless. Everything we've done has been useless.'

'No,' he said quietly. 'Don't ever let yourself think that, Irina.'

'Oh, David——' She ran to him, caught his hands, looked at him despairingly. 'There is only one thing for me to do. I'll go back. I'll leave——'

'You'll leave with *me*. And soon.' He put his arms around her. She was trembling. He held her tightly. 'There now, there,' he said as though he were speaking to a lost child. Gradually the trembling stopped. 'What do you think, Irina? Should we leave tonight?'

'Yes,' she said, her face almost smothered against him. 'Yes! Let us leave. Now!'

'Now? What about putting some clothes on first?' He heard the beginning of a small laugh. 'That's my girl,' he said. 'I'll order some food—we need that, too, you know—and get things squared away. You pack, and be ready.'

She nodded.

'I'll only be gone ten minutes, perhaps less. You won't start being scared again? Promise me.'

Once more she nodded, her head still lowered.

He lifted her chin with one finger. 'Keep that well up, will you? And lock the door.'

'Yes. But——'

He gave her an embrace that squeezed the breath out of her body and silenced her completely. 'Lock this door!' he warned, and was gone.

Again he used the staircase, his mind racing as fast as his feet. He glanced into the sombre dining-room, with an elderly waiter moving slowly around, and abandoned all hope. He tried the café across the lobby. Here, there were two waitresses dressed in black sateen, plump middle-aged women, waiting with crisp white aprons for after-dinner customers. He picked the one with a bright eye and a quick step.

For a brief minute, she listened to him. 'If you just bring a tray for two—goulash is fine—anything that's ready in the kitchen,' he said.

'Well,' she began, her round face perplexed. 'I don't know. The dining-room is busy, there is no room service now. Later——'

'I can take the tray upstairs. Just get the food on it. Please.'

That horrified her. 'I'll bring it,' she told him. 'If I can get away.' She glanced at the other waitress.

'I know you'll manage it. Room 204. As quickly as possible. My sister isn't well, she hasn't eaten all day.' He gave her a warm smile and slipped her a hundred *Schilling*. 'I'll pay now and save some bookkeeping.'

'That's too much! Seventy *Schilling* would be——'

'Keep the rest for your trouble. And thank you.'

'Thank *you*, sir,' she said to his retreating back. He gave a wave of his hand as he hurried out.

'Poor man, his sister's ill,' she told the other waitress, and bustled into the kitchen. 'Keep an eye on my tables, will you? I'll share the tip.' There was no argument about that.

David stopped once more at the desk in the lobby. There wasn't a public telephone in sight, but with some care his call to McCulloch would be harmless. The clerk was still fretting about having disturbed the lady. Possibly that made him excessively obliging. Certainly he could reach Geneva in a few minutes. 'Just get the main exchange,' David told him. 'I've left the Geneva number in my room, so I'll handle the call from there.' And before the clerk had reached the switchboard, David was on his way upstairs.

He braced himself to face Irina. She would tell him about that phone call, he was still persuading himself; she would tell him of her own free will. Whatever the message was, it had terrified her. Never had he held anyone in his arms and felt their fear pressed against him like that. That was a moment he would like to forget.

At her door, he paused. Then he took a deep breath and knocked.

Irina had changed her dress for the green one. She was a brunette again, pulling the stray curls into place with light fingers. 'I'll soon be packed,' she told him as she turned towards the suitcase.

'Good,' he said a little too heartily. No mention of that phone call; and there never would be, he realized. She was asking now where they were going, how long would it take, wouldn't he mind driving for another three or four hours? He answered easily, keeping his voice unworried, even conjuring up a small joke or two. But she wasn't the Irina he had once known. He resented the idea even as he forced himself to accept it; and doubt kept rising.

It was with relief that he heard the telephone ring next door. 'It's all right,' he told her as he made for his own room. 'I've been expecting this call.' The irony of the phrase struck him as he left her, standing very still, her eyes inquiring. And he realized, as he picked up the receiver, that he hadn't even mentioned Hugh McCulloch's name or Geneva. God, he thought, this isn't the way I hoped it would be.

It was only a matter of seconds, once he had given the Geneva number to the Swiss operator, before a woman's voice answered with 'Holz, McCulloch and Winterhouse.' Conscious of the open switchboard down in the lobby, David said, 'Mennery here. I'm calling from Austria. I'd like to speak with a member of the firm, or leave a message if no one is available.'

'Ah, Mr Mennery? I think one of the partners is still here. A moment, please.'

David's confidence began to reassert itself. The woman had played along with his little subterfuge so neatly that his despondency lifted. And when McCulloch's voice came on the line, with no identifying name attached, David's attack of pessimism was over. Here were people who knew what they were doing.

'Mr Mennery? So you are in Austria.'

'In Graz, at the moment.'

'Your business arrangements are going well?'

'Partly. The export problem is causing a few unexpected headaches, but I think I'll have them cured before delivery date.'

'Have you discussed them with your business partner?'

'Most of them. I saw him this evening. He will probably be calling you tonight, and give you a progress report. By the way, when you speak with him, tell him I'm speeding up the transit of that shipment. I'm advancing it by one day.'

'One day ahead of schedule?' McCulloch sounded puzzled.

'It's advisable. Be sure to tell him, won't you?'

'I will. And I'll have the full agreement drawn up at this end, ready for final signature.'

'The quicker the better.'

'Right away,' McCulloch said, and ended the call.

Well, thought David, I got that signal through all right: Saturday, not Sunday, in Merano. He picked up his raincoat and took out the map. He'd study the next stretch of road while he was having supper with Irina: a good excuse to keep from forcing conversation. *A few unexpected headaches.* And then some, he added bitterly. He drew out the small automatic. It was a ·22-calibre Beretta, and about as useful as a peashooter beyond close range. It was loaded. He checked its safety catch again before slipping it into the depth of his raincoat pocket. There he found the red tie. He thrust it under a sweater in his bag—he ought to have remembered to ditch it when he had dropped the bundle of Irina's old clothes in a thicket on that deserted stretch of road. Or perhaps he'd wear it some day—if he got through this journey with memories less bitter than his feelings were now. If he got through this journey: period. He chose a plain dark tie, inconspicuous and safe, and slipped it under his collar. Now the desk clerk would approve of him—he had glanced severely at David's open-necked shirt—and their abrupt exit would be more acceptable. What excuse for that? David prepared one as he knotted the tie; but only for use if absolutely necessary. Explanations too often sounded like evasions; and sometimes they were.

123

There was a discreet knock at his door. It was the waitress, with a tray piled like a pyramid. 'That's fine,' he told her, and helped her bring the heavy load down from her shoulder. 'Just splendid. Wonderful. We'll fix the table. You're in a hurry, I know. Please, no. We won't detain you any longer. *Vielen Dank.*' She left, still breathing heavily, but with a broad smile (relief combined with a sense of achievement?) and a stream of good wishes floating back along the corridor.

'Irina,' he said, knocking at her door. 'Food's here. Come and get it. It's picnic style, do you mind?'

Irina was dressed, ready to leave. She was calm, her face carefully made up and all signs of tears banished. She followed him to his room, helped him place the covered dishes on every available bit of free space. 'I like picnics. Do you remember, David, the day we went to visit the Moldau?'

'I remember,' he said. And there we go, right back to the far-off past, avoiding the present, escaping the future. 'We took almost as much food as this with us. Where do we start? Soup? And I think we should leave the talking to later. Let's concentrate on getting some nourishment into you.'

'Yes,' she agreed. 'These dumplings look good. One or two, David?' She delved into the tureen.

He shook his head, amazed at her recovery. Or was it all part of the act? He almost destroyed his own appetite with that question. 'We'll have to eat in record time. Like one of my friends in Vermont. A farmer. Eighty-two years old. He says, "I can eat a squar meal in ten minutes." ' And just listen to me, David thought: how's that for the carefree companion?

'A squar meal?'

'Direct quotation.' David translated it for her. She was smiling, asking him now about Vermont. Wasn't that where his grandfather had lived? She remembered him telling her about the maple trees and sugaring off. She had never forgotten that phrase.

Sugaring off. . . . That's what we are doing now, he thought. There wasn't one hint in those beautiful blue eyes that only half an hour ago they had been filled with terror. Whoever telephoned had traced her to Graz: still more worrying to David, she had been traced to this hotel. And only he had known its name, only he and Jo Corelli had known it in advance. Krieger had been told, up on the castle hill. Time enough to——? No, David decided angrily. You're playing right into Jiri Hrádek's hands. If we start distrusting one another, seeing some betrayal behind every unanswerable question, we'll split wide open. That was one way to take care of any opposition. Hrádek must know that dodge well. How else had he clawed his way up, in a tight power structure? And yet, and yet—who the hell knew about this hotel?

'What's wrong, David?' Irina asked suddenly. 'You're so silent.' She watched him nervously.

'Just trying to plan our route. I'd better have a look at the map.' He spread it out on the bed, took his plate over to the night table. 'Finish your goulash,' he told her. 'And then pour me some coffee. No strudel: it will put me to sleep.'

'How long exactly will you have to drive?'

'That's what I'm figuring out.'

She fell silent, and let him study the map.

By half-past seven, and waning light, they were ready to leave. There was a new desk clerk on duty, one who had his own private problems. The exit was simple, after all. The Geneva call was added to the bill, and passports returned. Irina had been given her instructions. She went ahead of David, the elderly bellboy insisting on carrying her small luggage (did he ever go off duty? too old for union rules?) and unlocked the Mercedes. (Ten yards from the door—less than ten metres, David told her.) She was waiting, all set, by the time he came out into the street. It was totally empty at this hour. Not a pedestrian in sight, no car moving out to follow them.

The route to Lienz—about one hundred and eighty-four miles, he had calculated—would be easy and direct, longer but simpler than his afternoon journey. Yet, even at the cost of an extra ten minutes, he made a small detour, watching the road behind him, driving south as though he were heading for Yugoslavia. Then, satisfied, he turned west and picked up speed.

'Is everything all right?' Irina asked.

'I was just checking. No one has followed us out of Graz.'

'They may not need to follow.'

'What makes you think that?' It was a good lead-in for her. Now she could bring up the telephone call quite naturally. But she didn't. She said nothing more.

David concentrated on the road and let her be the first to break the silence. It lasted almost sixty miles, practically a third of the journey. Her eyes were closed as if she had fallen asleep.

At last she stirred, stretched her cramped legs, eased her shoulders. 'How much longer?'

'Two hours or more.'

'It's so far away?'

'As far as we can get tonight. Safely.'

'And are we safe?'

'At this moment, yes. But you'll be in serious danger, and your father too—once you lead them to him.'

'Once I lead them——?' Irina was aroused. 'My father won't be in danger from them. They've never touched him. There would be bad publicity—an international scandal. He has too many friends in other countries.'

'Is that why he has hidden himself away for these last years? You'd better ask Jo about your father. She met him in London when he was still moving around openly. What changed his life-style, d'you think?'

'But——' she began, and stopped. 'I don't know,' she said at last. 'I haven't heard from him in all that time.' Then she added, 'Nothing will happen to him. They'd never risk that. It would be bad propaganda.'

'What about a simple little accident?' David persisted. 'Would that arouse public opinion? Something like a fire in his house, and both of you trapped in it.' Now I am being brutal, he told himself, but he kept on. 'And the completed manuscript for his new book destroyed. People would be shocked, regretful. They'd hold sad memorial services. But aroused and angry? Public protests? Denunciations? How could that happen with an ordinary everyday tragedy such as a fire?'

Slowly she said, as though she were still persuading herself, 'Jiri would never——'

'Wouldn't he?'

Again she fell silent. At last she asked, 'Alois—what happened to Alois?'

'It isn't a pretty story.'

'Tell me.'

And so he gave her Krieger's account.

'And those two men I saw on the staircase?'

'Acting under Ludvik's orders.'

'Ludvik?'

'And now,' said David, 'let me tell you what Krieger found out about Josef's death.' He gave her full details, sparing nothing.

'Ludvik.' This time she believed it.

Hurriedly he added, 'There is also some pleasant news. About your father. He's at work. There's a new novel—a big one—almost finished. It will be published next year.'

'If it survives a fire,' she said.

So now she could believe that too. 'We shall just have to out-think Jiri, that's all.'

'Out-think *him*? Useless—David, it's useless!'

'That is just what he wants us to believe.' When she didn't answer, he said, 'You know, people can persuade themselves into defeat. They can hold a trump card, and yet never play it on time. They're left with it in their hands, because they doubted, hesitated; they listened to some glib talk or were too impressed by their opponent. And what's a trump card when you're stuck with it, and the game has passed you by? It's useless. And that's the right meaning of that word.' He paused. 'Isn't it?'

'Yes.' Her voice was low.

'Another thing to remember, Irina, is simply this. When stakes are high—and there are no higher stakes than in power politics—your enemy plays for keeps. He will give you no credit for even a kind thought or hesitation. He will twist everything that you say or do, when it suits him, and use it to his own advantage. He intends to win. And in the terms of his tight ideology that means he intends you to lose. There's no real contest, as he sees it: it's only a matter of time. Your hopes against his plans.'

'Once, David, you were an optimist.'

'I'm still an optimist. I said we could out-think Jiri, didn't I?'

'But you also said there was no real contest.'

'As he sees it. I said that too, didn't I?'

'Yes.' And then she added. 'Perhaps I've become the pessimist.'

'You'd be fine if you'd get rid of that word "useless." '

'Tonight,' she said, 'Jiri had someone telephone me. When you were out, David.'

127

'I know. And if I had been there, they'd have cut off the call and tried again later. And again. Until they got you alone.'

'You knew?' And right there was one big difference between David and Jiri. If Jiri had known about the call, he might have waited, like David, to let her talk about it. But he would never have admitted he knew all along. He would have kept it to use against her.

'Clever set of bastards. Sorry—I'm getting just a little bit teed off by all this. Damned if I'm going to keep running and looking over my shoulder. They threatened you, of course.'

'No. They were friendly.'

'What?' He almost swerved over the line. He got his lights beaming straight again along the dark empty road. 'And that's what scared you?' She hadn't become as simple-minded as he had thought in his most depressed moments.

'That too. But chiefly because they had tracked us down so easily. And we had taken such care.'

'Just what you were meant to feel. Remember, Jiri was an expert in propaganda before he went over to the strong-arm department. What is propaganda? Just persuading someone to believe what you want him to believe.'

'They persuaded me—almost.' She reached out in the darkness and touched his arm, briefly. 'They said they were worried about me. So they would keep following, make sure that I was safe.'

'Safe from what, in heaven's name?'

'From Krieger. You are just a pawn, they said. So is Jo. Krieger is the one who cannot be trusted.'

'Trusted with what?'

'To deliver me safely. He doesn't want me to reach my father and give him my message from Jiri.'

For a moment David took his eyes off the road and stared blankly at her. He thought of her passport; he thought of the way she had been able to escape—no difficulties at all, seemingly—through Czechoslovakia. 'Did you make a deal with Jiri Hrádek?'

'Not a deal,' she said quickly. 'Just an agreement. He gave me the divorce; and the passport. And he promised to hide my disappearance for as long as it was possible. I was to ask my father to return to Czechoslovakia. That was all.'

'You were to persuade your father?'

'No—no! Just ask; that was all. Please—David, believe me.'

'Did you think your father would agree to return?'

'No, of course not. Not with all hope of democracy gone. He won't return. Why else did I bring out two of the notebooks he had to leave behind? I didn't tell Jiri about them. Why should I? I took what he offered me. And I'll keep my promise to him. That was the agreement.'

'And when your father refuses to return—what then?'

'Jiri said nothing about that.'

'What then?' he insisted.

'I plan to stay with my father, keep out of sight. Then when he has his book published—well, perhaps by that time—when it is too late for Jiri to take action—it may be safe for both of us to come out. Live normally.' She looked at him through the darkness, seemed uncertain. 'That could be true, couldn't it?'

'Yes. Except that these aren't plans. They're hopes.'

'And Jiri has his plans,' she said slowly, remembering David's words. 'My hopes against his plans.' She gave a strange small laugh. 'And I thought it was the other way round,' she added almost in a whisper.

'Let's get back to the telephone call,' he said brusquely. 'What else was said?'

'Only that they would find us wherever we went, as easily as they had traced us to Graz. I wasn't to be alarmed. It was for my safety.' She took a deep breath. 'They sounded the way Ludvik did—when he drove me to the Opera House this morning.'

Thank God she hadn't believed them, David thought; or else she wouldn't have been so terrified. 'Did you recognize the voice on the telephone?'

'No. He spoke in our language. His accent was real. He was a Czech.'

'Gentle and friendly?'

'Yes.'

The hell he is, thought David. 'The call came from the airport. Perhaps he had just arrived from Vienna.'

'Was that why we really left—before he could get to the hotel?' The idea delighted her.

'It did us no harm,' David said. There were too many maybes attached to be able to give a firmer answer. The man could have reached the hotel just as they were leaving, but perhaps he had gone to the garage to check on the Chrysler to reassure himself they were still in Graz; that might have seemed safer to him than hanging around a café or watching a small lobby. Or perhaps the man had driven straight on to Lienz—if he knew so damned much about their movements. 'But why talk of one man? There could be two of them.'

'The two who passed me on the stairway to Alois's flat?'

'Would you recognize them again?'

'I—I don't know. I only caught a glimpse; I drew back against the wall, didn't stare at them. I hoped they wouldn't pay attention to me.'

'Then we'll stop at the next town. We may as well get some gas, and you can wash up.'

'There's no need——'

'We'll stop,' he told her. 'And I want you to look at two photographs in a quiet place with a good light. Memorize the faces this time.'

'Of the two men?'

'It would be just as well to do that before you reach Lienz.'

'They'll be there?'

'I don't know.' But someone would be there, if not these two. Of that he was certain. 'In that telephone call were you asked about our route?'

'Yes.'

'And you said——?'

'I said nothing.'

'Did they mention Lienz?'

'No.' Then a new, and disturbing idea flashed into her mind., 'David—please! Don't you believe me? I've told you everything.'

'Everything, Irina?'

'Everything that matters.'

Yet something that might not seem important to Irina could be something that was absolutely vital to her safety. He let her answer go, asked no further questions. He could hear the exhaustion in her voice. Tomorrow, he thought, when she has had a decent sleep, I'll ask her to search her memory; I'll get her to tell me more about Jiri, about the way he approached her, about her permitted escape. For that was what it had been: a permitted escape.

The highway now followed the long line of a lake. There

were lights from a scattering of houses, well spaced within their gardens, that faced towards the water. Summer cottages, perhaps, and people behind their solid walls, looking at TV and thinking of tomorrow's boating. At the far end of the lake there was a glow of illumination, a town lit up for its holidaymakers. There would be a constant movement of visitors, and plenty of cars. 'That's where we'll stop,' David said. Then he had another impulse. 'We'll stay overnight.'

'And not go to Lienz?'

'Why should we?' Jo might be there; but Krieger would certainly telephone her tomorrow morning as arranged, and instruct her to move on to Merano. Krieger wasn't planning to meet him in Lienz anyway. 'We've come far enough: a hundred and five miles from Graz. That's about one hundred and sixty-eight kilometres,' he added helpfully. 'Okay?'

'Yes. But Jo will be alone—waiting for us. She'll worry. They'll *all* be worried.'

'I'll let Hugh McCulloch know we're safe.'

'You'll tell him where we are staying overnight?'

'I'm telling nobody except you.'

She laughed unexpectedly. 'Oh, David, you're going to confuse everyone, including Jiri. You know what you are doing? You are kidnapping me, just as he warned me. Only it isn't on Krieger's orders, is it?'

'No. Any objections?' They were reaching the town. Ahead of them was a handsome square, with low houses and town offices, where the road to Lienz branched to the right. He kept to the left, entered the main street. It was happy and busy—a pleasure place geared for the holiday money, but not in brass-ring Las Vegas style. Nor was it a beatnik heaven either. Everything looked comfortable, placidly gay: enjoyment on a leisured, middle-class scale. Above all, it looked safe. It had its quota of elderly couples, but it was mostly filled with smart girls and their tanned young men, and the distant sounds of old but well-played jazz.

'No objections,' she was saying. Bright lights were all around them, and he could see her face clearly now. She looked sixteen years younger. Even that smile was the same one he remembered from long ago.

'Too late for them anyway.' They had reached the end of the little thoroughfare and passed through the gates to an enormous spread of courtyard and gardens, guarded by a right angle of buildings that shut out town and streets. 'Scratch an Austrian hotel, and you find a castle,' he said with a wide smile. And even if it was a pseudo castle, the place still looked good. Everything looked good to David at this moment.

He drew up near the lodge inside the gates. Plenty of cars parked there; people strolling around the paths, admiring the rose-beds. 'We'll never be noticed,' he told her, and switched off the engine.

'I wish,' she said softly, 'I could stay kidnapped. Just you and I, David. No one else. They way we once were.'

Yes, her smile was the same. Her eyes, too, meeting his; no longer evading him.

'Do you remember——' she began slowly, almost hesitantly. But the way she came into his arms was sure.

'Everything,' he told her.

Chapter Twelve

WALTER KRIEGER'S HOTEL in Graz was near the Telephone Office, large, state-owned, and impersonal. It was a simple matter for him to step in there, after a hasty supper, and make his call to Hugh McCulloch in Geneva. A public telephone had a certain reassuring anonymity about it. He gave a condensed report of today's events, neatly edited and clear. McCulloch must have been startled by their development, but he listened in silence. (If he was following his usual procedure, he would be recording Krieger's words, and he would go over them carefully once the call was ended. If any questions arose, they would be put to Krieger when he next telephoned.)

'That's about all,' Krieger concluded.

'Not quite.' McCulloch's voice was strained. 'There is a message for you from David. It came at ten-past seven this evening. He is advancing his schedule by one day.'

It was Krieger's turn for silence. So something happened since Dave talked with me, he was thinking.

'It bothers me, frankly,' McCulloch said.

It bugs me, too, thought Krieger, but he said jokingly, 'Good. Then we can get some action out of your end.' Hugh was a careful man, deliberate and accurate: but at times, for Krieger's own inclinations, a trifle slow. Too much attention paid to the small print. 'Tell Sylvester that the meeting must be arranged for Sunday. Where?'

'Sylvester is still arguing that out with himself.'

Sylvester was another cautious type. 'Then you and I had better decide. And I say we do it right now. Plan A or Plan B? Which is it, Hugh?'

Plan A was the simpler one: Irina to be taken to her father's house. Plan B was a meeting elsewhere.

'We really should consult——'

133

'Hell, we've consulted enough.'

'It's difficult——'

'Not half as difficult as it could be for Dave. You heard my report. Don't you see that he could be next on the list for disposal, as soon as he has done his job?'

There was another silence.

Two dead men, Krieger was thinking angrily: Josef and Alois. Two important witnesses whose testimony could prove that Irina's escape was not concocted by any Western intelligence agency.

'As soon as he has done his job,' Krieger repeated. 'That's the pattern that has emerged. Isn't it?' he asked sharply.

'It could be,' McCulloch said. Then, 'More than we bargained for.'

'It's always more than we bargain for,' Krieger told him. 'I vote for Plan B. It's safer.'

'You are convinced they want her to lead them to the house?'

'Yes.'

'All right, then. Plan B. But which area?'

That was a guarded reference to two villages that had been selected as possible meeting places: one close to Zurich; the other outside Interlaken.

'Neither of these.'

'What?'

'Tomorrow we'll all be in Merano.' Krieger could imagine McCulloch's eyebrows shooting up. Merano meant Irina would be entering Switzerland almost at its south-eastern corner, mountains away from either Zurich or the Interlaken area.

'Whose idea was that?' McCulloch was testy.

'I wish I could say it was mine.'

'It's one hell of a way to reach——'

'We don't. Forget these places. Think of a village closer to that particular stretch of border, where there's a house I can borrow, any time, from my friend the candy merchant. Remember it? You liked it a lot two years ago. Said you could retire there.'

McCulloch remembered all right. Tarasp. A village off the main highway, on a dead-end road climbing up a hill. That was where he and Krieger had stayed on a visit to the Swiss National Park two years ago.

'Castle, painted walls, and window boxes?' he asked, to make sure it was that same village in the Lower Engadine.

'That's it.'

'Too remote—the back side of beyond.'

'There's an airport thirty miles away.'

'I still think——'

'No. This is it, Hugh. It makes sure of a speedy delivery. That's what we need now. And the more you look at your map, the better you'll like it.'

McCulloch heaved a heavy sigh. He was thinking of the new timetable he would have to work out. All his careful pre-arranged plans for either Zurich or Interlaken were being dumped like a load of gravel. 'Your friend will lend us his house?'

'Sure. He offered it to me for August. Just call him. He'll come through.'

'Where can I reach you next?'

'Lienz. I might as well drop in there and verify a few things.'

'More problems?' McCulloch asked sharply.

'There is a definite leakage. My headache. You just concentrate on things at your end, will you?'

'I'll start them moving.'

'All I ask. See you on Sunday,' said Krieger, making Tarasp final as he ended the call.

Krieger walked briskly out of the Telephone Office, just busy enough so that he didn't feel conspicuous. No one seemed to be paying any attention at all to him. Satisfactory, he decided: McCulloch would deliver as promised. Sure, Hugh loved a well-made plan and would still be shaking his head over this abrupt change. But plans were only as good as they were flexible. Here he was, himself, preparing to pick up his Chrysler and drive to Lienz, although this afternoon he had had no intention of stopping there. But a brief visit, face to face with Jo, would be a better solution to their problems than a telephone call early tomorrow. So let McCulloch worry about getting Jaromir Kusak to Tarasp, and Krieger would do the worrying about the way Irina had been followed to Dürnstein; and between them they might kick Jiri Hrádek's heels right out from under him. That would be one downfall that Krieger would like to see.

*   *   *

Krieger made one more telephone call before he checked out of his hotel—this time to David Mennery at the Grand. The desk clerk gave him a ready answer: Herr Mennery and Fräulein Tesar had left almost half an hour ago. Quick, thought Krieger, too damned quick. What had sent Dave off like that?

Krieger's sense of urgency grew. The distance from the station to the garage was short: normally he would have walked along the riverbank and enjoyed the cool evening air, but now he took a taxi and had it stop behind a couple of parked cars near the front of the hotel. That seemed safer than driving directly to the garage. He was short of loose coins, thanks to telephones and tips, and he had to search through his pockets, sitting in the dark cab while its driver protested he had no change either. 'Then get it in the hotel,' Krieger suggested, holding out the rejected bill.

'I'll wait here,' the driver told him. He was a pugnacious type. Either he resented a short fare or he hated nightwork. He was young enough to have a girl who wanted to go dancing.

Krieger prepared to step on to the dark pavement—a nice peaceful street with most people indoors, although it was just eight o'clock. And at that moment two men came down the well-lighted steps and began walking towards him. His hand froze on the door handle of the cab. His head tilted away from the pavement. His old green Tyrolean hat would disguise his hair: his light raincoat was slung over his tweed jacket's shoulder and possibly hid its colour. But if these two men were coming to get this cab, then all precautions were useless. They might only have seen him briefly this morning, in a baker's shop in Vienna, but their eyes were trained to remember. This damned moustache, he thought bitterly of his pride and joy.

But Milan and Jan weren't interested in getting a taxi. They stopped at the car parked twelve feet ahead of it. Milan pulled its door open, entered, while Jan hurried around to the driver's side. They were too angry, moving too fast, to give more than a glance at the taxi behind them.

'Something wrong?' demanded Krieger's driver.

'Just a cramp in my leg. Give it a couple of seconds. And put them on the bill,' Krieger said. It the man hadn't spoken he might have been able to catch a phrase from Jan as he had climbed into the white Fiat. All he heard was a rush of Czech, and then a rasp of gears. The Fiat backed, pulled out abruptly.

136

The cab driver was shaking his head. 'Damned foreigners,' he was saying. 'If it isn't Czechs or Slovaks, it's Hungarians or Croats. Makes you wonder why they ever stopped being Austrians if they come here so much.'

'A nice car.' It was brand new, with a Graz licence plate.

'Won't last long with that kind of drive-yourself.'

'So it's rented. How can you tell?'

'We've got these new white Fiats for hire at my garage. Too good for us. And just see what gets into them! Did you hear that gear-shift?'

'They seem in a hurry,' said Krieger mildly. He watched the Fiat's tail-lights scurrying south.

'Foreigners are always in a hurry. And they've always got plenty of money too. D'you know how much it costs to rent a car? Let me tell you——'

'Yes,' said Krieger. 'I think the cramp has gone. I'd better get some change.'

'I'll do it,' said the driver. His bad temper had vented itself: he was now an almost amiable young man with a perky grin. Krieger didn't argue. He waited inside the safety of the cab and thought about Milan and Jan. They had traced Irina, not only to Graz, but to the exact hotel. It was only small consolation to learn that Dave had outwitted them slightly. Very slightly. The direction they had taken could lead to the road to Lienz.

He let the taxi drive off before he picked up his bag and headed round the corner. The garage was deserted except for one thin-faced mechanic working on his motor cycle. The Chrysler was neatly parked among a dozen cars. There was no objection made about driving it out: Krieger had the official receipt as well as a reasonable explanation, and the mechanic raised no problem beyond an extra charge for the gasoline and oil which had been ordered. (One up for Dave, thought Krieger.)

'Lucky I filled it up right away,' the mechanic said. He was hollow-chested, long-haired, with gentle eyes and a sad smile. 'I didn't expect anyone to drive the car out until tomorrow morning. You had better let your friends know.'

'The American who left it here?'

'No—his two friends who came round asking about the Chrysler, and when it was leaving. I told them tomorrow morning.'

'A big fellow with fair hair, and a thinner man with dark hair?'

'That's them. Hope I didn't——'

'No, no. We'll let them know. What kind of car were they driving?'

'Didn't have any. Came here by taxi from the airport and wanted us to rent them a car. But we don't handle that. Too tricky. I sent them to a hire agency near the station. Did they find something?'

'I'm sure they did.'

'But nothing like this one.' The mechanic gave the Chrysler a pat on its hood, and then a wave, and went back to his motor cycle.

Perhaps, thought Krieger, he had married his girl who liked to go dancing in the evening, and was glad of nightwork to pay for the rent and the diapers.

Krieger edged his car carefully into the empty street, and picked up speed as he turned the corner and took the road south. His thoughts were miserable company. It was no longer possible to argue that Jo must have been careless and led Ludvik to Dürnstein, or that Dave had been so absorbed in Irina that he hadn't paid enough attention to a car following him all the way from Dürnstein to Graz. These two, Milan and Jan, had been sent from Vienna direct by air. They had known exactly where to pick up Irina's trail. They had even known about the Chrysler. No doubt left: there was an informer.

The highway was well made, but hedged in by small silent factories and little box houses where people gathered in barely lit rooms around television sets. And then the hard dark shapes scattered, thinned out, and fields and farms and trees took over. The road swept round to the right, a clear stretch free of traffic, and headed west.

Krieger put on more speed. Be careful, he told himself: don't drive on anger. Or perhaps he should let his temper break, get rid of it before he reached Lienz. An informer—God damn him to everlasting hell.

Krieger had always liked Lienz. It was a country capital, where fields and hills and woods sloped up and down around an old town. The little shops along narrow streets had crowded displays of local products—plain foods and simple wines as well as

Tyrolean jackets, cocky hats, decorated leather belts, wide-skirted dirndls, embroidered shawls—and none of them aimed particularly at the tourist trade. Nor were the windowfuls of guns and rifles and hunting knives. People here had a life of their own, and held to their routines: most of them were early in bed and halfway through their sleep by midnight. It was a scattering of visitors who still wandered aimlessly around, perhaps car-weary and eager for a breath of fresh cool air before they turned in.

The old market-place—a lopsided kind of square—was filled with foreign automobiles, all ready for another three hundred miles tomorrow. Krieger added his Chrysler to a row of them, picked up his bag and raincoat, and threaded his way haphazardly towards the sidewalk, his eyes searching out all white cars, checking each Fiat for a Graz registration. One from Milan; another from Geneva; a third from Rome. Possibly, he warned himself, the two Czechs had parked elsewhere—if they had driven here at all. But, his instinct insisted, if they had been told about Dave's destination, they probably knew the name of the hotel too. In that case, it was more than likely that a couple of tired strangers arriving late in this town would park as close as they could to Die Forelle, particularly when there were plenty of cars around to give a sense of protection. And there it was, a white Fiat powdered with fine dust, Graz licence plate and all.

Krieger kept his even pace, reached the broad sidewalk with its masses of geraniums and petunias trailing thickly from window-boxes, and headed for the gentle lights of the inn. Placid and peaceful: a place where—if it weren't for a white Fiat from Graz—one could enjoy a good night's rest. But at least there was one comfort: he hadn't seen any sign of Mennery's car. Dave was being careful; more careful than these two action boys from Prague.

And with that thought Krieger passed under the inn's gilded sign—a leaping trout—held out in stiff but shining welcome, and entered the small lobby.

Nothing had changed much in two years. Krieger crossed over a polished floor to the reception desk. Around him were panelled walls, shaded lights, gleaming brass ornaments. Flowers, too, of course—this was the East Tyrol. And the lingering but tantalizing aroma of venison stew.

Behind the desk a middle-aged man laid aside his book and raised his massive bulk out of an armchair. He stepped majestically forward, a tall figure doubly impressive in Austrian dress—grey wool jacket with a forest-green collar, green leaves stitched on to lapels as decoration, elkhorn buttons. He was very much the master of the inn. He hadn't changed, either, in two years: same shrewd eyes, same genial smile. Krieger could remember everything about the man except his name. Yes, I'm tired, Krieger thought; and hungry too. He let his bag drop on a wooden stool and managed a smile.

'Too bad that the kitchen is closed at this hour,' he said tentatively.

'Too bad,' the man agreed, formal but definite. 'Also too bad that there isn't a room available. Everything is occupied.' He pointed to the register, filled with names.

'Even that small sitting-room you keep for emergencies?'

The man's round red-cheeked face looked up from the register, studied Krieger. 'Ah,' he said suddenly, 'two years ago? Herr—Herr Krieger?'

'That's right.'

'From Switzerland?'

Krieger shook hands. 'That's a good welcome even if you haven't a room for me. Is there a Miss Corelli staying here, by the way? I'd like to call her——' He broke off, as the man smiled approvingly past him, and turned to see Jo Corelli standing at the doorway of the dining-room, hesitating, not quite her usual poised self. She was obviously startled, perhaps even shocked. But otherwise she made as pretty a picture as ever, quietly chic in a white sweater and skirt, with her dark hair smoothly brushed and held back in place by a chiffon scarf.

She didn't look like a girl who had spent this long day in travelling over the greater part of Austria.

'Jo!' Krieger said. 'Now isn't this nice? Had a good trip?'

She recovered enough to smile, and came across the hall to give him a brief hug. 'Very, very nice,' she murmured. 'I've been waiting for you in the dining-sitting-room-bar for the last half-hour.'

You have, have you? . . . 'Yes,' Krieger said, 'I'd like a drink unless—' he looked at the man behind the desk—'the bar is closed too?'

'I'll make arrangements,' the man said, and left in the direction of the kitchen. 'Wine or beer?'

'Beer tonight. And plenty of it.'

'That kind of day?' Jo asked as she led the way to a table near the window in the almost-deserted dining-room. The only remaining guests were a group of tourists arguing in Dutch, but far enough away to be ignorable. Wall-lights had been lowered, perhaps as a gentle hint that it was time for all good people to push off to bed. But the dim effect was easy on tired eyes, and Krieger welcomed it. The corner which Jo had staked out for herself with her handbag and a flask of wine was partly shielded from the street by half-drawn curtains.

'Cosy,' Krieger said, and relaxed into a solid chair.

'And practical. You can see some of the square from this window, but no one can look inside—at least, you didn't notice me, did you?'

Krieger glanced out between the curtains. And of course, he would have to see the white Fiat to remind him that life wasn't a matter of shaded lights and a comfortable chair and a pretty girl watching him with a sympathetic smile.

'You saw me arrive?'

'Of course. I was waiting for you, wasn't I? You were alone in the Chrysler. You parked out of sight. And then, a few minutes later, you came zigzagging through the cars towards the front door. You looked sad, Walter. Even—grim. Why?'

'I always look a touch grim when it's midnight and I've been on the move since early morning.' Particularly, he thought, when I've just driven almost four hours with enough anger in me to last for four weeks. 'But if you saw me arrive, why did you look so startled when you met me?'

'Because you made me feel like a complete idiot.'

'I did?'

'You did. Here I was planning all kinds of little stratagems—how I'd let you notice me in the lobby without drawing anyone's attention to our meeting—and there you were, walking into a place where you were *known*, asking for Jo Corelli without batting an eyelid. Really, Walter—after the way we dodged around Vienna—I ask you!'

'And I'd say there has been a change in tactics. I've decided we'll play things a little differently.'

'So has Dave,' Jo said angrily. 'He chose Lienz, didn't he?

He brought us here—and one ghastly journey it was, too—and now he isn't going to turn up.'

'Isn't he?' Krieger's eyes were thoughtful as they studied Jo's face. 'What makes you so sure of that?'

'Hugh McCulloch telephoned from Geneva——'

'When?'

'Eleven-fifteen. With an urgent message to be given to you as soon as you arrived. He had just heard—very briefly—from Dave. Not to worry. Dave and Irina are safely out of Graz. Dave will contact you in Merano.'

So McCulloch had mentioned Merano. Inescapable, of course. Lines of communication had to be kept clear, but with every clarification came another break in security. 'Where did you take McCulloch's call? Not, I hope, from the desk in the lobby.' And had she repeated *Merano*, just to let McCulloch know she had got it correctly?

'Oh, come on, Walter. I'm not all that stupid.'

'Sorry,' he said abruptly.

'I should think so.' She looked at him, both puzzled and hurt. 'You're acting like a stranger.'

He watched her unhappily.

'Who has broken security, Jo? Frankly, someone has been careless.' Or worse. But he left that unspoken. 'Too much talk, perhaps.'

'Not me!' she said emphatically. 'I wasn't in the lobby when Geneva telephoned. I was in bed. I took the call there. Then I got up and dressed and fixed my hair and came down here to wait for you. Of course, I checked Mark's room first, to tell him about McCulloch's latest bulletin, but he wasn't in. He's still out——'

'Mark Bohn? How did he get to Lienz?'

'With me.'

'And where is he now?'

'I don't know. I really don't care either. We saw an awful lot of each other today. You know what? Mark is great fun for ten minutes at a cocktail party, and amusing for the soup course at dinner, but——' She shrugged her shoulders. 'We arrived here just after sunset, and Mark decided we'd split up and come in separately, stay apart. Then you breeze in, changing all tactics. And Mark and I have custard pie all over our faces.'

'What good were our old tactics?' Krieger asked quietly.

'You were followed to Dürnstein, in spite of all our secrecy. And what about your journey here?'

'Partly followed.' She was worried now, and trying to hide it.

'Partly?'

'It was strange—I just can't fathom it. When we left Dürnstein the grey Fiat had already gone. I thought we were safe. Then I saw it as we were about to cross the Danube, just below Melk. There was a crowd of cars, but it was the last one getting on to our ferry. And Ludvik was driving. Mark said I must be crazy. But he's nearsighted, and no help at all. I saw the Fiat once more—as we drove into Salzburg.'

'And then?'

'Nothing. I turned in our car, while Mark went to inquire about chartering a small plane. I wanted to fly to Lienz—save time and energy. I also thought that was one way we could really shake Ludvik. But——'

She broke off as Krieger's hand pressed lightly on her arm. The innkeeper was making his way towards them with the broad smile of success curving over his ruddy cheeks. Behind him was a girl, tired but willing, with a large tray on her thin shoulders.

'Kröll,' Krieger said softly. 'That's it!' Then, to the innkeeper, 'My admiration, Herr Kröll—you really did make arrangements.' The tray had two large tankards of beer and a plate of open sandwiches.

'And when you have eaten,' Herr Kröll said, his voice lowered to a stage whisper as if that could hide this infringement of his rules about serving no food after midnight, 'Elsa will take you to her mother's house. It is quite near—two minutes through the back courtyard. You will find a good bed there. It's being prepared right now. No, no, no——' he added, brushing aside all thanks. 'The least we can do, Herr Krieger. At your service.' And with a quick bow he retreated to the hall and his armchair.

'I'll be ready in half an hour, Elsa,' Krieger told the young waitress. He could only hope he hadn't bumped her out of her own comfortable bed for this night. If he had, her patient smile didn't show any resentment. 'Can you stay awake that long? I'm sorry to give you all this trouble.' She melted completely, laughed, and wished him good appetite as she hurried back to the kitchen.

143

'As my father, the expert diplomat, used to say,' Jo murmured, 'when you apologize, lay it on with a trowel. And as my uncle, that wily Englishman, would add, there's nothing like the old-boy level for solving the headaches of travel.' Then she said, 'I wish we had someone like Herr Kröll around to get us a small plane this afternoon.'

'Bohn had no luck?'

'Everything was already chartered. And of course there are no regular flights to Lienz—or rather to Nikolsdorf. The airport there takes only light planes. So we hired ourselves another car, and drove like crazy. We just managed to get over the Grossglockner while the light was still good. There was a lot of mist today—it kept falling and rising—really weird. Mark let me drive over the pass, and he took the lower stretches.'

'Very gallant of him.'

'Actually,' Jo said in Bohn's defence, 'he *was* being gallant. He wouldn't let me set out alone for Lienz, insisted someone had to be with me.' She smiled suddenly. 'Poor Mark! He hadn't bargained for a road skating its way between ice floes. Of course, when we got down to flatter ground and he took the wheel, then it was my turn to close my eyes and suppress my groans. He's the most erratic driver I've ever sat beside. Still— we got here.' Her amusement left her. Her dark-blue eyes were wide and troubled. Her voice was low. 'No one followed us out of Salzburg. No grey Fiat anywhere along that entire route. And yet the first thing I saw, as we drove into this main square, was a man standing against the wall of the old *Rathaus*—that's the building just across from this inn. It was Ludvik. Already here. Waiting for us.'

Krieger paused in lifting a second sandwich. 'He still didn't care if he was seen?'

'Not any longer. The moment he glimpsed our car, he must have moved away. At least he was gone by the time I drew into a parking place and could look around, and that was only a matter of a few seconds.'

So they've changed their tactics too, Krieger thought, and took a large bite of ham and cheese.

'It was Ludvik,' Jo insisted.

'I believe you.'

'But how could it be? He came into Salzburg just behind us.

'And once he was told about Leinz, he managed to charter

one of those light planes that were so scarce.' How hard had
Bohn tried? Krieger wondered.

'Ludvik was told? By whom?'

'Who knew about Lienz? And who knew about Graz?'

'Graz? Did someone follow Dave there? Oh, no!'

'Two friends of Ludvik flew into Graz from Vienna. And
as soon as they discovered Dave and Irina had left, they drove
here.'

'Oh, no!' Jo repeated softly.

'Their car is outside,' Krieger said curtly, and pushed away
the sandwich. He drank some beer, lit his pipe.

'Which is it?'

'The white Fiat next to that red Volvo.'

'I saw it arrive. Twenty minutes before you did. There were
two men. They came in here, stood at the door for a moment,
scanned the room, and left.' Jo took a deep breath. 'Who were
they looking for? Dave?'

'I don't think they'd expect to find him and Irina sitting
downstairs in a dining-room.'

'Who were they looking for?' Jo persisted.

'Someone who could give them information about our next
move.'

'I've told no one about Merano.' She was avoiding all mention of Bohn. 'Oh, Walter, I can't believe it. I just can't believe
it. What do we do?'

'We find out. Definitely.'

'How?'

'By dropping the name of Merano and seeing if it reaches
them.'

'Too dangerous.'

'How else do we know where they are getting their information?'

'And what about Dave and Irina? Can we keep them out of
this?'

Krieger smiled, watching her anxious face. 'Yes,' he said
gently. 'We'll run some interference for them. That's all.' He
gripped her hand. 'Just leave the talking to me, will you, Jo?'

She nodded, tried to smile. Then her eyes left his, glanced
towards the lobby. 'Oh, Walter, let me drive with you tomorrow. Please?'

Krieger looked towards the lobby too. Mark Bohn was

standing at the threshold of the dining-room, as if he didn't know whether to enter or to stay out.

'Why not?' Krieger answered Jo. 'We leave at nine.'

He waved to the doorway. Bohn took his cue and started towards them. Jo picked up her handbag and left before he could reach the table.

She passed him without a glance.

Much amused, Bohn said, 'Jo is really carrying the Mata Hari bit too far. I told her we'd play-act strangers here, but at this time of night—who's watching? And what are you doing here? Didn't Graz hold any charms?' He dropped into the chair opposite Krieger.

'I just wanted to be sure of an early start tomorrow.'

'Oh? And where are we bound for?'

'Merano.'

'Merano? Then Jo and I have both lost our bets. We thought we'd be heading into Italy.'

'Merano is in Italy. Or are you forgetting the peace treaty after the First World War?' That was when Merano and all the South Tyrol had been ceded to the Italians and Meran became Merano in the Alto Adige.

Bohn mastered his irritation. 'Of course not. You know what I meant: some place more central, like Rome. Merano is far to the north——'

'But a pleasant town where we can all relax for a day or so. Irina is tired.'

'Isn't it something of a dead end?'

'There's a good road south from Merano, right past Lake Como.'

'To Milan?'

Krieger put a hand up for caution, glanced over at the voluble Dutch.

'They aren't listening,' Bohn told him impatiently. 'Aren't we taking the long way round to Milan? Who thought this up, anyway?'

'Dave.'

'Ah—the inspired amateur. I never knew he was such a devious character. Did he and Irina arrive with you?'

'No.'

'They're still in Graz?'

'To tell you the truth, I'm not sure where they are.'

Bohn stared. 'You're full of surprises tonight.'

'It has been a day of surprises. I thought you were heading for Munich after you reached Salzburg. What about your assignment on the Olympics? Haven't you got some interviews lined up?'

'The Games don't get really under way for another ten days. And I thought Jo needed company. She's a bit rattled, did you notice? Something's troubling her. Any idea of what is wrong?'

'Just needs some rest, I think. I'll drive her to Merano tomorrow. You can follow us in that car you brought here from Salzburg.'

Bohn was silent. Either he didn't like the idea of driving around the Dolomites by himself, or he was worrying about the meaning of this change in plans.

'That is,' Krieger continued, 'if you want to join us in Merano at the Hotel Bristol. That's the gathering spot.'

'I'll be there. After all, if I've come this far——' Bohn shrugged his shoulders, smiled, then added, 'What kind of road is it? Nothing like today's journey, I hope.'

'No ice floes,' Krieger assured him with a grin. 'Plenty of scenery, though. The Dolomites are beautiful brutes. The road is good. You won't get lost.' And too bad, thought Krieger.

'I'll make sure of that by keeping close on your tail.'

'I'd rather have you than Ludvik.'

'Ludvik?'

'Yes, he's in Lienz. And so are a couple of other murderers—friends of his.' Krieger's calm voice was as matter-of-fact as the way he knocked out the ashes from his pipe. He pocketed it and rose to his feet, glancing at his watch. 'Time to turn in, I think.'

'Murderers?' Bohn asked. He followed Krieger to the lobby. 'You are joking, surely.' His voice was troubled, his eyes grave.

'I'll give you the full story in Merano. It's one for the books. But I don't think we'll be pestered much more by these thugs. The Austrian police will pick them up here early tomorrow.'

'They're wanted by the Austrian police?'

'Yes.'

Bohn was studying Krieger's face. 'You really aren't kidding,' he said at last. Perhaps he was remembering Krieger's unexplained session at Vienna police headquarters that morning.

'Definitely not. I'll be one of the witnesses against them.'

They had reached the lobby. Herr Kröll had retired for the night. In his place at the desk was a thin-faced boy guarding Krieger's bag and coat. 'You actually saw——' Bohn began.

'I did,' Krieger said, his lips tight.

There was a short silence. 'See you tomorrow,' Bohn said. 'When?'

'Nine o'clock. Prompt.'

'Then it's bed for me now.' Bohn did look exhausted, his face white and strained even in the warmly shaded light of the hall. He left for the small elevator at the back of the lobby, without another minute wasted on good nights.

Krieger waited, tired elbows resting on the reception desk, while the boy went to fetch Elsa. Inside the dining-room the Dutch were still drinking beer and resisting sleep. High life in Lienz, Krieger thought. Elsa came at last, a shawl over her shoulders, ready for the night air. And as he followed her towards the back door for his two-minute journey, the switchboard was signalling. I can only hope it isn't Bohn who's making that telephone call, thought Krieger as he stepped into a narrow alley, cool and dark. Ahead of him, Elsa's solid shoes clattered over the cobblestones.

The room was at the top of the stairs, three flights up, but clean, with a white bed that looked invitingly soft, and one small window. Elsa's shoes creaked on the wooden steps as she started down. There was no disguising of sound in this old house, thought Krieger, no chance of a short trip outside without wakening the whole family. He was shut in for the night. He laid his bag carefully down on the wooden floor, switched off the light, and moved quietly over to the shutters to push them fully open. His luck improved: the room was at the front of the house and overlooked the square. From this high perch he could see a good deal, almost as much as from an alley or a dark doorway; and certainly less detectable. How long should he give them? Fifteen minutes, half an hour, even a full hour? He focused his eyes on the white Fiat. He took out his pipe, hesitated. Matches flared. Better not. . . . He replaced the pipe in his pocket.

Patiently he stood, his arms resting on the sill, his coat draped round him to keep off the night chill, his shoulders within the shadow of the overhanging eaves. Every five minutes or so he'd change his balance, stretch his back and neck, tighten his leg muscles. A false hunch? A stupid expectation? He would wait until one-thirty and find out.

Down in the square, partly moon-shadowed, partly lit by street lamps, there was little to break the night's silence. Two motor cycles ripped through. A small group of heavy-booted hikers, English voices rising up to his window, wandered back to their *Gasthof*, studying the cars as they went. A man in Tyrolean dress took off in a Volkswagen. That was all. By half-past one the square had seemingly bedded down for the night. Krieger was almost asleep himself, eyelids drowsing. He blinked them open, decided on another ten minutes to give himself every possible chance. (In the past he had found that when he had talked himself out of playing a strong hand, he had invariably lost.) Perhaps fifteen minutes, he thought, unwilling to admit defeat.

But he needed only five of them.

From the mouth of a narrow street some distance off, two men stepped out of the shadows and made their way to the cars. Their footsteps gave no echo on the pavement: they were moving with exaggerated care, lightly, quickly. They were travelling light too. Each carried a small hand case and nothing more. Their heads were bent forward, faces hidden from high windows. They had to pass an edge of light, widely cast by a street lamp, and for that moment the colour of their hair was distinguishable: one dark, one blond. Their heights were right, too: medium-sized Milan and six-foot Jan. They stopped at the white Fiat, unlocked it as they glanced around them—a searching look that swept ground level and then rose to the upper windows of Die Forelle—and stepped inside. Cautiously, the engine started up, its noise controlled. Gently, the Fiat backed out of the ranks and pointed west. And that was the direction of the Italian frontier. Krieger drew a long satisfied breath.

He still didn't leave the window. He wanted to keep an eye on that car until it left the square. Yes, it was definitely going to take the road west. And then to his surprise, it halted at the corner, its engine still running. A man hurried out of the last doorway on the square—how long had he been there?—and was across the sidewalk and into the Fiat before Krieger could lean out for a better view. It could have been Ludvik—the man was the correct height and breadth. And it probably was Ludvik, Krieger decided as the car moved out of sight. Ludvik would want to get out of Austrian territory just as quickly as Milan and Jan.

Well, he thought, I pushed a little and they gave.

He left the window, switched on the light, found his flask of brandy under his shaving kit. Tomorrow, he must allow himself enough time before leaving to put a call in to Vienna. What working arrangements were there between the Austrian and Italian police—any chance of speedy extradition? Possibly not; but it might make a useful threat. Anything that made Ludvik's life more complicated was a handy idea. And if any confirmation of the Pokorny murders had been needed, it had been given right here, tonight, in a panic flight from Lienz.

Tomorrow morning, too, he'd better have a check made on the Chrysler: Ludvik had stationed himself too damned near it. Yet it was more likely that Ludvik would wait until he was well out of Austrian territory before he took any action against Krieger. There could be hell to pay in Merano. A witness, Krieger had called himself, and witnesses weren't much tolerated by Ludvik and his goon squad. Krieger had a third swallow of brandy and chased that thought away. The chill was out of his bones too. But quite apart from the brandy and its warmth, he hadn't felt better in years.

He was soon in bed in spite of strange territory and its creaking floor, his sleep was deep and dream-free, a blissful forgetting inside a cloud of white eiderdown.

The morning brought clouds and threats of rain, but nothing dampened Krieger's upbeat mood: bad weather could be a discouragement to weekend drivers, and mountain roads might be less cluttered with Saturday traffic. By nine o'clock he was ready—car checked, Vienna telephoned, and a brief call made to McCulloch too.

Jo, usually punctual, was a few minutes late. She got into the Chrysler with only a small nod in exchange for his greeting, and sat beside him in marked silence. He started the engine, began edging around the square, avoiding a minibus with problems in loading—suitcases scattered around it along with some half-awake Dutchmen. A lot of other cars were pulling out too; soon the square would be given back to the Lienzer.

But he could see no sign of Mark Bohn at the doorway of Die Forelle.

'We've mislaid Bohn,' he said cheerfully.

'No such luck.' Jo was still on edge.

'A bad night?'

'Yes.'

'Had any breakfast?'

'Two mouthfuls—before Bohn dropped into my room with a message for you. Why didn't he come down here and deliver it himself?' (A messenger girl, that's what I am, Jo thought angrily.) 'He's been detained. He has been trying to reach Munich—something about his assignment there, exact dates, et cetera, et cetera, et cetera—and he's now waiting for Munich to call back.'

'So,' Krieger said softly, 'he has bugged out.'

'Not Bohn! He'll meet us in Merano.'

'I wonder.' Krieger concentrated on the narrow shopping street they had entered, a bustle of business and weekend marketing.

'Why?'

'He's scared, Jo. He's way in over his head, and he has just realized it.'

'But how——'

'A mention of murder.'

She drew a deep breath. 'That isn't funny,' she said, her annoyance growing.

'It wasn't meant to be.' He tried to calm her, and added, 'Sorry, Jo. I haven't told you much about Vienna, or——'

'You've told me nothing in these last twenty-four hours.' There was deep reproof in her voice. 'This is *me*, Jo.'

So that was where the hurt lay. 'But now I can,' he said. And thank God, we can leave suspicions and doubts behind us with Mark Bohn. 'Twenty miles to the frontier, and a decent breakfast for you, and a lot of talk. How does that sound?'

It sounded fine, thought Jo. She gave her first smile of the morning.

Chapter Thirteen

PEACE WAS EVERYWHERE: in his heart, most of all. David
stood at the window, looking down at the silent garden, a vast
stretch of green with wandering paths and circles of flowers and
clusters of trees turned to sharp silhouettes against the early sun.
The surrounding buildings were hushed, no sign of life behind
their curtained windows. Only at the lodge near the entry gates
was a discreet stir of activity, preparing for a new day's business. Except for the hotel staff, most people were still asleep.
Like Irina.

He turned away from the window, came over to the bed
where she lay outstretched, face half-buried in the pillow, hair
loose and golden, a twist of sheet barely covering her hips.
Lightly, trying not to wake her, he kissed her neck, her
shoulders; felt the smooth curve of her waist, the gentle round-
ness of her breasts. Suddenly, her hands caught his wrists and
she laughed as she turned to face him. Her arms went round
him, pulling him towards her, her lips meeting his.

They came out of their dream as a brisk knock was repeated on
the door. David opened his eyes, became fully awake as he
heard a third knock, sharp and peremptory, and a voice calling
'*Guten Morgen.*'

'I was too damned efficient last night,' he said angrily, and
drew on his dressing gown. Everything arranged for an early
start this morning: a large hot breakfast to let them reach
Merano without worrying about food. He glanced at his watch
as he crossed the room: seven-fifteen. The waiter was late.
And thank God for that, he thought, and opened the door in a
better mood. Behind him he heard the rustle of bedclothes as
Irina pulled them over her head.

'Come out before you smother,' he told her as room service

retreated back into the corridor, and he began uncovering the dishes set on a table by the window. He paused, watching her as she came to join him. His smile faded. He said softly: 'You really are the most beautiful woman.'

She looked at him for a long moment, her eyes wide and warm. Then she shook her head and laughed. 'I'm just the happiest woman.' She put her arms around him, held him tightly. 'Never leave me again, David.'

'Never again,' he said. 'We were cheated of sixteen years. Never again.'

They breakfasted and dressed and were ready to set out by twenty minutes past eight. By that time, the lodge was busy with departures and bill payers.

'I'll call McCulloch later,' David said, as he dropped their baggage on the back seat of the car, and helped Irina safely in. Even the touch of her hand sent his heart leaping.

'Again? Didn't you call him last night?'

'Yes. But I didn't talk with him. I left a message just to keep him happy.' David smiled as he read her thoughts. 'It was enough,' he assured her. 'You're too dutiful, Irina. Besides, I was worried about having to leave you alone.' He laughed, remembering his return. 'If I hadn't come chasing back to you, you'd have floated out of that bathroom in a sea of foam, and right down the staircase. What did you empty into that tub?'

'Everything that was lying around.' She laughed, too. 'There were so many free samples all waiting to be used.' And why not? My first hot bath in twelve days, she thought. And the first morning in years when I didn't awake with fear sliding back into my mind. Fear and a sense of hopelessness.

'Converted to capitalism, are you?' he asked lightly, trying to drive away the cloud that now shadowed her face. He succeeded: the smile came back to her lips.

As he slowed the car to pass through the gates, she looked over her shoulder to have one last glimpse of the green garden with its blaze of brilliant flower beds and the tall trees standing sentinel. 'I was happy there,' she said softly. 'Something to remember always.'

He nodded. 'Why the past tense? It isn't over. It is a beginning.'

'But——'

153

'But nothing. Who's going to stop us from planning our own lives? Your father? No. I don't think that's his style. Now, if we were dealing again with your mother, we'd have a real battle on our hands.'

'David, David——' She was shaking her head.

'What's wrong with all that?'

'Me. I've lost the habit of thinking about the future. I live day by day.'

'That isn't enough.'

'It is, when you are afraid of the future.'

'Why afraid? Because it is unknown?'

'Yes. So many paths to choose and none of them certain.'

'But the freedom of choice is yours.'

'And if you make a wrong choice?'

'You admit it—the sooner, the better. You cut your losses, choose more carefully the second time.'

'What if you keep making other mistakes?'

'Then you probably didn't admit you were wrong the first time,' he said half-jokingly. 'That's one sure way of repeating your errors. I know. I've done it.'

'And you still want your freedom of choice—even if it's the wrong choice?'

'Who's to say that a choice made for me would be any less wrong? No, thank you. I'll take my chances on my own decisions. And you're going to do that too, Irina.'

'I'll learn. I suppose. But now—it's frightening in a way.'

'I know.'

'Do you really know, David?'

'We all have some controls over our lives.'

'But are you told what town you must live in; what job you may have; where you will work; where you can travel, even within your own country? Everything is done by Prague: the choices are made for you, for everyone—and it all begins to seem inevitable.' She drew a deep breath. 'In my whole life, I've only made two really important decisions for myself: to separate from my husband; to leave my country.' And even that escape wasn't my own decision entirely, she thought: it might never have happened if Jiri hadn't allowed it to come true. 'Why did he let me?' she asked, almost of herself.

David slowed the car to avoid a trail of teenagers, with picnic baskets and phonograph, making their carefree way to one of the marinas lining the shore of the lake. 'Who? And let you do what?'

'Jiri. Why did he allow me to escape?'

David looked at her sharply, then made a left turn through the empty square to reach the main highway. 'How long have you known that?'

'I'm only beginning to realize it, Jiri——'

'I don't want to talk about Jiri. I want to talk about us. Come on, Irina—get rid of that ghost. From now on, everything is *not* done by Prague.'

'You sound so confident.'

Confident, am I? He let that go. The only thing he was sure of, at this minute—apart from his own feelings about Irina— was the fact that they were on their way to Merano. The little lakeside town of Velden was behind them, its people waking up to another day of sailing, swimming, tennis, eating, drinking, dancing, and general jollification, all worries pushed aside until vacations were over. He thought, with an unexpected touch of nostalgia, of a stretch of white sand pounded by huge breakers, of high dunes and green-gold grass. 'You've never seen the Atlantic, have you, Irina?'

'The only ocean I ever saw was the English Channel.' And then, as he laughed, she said, 'But it isn't an ocean, is it?'

'No. It isn't even a very big bit of sea.'

'It was enormous to me. Is an ocean so different?'

'You'll find out. I have a small cottage where I spend weekends.' And he began describing East Hampton.

Just outside Villach, their last big town on this route, David slowed down as they approached an efficient-looking service station that was quite empty of customers at this hour. 'One thing I've learned: keep your car tanked up on country highways.' And then as she looked puzzled, he explained less cryptically. Irina's English was excellent, but it didn't extend much to American short cuts. He had the feeling she had to guess the meaning of one quarter of his phrases. Darling Irina, he thought, watching the smiling eyes, the slightly raised eyebrow, the parted lips breaking into a laugh, you've got so many things—small as well as big—to learn all at once. 'Look,' he said, 'would you be all right if I were to leave you for ten minutes? I see the garage office over there, and it must have a

telephone. It might be an idea to check in with McCulloch—
let him know we are on our way.'

'I'll be all right,' she assured him.

He still hesitated. 'Come and stand beside me,' he said.
'We'll make the call together.'

'I'd be less noticed, sitting here.'

True enough. 'I'll keep an eye on you,' he said as he got out.
He could do that easily once he'd been given permission to use
the telephone: the office window was wide and the car was
clearly in sight. She had tied her blue-and-green scarf to hide
her hair, and she was keeping her head bent as if she were
reading something. No one from any of the passing cars could
recognize or remember her. Reassured, he made the call to
Geneva.

He really worries about me, Irina had thought as she tied the
scarf in place. It was a good feeling. She reached into the back
seat, found her automatic pencil jammed down the side of her
handbag, left the bag where it lay beside the luggage, and with
the pencil to help her, she began studying David's road map,
trying to measure distances and translate kilometres into miles.
I'll have to learn about miles, she told herself. I may as well
begin, right now.

By the time he returned, the car, with tank filled and oil
checked, was ready to leave. He didn't look altogether happy.
Something was annoying him. Irina slipped the pencil into her
pocket, said quickly, 'We are now about twelve miles out of
Velden, and still sixty to go to Lienz. Then it's only another
twenty to the Italian frontier. Am I right?'

'Close enough,' he said with a grin. She had dropped seven
miles somewhere between Velden and Lienz. He noticed the
calculations she had lightly jotted down in the map's margin,
and they touched him. It had been quite an effort. 'In fact,
perfect.'

'How long will it take?'

He measured the traffic ahead of them on the highway, not
compressed as yet, and moving at a steady pace. 'We'll make
the border easily by ten-thirty. Weather permitting,' he added
as he looked at the dark clouds gathering ahead of them, and
hoped they were not symbolic.

'Are we going to stop at Lienz?'

'Why should we?'

156

'Jo may be waiting there for us.'

'Jo isn't alone. Walter Krieger is with her. He reached Lienz last night.'

'Expecting to find us?' Irina was dismayed.

'Yes. But he's probably delighted we didn't turn up. Ludvik was there, expecting us. And so were these two.' David reached into his pocket and found the photographs of Milan and Jan. 'Better look at them now. They are the men you passed on the stairway to Alois Pokorny's flat. Milan is the dark-haired one. The big fellow is Jan. Recognize them?'

'The man with light hair—Jan?—Yes,' she said slowly, 'that was the one who passed very close to me. At least I think so. Perhaps if I saw them again together, I could identify them.'

'Just keep their faces in mind from now on.' And I thought I had ditched them neatly in Graz. How did they find out about Lienz?

Irina was troubled too. She handed back the photographs; said nothing.

'The three of them have left Lienz. I don't know why or how. McCulloch had other things to talk about. Krieger will brief me completely, in Merano.'

'Will Ludvik and his friends be in Merano?' Irina asked, very quietly.

'If they've found out about that, too—yes.'

'If? They seem to know everything.'

'Well, let's hope that they haven't heard of Tarasp.'

She looked at him, her eyes questioning.

'It's a village just over the Swiss border. That's our destination. Krieger will tell us about the exact house where——'

'My father's house?'

'No. He lives somewhere else in Switzerland. He's coming to meet you. I wasn't given the reason —McCulloch says Krieger will explain it all.'

'And when do we reach Tarasp? Tomorrow?' So soon, she thought. And where does David go then?

'Perhaps earlier.'

'Oh, no!' she exclaimed. There was pain in her voice, disbelief on her face. 'Tonight? Oh, no——'

'That's how I felt.'

She said nothing at all.

'Do you go with your father or do you stay with me?'

She shook her head. 'I know what I want to do. But——'
She didn't finish.

His lips tightened. If there was a conflict in Irina between
'want' and 'ought', he could guess which would win. And I'll
be asked to wait for her, and she will promise to come to me.
Will she? What if her father falls ill, needs her—delay after
delay?

Irina said, 'But it's too far to drive to Tarasp. You *can't*
cover that distance in one day.'

She's postponing her decision, he thought. 'Look at the map
again, Irina. From the Italian border to Merano is only a
hundred miles. We'll reach there by two o'clock, perhaps
sooner.'

'But all these mountains!'

'Our road goes round them, not through them.' And another
pleasant plan sent skittering. He had looked forward to taking
a more complicated route, between the giant Dolomite peaks—
a slower journey, but incredibly beautiful, something for them
to remember always.

'And from Merano to Switzerland?' She was still gazing at
the map. She folded it back to see the exact section more clearly,
and took out the pencil as a pointer. Angrily she said, 'I can't
find this Tarasp.'

'It's there all right. It's in the Engadine—just west of the
Swiss National Park. According to McCulloch, about eighty
miles from Merano.'

'So near?' The Engadine. . . . There it was, and the
National Park. Her pencil followed the road that circled it.

'Near enough. Your father is reaching Tarasp tonight.'

The pencil stopped abruptly, a sharp jab to match her feelings; its lead broke off. Yes, that was Tarasp. And it was close
to the border. No distance at all. She laid the map on the seat
beside her, pocketed the pencil, and frowned. 'But why all the
change in our plans? This isn't the way it was meant to be. Is
it, David?'

'No,' he said. 'It isn't the way I hoped it would be.'

'But why——'

'Darling, I don't know why. Not until I see Krieger in
Merano. We'll stop there for a couple of hours.'

'I don't think I like your Mr Krieger. He has arranged
everything, hasn't he?'

'Possibly. Don't tell that to Hugh McCulloch, though.' He put on speed. No more sweet delays. He would have rebelled if he didn't sense that Krieger had some very strong reasons for this urgency. But they had better be good ones, he thought angrily. Then, if only to arouse Irina from her depression, he came out of his black mood and got the conversation back to a more normal level. By the time they passed through Lienz, she was even smiling at the comic anecdotes he was managing to dredge up, about crazy conductors and maddened musicians. One thing about the world of music: it provided plenty of light relief as well as heavenly sound.

The last stretch of road, heading west to the Austro-Italian frontier, was as straight and dull as the single-minded railroad track that ran beside it through a flat broad valley of empty fields, with the mountains now pushed far back to the south and north. The cars ahead were beginning to slacken speed.

Irina watched them unbelievingly. 'They hardly stop. Are you sure that's the frontier, David?'

'That's the border, all right.' And they had made it in good time, in spite of a heavy shower of rain as they had passed through Lienz.

As they came closer to the small scattering of buildings, Irina could see the cars more clearly. 'Some have been stopped.' She was nervous. 'Why?'

'Their own choice. They probably need gas, or are changing *Schilling* into *lire*. Not a bad idea, come to think of it.' He put a reassuring hand on her arm. 'All you have to do is show your passport and smile and say thank you as you're waved through. The Italians, farther along the road, will probably throw you a salute. Don't worry, my pet. No barbed wire here.' As he approached the tail end of the small procession of cars, David slowed down. But his attention was caught by the man in the yellow jacket who stood at the edge of the road, with a bag propped beside his feet, watching each car as it passed him. David had seen the blob of yellow—who could have missed it? —two hundred yards away or so, and decided it was some new-style hitch-hiker. As they came closer, David could see the man more clearly: large round eyeglasses, long dark hair ruffled by the breeze through the valley, grey sideburns bulging out from

159

thin cheeks. 'Mark Bohn,' David said incredulously. 'Damn it all, it *is* Mark Bohn.'

Bohn was now studying the green Mercedes as it neared him: his face was blank, showed no sign of recognition. But then, David reflected, no one knew what kind of car he was driving except Walter Krieger. He sounded the horn lightly, briefly, and put out his arm to give one small wave. 'I think,' he said without much enthusiasm, 'we are about to be boarded.' This was one journey on which he could do without Bohn and his incessant stream of talk—or anyone else, for that matter. There went another romantic notion: to drive, alone with Irina, through the Dolomites. He passed Bohn, pointing ahead to a place where he could safely draw the car off the road. And what one hell of a spot Bohn had chosen to stop a car— what did he want, a pile-up? Of course he had been noticeable: that was probably all he had thought about.

David pulled up behind a small group of cars parked near a service station, glanced back. 'He didn't get my signal,' David said, and shook his head. Bohn was hesitating, slightly bewildered, and a little pathetic. His bright smile of recognition had died away into a blank stare. Then, as he saw the Mercedes definitely stopped, his smile came back. He picked up the bag at his feet and started towards them.

Irina said, 'Is he a friend of yours?'

'Yes. And a friend of yours too. That letter—by the way, I've wondered. Why did you send it to Bohn? Why not to London —to your father's publisher?'

'A year ago I sent a letter to London. Nothing secret in it. Only family news. It was stopped.'

'Where?'

'I don't know, Jiri brought it back to me. He said——' She fell silent as Bohn reached them.

Jiri again, thought David: there was always Jiri Hrádek cropping up somewhere. He was sick of that damn name. Jiri, Jiri, the hell with Jiri. He got out of the car, greeted Bohn casually.

Bohn was saying, 'I thought you weren't going to stop.'

'Why not? You looked like a man who needed a lift.'

Bohn smiled broadly. 'That's Dave,' he said, 'putting two and two together, scoring a solid four.' The way he said it, though, didn't make it sound much of a compliment. But that was Bohn's style, David reflected, particularly when his mood was sour.

Bohn reached past David, his hand outstretched for Irina. 'So you're safe and well, and twice as beautiful as when we last met.'

Irina stared at him, politely let her hand be shaken.

'Have I changed so much?' Bohn went on, his mood now bantering. 'More hair, of course. And four years of added worry lines. And a tendency to get tired from too much standing.' He sat down on the driver's seat. 'I waited a good half hour for you, maybe more. You had to come this way. A matter of simple deduction that even I——'

'And how did you get here?' David cut in. 'On foot?'

'With that damned asthmatic machine.' Bohn gestured to a Citroën drawn well to the side of the service station. 'It coughed itself to death just as I reached this point. One of the mechanics said he could give it a thorough overhaul—by three o'clock. But now that you're on the scene, I'll leave it here for Salzburg to pick up. That's where Jo rented it yesterday.'

'And where is Jo?'

'Halfway to Merano with Krieger, I'd imagine. I was delayed in Lienz—had to wait for a phone call from Munich—I must be there by tonight if possible. Serious work starts tomorrow. No more gallivanting around scenic countrysides.' He looked at Irina, said with obvious enthusiasm, 'And how are you? I'm glad it all worked out so well. Really splendid.'

'It isn't over yet,' David reminded him. 'And if you'll just stop blocking the way, I'll get this car moved over to a gas pump.'

'What's the rush? We've all day ahead of us.'

'We don't,' David said shortly. 'Irina, have you any Austrian money you need changed?'

'Plenty of time for that in Merano,' Bohn said, but he slid off the front seat.

David got back into the car, edged it into position, talked briefly with the attendant, and set out for the exchange booth. In Merano, there would be little time for anything beyond making contact with Krieger and hearing the details about Tarasp.

'Not wasting one minute, is he?' Bohn remarked as he rejoined Irina. 'Perhaps he doesn't intend to stay in Merano at all.' He laughed outright. 'Like the way he ditched us all in Lienz. We began to wonder just how reliable old Dave was.' Bohn's eyes flickered over her dress—green wool, and surely too warm for any southward journey?

'There was no need to be in Lienz,' Irina said. She was embarrassed. Now he will ask where we spent the night.

But there is need to be in Merano, Bohn was thinking. He reached into the car and picked up the map that lay on the seat beside her. He looked at it, shaking his head. 'You folded this, I bet. Newspapers and maps—women never get them back into the right creases. Do you want me to straighten it out for you?' His eyes were on the section that faced up. It showed the highway that ran west from Merano and then divided, one route turning north to cross eventually into Switzerland. (The other route travelled south, but it was only partly shown on this section of the map, and therefore less important.) His eyes were now following the Swiss highway that continued from the frontier and curved around the National Park. And what was that—a pencil mark? Yes, a pencil mark, a jagged dot, under the name of a village. 'I like that dress you're wearing,' he said as he shook out the map. He folded it back into its original shape, but not before he had a second glance at the marked village. 'Will it be warm enough for the journey?'

'Quite warm enough.'

Certainly not Italy, then, where the August sun turned humid valleys into a hot stew. He ought to have guessed that Krieger would be handing out false leads to everyone. So screw Lake Como, Milan, and Walter Krieger. 'You'll need a coat, too, for Switzerland, won't you?' He dropped the neatly folded map back beside her. Trasp, Tarsp, something like that. He'd check later, on his own map.

'I have one.'

'Oh yes,' he said, looking now at the back seat where a blue wool coat, folded along with David's raincoat, lay beside two pieces of luggage and a bulging shoulder-strap bag. 'Not much room for me there. Hand me the car keys, Irina. I'll get these things moved into the trunk, and save Dave's precious time.' He reached for the handbag.

'I'll take that,' she said sharply.

It slipped out of his hands on to the floor. He released its catch as he bent to pick it up and held it out to her, upside down. Before she could grasp it, it spilled open and a clutter of objects scattered over the front seat. 'Sorry, sorry! I was in too much of a hurry.'

She rescued a notebook, a diary perhaps, leaving powder and lipstick and passport and wallet and all the other inevitable items strewn around. 'Where's the other one?' she asked worriedly, her voice sharp.

'Still inside the bag—jammed at the bottom.' He pulled it out. 'This it?' He opened it, riffled through its pages. They were closely written, in Czech. Dates, names—that he could see, even in this brief moment. And they were not in Irina's handwriting, either, as far as he could remember it from her letter. 'Don't tell me you've smuggled out some of Jiri's memos,' he said, and grinned widely as he handed her the diary.

She put both notebooks back into her handbag, began packing the other articles on top of them. 'I took nothing of Jiri's,' she said. 'These belong to my father.'

'Oh, all the facts and figures he gathered about your politicians?' Then, as she flashed a startled glance at him, he said, 'Sure, everyone knows about that.' His eyes fell on the passport she was adding, last of all, to her bag. British. And ready for use.

'Everyone?' she challenged him.

'All of us who've been interested in Czechoslovakia. But I thought his papers and notes were seized in a house search when——'

'These were well hidden.'

'And they're dynamite, too?' he asked with another broad smile.

She said nothing, but closed her handbag and set it safely beside her.

'Have you met Krieger?'

Bohn's voice was strangely sombre.

With surprise, she said, 'No.'

'Between us, Irina—be very careful with Krieger. He's playing some double game of his own. He isn't interested in you. He's only interested in drawing your father out of hiding.'

'But David says——'

'That he's an ordinary citizen? Don't you believe it. Krieger is an intelligence expert, a hard-boiled professional agent, and as clever as they come. Don't even let him know that your father's diaries exist.'

'He is my father's friend,' she protested.

'He was. Thirty years ago. Trust me, Irina—I have sources. I know what I'm talking about.'

'Then why did you choose him to help me?'

'I didn't choose anyone. McCulloch took that job over, didn't even let me——' Bohn looked round as he heard footsteps behind him. 'Hello, Dave. Just in time to help me put the luggage in the trunk.'

'Later,' said David. 'Let's get moving.' He had several travel folders in his hand, advertising the beauties of Austria.

'Look—if you could spare another ten minutes.'

'We can't.' David jammed a folder into his pocket as he took his seat. Its title, *Meran in the South Tyrol*, wouldn't exactly please the Italians, but it was all he could find on this side of the frontier. The others he tossed on the floor behind him, and hoped they had served as a slight diversion for anyone too interested in his movements.

'But I'd like to make a phone call, let Salzburg know where they'll find their Citroën.'

'Later,' David repeated. 'Are you coming or aren't you?'

Bohn jammed his bag on the floor of the back seat. He got in, lips tight.

They passed through both frontiers without much more delay. 'Where do we drop you?' David asked.

'Anywhere on a railway line where I can catch a northbound express.'

'Brixen?'

'That would do.' And I can telephone my information from there, thought Bohn. My last small flourish as I bow out. As far as I'm concerned, this assignment is over. Murder is more than I bargained for. And Jiri Hrádek knows that too. 'If it isn't too much trouble for you,' Bohn added.

'No sweat. It's on our route. I won't guarantee I can take you to the station, though.'

'Oh, just drop me where I can find a taxi. Wouldn't want to delay you. Are you going to drive to Switzerland tonight?'

David was taken by surprise. Then he said, 'Switzerland? Is that where we're going?' He tried to sound amused.

Yes, thought Bohn, that is where you are definitely going.

And tonight—why else was Dave in such a tearing hurry? 'You're a glutton for punishment, Dave. Night driving is my ideal of hell. And over a mountain road! No, thank you.'

I've no good reason to dislike all these undercurrents, David thought, and yet, somehow, they are disturbing. Krieger is right: people talk too much; and Bohn is a gossip by nature, a name-dropper by habit. 'No, thank you, too,' David said briskly. 'Night driving is a waste of good time.' He glanced over his shoulder at Bohn, shook his head with amusement.

'Then what's all the rush?'

'Because I'd rather be in Merano than heading along this damned highway with two hands on the wheel!' He turned to Irina, strangely silent, her eyes following the rise of precipices above deep forests and undulating fields. 'From now on,' he told her, 'you won't find one stretch of horizon without mountains towering into the sky. The best time is early morning— just after the dawn begins to spread. You'll see.'

'Then we don't leave till tomorrow?' She was smiling.

He put an arm around her shoulder, pulled her close. 'We'll leave when we feel like it.'

Bohn spoke softly. 'And what will Krieger have to say about that?'

'What did he say at Lienz?'

For a moment Bohn stared. He took off his glasses, polished them with his silk scarf. 'Nothing much.' He stuck them into his breast pocket, and closed his eyes. 'If you don't mind,' he said, 'I'll catnap. Vertical mountains aren't my idea of excitement. Give me a city street any day.' He didn't sleep at first. He kept his eyes closed and listened, but there was nothing worth adding to his report. Certainly, Switzerland. Probably the Engadine. Possibly tomorrow at dawn. Two dangerous notebooks being smuggled out. A British passport. As for Dave and Irina—why mention their affair? If Jiri Hrádek heard how things were developing with them, there could be action. And not my kind of action, he told himself: if there is anything I abhor it is violence. His conscience clear, he even fell asleep, cramped as he was in the crowded back seat. When he woke up they were at Brixen.

'See you in New York,' said David.

'And Irina?'

'I don't know,' she said unhappily. 'It depends——'

'Well, when you meet your father, give him my best wishes. And ask him if he would let me interview him—sometime when it suits him, of course.'

'Why should he?' David asked bluntly.

'Well, after all, I did start his daughter's escape, didn't I?'

'And thank you for that,' said Irina. 'I'll tell my father——'

'Goodbye,' David said. 'You can telephone for a taxi here.' He nodded to the busy café where he had halted the car, keeping the engine running.

'I can take a hint.' Bohn was smiling. The smile still lingered as the car moved off. He picked up his bag and went to inquire where he could make a long-distance call to Vienna. His message would be relayed to Czechoslovakia, and not too late, thanks to Dave's driving. Lord, what fools these mortals be. . . . Bohn checked a sudden laugh. If he had left Lienz this morning, deep in worry (that bastard Krieger, how much did he know?), he was now on the topmost pinnacle of one of Dave's god-awful mountains. What fools, all of them!

Chapter Fourteen

DRIFTS OF LIGHT MIST still floated vaguely around some of the giant peaks, but the heavy blanket of rain clouds had lifted. So had David's mood. The traffic had eased, most travellers now standing in line for a midday meal—the eating places, far-spaced along this route, must be jammed tight, judging by the pack of cars and buses that had drawn off the highway. The road was clear, well made, skid-resistant. And Mark Bohn's intrusion was already slipping away behind that huge barrier of mountains. It isn't, thought David, that I dislike Bohn. But sometimes he can irritate the hell out of me. That damned curiosity of his. Always wants to know, even things he has no need to know. Why that interest in Irina's passport at the frontier, for instance? 'A false passport, Irina?' Bohn had asked with a touch of mockery. 'Don't you know that's illegal? You'll get us all arrested.' Irina had looked at him coldly. 'It is perfectly legal,' she had said, cutting him off so abruptly that his only comment was a startled eyebrow and an apologetic smile.

David laughed out loud.

Irina, sitting close to him, raised her head from his shoulder, asked in surprise. 'Now, why?'

'Bohn. If anything might have had us stopped and questioned, it was his voice bleating about false passports.'

'He kept his voice low.' But something had been haunting her thoughts ever since they left Bohn on the outskirts of Brixen. Now she tried to make light of her worry. 'He would have had an explanation ready if we had been questioned. Wouldn't he?'

'Yes, he's quick with explanations. Still, you don't make off-beat jokes to frontier guards. Or to income-tax collectors, or customs officials. Or to anyone who can raise or lower your salary. No future in that.' He had her smiling again. 'Darling,' he said gently, 'what is bothering you about Bohn? After all, you did send that letter to him.'

'There was no one else who could help.'

'Not even me?'

'You didn't know anyone in the CIA. Did you?'

'No. At least, not that I'm aware of.'

'Bohn knows everyone. And I was given his address in Washington. I didn't know where you were. I did not even know you were his friend. It was such a shock—such a wonderful, wonderful shock—to find he had sent you to Vienna.'

Not Bohn, David thought. McCulloch had made that choice. Bohn, not too enthusiastically, had gone along with it. Bohn had kept saying—now, what had he said that night at East Hampton? Amateurs were useless. Something like that.

'What is it, David?'

It was sweet to hear the concern in her voice.

David managed a smile, kept his voice easy. 'Didn't you tell him about me, back in 1968? When he visited Prague and you met him?'

'I didn't meet him in 1968.'

'What?'

'I didn't meet him until 1970. And it was a very brief meeting.'

'1970? He was in Prague in 1970?'

'And last year too.'

Now it was David who was troubled. He was remembering 1968. September it had been, when Bohn had descended on East Hampton for a quick visit. Damnation, David thought, his whole reason for that unexpected appearance had been to bring me news of Irina. 'You never met him in 1968? At the time Dubcek was——'

'No.'

That was definite.

'All right,' said David, 'what about today? Why are you worrying about Bohn?'

'I don't know. And that worries me too. You see, there's no real reason why I should feel like this. Just so many little things, none of them important. He could not have been more friendly, more helpful. Yet always—always with questions. Sidelong questions. Why is he so curious?'

'He always has been. It's his way. What did you talk about?'

'Oh, maps and clothes. And father's notebooks. I think that was what really upset me. I didn't want anyone to know about them. Except you.'

For a long minute David was silent. 'Tell me about maps and clothes and all the rest of Bohn's jokes.'

'As they happened?'

'Yes. From the beginning—as they happened.'

'But they were really nothing.'

'And yet you're worrying about them.'

'I've become too anxious about everything.' Her voice faltered as she added, 'Too suspicious.'

'Then let's get rid of your worries by talking them away. Come on, darling. Tell me what happened.'

'You won't laugh at me?'

'No. I won't laugh.' David listened intently to the soft hesitant voice, kept his eyes on the winding road. Sun-shadowed meadows rose and fell on either side, ending in thick dark forests that climbed steeply to the precipices falling away from sheer mountain peaks, giant ramparts of jagged rock upthrust in ancient convulsions of the earth. The highway was a curving piece of white string; the cars rushing along it were small coloured beads; and the people inside them, each a world in himself, were less than grains of dust to the stone giants towering above them.

'And that,' Irina said, as she ended her small story, 'is really all. Have I talked the worries away?' She liked that phrase. It could be possible, too: she felt better. 'They aren't important, are they? I only wish he hadn't been so quick to remark about father's notebooks. That was what really upset me.'

So it had been the small incident with the notebooks that had started her chain of doubts, David thought. Without that, Irina might have forgotten all the rest of Bohn's questions, or put them aside as small talk.

Taken one by one, they did seem negligible. Together, they made a disturbing pattern.

'Because,' Irina went on, 'everyone does *not* know that these notebooks exist. Only Jiri's men, who seized father's books and papers when he escaped—he was in Prague at the time, and couldn't get back to his home at Rajhrad where he stored most of his documents—only these men could know. They thought they had found everything. But the two notebooks I have with me—they are the most important. That was why my father hid them so securely.'

'In the drawer where you discovered the Beretta?'

'It was not really a drawer. I had to call it that when I spoke about it in front of Jo. I did not know her well enough. You understand?' she asked anxiously.

'Then where did you find——'

'In the leg of a table.'

He stared at her, but she was serious.

'It was a dining table that had belonged to my great-grand-father—a heavy piece of oak resting on thick square legs. There were some primitive wood carvings around the edge of the top, and the pattern trailed down the four legs. Not elaborate. Just peasant decorations carved on the solid wood. But inside one of the legs there was a concealed compartment. It was not large— just hollowed out enough to hide a few objects—so that if you were to rap on that part of the leg, it sounded solid.'

'Your great-grandfather had an inventive carpenter.'

'There was need of them even in those days.'

'How did you get into the compartment? I suppose it had a panel that opened?'

'Yes. You pressed two pieces of the carved decoration, and a small panel swung out. When it was closed, it fitted into the design so perfectly that you could not guess it existed.'

No sign at all, either by sight or by sound: a neat piece of work. David said, 'So when you went to your father's house, after it had been searched and his papers removed, you opened the panel and——'

'No,' she said quickly, 'not then.'

'Why not?'

'I was afraid there might be a concealed camera in the room. And also, what would I do with any documents my father had hidden? There was no safer hiding place than that table leg. I let it alone until I knew I was going to leave. On the night before I began my journey, as soon as it was dark, I took a flashlight and shielded it with my hand and opened the table leg and groped inside. There was a pistol, propped upright in the shallow space, with two thin notebooks behind it.' A small smile played over her face. 'I took them to bed with me that night. I read them by flashlight.'

170

For a moment David could say nothing. Another world, he was thinking, a world where you moved in darkness like a thief in your own house.

'What do they deal with?'

'Names, dates, places, events. The history of conspiracies and plots in 1968, before the Soviet tanks came over the frontier.'

Background material, David thought. 'But your father is working on a novel, isn't he? Does he need that kind of detailed documentation?' It troubled David, angered him too, that Irina had increased the danger to herself by smuggling two small books out of Czechoslovakia, all for the sake of a piece of fiction. 'Surely his memory is enough.'

'It is good; but memory is not enough when he faces critics who will say he is too prejudiced against the Communists, too fantastic.'

'But——'

'I know how my father works. He has never tampered with history. If he does not have the exact facts about critical events, he will not use them as political background. The novel he is writing is his first big work in years. Years, David.'

'I know.'

'And it must not have any gaps in it—especially about that period before the invasion of Czechoslovakia. It has to be the climax of the novel. It leads into the title—*The Prague Winter*.'

David said, 'But surely the political background of that period has been reported and published. It's common knowledge, isn't it?' More or less, he added to that.

'Not the part played by Jiri and his friends—the Stalinists, the hard-line Communists. They not only plotted against Dubcek and his liberals—they are openly proud of that—but they also were planning secretly to eliminate the men who weren't "progressive", just middle-of-the-road Communists.'

'The men who are now at the head of the government?'

'Yes. Russia chose them—not Jiri's group—and put them in power: she could handle them more easily, perhaps.' Irina paused, shook her head. 'Strange; and comic, too. Jiri had even let Soviet intelligence agents install themselves in his Prague headquarters, the week before the invasion took place.'

'What?'

'Yes, that happened.'

'Preparing for the takeover?'

'Yes.'

'Well, that may explain why the Russians didn't exactly kick Jiri out. He is still an important man, isn't he?'

She half smiled as she said, 'Even the Russians did not know the full story. Besides, Jiri seems to have changed—become more moderate. He now works along with the men he once plotted against.'

'How many people knew he was involved in that conspiracy?'

'Very few.'

'Are they still alive?'

'Not many. And those who survived, like Jiri, were so deeply implicated that they will not talk. Their safety depends on complete silence.'

'That's a dangerous little power grouping right there.' Conspiracy seemed to get into a man's blood, a disease that flared up again and again unless it was fully exposed. And now the importance of Kusak's notes, the exact recording of names and dates and facts, struck David fully. The material might not be acceptable in a court of law—much of it must have been supplied in bits and pieces by friends of Dubcek, and they were imprisoned or dead—but in the hands of a writer such as Kusak, it would certainly cripple any future plans of Jiri Hrádek and his surviving allies. 'What are they doing—biding their time?'

'They seemed to have changed. They have become less extreme.' But she sounded uncertain.

'Like Jiri?'

She was silent.

'Do you really believe he has changed?' David persisted.

'Two weeks ago I hoped he had. But now—no, I don't think so. Or Josef and Alois would both still be alive.' She fell silent, her eyes watching the upsurge of stone mountain, hard and naked, that rose straight from green meadows and forests. When she spoke again, her voice had lost all emotion. It was cool, detached. 'How easy people—like me—make it for Jiri. We see, but we close our eyes. We hear, but we try not to listen. It was only when I read my father's notebooks——' She looked at David. 'I know. I told you yesterday that I had only glanced at them. I was trying to make them sound not very important. Evasion—or lies—that's something I have learned

172

too well. It has become a way of life: never the full truth, always something kept back, something for safety.'

David's hand held hers. 'It was only when you read your father's notes——' he prompted her gently.

'When I read them, all the things that had not been clear to me—everything I had tried *not* to believe——' She didn't finish the sentence. And then she said, 'Even two weeks ago, as I packed the notebooks, I was deciding to ask my father not to use anything in them that might endanger Jiri's life. Because of the help he had given me to escape.'

'What help actually?' Perhaps, David thought, I'll learn the whole truth at last.

'He looked the other way. He knew what I was planning. He could have had me arrested for trying to leave the country. He didn't. He gave me a message of good will for my father; my passport; soft words; and a smile. Yes, people like me make it easy for Jiri. We keep seeing signs of change so easily, because that is what we hope to see.'

'He gave you no other help?'

Again there was a long silence.

'Advice.'

'About what, Irina?'

'My letter. The quickest way to get action was to send it to an American who had connections in Washington and who had met me. Someone who had been a journalist and travelled abroad a good deal and knew Czechoslovakia. Someone who understood the situation, and would believe me.'

'Mark Bohn?'

'He is the only American journalist I know who lives in Washington, and has visited Czechoslovakia, and has met me.'

'And his address? Did he pass it on to you?' That had been Bohn's story.

'Jiri knew all the writers and correspondents who came to Prague. He knew all their addresses. He had a list of them. He left it with me, laid it casually on my desk. All I did was to pick out the name of Mark Bohn.'

'You didn't tell Jiri whom you had chosen?'

'No.'

'And he never suggested Bohn?'

'No.'

'But he knew Bohn had met you?'

173

'No. I don't think so.'

'If Jiri knows all the journalists who come to visit Czecho-slovakia, wouldn't he know their movements? Whom they met, whom they talked with?' I'm damned sure that Jiri Hrádek has more than a list of their home addresses.

Her eyes widened. She said, 'But Jiri never mentioned Bohn to me. I never saw them together.' She stared at him. Then, slowly, bitterly, 'Jiri planned everything.'

David said nothing.

'Didn't he?'

'He planned a lot. But we've no real proof about Bohn. He could have been used, too.'

'He is your friend. Surely he would not——'

'Surely,' David said. His voice was even, but his thoughts were jagged and broken. He tried to piece them together, but it was difficult. A touch of guilt at even harbouring any suspicion about Mark Bohn kept his mind off balance. And there was a background feeling of hurt pride, which didn't help any rational judgments. Had he been completely fooled; or was he drawing too many hasty conclusions? Either way, he didn't enjoy his emotions at this moment. Impossible to think straight. Not with a good half of his mind needed for this road. He was driving badly. That last corner had been taken care-lessly.

'Let's get a breath of fresh air,' he said, slowing down, his eyes watching for some broadening of the highway, for a space where he could safely edge off the paved surface.

He found it, a place with a view, waiting for photographers and picnic makers. A couple of pint-sized cars were already there, two loads of families setting up folding tables and chairs —where could they pack all that stuff in?

'Over here,' David said, his arm around Irina, leading her to the side of the small clearing, farthest away from the massive display of pink flesh (shirts were coming off for a lunch-hour sun tan), where a brave stand of pines still held on to the top edge of the precipice. It looked brittle. David pulled Irina back a little, caught her in his arms. Far below them was the deeply carved bed of a surging torrent; beyond it, more cliffs and crags plunged from mountainsides.

They stood close together, looking in silence at the vast stretch of brooding peace.

The sadness and strain left Irina's face. She was young and happy again, with the wind blowing through her hair, her arm around David, his arms holding her close, her kisses meeting his.

'This,' he told her, 'is what I've wanted to do for the last hundred miles.' He kissed her once more, long and deeply. At last, he released her. 'I love you, Irina. Never forget that.'

Then he turned away abruptly, caught her hand, picked up her handbag from where she had dropped it, and started back for the car. His face was tense.

By the time they reached the road, he was in control once more. He pointed to the happy picnickers, deep in potato salad and beer.

'Shall we tell them a thunderstorm is blowing up?' (The clouds were darkening, light mists thickening over nearby peaks.) 'Or that they are sitting practically on an overhang above a precipice?'

Indeed they were, quite oblivious to the bite in the rock face below them, where rain and wind and sun and frost had nibbled away for years. No immediate danger, David decided: next spring, another piece of mountainside would crumble away, shaving off a chunk of picnic ground. But at the car he called back to the merry group. 'You're too near the edge!' Only one man paid attention. He laughed, shook his head, said something to his companions that sent them all into a fit of amusement. David, it seemed, was a very funny fellow.

'Okay,' David said, and got into the car.

'Are they really in danger?'

'They'll be driven back to the road when the rain starts pouring down.' The wind, ominous herald, had begun to rise. 'Let's run ahead of the storm.' He got the car back on the highway, accelerated. Driving was easy again. 'Another hour at the most,' he said. 'We'll be in Merano by one-thirty with luck.' Certainly before two o'clock. Then the problem would be to find a safe room, where Irina could rest while he met Krieger. He pulled the travel folder out of his pocket and handed it to Irina. 'Time to start studying this. It has a good street plan of the town. It also has a list of hotels, each of them with a number attached. So find the Bristol on that list, note its number, and then look for that number on the street plan. Got the idea?'

She nodded, smiling. She had taken out her pencil to help

175

her check the long list of names. It needed more lead, she noticed: she must have broken off the point when she used it last. 'Bristol . . .' She found the name, memorized its number and location, tracked it to its street.

'Here it is!' she said at last. 'It is quite central. See?' She held out the map.

David glanced at it, noting the hotel's general situation. 'Now we know what to avoid.'

'You don't want to go to the Bristol?'

'No. Krieger is staying there. We'll find something near enough, but not on top of him.'

'But won't he expect us to stay at the Bristol too?'

'I guess he does.'

Irina's eyes widened. 'Don't you trust him?'

David smiled. 'I think we can trust Krieger.'

'Because Mark Bohn distrusts him?'

That might be a very good reason, David decided. He said, 'I've met Krieger. I know how he thinks.'

'But you have met Bohn too.' Bohn . . . Had he noticed where her pencil had broken on the map? Oh, surely not. Certainly he had looked at the map as he folded it, but his face had shown no interest at all—quite unlike the way he had riffled through her father's notebook. That really had caught his attention. Irina slipped the pencil back into her pocket. David had been long in answering her: perhaps he didn't want to talk about Bohn. Yet she did: a strange compulsion she couldn't even explain to herself at this moment. 'You have met him many times. Haven't you?'

'Off and on—yes, we've met.' David paused, then admitted frankly, 'And I've never known how he thinks.' Just a sum total of amusing talk, easy camaraderie, a touch of wit, currently fashionable phrases, name-dropping and general know-it-allness; and nothing solid to remember him by. 'I don't even know how he'd handle himself in an emergency. He's as nebulous as those mists on the mountaintops—and as full of surprises.'

'Isn't Krieger?'

'Yes. But his surprises don't baffle me. They've got hard sense behind them. They aren't—' he searched for the right word '—they aren't erratic.'

'Is that how you think of Mark Bohn—erratic?'

176

'Right now, it's the kindest judgment I can make about him.'

Perhaps too kind, she thought. She put out her hand, laid it along the side of his cheek, held it there for a few moments. Then she went back to studying the travel folder, a small pretence to cover her sudden display of emotion. 'And I love you, David,' she said very softly. 'And you, too, never forget that.'

Chapter Fifteen

THEY OUTRAN the rapidly advancing storm, leaving the lightning flashes crackling around the savage peaks behind them. They came to Merano, its surrounding hills terraced with vineyards, its half circle of gentler mountains open to the warm south, its spread of red roofs giving a merry welcome under the sparkling sunlight. A fast-flowing river, edged by flowers and trees and promenades, swept through the town, cosying a central mass of houses within the curve of its arm. This was the old section, six hundred years old at its core, pressed back against a steep hillside covered with vines.

'We'll head in that direction,' David said. 'Not actually into the Old Town, but just outside its gates.' The Old Town itself would make a good rendezvous: narrow sidewalks sheltered by arcades, busy little shops, Saturday crowds in local costumes from neighbouring villages, dark wine rooms, small inns, and a general feeling of country market. 'As far as I remember, there's an inn—three hundred years old—just in the right spot. The Golden something or other. I'll recognize it when I see its sign.'

'You've been here before? You know Merano?' Irina was relieved. The twists and turns of the streets, so closely packed together, were bewildering. They might spend hours wandering around, she had thought, searching for some place to rest.

'A little, but enough. A two-day visit sixteen years ago.'

After Vienna, she thought . . . He came here after he had waited for me in Vienna. 'If I had been with you then——'

Yes, that would have saved them both a lot of heartaches. 'You are here now.'

'Was that why you chose Merano?'

The old subconscious at work? He laughed and said, 'Could be.'

They had passed through a busy thoroughfare, short like all

the distances inside this town, and were now climbing a curving street that was densely packed with houses and small shops. David slowed up, his eyes on a quiet service station. There should be an inn just beyond it: Goldener Adler, he remembered now, in one of those strange leaps back into the long ago. But he couldn't see its sign, only the name of an Italian café.

He drew up at the service station, noticed that it fronted on a small garage. Now, if only the inn were near here, this would be a useful setup.

'So soon?' Irina asked. One minute they had been inside a bustling city: now, within easy walking distance, they were in a country town. 'But where is the inn?'

'My memory wasn't so good,' David said, getting out of the car, trying to make light of his disappointment. The Golden Eagle would have been perfect.

But once the fair-haired and blue-eyed Austrian—the only attendant in the garage, it seemed—came over to talk with him, it turned out that the Caffè d'Oro had replaced the Goldener Adler.

'They gave up and moved away. Went to live in the North Tyrol.' The young man shrugged. He had learned to live with Italian street signs and Italian spoken in schools. He could always talk his own language when he was with his own friends, or—as now—with a foreigner who made the effort and wouldn't report him. He studied David, and the Mercedes, and the pretty girl who still sat in the car.

'Looking for a room?'

'Just for a short stay.'

'My mother has a free room. Nice place.'

David eyed the man in turn: a frank open face; no guile, the smile friendly. 'Where is it?' It could be a mile away or more.

'Just back of here. You can reach it by driving up this street, making a right turn, and then——'

'No direct way through the garage?' David asked, noticing a rear door, half-open, leading into a yard.

'You'd have to walk.'

'Yes,' David said, and resisted a comment.

'Only a few steps. A short cut. How much do you pay?'

'How much does your mother charge?'

The young man laughed. It was all settled as far as he was concerned. 'She won't ruin you.'

'Running water?'

He nodded. 'But not in the room.'

'Any telephone?'

'Over there.' He pointed to a corner of the garage. 'That's extra, of course.'

'Of course,' David said gravely. 'Show us the way, will you?'

The young man did more than that. He helped David get the luggage out of the car and even carried the two coats as far as the back door. 'Can't leave here. The other fellow is off; Saturday. Just cross the courtyard and take that alley directly opposite. Turn left, and you'll be at the house. There's a notice in the window: *Zimmer Frei*. Got that?'

I hope so, David thought.

'The name is Hartmann. Tell her Franz sent you. And don't worry about your car. I'll put it in the garage for you. Need any work on it? It could do with a wash.'

'Okay. Gas and oil. And check the battery and brakes.' That should keep Franz happy for the next hour, David thought. He'd be too busy to pay much attention to any phone call.

The courtyard was small, and the alley—a dark slit separating two gable walls—was short. 'If we don't like the look of the place,' David said quietly to Irina, 'we leave. With thanks and apologies.'

But a few seconds down the alley brought them to a road, squeezed between a row of houses and a terraced vineyard that climbed the hill opposite. David turned left, and there, at the corner of the alley and the road, was the Hartmann cottage with its *Zimmer Frei* carefully displayed between pots of geraniums. It was old and pleasant; white walls and red roof, window boxes heavy with bright petunias.

'I love it,' Irina said. And I love that road, David thought, as he saw it ended in a busy street only a minute's walk away: it gives us a second exit out of here. His fears that they might be trapped by an alley leading into some cul-de-sac began to disperse.

Frau Hartmann also was reassuring. She had deep troubles of her own, and paid only polite interest to the strangers. Except for one bad moment.

'You are not married?' she asked, noticing Irina's hands bare of any ring. Her anxious frown deepened, her melancholy blue eyes were horrified.

'The room is for my sister,' David said quickly. 'A place to rest, and wash, and change her clothes. We have been travelling all day. She is very tired.'

Frau Hartmann softened a little, back to her usual patient suffering. 'But I have only one room to let.'

David pressed his case. 'We shan't be here very long. I'll pay for tonight in advance.'

'There are two beds.'

The frown was deepening again. A nervous hand pressed the faded blonde hair more tightly into place.

'I'll pay for both of them.'

'But you will not use——'

'For both of them,' David said firmly, taking out his wallet. 'It is worth it to have a quiet room where my sister will feel safe.'

'She will be very safe here. No one will disturb her.' And that seemed to ease Frau Hartmann's conscience about any extra payment for an unused bed. She led the way up a wooden staircase, scrubbed white, to a small and equally scrubbed room with spotless linen and a view of the vineyard. There was a parting smile, surprisingly warm even if brief, but no more conversation. Frau Hartmann had the habit of silence. And there will be no asking for passports, either, David thought with relief: no problem about getting them back in time for a quick departure.

'I'm going to telephone Krieger,' he told Irina, 'and I'll pick up something to eat at the café. Can you hold out that long? I'll be back in ten minutes.'

'Twenty minutes,' she said with a laugh. 'Don't worry, darling. I couldn't feel safer. Isn't this a wonderful place?' She kicked off her shoes, flopped on the bed. He bent over, kissed her, caught her in his arms. 'Still more wonderful if you did not have to telephone.'

Half an hour later he actually was on his way to the telephone. Damn this living by timetable, he thought, but his mood was high. There was no interference from Frau Hartmann either: she was busy in the kitchen, judging by the clang of pots. And none, too, from Franz, who only stopped work to ask, 'Everything fine?'

'Everything's fine,' David said, and put in his call to the

Bristol. It went through with no delay. Krieger was there, waiting.

'What the hell kept you?' Krieger began. 'And where are you?'

'We're in Merano.'

'Not on your way here, I hope.'

'No. We found a room.'

'Nearby?'

'Just outside the Old Town.'

'Good. A big hotel? Or an inn?'

'It's a room in a cottage behind a garage.'

'Well—that's original. Safe, too.'

'It feels that way.'

'The only snag is—how does Jo find it? I don't want to hear street names——'

'Does she know this section of town?'

'I do.'

'Well enough?'

'Yes. And if you don't trust my memory, I've got a street map. Have you?'

'Yes. Remember the Golden Eagle?'

There was a slight pause. 'I know where it is.'

'It's under new management. Now a café. The garage is almost next door. Franz Hartmann owns it. He will show Jo the way to his mother's house. But why send her——?'

'You and I have to meet.' There was silence, and then the sound of muffled voices. Jo must be with Krieger, David thought. He's probably briefing her. But what's the haste? 'Are you there?' Krieger's voice came clearly back.

'Yes,' David said with marked patience.

'You'll reach the arcades in the Old Town in a few minutes. Wait for me in the Red Lion. It's on the left-hand side, up-street. Leave right now, will you?'

'I'll leave as soon as Jo arrives here.'

'I thought you told me the room was safe,' Krieger said testily.

'It is. But right now I'm going out to find some food. We've had nothing since breakfast. And that was seven hours ago.'

Another small pause. 'Be careful, then.'

The warning note in Krieger's voice caught David's attention. 'Trouble?'

'In three sizes.'

'They're *here*?'

'All over the damned place. The sooner we meet, the better.'

'Then get Jo to move that pretty little——'

'You too,' said Krieger, and rang off.

'Jo is coming. Any minute,' David told Irina as he returned to the room. 'Better get dressed, honey. And here's something to keep us going.' He produced golden-crusted rolls, a quantity of thinly sliced dark ham, outsize peaches, and a bottle of Chianti. 'Not fancy,' he said as he split open two of the rolls with his pocket-knife and slapped some ham in place, 'but sustaining.' He poured the wine into a tooth glass, tasted it, and said, 'Well, this is no time to fuss over vintages. It won't poison us, at least. Or will it? I just grabbed the first things the café had for sale.'

All this light talk, thought Irina, is covering something. He's worried, and he doesn't want me to know. 'How was Krieger?' She pulled on her dress, brushed her hair.

'I have to meet him as soon as Jo arrives.'

'Oh.' She picked up her sandwich from the dressing table. 'Well, this looks beautiful. I'm starving.' And then she said, 'David—what about the notebooks? Will you tell Krieger about them?'

'Why not?'

She managed to make a first bite into the roll, laughed at herself as she struggled with it. And then, once the mouthful was swallowed, she said, 'What if he asks for them? Would you give them to him?'

'No.'

'Would you carry them for me?'

'They are safer with you. But not in that handbag.'

'Yes. I know. I forgot all about that bag today when we stood near the precipice. I could have walked away—left it there.' She shook her head, smiling. 'Really, David——' She bit into the golden crust once more. It was hard to believe, she thought, how relaxed she had become in a matter of twenty-four hours, even less: relaxed and unthinking, since David was there to do all the worrying for her. 'Do you like Jo?' she asked.

'Yes.'

'And you trust her?'

'Sure.'

'Then I can talk with her. Quite naturally. I hate feeling that I have to be on guard. It is so—so easy being with you, David.'

'Then let's make it a permanent——' There was a voice on the staircase, light footsteps. 'Jo,' he said. He made a grab for Irina, gave her an intense kiss. 'That's to keep you thinking about me until I get back.'

He rose from the bed and was standing casually at the window as Jo pushed the door wide.

Jo unbelted her trench coat, took off her dark glasses, pulled her scarf away from her hair. She was sparkling with her triumph. 'Twenty-two minutes flat,' she said. 'And that included a short trip in a taxi, and some backtracking through twisty streets to where I had parked my car—it's rented, of course; a tan Ford coupé—you'll see it in the garage downstairs—and—well, here I am. Just in time for a picnic. These peaches! They smell like gardenias. I knew a girl once who ate gardenias, kept them in her refrigerator and had them petal by petal.'

David watched Jo with amusement. She is very much like me, he thought. All this talk to conceal embarrassment. Or perhaps some real anxiety.

'Who was watching the hotel?' he tried.

'Ludvik. Disguised by sitting behind a newspaper in the lobby. Earlier this morning it was the tall fair-haired man—Jan. Didn't see the dark-haired one called Milan. But he's around. Possibly they have some reinforcements as well. Krieger will explain.'

David took the hint. He moved to the door, his half-eaten sandwich still in his hand.

'Better carry your raincoat too,' Jo said. 'It looks like thunder. That's all we need now, isn't it? One good drenching downpour to soak us through.' She looked from David to Irina, and then at him again. 'If,' she said casually, 'you're late in getting back here, David, I'll take off with Irina. Okay?'

Irina glanced at him worriedly.

'I won't be long,' he assured her. He photographed her in his mind, sitting on the bed, hair falling loosely over her cheek, blue eyes wide and questioning. Crisp white curtains on the window behind her, red geraniums; a picnic scattered on the dressing table: a sweet interlude while it had lasted. He gave a cheerful wave of his hand, saw Irina smile, and ran down the steep narrow stairs. Outside the road was empty, the alley dark and peaceful. A safe house, he thought, and felt better.

He finished the sandwich as he crossed the yard, and slung his raincoat over his shoulder. One pocket bumped hard into his ribs: that damned automatic he had been carrying around. It brought him back to less pleasant realities. You're another of these clowns, he told himself, picnicking near the edge of a thousand-foot drop, thinking the ground is solid because it doesn't tremble and crack underfoot. A safe little room, is it? Nothing is safe while Ludvik and his friends are prowling around this town.

In the garage there was the same feeling of peace and quiet, time ticking away unnoticed. Franz was at the entrance, enjoying the air and a cigarette. Work on the Mercedes was finished. And near it there was a tan-coloured Ford. A British-made Consul, he noted: not new, but in good condition. Excellent tyres. Trust Jo to get some traction for a mountain journey. In fact, he told himself, trust Jo altogether: she'd take care of Irina. The deceptive thing about Jo was the fact that she was young, pretty, and elegant. With all that going for her, she didn't need brains, but she had plenty of them too. What did she mean by that small remark, seemingly offhand? *If you're late in getting back* . . . Who's going to be late? he thought, as he headed for the street.

Franz was following him out, asking, 'Did Fräulein Schmidt find you?'

Schmidt? Good old Smith. In any language, a useful name. David glanced along both sidewalks, checking the nearby doorways and parked cars. 'She did.'

Franz halted at the gas pump, looked at the sky, shook his head. 'Heavy clouds. They'd better start breaking them up, or else we'll lose the grapes.'

David stared at him, saw Franz was going to launch into an expansive talk about vine harvests. He said, moving away, 'Got to buy some aspirin.' Behind him he could almost feel Franz's disappointment—resentment?—at being so unexpectedly cut off at the beginning of a ten-minute lecture. Sorry, chum: another time. Now is for keeping my eyes open and my memory sharp. If I cut down to the right I'll reach the Corn Market; then turn left and I'll be at the beginning of the arcades. Simple enough. But these crowds—good God, the whole countryside has come into town for Saturday afternoon —well, if I'm finding it difficult to see anything but a mass of heads, all unrecognizable, it may just be that Ludvik and friends are having the same trouble. I'll take that as some consolation; not much, but it's all I'm going to get.

Slightly encouraged, he increased his pace and headed for the Old Town.

Chapter Sixteen

DISTANCES WERE SHORT in this closely built section of Merano, recalling days when safety lay in houses and streets clustered tight within strong walls. In less than three minutes David reached the Corn Market, an open square that at first seemed vulnerable. But the constant movement of people was a comforting sight, especially when he still saw no sign of Ludvik. Or of Milan. Or of Jan. Quietly, without looking too much in a hurry, he dodged past groups of farmers dressed for town in their white shirts, black waistcoats with silver buttons, feathered hats; past their red-cheeked wives in dirndls and bright neckerchiefs; past flaxen-haired children and huge shopping baskets; past tourists in their own distinctive fancy dress. There were other local people too, possibly Italians, in three-button suits; girls in miniskirts; teenagers in blue jeans. And there were enough men in light tweed jackets, with open-necked shirts and raincoats over their shoulders, to make David feel he fitted into the over-all picture. At least no one was giving him a second glance. Thank God, he thought, I'm not six feet four with a mop of red hair.

But it was with relief that he reached the narrow street that sloped steadily uphill towards the heart of the Old Town. It was made all the narrower by the heavy stone pillars on either side that were spaced along the curbs and bore the weight of the houses' second floors as they stretched over the sidewalks. They formed continuous arcades, low and vaulted, where shops and doorways and inns and taverns drew back under deep shadows. A secret place, giving a feeling of protection and mystery even if the small stores were brightly lit and crowded with weekend shoppers: modern life in a medieval setting. David halted by one of the massive pillars, lit a cigarette, and took his bearings: people, the same mix as in the Corn Market;

narrow doorways leading to the houses overhead; window displays of sausages and cheese, wine and bread, pots and pans, aprons and dirndls, boots and lederhosen; cafés and taverns; the gilded sign of an inn called the Golden Rose; all very simple and comfortable and domestic. Impossible in this crowd to recognize anyone unless you came face to face with him, and perish that thought.

There was a long screaming hiss, a violent explosion. David dropped his cigarette and looked around. No one was paying any attention, except the foreigners. They had flinched too, like David; some had visibly jumped; and one girl in a mini-dress let out a scream. Another strange high-powered hiss, another hideous bang. A small boy in short leather pants clapped his hands in delight. 'Rockets, rockets, I want to see the rockets!' He made a dash past David into the middle of the street. His mother, with rose-patterned apron over a green dirndl, lunged after him. 'Excuse me, please,' she said to David, politeness lingering even in a small crisis. And then, seeing his bewilderment, she added, 'Rockets, that's all. From the hilltops.' And she was on her way to rescue her son from the traffic.

Rockets—but of course: to break up the clouds, prevent a massive downpour of rain or perhaps a hailstorm, and save the grapes. The sudden vision of squads of men, with fancy vests and silver buttons and eagles' feathers topping their hats, gathered on the surrounding hills to fire off rockets at big black clouds, delighted David. Damnation, I wish I were out in the open, he thought; some place where I could enjoy the fireworks.

But only a few doors away he could see another dangling sign of an inn. This one had a gilded lion's head.

He started pressing through the crowd as the Meraner were doing, leaving the strangers-in-town to stand and exclaim in half a dozen languages. There was a third explosion, more violent than ever; then a fourth almost on top of it, sending a double jolt through the arcades. Immediately ahead of him two men halted abruptly, swore, laughed, exchanged comments as they walked on. There was nothing remarkable in that—others, including David, had done much the same—but the language in which they had spoken was something else. Czech. Unmistakable. David froze, drew close to the nearest pillar, made an excuse of searching for another cigarette while he tried to keep the men in view.

He had never seen them before. Medium height, both of them: square-shouldered grey suits, almost identical in cut; shirt collars worn open, turned precisely back in old-fashioned holiday-at-the-seaside style; hair (one head light brown, one dark) cut straight across the neck. Perhaps, he thought as he lit his cigarette and saw that they were now approaching the Red Lion, perhaps he was too damned suspicious. They could be ordinary Czech tourists, good party members given permission to travel; or they might even be refugees who had found jobs in Merano. But whatever they were, he would play it safe, and let them wander up the street before he stepped into the Red Lion. One thing was strange, though: they hadn't glanced at any of the shop windows they were passing, or even noticed three Junoesque blondes in bright dirndls. Then the two heads swerved to look at the doorway of the inn, a long and definite stare as if they were memorizing its sign. They walked on. Not far. Just to the next pillar. There they halted, turning to look down the arcade, their eyes searching the oncoming pedestrians.

David swore under his breath, dodged behind the cover of a heavy column of stone. Beside him the three startling blondes met two women, stopped to talk, and blocked him off from the rest of the arcade. He noticed one man—light-haired, tall, wearing Tyrolean green—making his way with more determination than politeness through this sudden clot in foot traffic. The man ploughed through, reached the two who waited. They grouped together, talking. Briefly. Then the grey suits continued walking up the arcade, while Green Jacket stepped into the street, crossing to its other side.

David reached the narrow doorway of the Red Lion, stepped over its dark threshold, turned to look out at the street. So far he had seen only the back of the Tyrolean jacket. But as the man reached the arcade opposite, no more than thirty feet away, he looked over his shoulder as though he were gauging his line of sight. He must have been satisfied with the view: he could see anyone coming out of the Red Lion's doorway. He drew close to the nearest pillar, and stayed there. And that, thought David, was most certainly Ludvik.

* * *

The ground-floor room of the Red Lion, two steps down from the threshold, was long and narrow, stretching away out into some back area of the inn. It was sparsely lit. Tobacco smoke lingered under the low raftered ceiling, turning it blacker. The smell of food still hovered, although most patrons had eaten and left. There was only a residue of three farmers arguing about prices in the wooden booth nearest the door, while four younger men in lederhosen huddled in earnest talk at another bare wooden table, voices dropped almost to a hoarse whisper.

That was all. Except for Krieger, who sat in a booth, well removed from the other customers, and faced the door. He was lighting his pipe, and ordering beer from the one waitress still on duty, middle-aged and buxom.

So he has just arrived, thought David. The incidents in the street began to hang together. 'I'll have beer too,' he told the woman. Hooking his raincoat on one of the iron prongs that were lined along the wall above his head, he slid along the wooden bench opposite Krieger. This was a place where muffled conversation was quite in order: the hoarse whisperers now had their four heads together practically in a knot.

Krieger noted his glance at the young men. 'Politics,' he said, still speaking in German. 'Always a tricky business, if you're a strong nationalist.'

'The bleeding heart of the Tyrol?'

Absent-mindedly, Krieger nodded, watching the waitress clear a neighbouring table of empty wineglasses before she bustled off. When she was out of earshot, he spoke in English. His voice was low, rapid. 'You were late. Any difficulties?'

Late, was I? What about you? David repressed a smile, said, 'A small delay. A couple of strangers speaking Czech took a hard look at the Red Lion. I have an idea they were following you—if you arrived about the time of that double explosion.'

'Just around then,' Krieger admitted. 'And what gave you the idea?'

'They're friends of Ludvik. They waited for him, talked a little, and then——'

'Are you certain it was Ludvik?'

'Pretty sure, in spite of his new Tyrolean jacket.'

'That's him.' Krieger swore. 'I took a lot of trouble getting here. He was tailing me, of course. I managed to ditch him. Arrived clean—I thought.' He took out his pipe and filled it.

'But when he dropped well behind, his two men must have taken his place. They followed me and he followed them. Clever bastard. Where did he go?'

'He's across the street right now, propped up against one of those pillars. His two friends headed up the arcade.'

Krieger frowned at his pipe. It wasn't drawing well. 'What did they look like?'

'Mid-grey suits, off-the-peg cut, stiff material. One light hair, one dark; both square-trimmed at the neck. Open collars. Nondescript features, nothing remarkable. Medium height; husky.'

'Reinforcements,' Krieger said softly. 'But that's to be expected. Ludvik had time to bring them in. He has been in Merano since early morning.' He relit his pipe, got it going at last.

'How the hell did he learn about Merano?'

'I passed the word to Mark Bohn.' Krieger noted the appalled expression spreading over David's face. 'I knew what I was doing,' he added testily. 'How else could I trace the leak? Don't look so damned startled. It was Bohn all right.'

For a moment David was silent. He said heavily, 'Bohn——'

'Careful, careful. Here comes the beer.' Krieger began talking in German. About the rockets. And the vines. He raised his huge mug of light beer. 'To the grapes, safe again, ripening for next month's vintage. Now that's the season to come here. General jollity.' The waitress smiled her agreement and stumped off, the full skirts of her dress and petticoats swinging around her solid hips.

David said, 'We've got to get——'

'First things first. Tarasp. I'll give you the quick details now. in case we are rudely interrupted.'

'But we've got to get Irina out of Merano. At once. Bohn——'

'Couldn't agree more. So listen carefully.' Krieger plunged into a brief description of Upper Tarasp, a small village sharing a hilltop with a castle, and added directions to the house where Irina and her father would meet. Rooms at the inn had been booked for Jo and David. 'Got all that?' he asked as he ended.

David nodded. 'And then?'

'They will disappear: merge into his pattern of life until the new book is published. By that time, with a million people knowing what it contains, it should be pretty hard even for Jiri Hrádek to silence its message.'

They will disappear . . . merge . . . David stared down at the table. I found her and I'll lose her. All over again. He roused himself. 'What about revenge? An old-fashioned word, but Jiri Hrádek is the type to believe in it. Irina—well, there's a personal thing there; a challenge. I don't think he's going to let her slip away from him as easily as that. And there's one added danger: she has smuggled out two of her father's notebooks—important—details about Jiri's political manœuvres in 1968. What does he do when he hears about that?'

'Kusak's notes? She has them with her?'

'Yes.'

Krieger recovered from the shock. He said slowly, 'Yes, that's a new danger. Definitely. If Jiri Hrádek knew—but thank God, he doesn't.'

'He knows. We left Bohn telephoning at Brixen.'

'Bohn?' The name shot out like a bullet.

'He picked us up at the border. He saw the books by accident.' A well-calculated accident: that I know now. 'He was alone with Irina for several minutes.' David rose, reaching for his coat. 'I'll give you all explanations in Tarasp. Now, I'm getting Irina out of Merano.'

Krieger's hand was an iron vice on David's wrist, locking him in place. 'She has left,' Krieger said very quietly. He released his grip.

David stared at him, sat down.

'She left with Jo.' Krieger glanced at his watch. 'About ten minutes ago.'

Still David said nothing.

'It's the safest way, David. Speed. Unexpected moves. That's all we have on our side. The opposition have the gadgets and the cute little devices. We've got our wits and some fast footwork. That's all we've got.' He paused, watching David. 'And to keep Irina safe, tell me about Bohn. All of it. Every detail. What did he learn?'

Ten minutes ago . . . I ought to have guessed, David was thinking. Jo's last remark—the one that puzzled me—that was her warning. His anger broke. 'You know, you're a real son of a bitch, Krieger!'

'Someone has to be that, every now and again. What about Bohn?'

'Jo could have told me openly.'

Krieger masked his impatience. 'She wanted to. I was against it. What would have happened? Arguments. Delays. In the end you would have had to come here to get the details on Tarasp. What's more, you wouldn't have arrived here in time to see Ludvik taking position across the street. He would have spotted you—had you followed on your way back to Irina. Because, of course, you'd have insisted she should wait until you returned. Right?'

Yes, Krieger had a point there. Several points. David swallowed his anger, calmed his voice. 'I'll qualify that description of you. You are a persuasive son of a bitch.'

Krieger nodded. 'What about Bohn? But keep it short. I want you on the road in the next half hour.'

'Suits me. I'll put on some speed and catch up with Jo before the border.'

'Well before that. As planned. She's taking it easy along Highway 38—due west. When it branches south, she'll follow Highway 40 to the north. But only for three or four miles. She'll stop and wait for you, near a pilgrimage chapel—St. Mary's—you can't miss it. It's on a small hill, prominent, stands alone. Look for Jo's car drawn off the road at a picnic area just below it. You'll take over for the mountain passes. She had a rough day yesterday. Besides, she doesn't know the details about Tarasp. The fewer who know about them, the better. In case of accidents.'

Such as being caught by Ludvik. Then David had a new worry. 'Irina knows about Tarasp. I told her.'

Krieger asked quickly, 'And did she tell Bohn?'

'No.'

'What did she tell him?' Krieger's voice was sharp.

'That wasn't the way it happened,' David said, coming to Irina's defence. 'She didn't actually say anything. Bohn just extracted——'

'All right,' Krieger broke in, 'what did he extract?'

David stopped his justifications and gave the straight story.

Now I know two things, thought Krieger as the condensed account ended with David already on his feet, unhooking his raincoat. One is a new complication and I'll leave it unspoken:

he's still in love with her and she with him. And the second is that I made a bad mistake about Bohn: he is deeper in than I imagined, and more than he may realize. If Jiri needs Bohn, he'll use him again. 'I was wrong about Bohn,' Krieger said softly. 'I was so damned sure he had bugged out.'

'He has, now.'

'He may want to, but——' Krieger shrugged. 'Are you sure he didn't learn about Tarasp?'

'Irina would have told me.' David was about to leave. 'Anything else?'

'Use the back door. I'll wait a little, try and string Ludvik along. If he sees me hanging around, he may think we're still resting up for the next stage of the journey. By the way, they'll be on the lookout for a green Mercedes. You know that?'

'Yes.' Damn Bohn's eyes to hell. 'I'll keep a sharp watch for anyone following closely.'

'They may still be driving a white Fiat—they don't know we spotted it in Graz. So good luck. Wait for me in Tarasp. I may be a little late. But——' He broke off as a draught of fresh air stirred round his ankles. The back door at the far end of the restaurant had opened.

'Two men,' David reported. That was all he could identify in that unlighted portion of the room; two men briefly silhouetted by the opened door, becoming two shadows as they closed it. They stood there, accustoming their eyes to the long stretch of gloom.

'Move!' Krieger's voice was low, urgent. 'Get away from me. Move!'

David moved. He made his way towards the back of the restaurant, but he was taking his time. Nonchalance, that was his best bet. Far behind him the voices of the three farmers were raised, calling for the waitress, who got up from the table where she had been counting her tips. With a jingle of coins being dropped back into her purse, she passed David, and, misguessing his direction, pointed helpfully to a door marked *Herren*. He stopped beside it as though he were about to enter, letting the two men draw level with him. Yes, they were the same two who had headed up the arcade. So they had circled round to reach the rear of the Red Lion. Either they were tired of waiting in some back alley, or they were checking to see if Krieger was still around. Krieger was their target, that was certain. They didn't even give a second glance at David. 'Be with you soon!' the waitress called to them. 'No hurry,' one replied.

David changed positions again, choosing the moment when their backs were completely turned to him, to slip into the nearest booth. From there he could see the front edge of Krieger's table. Krieger himself was not in sight. Neither were the two strangers, now sitting just beyond Krieger. It wasn't much of a view, David thought, but at least he was unobserved. They hadn't noticed his little manœuvre. Of that he was sure.

It was the only thing he was sure about at this moment. Krieger, if he could have seen him, would be cursing into his beer. I know, I know, David thought angrily: I'm supposed to be walking down a back alley on my way to the Mercedes and a neat departure from Merano. But however much I'm trying to persuade myself that Krieger can handle this situation, he is sitting there alone. How do you leave a man to face two goons by himself? Sure, Krieger chose it this way: he's running interference for all of us. But I don't like it, I don't like any part of it.

A minute passed. All was gas and gaiters in the front half of the room. The farmers were about to leave. He could hear the solid clunk of their heels on the wooden floor. Then they stopped, made some more jokes, and set the waitress giggling again. A young man's voice called to them in a thick dialect. A reply from one of the older men. Loud laughter; another comment; a shouted dialogue beginning, half argument, half joke.

A second minute gone, David thought anxiously as he kept his eyes on his watch and his ears open for the smallest sound. Krieger hadn't stirred, while the two strangers seemed determined to sit and wait until they could follow him out. Nothing more than that? David hesitated. He felt slightly foolish. Time to leave?

Suddenly, the two men rose, walked swiftly over to Krieger's table. David reached into his raincoat, gripped the automatic, watched them. One was thrusting his hand into the pocket of his jacket, bulging it ominously. The other, as they turned to face Krieger, hemming him in, was saying a few sharp words. His thumb emphasized his command with a jerk towards the rear door.

Carefully David eased himself away from his table, his eyes still fixed on the men. Their backs were partly turned to him: their attention was riveted on Krieger, who was rising with calculated deliberation. He was talking too—just enough to keep them concentrating, wary of some trick. It gave David the few seconds he needed to reach the man with the gun in his pocket. The other glanced round, exclaimed a warning. It came a fraction too late. David lunged forward and hit hard with the butt of the automatic at the back of his man's neck. Krieger smashed his beer mug against the other's mouth. The two men slumped almost simultaneously: one on the floor, out for a very long count; the other over the table, his hands at his face.

Krieger only stopped to drop some money beside the moaning man. 'That will pay for the beer mug too,' he said as he followed David towards the back door.

They stepped into a windowless alley. Krieger pointed to the left. 'Your quickest way. I'll take this route.' He moved off to the right. Stopping for a moment and looking back, he shook his head and said, 'You're a stubborn fool. But thanks.'

David smiled, broke into a run along the alley, winding its way like a deep-bedded stream between high banks of three-storied walls. It was shadowed here, and quiet. The strip of sky that could be seen far above the rippling edges of red tiles was now blue and storm-free. He reached a street curving north, and there slackened his pace to a brisk walk.

Chapter Seventeen

IRINA HAD LISTENED to David's footsteps running down the wooden staircase. She rose from the bed, the sandwich still in her hand, and crossed over to the window. But he was already out of sight. Nothing down there except an empty road and quiet vineyards. She came back, avoiding Jo's eyes. 'You were right,' she said. 'It looks like thunder.'

'Finish your lunch.' Jo was tidying the dresser, wrapping up the uneaten food, stowing it carefully away in the paper bag. There was a lot more inside it, too. That was one thing she had learned on this trip: go prepared.

'Have some. Or are you not hungry?'

'Later,' Jo said. 'We can have a picnic later.' Perhaps her nervous stomach would be under control by then: her attempt to eat at noon had been disastrous. I wish I could really be as calm as I look, she thought as she got the room straightened. Fortunately Irina hadn't unpacked much. 'Did you throw that wig away?'

Irina was horrified. 'Throw it away? I don't like it, but I would not do that.' She finished her sandwich, and then the wine. The peaches were already packed. Jo was really too efficient. 'I'd like a peach.'

'Later. It takes too long to eat. All that juice. Messy.'

'But we've plenty of time——'

'We don't have any. Come on, Irina, put on that wig. It does help to change you.'

'No. I can tie my scarf around my head.'

'Then do it.' Anything to stop an argument, Jo thought. She can put the wig on later, once we are out of town and I'm changing to a redhead for St Mary's benefit.

'Do it!' Jo repeated sharply.

'Now?'

'Now. And powder your face—make it pale. No lipstick, either.'

'We're leaving? Without David?'

'We're leaving. Ludvik and Milan and Jan aren't sitting around in a cosy little bedroom waiting for the weather to clear. Please Irina—believe me. This is the only way to——'

'I'm not leaving.' Irina was definite. 'You go. I am staying.'

Jo sat down on the bed. 'I feel sick.'

Irina's face changed. The hostile look was gone. 'Then rest, Jo. Lie down for a little.'

'I can't. And you can't. We've got to keep moving.'

Irina looked at Jo's white face, heard the small break in her voice.

She said gently, 'But I want to wait for David.'

Jo took a long deep breath. 'You're as stubborn as your father. But he would always listen to reason.'

'You have met my father?'

'In London. I was staying at my uncle's flat when your father got out of Prague. I was with him when he was almost murdered.'

'*What?*'

'I'll tell you in the car. We'll have plenty of time to talk before Dave catches up with us.' Jo rose, picked up her rain-coat. Thank God, she thought, that Dave was joining them: the road west had looked easy enough on the map—until you turned north for Switzerland. 'We'll wait for him at St Mary's. It's only thirty miles out of town.' Irina had made no move. 'Coming?'

Irina shook her head. 'I am waiting for David here.'

'And have him killed, like Josef and Alois Pokorny?'

Irina's eyes widened. Now I'm being brutal, Jo thought, but there's no other way. 'Or perhaps you haven't noticed that everyone who has spent a lot of time with you ends up in a fatal accident? Why? Ask your Jiri about that. He's building up a neat legend about your escape and can't have it exposed as a fake.' Jo paused. 'Now cover up your hair. Put on my coat. I'll wear yours. A little confusion never hurts.'

'What legend?' But Irina was binding her scarf tightly round her hair. She even pulled on the raincoat.

The knot in Jo's stomach untied. The battle is won, she thought. 'Come on—let's move. I'll give you the details later.'

But Irina took no step towards the door. She faced Jo, her eyes questioning. Jo said, 'Today's newspapers have a report from Prague—about you and a political kidnapping.'

Irina stood very still. 'A kidnapping?'

'That's Jiri's angle. Krieger was expecting something tricky. So stop worrying, Irina. Trust Krieger. He will think of——'

'Trust Krieger?' Irina was bitter. 'He planned this, didn't he?' She pointed to David's bag, which Jo was about to carry downstairs along with the food.

For a moment it seemed as though Irina was going to strip off the raincoat.

Jo's anger broke. 'Krieger,' she said, her voice becoming more clipped, more English, 'is staying in Merano as long as he can. And every minute of that delay could be dangerous. In fact, my dear Irina, he may very well end up dead, and all because of helping you. So cut it out. If you've got to hate someone, start hating Ludvik and his friends. They are the ones who murdered Alois. And Krieger is the witness who could have them hanged for it.'

With that cold outburst, Jo opened the door. She looked back impatiently to see Irina still fumbling with the raincoat. She wasn't taking it off, though. She was transferring two small books from her handbag into the coat's deep inner pocket.

Irina closed her bag. 'It was too full,' she said. 'And it could easily be stolen.' She looked down at the raincoat for one last check.

'Doesn't show one bulge,' Jo assured her. Strange girl, what on earth was she hiding? Worrying—at a time like this—about purse snatchers? But at least she had taken Jo's straight talk well. And Jo herself felt the better for it. The truth is we both needed it, she thought. The mutiny is over and my nausea has gone. 'I'll do the explaining to Frau Whosis and her son,' she told Irina as they went downstairs. 'That way we won't get our stories crossed.'

As they reached the little hall, a violent explosion rattled the windows. Jo missed the last step, almost tripped, Irina flinched. They looked at each other, and went on. There was no sign of Frau Hartmann. 'She has probably locked herself in a closet,' Jo said. 'My mother always does that when there's a thunderstorm.'

'It's close,' Irina said.

'Too close.'

In the alley they heard a long hideous hiss, ending in another enormous explosion.

'A gas main blown up?' Jo asked. 'Then we could have traffic problems.'

They started running.

The garage was empty except for the two cars. Franz was out in the street, head bent back, eyes on the sky. A third wild hiss and a stupendous bang were followed by a fourth hiss, a fourth explosion.

This time, they both jumped openly. 'Could they be rockets?' Irina asked. 'A celebration?'

The tension was gone between them. They laughed together.

'Anyway,' said Jo as they dropped the baggage, David's included, into the back seat of the Ford, 'I think Herr Hartmann is too busy counting the bangs to pay us much attention.' And that will save a five-minute delay, she thought thankfully.

But he had keen ears. As soon as he heard the engine turn over, he came running into the garage to see who was tampering with one of its cars.

Jo was just about to move out. 'My friend is not feeling well. I'm taking her to the country for the weekend,' she explained. 'Please thank your mother for us. And tell Herr Mennery, when he comes to get his car, that we've got his luggage with us. We'll expect him at my aunt's house—just south of here, near Bolzano.' She had been speaking in German, but the Italian name had slipped out. 'Near Bozen,' she corrected, and hoped she was forgiven.

'What about the petrol? I filled your——'

'He will pay for that along with his bill.' With a bright smile and a wave of her hand, Jo drove slowly out of the garage and made ready for a right turn, the quick route for the westbound highway.

Franz Hartmann shouted. 'Fräulein Schmidt!' She stopped. 'Not that way!' he called as he ran up to her. 'If you're going south, you turn left——'

'And drive through the busy Corn Market? No, thank you. I can reach the road to Bozen more easily than that.'

'But you are taking the long way round. You will have to——'

'Better than struggling through the Old Town. *Auf Wiedersehen.*'

Franz Hartmann stood at the door of his garage, watching the Ford drive off. So the room wasn't good enough for them, was that it? The American's sister was ill, that was Fräulein Schmidt's story, and perhaps true; the blonde had looked as pale as if she had dipped her face in a flour bin. In that case, better not have anyone turning that room into a hospital— good riddance to them. Yet he didn't like it. He wished he could risk leaving the garage for a couple of minutes, but at that moment a car stopped at the pump, demanding five gallons of petrol.

While he was busy with that job he saw Willi, the neighbour's boy, coming to borrow a wrench as usual.

'Willi!' he called out, 'nip around to the house. Tell my mother that the women have left. She'd better check the spare room, see if anything's missing.'

A second car drew up, needing four gallons of petrol, and a third had pulled up at the kerb to wait till he was free. Willi came chasing back, heavy shoes clattering through the garage, and picked up the wrench.

'Your mother checked,' he reported. 'Everything is fine. I'll return this in five minutes.' He waved the wrench and darted away to his own yard.

Nothing missing, Franz thought. The room just wasn't good enough for them, that was the truth. Angrily, he gestured to the third car to move over to the pump.

The car did not move. Instead, two men got out. More foreigners; and as usual in need of directions. Franz hooked up the pump, wiped his hands on a rag, and went to meet them. They came from Graz—that was what the licence plate of their white Fiat said—but they weren't Austrian, even if the tall one had light hair and eyes. The other, a darker type, was going to do the talking.

He was speaking in Italian, carefully, as though he had learned his little piece by heart. But he wasn't asking about a street name or a puzzling address. He was looking for a friend who had just arrived in Merano, driving a green Mercedes with a Viennese licence.

'Why don't you try at the hotels?' Franz asked.

'We've telephoned all the hotels and inns.'

So now, thought Franz, they are checking the garages. This is more than a search for a friend. Police business. I'm not going to get mixed up in that. Not me. They are not Italian police, that's for sure; but they all work together. One complaint from them to the Italians, and I've had it.

'A green Mercedes?' he asked.

'That is what I said.' The speaker could make even Italian sound cold and hard. 'Driven by an American. He has a girl with him, a pretty blonde.'

The dark eyes were studying Franz, but it was the movement of the other fellow, abruptly walking into the garage, that gave Franz the final prod. He said, 'An American? Yes. He was here.'

'He *is* here,' called back the light-haired man. 'At least his car is.'

His friend moved into the garage. Franz followed. But they didn't touch the car: they simply checked its licence plate. The light-haired man took a step towards Franz. His friend stopped him; then he asked, in that cold hard voice, 'Where is the American?'

'Not here.'

'Where?'

'He went into town.'

'With the girl?'

'No.'

'Then where is she?'

With relief Franz said, 'She left with a friend.'

'Who?'

'Another girl. They left about ten—maybe fifteen minutes ago.' And God be thanked that I don't have to mention the room to them. These two would scare mother to death. There's something about that big fellow that scares even me. They'd have searched the house, no doubt about that; from cellar to attic. Franz felt a cold sweat break out over his brow.

'What kind of car?'

'Ford. Tan colour, Meran registration. They were driving south to Bozen.'

'South? That's a good one. And she took the direction west?'

'Yes. But she wanted to avoid the traffic in——'

The men laughed, walked out.

And what about the American? Franz wondered. Weren't they going to wait for him?

It seemed they had no more interest in the American. Franz saw the white Fiat drive past, travelling towards the west.

He was still standing there, trying to puzzle it all out, when Willi brought back the wrench. Willi said, 'Something wrong?' Franz shook his head, didn't answer.

He still was not in an answering mood when David arrived back at the garage. He presented his bill with a minimum of words. 'They left. Took your luggage with them. Headed for Bozen.'

David checked the bill. It had been carefully made out, honest to the last *lira*. The extra charge for the petrol for Jo's car was probably accurate, too. It was all on the same expense account, anyhow, he thought. He tried a small joke about men being sometimes left to pay the bill, but it collapsed and fell flat on its sad face. What's bothering Franz? he wondered. 'Sorry I had to dash off. I just wanted to get that aspirin before the thunderstorm broke. But it didn't, did it?'

'No.' Franz was intent on counting out the change.

'That was quite a performance with the rockets. Did the girls leave while it was going on?'

'Soon after.' Franz re-counted the change, this time into David's hand.

'Something wrong?' David pocketed the loose coins. Franz was too open-faced a character to be able to disguise his worry. Something *is* wrong, David decided, and tried again. 'Were the girls all right? No delay?'

'No delay.' Franz turned away, walking towards the small wooden table that served as his office.

The hell with this, thought David, and got into the Mercedes. As he drove out, he braked for a moment near the table.

'Many thanks,' he said, and tried a friendly grin. 'Next time, we'll——'

'Next time you don't come here. We don't need your kind.'

David switched off the engine. 'And what kind is that?'

'The kind that brings trouble.'

David restrained his rising temper. 'What trouble?'

Franz glanced over his shoulder, made sure Willi was not hovering near the door. 'Two policemen. In plain clothes.'

Milan and Jan? David's face was grim. He asked, 'One had dark hair and eyes; the other, taller, with light hair?'

Franz stared, then nodded.

Yes, it could be Milan and Jan. So they had come searching for a green Mercedes. David drew a sharp breath. 'What about the Ford? Did you tell them——'

'They didn't see it,' Franz said abruptly, and walked into the street.

'But did you tell them about it?' David called after him.

Yes, David thought, he told them; and he won't admit it. This is all I'll get out of him. But again David tried, once he had the Mercedes moving out of the garage. 'What kind of car?' he asked as he drew up beside Franz. 'These two men—what kind of car?'

The intensity of David's low voice jolted an answer out of Franz. 'White Fiat.' Then he noticed the American's eyes, anxious, desperate, as they searched the street. He relented still further. 'They didn't wait for you. They travelled——'

The Mercedes made a right turn, shot into an opening in the traffic, and headed west.

'But how did he know?' Franz asked aloud. How did the American know they had travelled west? And why should a wanted man chase after two cops? Franz stood there, hands on hips, brows drawn into a frown, and watched the Mercedes vanish from sight. None of your business, he told himself: they're a crazy mixed-up bunch, these foreigners: no sense, no meaning to the way they behave. You're well out of it, Franz, my boy. There will be no policemen prowling round the garage —or the house. Not now. No questions, no search. No gossip among the neighbours; no feeling of being watched. But now you've got to do one thing for sure: get those guns and the dynamite out of the cellar. Let your friends find another hiding place for all their stuff. Tell them that, tonight—you'll see them at the dance—tell these damned hotheads to leave your house alone. This time they will listen. Franz, you've got one real solid excuse at last to move them out: police.

A Volkswagen was arriving at the gas pump. 'Three gallons? Right away.' Franz Hartmann's grin was cheerful, his face as cloudless as the sky overhead. Yes, he thought happily, you've got one perfect excuse. There will be no arm twisting, no more persuasion, no more being called a sneaking coward. My God, when friends go political, they can make your whole life one sweating shivering misery.

'Hey, Willi,' he called across the street, 'tell your sister to be ready at eight o'clock. We're going to the dance tonight.' Perhaps, he thought with a wide grin, I ought to be thanking the American. He began whistling a dot-and-carry-one polka.

David left Merano and its last busy street, and his anger cooled along with the traffic problems. His mind grew clear, like the straight highway ahead of him: no more tortuous turns and backtrackings to make sure a white Fiat hadn't been following him.

No use blaming Franz Hartmann for talking too much: the guy had simply not known what was at stake. If there was any blame to be dealt out, it was Mark Bohn who should have it all. Bohn saw the Mercedes; he reported it; the report was relayed to Ludvik and Company, possibly within an hour after it had been received. (They have the gadgets, David remembered: they have two-way radios and scramblers and God knows what else in helpful devices.) In that case, Irina and I were lucky not to have been seen coming into town. Except, of course, that I had not taken the usual route to Merano by way of Bolzano: I didn't come in from the south; I chose the road, less travelled, more difficult, that came down to Merano from the north. All that insufferable damnable trouble for nothing. Because all the cars we've taken, all of Krieger's plans, made one big zero when Franz opened his fat mouth. Or hesitated in replying. It all came to the same thing. Milan and Jan had only to watch that guileless face trying to be crafty, and they would head straight into the garage. And there—somehow or other—they had found out that Irina had left. The one thing we were trying to hide, the one thing; and they found it out.

Krieger, he thought instantly, what's the point of Krieger hanging around Merano? He's risking his neck. Those two Czech imports in the Red Lion, even if they are bashed up a bit, have some definite business with Krieger: they, or Ludvik, will not leave it unfinished. Why? Krieger didn't have time to tell me, but there is some reason behind it all. Perhaps—it just could be—they've learned he saw Milan and Jan leaving the murder scene. But how? Oh, stow it: you've got enough to worry about without shooting off half-cocked guesses. But you'd better waste three more good minutes by stopping at the nearest telephone and passing the word to Krieger. Where is he anyway? You don't even know that. But sometime, he'll go back to his hotel. And just hope your message isn't too late.

He drew up at the next village, where a neon-lit café looked as if it might have a men's room as well as a telephone. His message was ready in his mind, all translated into clear German, and as innocent as he could make it. 'Results disappointing. No reason now to prolong your stay.' The hotel porter sounded intelligent and brisk. He repeated the two sentences accurately. Certainly he would see that Herr Krieger had the message as soon as he returned to the Bristol.

David got back to the car. At least this brief stop had its other uses. The white Fiat he had noticed some distance behind him had only contained a close-packed family, now spilling out from it to get beer for the parents and ice cream for the kids. And there was no other Fiat in the parking space, waiting to follow him out. Of course they would know the road he would be travelling. Mark Bohn had reported that too.

Before he turned on the ignition, David reached for his map. Might as well see where he was going. He folded it back to the section he needed: the bold red line ran across it, west from Merano, and then split into two just where Highway 40 branched off to the north. And this is what Bohn saw, he thought, a road leading right over the frontier into Switzerland. Immediately, his eye was caught by Tarasp. His spine stiffened. Tarasp was marked. Definitely. A pencil smudge around a small hole punctured by a sharp point.

He forced himself to study the route directly ahead of him, and found Santa Maria clearly marked on its perch above the highway. Yes, that was St Mary's, all right. Jo could already be there. And that damned Fiat? It had no interest in him, that was certain. His worry increased. He dropped the map as he started the motor. He swung out on to the highway. Once he had passed the string of villages that edged it for the next fifteen or twenty miles, he could let the speedometer climb. Patience, he warned himself: *piano piano va lontano:* you'll make better time if you don't have to argue with an Italian cop. They were around; he had already seen two of them on the prowl, and one automobile stopped. So he resisted his impulses, and kept to a normal speed, cursing every mile of the way.

Chapter Eighteen

'KRIEGER WAS RIGHT,' Jo said, pointing to the chapel of Santa Maria, miniature in size but indomitable in its stance, poised high over the road on a huge promontory of rock. 'We just couldn't miss that, could we?'

Irina, for once, didn't flinch at the name of Krieger. David, she thought thankfully, would see Santa Maria clearly too; he would be able to find them, after all. No delays, no difficult search. Her doubts began to leave her. Ever since Jo had driven into this long valley, a strong wind whistling past the car even on this bright blue-skied day, the little pilgrimage church with its tiny steeple had been visible, standing firm against a background of brutal hills rising into savage mountains. It was still some distance away, but its details were now sharpening, changing in emphasis. The frontal precipice, looming larger and larger, seemed to fall straight towards the highway. 'Like the prow of a tall, tall ship, just about to cut through the road,' Irina said.

'That will take a few years,' Jo said reassuringly. Fortunately, she thought, the highway skirted that bulge of cliff with considerable respect, drawing away from the outthrust of sheer rock as far as it could without being pushed into the small river that rushed down the valley. Even so, there was a lot of spillage from the face of the precipice: splintered stones and pulverized fragments of rock fell in loosely packed screes, to pile at its base in dumps of jagged flints. The warning signs were already giving advance notice along the road: *Caduta Massi*. 'Rockfalls,' Jo translated for Irina. 'Don't worry. We won't have to climb up there.'

'How do the pilgrims manage it?'

'They don't tackle it face-on, that's certain. There's a picnic area. Krieger says, at this side of Santa Maria. We should almost be at it now.' But where? The woods, flanking the highway, hid everything. In front of her, the stream of cars that had passed her (drive slowly, Krieger had advised) was already rounding the curve of the precipice. Behind her, a huge trailer-truck was pulling out impatiently. 'Not now, buster,' she told it angrily. 'You damn well keep behind me and give me some cover. Oh, blast these Turkish drivers! They're always trying to edge you off the road. They haul these loads all the way from the Balkans to Hamburg and Amsterdam, and it does something to their egos. If anyone is driving something as fancy as a Cadillac or a Jaguar, he gets sideswiped into a ditch. Keep back, damn you, will you?' She almost missed the entrance to the clearing that lay just off the road, and had to make an abrupt right turn on to the patch of rough meadow nestling under Santa Maria's bastion. Behind her there was a Turkish yell and a blare on a horn. 'And to you, my sweet,' Jo finished, her eyes now searching out the most hidden place where she could park.

Not far inside the meadow, two lightweight buses of local vintage had been drawn up parallel to the highway. Beyond them, picnic tables and children and benches. Well beyond those, a cluster, badly grouped, of three slightly aged Volkswagens. The buses, Jo decided as she noted the gap between them, allowing just enough space. The Ford fitted neatly into the vacant slot. Now, she thought thankfully, it can't be seen from the highway.

The only trouble was, she couldn't see the highway either, and keep watch for that white car which had been lagging behind them for the last half hour. 'Quick!' she urged Irina. She slipped out of the driver's seat, pulling the blue coat around her shoulders, smoothing the curls of the auburn wig against her cheeks. She lifted the bag of food. 'Might as well have that picnic now,' she said cheerfully, and edged her way out between the buses towards the nearest table, where the drivers were sitting at one end. The other two tables were completely occupied, small girls in neat rows waiting patiently under the watchful eyes of three nuns. Jo sat down, avoiding the bus drivers' appreciative stare, and waited for Irina.

Irina had smiled at the conflict between Turk and infidel, had laughed as the Ford bumped over the meadow and set the luggage bouncing on the back seat. But now, with Jo's trench coat tightly belted around her waist, her fake dark hair obediently in place, her bag slung over her shoulder, she was showing signs of a second mutiny. Her lips were set, her eyebrows down. But she had the good sense to keep her voice low. 'David will never see the car,' she began. 'He won't even notice us with all this——' She gestured to the twenty pairs of young eyes, round and wide, studying the newcomers with interest.

'And I hope no one else will, either,' Jo said quietly. 'Sit down, Irina. Keep your back to the road. I'll watch out for David.'

'Will you be able to see——'

'Just barely. But enough—if you'll only sit down and stop blocking my view.'

Irina hesitated, then did as she was told. 'What else are you looking for?'

'A white car.'

'We were followed?'

'I don't know.'

'You must know *something*.' Or else Jo would not have been taking all these precautions. 'Please——'

'Come on, let's laugh it up a little. We're on a picnic, aren't we?' Jo bowed and smiled to the two men at the other end of the table, who might not be able to hear the softly spoken words, or even understand them if they had been audible, but were openly fascinated. 'Relax,' she told Irina. 'The natives are friendly. They just can't place us, that's all. We are out of another world.' And at this moment, she thought, I wish I belonged to theirs—a simpler, less complicated universe. 'Have a peach? There's chocolate, too—slabs of it. Or do you want a ham sandwich? Cheese? Good Lord, Dave must have been buying for a real party. But men are like that: put them in front of a food counter and they grab everything in sight. My mother, who's a very sharp housekeeper, won't let my father go near a supermarket.' She brought out the bottle of Chianti and plonked it down on the table. 'Now we really do look festive.' But she kept watching the highway.

'Please—' Irina said again, 'don't treat me like one of those children.' She glanced at the two tables of quiet little faces, and smiled for them. Who were they, all in the same plain dresses, with crisply braided hair and large friendly eyes? The nuns admonished gently: the eyes stopped staring. 'What is worrying you, Jo?' It can't be much; not in this innocent setting.

'I was driving slowly. We were passed by every car on the road, weren't we?'

'Except that truck,' Irina teased.

'Until then, every car passed us. All but one. It kept falling back whenever it caught sight of us.'

Now Irina was serious. 'A white car?'

'Yes.' Jo had first seen it just after they made that brief stop, well outside of Merano, to settle the wig problem.

'There are so many white——'

'I know. But——' Jo hesitated, then said, 'A white Fiat was in Graz yesterday evening. It turned up in Lienz last night. It left before dawn.'

'Who was in it?'

'Milan and Jan. Ludvik joined them in Lienz. They headed for Merano.' Jo watched Irina carefully: no panic; she was taking this calmly. Encouraged, Jo went on, 'So you see why I'm puzzled by a white car that should have passed us like all the rest, but didn't.'

Irina roused herself from her own thoughts. 'Clever of you to drive slowly,' she said, trying to appear unconcerned. So they were in Merano, she kept thinking. For hours.

'Not my idea. It was Krieger's.' And I thought he was out of his skull for suggesting it. He knows how I hate dawdling along a highway like an old farm woman taking her eggs to market. Jo almost laughed, partly at herself, partly with relief: Irina was handling this piece of news well. Let's be normal, she decided. Either that car was following us, or it wasn't. And what if it was? We sit tight and wait for Dave. She said, 'I could have been overworrying. I do that a lot: bad habit. And it doesn't seem as if we are being followed, after all. That white car ought to have passed by now. Perhaps it turned off on a little side road to have a picnic of its own.'

'Perhaps.'

'Why else should they delay like this?'

'To send a message back to Merano. To ask for further instructions.'

'Oh, come on, Irina. Your imagination is even wilder than mine.' She lifted a peach. 'Have one? Specialty of Merano.' Let's be normal, she told herself once again.

'No, thanks.'

'Then what do we do with these peaches? Give them to the children? I couldn't swallow a mouthful with all those eyes watching it disappear down my throat.' Irina nodded her agreement. 'Okay. You keep looking at the road.' Jo rose, gathering up all the picnic, leaving only the Chianti bottle on the table. 'And if we have been followed here—well, at least we can't pin the blame on Mark Bohn this time.' She noticed Irina's face, tense, incredulous. 'Yes,' Jo said, 'he was the informer.' Her lips tightened. She picked up the bag of food and walked over to the nuns.

Irina drew a steadying breath. Yes, David and she had been too kind about Bohn: David out of friendship, and she, because of—because of what? Stupidity? Embarrassment over such an idiotic mistake with the map? No one would pay it any attention, she had thought. But Bohn did. She knew that now. The moment of shock ended, leaving her strangely calm as she kept watch on the small section of highway that was visible from where she sat.

She listened to Jo's flow of Italian, to the nuns' chorus of replies, to the children's burst of chatter: she noted the cars that flashed past—one blue, one brown, another blue, one grey; and she kept asking herself the same question over and over again. Why was she still being followed? Mark Bohn had made his report to Vienna hours ago. It must have been relayed from Vienna to Prague and then to Merano. By this time Ludvik must have learned that her destination was Switzerland. So why were they still following her? Perhaps, of course, Jo had been mistaken. That was what Jo was now trying to make her believe. Perhaps that white car had already turned off the road, perhaps it was only——

And then she saw it. Travelling at high speed. She sat very still, staring at the patch of highway now empty once more.

'Just as I thought,' said Jo as she returned, 'it's a group of orphans, a special outing, a Saturday treat. Poor darlings——' She broke off. Irina's eyes seem hypnotized by the road. 'You saw it?' she asked unbelievingly.

'Yes.' Irina recovered herself. 'Yes. I saw it.'

'A white Fiat?'

'I can't tell one car from another. But it was white. There were two men in front.'

'Wouldn't you know?' Jo said in dismay. She glanced back at the orphans. Well, at least they were happy. And stupid me, she thought: one small good deed, and as a reward I fall flat on my funny face. I ought to have remembered there were people in the world who couldn't tell a Rolls from a pancake. Jo gathered her wits. 'Well, did the car stop—slow down?'

'No, It was travelling fast.'

'Did they look at us—or just glance?'

'Glanced briefly.'

'Oh, what does it matter?' Jo asked, trying to control her rising anxiety. 'Neither a look nor a glance would help them. All they saw was a dark-haired girl sitting near two bus drivers, and a redhead with a batch of children and three nuns. They couldn't have seen a tan Ford, not from the highway. So we'll relax, and wait for Dave, and let Milan and Jan go chasing all the way to the Swiss border.' But they won't have to travel very far before they know they've lost us. They'll come back, keep checking every turn-off area. How many are there, I wonder, on this road to the north?

'When will David reach here?'

'Half an hour. Perhaps less.' Perhaps more, but let's not bring that up. 'And meanwhile we can count ourselves lucky. This is as safe a place to wait as any.' She looked along their table, caught the drivers' attention. (It had never slipped far.) She smiled, holding out the bottle of Chianti. 'Please,' she said, and broke into a stream of Italian. They accepted the wine with a graceful speech. Yes, they agreed, this was a pleasant spot to spend an afternoon. Were there any other picnic areas north of here? No, they told her, this was the only one for many many kilometres. Yes, the road ran fairly straight; good visibility most of the way until you reached the high passes. And with that last piece of information Jo left them to enjoy the wine.

'So,' Jo said as she ended translating for Irina, 'we can expect these two men quite soon. If, that is, they really are Milan and Jan. There isn't much to keep them searching on this highway. But let's not panic if they drive in here to make a thorough check. They probably will. They won't make the same mistake twice.'

'And then?' There was a strange smile on Irina's face.

Then what? Jo made a good attempt at nonchalance. 'They may stay, hover around, wait for us to leave. They'll look innocent. They think we know nothing about them, or about any white Fiat. And we'll string them along, play the game their way, pretend they're just a couple of tourists. When Dave arrives, that is the time to stop them. We'll evade them.' But how? Jo wondered. At this moment she had a strong impulse to run. A stupid reaction, she told herself, as she glanced around her, pretending to admire the scenery. Just beside them, sheltering them from the stiff northern breeze that had funnelled down the valley, rose the mass of rock covered with bushes and sparse trees, concealing the rough path to the chapel so far above that it was out of sight. To the east and south of the meadow, hills climbed steeply, densely wooded, heavy with larches, impenetrable. To the west was the highway. They were nicely protected, or nicely trapped, depending on which way you looked at it.

'Play the game their way,' Irina said and looked at Jo with amusement. She shook her head. 'It is no longer a game, Jo. No more hide-and-seek, and who is the clever one.'

'It was only a figure of speech,' said Jo defensively. Her cheeks coloured angrily. 'Have you any suggestions?'

'No. Just a question. Why are they still following me?' She paused, and added, 'There is no need.'

'No need?' Jo stared at her.

'Not now. I am of no more use to Jiri Hrádek.'

'Jo's stare widened. She's getting mixed up in her English, Jo thought. Or I am. Yet her voice is cool, detached. I'm the one who is about to panic. 'You damned well are,' Jo said, 'and you know it. Hrádek is ready to score my name off his little list, and Dave's too. We are expendable. But you, Irina, are definitely not. Not until you lead them to your father.'

'Jiri knows where my father is. Mark Bohn gave him that information four hours ago. Time enough—yes, plenty of time, to change his instructions about me.'

The story she told me about Bohn, and the map, and the section showing the route into Switzerland—is this what's bothering her? Jo said, 'That's a wild guess. And what if Jiri Hrádek did receive Bohn's information? He would only be given a general direction: Switzerland. His men would still have to follow you to the exact meeting place.'

'But if Jiri has learned that too?'

'How? Why, even I don't know where it is.'

213

'It's a place called Tarasp,' Irina said.

'But who told——'

'How well does Bohn see with his glasses?'

She's crazy, absolutely crazy, Jo thought.

'How well?' the quiet voice insisted.

'They magnify.'

'Strongly?'

'Yes.'

There was a brief silence.

'Then Jiri knows,' said Irina.

This time the silence was longer. At last Jo said, 'I hope I'm wrong, but I think you are trying to tell me that these men have been sent to kill you.'

'Today instead of tomorrow. What is the difference? To Jiri there is none.'

'You *are* crazy,' Jo said. But she forced her eyes back to the road.

From high above, a bell tolled lightly. The children's voices broke into excitement and they began clambering out from the benches. The two drivers finished the Chianti with one last gulp. The younger one, already on his feet, flashed a smile of thanks at Jo.

'Leaving?' she asked them.

'Yes. That's the signal.' He pointed overhead in the direction of the chapel. 'The pilgrims up there are now coming down. When they reach the meadow the children can go up. The church is too small, the staircase is too narrow, so——'

'The only path?'

'From here, yes. The steps are cut out of the rock.'

'And no other path up to the church?'

'Sure, but it isn't used. The stone steps are the safest. You just keep to them and you'll be all right.'

He gave a wave, moved off, climbed into his bus. It was the one nearer the road.

'I don't like this,' said Jo quietly. Once that bus moved out, the Ford was in plain view to anyone passing on the highway. And there went one faint hope that a white Fiat might not enter this picnic area after all, that Milan and Jan might not think this place worth a real search. 'Look, I think we'll get into the car and start driving back to Merano. Meet David on the way.' It's a complete mess-up, Jo thought: everything is going wrong. And for once she found herself without any other ideas beyond that simple-minded notion of running. 'Come on,' she urged, conscious of a long trail of women, appearing one by one as they stepped down from the rock-hewn stairs, intent faces breaking into laughter when they reached the safety of the flat green meadow.

'Why draw David back into danger?' Irina asked. He was out of it at this moment.

'He has never left it,' said Jo shortly. 'We'd better move. There is no shelter here for us. Not now.'

'The women?' Away from the discipline of the rocky path, they were spreading out, rejoining special friends. Around the bus there was forming a happy mob scene.

'We aren't wearing dirndls and blue silk shawls and wide-brimmed black hats. Nor are we middle-aged and thickset. Apart from that we could mix with them and giggle our heads off. Did you ever hear such girlish laughter? And not one of them under forty.' Then Jo found she was smiling too: at least, she thought, some people have been enjoying themselves this blasted Saturday afternoon. 'Let's move out before that bus blocks the exit.' She glanced at the road, or what she could see of it between the mass of wide-skirted dresses, a swirl of petti-coats and aprons above strong ankles and silver-buckled shoes. And she stopped smiling. Trying to edge its way into the picnic ground, and failing, was a white car. 'A Fiat,' she said softly. 'And it's angry,' she added as it gave two sharp blasts on its horn. Thank God, the women were paying no attention at all.

Quickly, Jo looked back at the meadow—too wide, too empty, in its stretch to the wooded hills—and then at the children. The last of them were near the stone steps, impatient, restless, discipline breaking down into laughter and rising voices, as they waited to follow those who had started the ascent and were already lost from sight. One nun remained to bring up the rear of the column. She was nervous, and obviously worried by the break in discipline. Her voice rose as she repeated her warnings to those at the end of the line: single file, keep to the path, do not step off. 'I think she needs some help,' Jo said. 'Shall we volunteer?'

Irina nodded, began running towards the staircase carved out of the rock. A few steps up that path, and the greenery would shield them. And after that? Later, she thought, we'll think of something later; now, it is enough to get out of sight. Jo followed her, pausing only to lift the empty wine bottle from the table and leave one bemused driver staring after her. Then his attention reverted to the mild chaos around the bus —not his, thank God. He was well out of it.

The women were now being persuaded to board, but some of them were still angry with a Fiat that had tried to nudge them aside. And of course, the ladies who had driven their Volkswagens here—purse-proud show-offs, these ones, with more lace at their necks and aprons of real silk—had chosen this moment to move out. Women drivers, he thought with amusement as he watched the jam at the exit to the road; but these ones would get their way. That Fiat might as well wait. What was it so impatient about, anyway? None of your business, Tommaso, he told himself, suppressing a twinge of sympathy for his fellow bus driver; you're no traffic cop. He stretched himself out on the bench, pulled his hat over his eyes, listened to the voices that died away as motor engines started up, and thought now of a little sleep in the warm sunshine. From high overhead he could hear the children singing as they climbed. Peace at last. Beautiful.

Chapter Nineteen

MILAN KLIMENT and Jan Bruzek drove into the meadow, but not before they had to back their Fiat on to the road and let three ancient Volkswagens and a decrepit bus have right of way out of the bottleneck. Their tempers, simmering ever since they had discovered that the tan-coloured Ford was lost, vanished without one trace in broad daylight, were now at boiling point. The sight of the car standing calmly on the meadow beside another rickety bus did nothing to cool them.

'They are here,' Milan said, his voice as grim as his face.

'They've been here all the time,' Jan exploded. 'Couldn't you have seen that when we passed this damned place?' He had been driving; Milan had been in charge of maps and directions.

'No more than you could. What the hell made you drive at such a speed?'

You know the answer, Jan told him silently. We lost sight of them because you insisted we stop and make radio contact with Merano. A couple of minutes, you said: five at most. The women are travelling at a snail's pace, we'll easily catch up; and we've got to get the verification of Bohn's earlier report back to Merano. But it had taken more like ten minutes, what with that East German relaying all messages from his listening post to Ludvik. And Ludvik had new instructions to give, too. So how did you expect me to drive, once we were back on the highway and no Ford in sight? They must have put on speed, you said; and that's what I did.

'Come on, come on!' Milan's irritation grew with each passing second. Jan had brought the Fiat to a halt on the opposite side of the meadow from the bus. Now he was reversing, so that he faced back towards the road. It would make their departure quick and easy—if that were needed—but the small delay was a further aggravation. Milan was out of the car even before the ignition was switched off. 'Come on,' he repeated, looking across the meadow at the man who was stretched out on a bench. 'We'll wake up that bastard, shake some answers out of him.'

They started towards the picnic table. Milan's thoughts were bitter. Bad luck all the way. (Prague would have another name for it.) He might as well face it: there had been nothing but failure—except for those moments of triumph in Merano when they had at last found a green Mercedes. Hopes raised, hopes dashed. 'This,' he told Jan, 'is where failure ends. We've swallowed our bellyful of it.'

'We didn't fail in Vienna,' Jan protested. Alois Pokorny had been neatly handled.

'What do you call leaving a witness behind?'

'We weren't the only ones to underestimate Krieger. Ludvik——'

'Sure.' Two of Ludvik's men now out of the picture: one with a severe concussion, the other with a broken jaw and a mouthful of loose teeth. 'That will put him in an understanding mood.'

'Especially with that damned German listening in. Why the hell did we have to use him, anyway?'

'Because,' Milan said with biting sarcasm, 'we are all such great and good friends. Also, the East Germans have a nice set-up in Merano. We borrowed it. An emergency. Or hadn't you heard?'

'It was a blunder all the same. We should keep our own communication system——'

'Tell that to Hrádek.'

Jan turned his resentment on to a safer target. 'What are the East Germans doing in the South Tyrol, anyhow?' They are here and we are not. And I never could stomach them, anyway, he thought.

'Encouraging the nationalists to make life miserable for this kind of slob.' Milan looked down with contempt at the Italian lying peacefully on the bench. He put out a hand and gripped the bus driver's shoulder.

Tommaso had kept his eyes closed. If he seemed to be asleep, the foreign voices would go away. (He was a placid amiable man, now nearing forty, and a little heavy around the middle

218

with his wife's excellent lasagne.) Besides, he couldn't understand a word they said, so how could he talk with them? Then
a hand grasped his shoulder, shook him roughly. *Porca miseria!*
This was no way to treat anyone. He opened his eyes, pushed
his hat off his forehead, looked up at two angry faces. Now
what have I done? he wondered. He sat up, gave them back
a hard stare.

The dark-haired man spoke. 'Where did they go? The two
women who came in the Ford—where did they go?' His Italian
was slow, searching for the words. Tommaso felt better. He
replied with a torrent of phrases, purposely hurried, and felt
still better as he saw the man was baffled.

'Not so fast! Where did they go!'

Tommaso looked at the hand on his shoulder. The man
released his grip. Then Tommaso looked around the meadow.
He shrugged. 'I was asleep.'

'They were here. A blonde in a blue coat, and a brunette,
taller, with smooth hair.'

'I didn't see any blonde.' Tommaso's shoulder was gripped
again, this time by the big fellow. His hand was strong, and the
pressure painful. 'No blonde. No tall brunette.'

'But there was a blue coat?'

Hurriedly, as the fingers dug deeper into his shoulder,
Tommaso said, 'There was a tall red-haired girl in a blue coat.'

Jan said to Milan, 'I saw a redhead with a bunch of kids.
What did they do—switch coats, wear wigs?'

'And the other woman?' Milan persisted. 'She was of
medium height. What colour of hair?'

'Black.'

'Wearing what?'

'A raincoat.'

'They drove here in the Ford? And they went up there?'
Milan pointed to the stone steps.

Tommaso hesitated. The thumb on his shoulder found a
nerve. He gasped.

'Everyone goes up there,' he said. He cursed himself for the
tears of pain that welled up in his eyes.

'Now,' Milan said to Jan, 'we know exactly what we are
looking for. Come on! We've wasted enough time.'

Jan slowly released his grip on the Italian's shoulder. 'He
wasted it for us. How would he look with his jaw broken?' Jan

moved away, smiling broadly. 'But why the rush? We've got them trapped. They are stuck on that rock pile.'

Milan had an afterthought. He halted, came back to the bus driver.

'Is there any other path down from the chapel?'

'There is one that leads to the highway on the other side of the hill.' And just let them try that one, thought Tommaso with considerable satisfaction.

'I didn't see it when we drove down the highway.'

'There are trees that hide it.'

The two men exchanged glances, and then moved briskly towards the steps. 'I'll break more than a jaw,' Jan was saying to Milan, 'if that dumb peasant gave them time to get away.' He took a silencer out from one pocket, a revolver from the other, and fitted them together. 'Might as well be prepared,' he said. He began the ascent. 'Why the change in our instructions?'

'You heard Ludvik.'

'But he didn't explain.'

'Why should he? Prague doesn't explain to him.'

They climbed on. 'What's so important about a handbag?' Jan asked. 'We have to bust our guts getting it, but we don't examine the contents. Repeat don't.'

'That's right.'

'And we don't go into Switzerland.' Jan mimicked Ludvik's voice: 'Prague is sending in a new team.'

And no explanation of that either, thought Milan. They don't think we're good enough for the final play-off.

'Any idea who they will be?'

Milan had his ideas. 'No,' he said. 'And save your breath. Keep your eyes open for a raincoat and a black wig. That's the main target.'

'Full of tricks, aren't they?'

Milan saved his own breath. At the pace Jan had set, he needed it. The stone steps were irregular, the spaces widening between them. The trees were thinning out at this level. Visibility became surprisingly good. He could see no movement. The two women must have climbed right to the top. They would hardly have risked stepping off this staircase, rough as it was: for on either side the ground sloped steeply, boulders and slabs of rock balancing on rough terraces, roots of shrubs and trees holding the whole precarious mixture from sliding downhill.

Now the summit was near. There were no more stone steps, just a path of pine needles weaving between the sparse trees. 'Remember this well,' Milan told Jan. 'They have never seen us. They do not know who we are or why we are here. So we can work quite close.'

'Suits me.'

'But not in sight of any witnesses. Got that?'

'No witnesses this time,' Jan agreed with a jagged grin. He almost laughed as his mind jumped to Krieger's brush with Ludvik's two special agents. Ludvik should have used us, he thought: Krieger would never have left us on the floor of the Red Lion. 'Hey,' he added, 'what about that other American —the young one? Where is he now?' Krieger was back at his hotel: so Ludvik had reported. But David Mennery?

'That's Ludvik's problem. He'll solve it.'

'Unless Mennery gives him the slip.' Graz still rankled with Jan.

'Quiet!' warned Milan. The path had eased into an open patch of meadow, long grasses bending before the breeze. In its centre was a very small church, complete with miniature steeple. A separate bell tower, covered on top, open at its sides, stood almost at the opposite side of the clearing. Just beyond it, Milan could see the beginning of the other path that led down to the highway. The bus driver hadn't lied after all. There it was. And presenting a new problem too: had the two women already started down that second trail? No, Milan decided. They didn't know they were being followed, so why should they run?

'Keep that gun out of sight,' he warned as a stream of children began pouring out of the church. Three nuns were trying to shape them into a single line. An old man with bent shoulders was hobbling over to the bell tower. There was no sign of the two women.

'What the devil are they all doing up here?' Jan asked angrily. The whole situation was beyond him. The bell began ringing. 'And what's that for? Someone dead?'

'We'll try the church,' Milan decided. It was no more than twenty full paces away from them. The bell tower was even less. It was a tight squeeze, up on this one flat stretch of ground.

And all the better. 'We'll take them out with a gun at their ribs and get them on to that other path.'

Easy, thought Jan as he followed Milan across the grass. Women always listened to threats: one scream and I'll shoot into the children. They'd believe that too; just long enough, anyway, to let us start down towards the highway. Then after it's all over, Milan and I will keep on going, reach the road, walk back to the picnic ground. 'We missed our friends,' we'll tell that fat Italian if he is still around. 'Too bad.' Yeah, too bad. And almost too easy. Ludvik should have sent us after Krieger and Mennery, and let the new help—so sure of themselves, weren't they?—take care of the kindergarten.

Milan stopped to speak to a nun. Just checking, Jan supposed. A careful type, Milan, but he worries too much about failure. Bad luck, that's what we've had. Until now. Get a move on, he told Milan silently: you're wasting time.

But it hadn't been wasted. It saved them a useless search in the church. Milan was saying, his voice low and clipped, 'They were here. Ten minutes ago. The nun says they must have gone back to the meadow.'

'Like hell they did.' Jan's anger exploded into action. He turned, headed past the tower, brushed aside the old goat with his ding-dong bell. Milan moved with equal speed, the long grass switching at his ankles. Behind him a nun called anxiously, 'Not there, *signore*!' Without a backward glance, he hurried on. 'Not there, *signore*!' echoed the old man, pausing in his rope-pulling to make his warning heard.

Fools, Milan raged as he plunged down a path carpeted with pine needles. Don't they have enough brains to realize that we'd have met Irina Kusak and the American girl if they had gone back to the meadow? No, this is the direction they took. And perhaps by plan—to reach the highway and circle back to get their car, drive on to Switzerland. Another failure? Not if we hurry. They are only ten minutes away, even less by now. They can't match our speed. They'll be careful on this trail; it's rough going. We'll catch up with them before they reach that damned road. 'Hurry!' he urged Jan's broad back. Unnecessarily. Jan was really travelling, his revolver now in his left hand to leave his right one free to steady him against a jutting crag, a gnarled trunk, a steep bank.

Rough and getting rougher, Milan thought. Could the

women have come down here? Yet they must have. There were only two paths down this forsaken hill, and they didn't take the one we came up. That's certain. So we've got them, he told himself, glancing at the steep drop on his left. On that side, with only a soft shoulder of earth and gravel to edge the path, an emptiness where bushes and trees had been swept away by a fall of boulders, the ground now sloped into a naked precipice. Safe enough, he reassured himself, if you kept close to the uphill bank where bushes and trees still grew, and steadied yourself with a firm right hand as Jan was doing. Underfoot the pine needles had given way to loose stones. He preferred that: it seemed a better grip for his lightweight shoes and their smooth leather soles. He was controlling his slips and slides as expertly as Jan. He was keeping up with Jan, too. Descents were easy. He might not know much about mountain climbing, but this place was only a rocky molehill compared to some of the giants he had seen today. 'Careful!' he called out once. Unnecessarily, again. Jan regained his footing easily, grinned, said over his shoulder, 'Any minute now. I think I saw something.'

And just then, the path curved to the right, around an outthrust of bank whose side was deeply eroded, exposing a tangle of dry roots from the dying trees above. Jan suddenly braked, almost fell, his arms outstretched in warning. Milan tried to halt, but the thick layer of loose stones slid with him, and his feet could find no hold. He toppled forward, his full weight coming down on Jan's shoulders to send them both sprawling. But they were still on the path. Milan stared at the edge, only an arm's length away, and tried not to think of the sheer drop beneath it.

Carefully he got on to his knees, ignored the sharp bite of jagged stones, concentrated on rising to his feet without dislodging another small avalanche. His right hand stretched out to the bank and caught hold of a tendril of root. It held. And it gave him confidence, helped to pull him up. He could stand, legs still trembling with the effort; but his feet were secure enough to let him raise his eyes and look down the path ahead of him. First, he noticed the revolver gleaming in the sunlight. It had been jerked from Jan's grip by the force of his fall and landed behind him. Jan was already on his feet, legs straddled to balance his stance on a loose bed of gravel. He was out of reach of the bank, and—like his revolver—too near the brink. But it wasn't the precipice that worried Jan. He was pointing ahead. 'There!' he shouted back, his eyes fixed on something farther down the path. 'There!'

The curve of the bank blocked Milan's view. He edged out. The stones underfoot were safe enough if he stepped with care. He stopped, appalled, as he saw what must have halted Jan so abruptly. Part of the hillside had slipped away. The path was gone, obliterated by a scree of smashed rocks. Beyond that, nothing: only the sky, and the far-off treetops on another hill.

For a moment, Milan's mind was blank. Then his first thought was of the women, those goddamned women. We've lost them. They've tricked us. They are—'But where *are* they?' he cried out in anger.

'There!' Jan shouted again. 'You blind fool, don't you see them? We've got them. We've got them!'

Milan let go of his hold on the root, took a few cautious steps around the curve. Now he could see. Standing squarely on the path between them and the rockslide, were two women.

Chapter Twenty

'NO!' IRINA SAID, as she and Jo had reached the doorway of the little church. The children had already crowded in, the nun trying to hush their excitement. Irina backed away. 'No, no. Useless. We'll be trapped.'

Jo gave one last glance inside Santa Maria. There were no elaborate hiding places here; no corners concealed with screens; no other doorways. Still, the church was shelter, and the small field that lay in front of it was wide open. Better to stay in the church with the children, wait until Dave came climbing up to Santa Maria. He would. Once he arrived at the picnic grounds, saw their car *and* the Fiat, nothing would keep him from climbing up here. 'Look,' she said, as she caught up with Irina, 'there is such a thing as sanctuary.'

'To these men?' Irina shook her head.

'But they couldn't make any move against us with all these children and nuns around.'

Irina almost laughed at her simplicity. 'Wouldn't they?' Her eyes searched round the field.

'Then where do we——'

'Over there. That other path—beside that bell tower.' Irina was already on her way. 'It's the only choice.'

There was no use wasting time on argument. Jo capitulated, followed at a run. She even volunteered to go first, once they reached the new trail. But as she manoeuvred down a slope of pine needles, she couldn't resist saying, 'You're so damn sure.'

'About these men—yes.' And as Jo didn't answer, Irina said, 'I know their type. I've seen them at work. You haven't. They'll keep following.'

'Even down here? They'll have more sense than——'

'Once they have searched the church, they will follow. They never give up.'

But I do? We'll see about that. 'I hope you're wrong,' Jo said, her voice sharp and abrupt. Irina didn't reply. They clambered down the path in silence.

Their pace was surprisingly good. Jo tried to keep it steady: eyes ignoring everything except the ground in front of her, one careful foot before the other, even steps, no skips or jumps. This really would surprise Bob Whitfield, she thought as she remembered her handsome Englishman of three years ago, that mountaineering maniac. She had been his despair every time they started down a hillside. ('Leaping like a bloody mountain goat,' he had called out in disgust. 'Stop it, you idiot!' he kept yelling after her. 'Take it easy. Easy!') Where was Bob Whitfield now, just when she needed him? What would he have done at this spot, for instance? The left side of the path had developed a precipice.

'I'm sorry,' said Irina, breaking their long silence. 'This was my decision, and it was not a good one. This trail——' She shook her head. 'I never imagined it would become anything like this.' She looked in dismay at the rough ground under foot. No more pine needles and soft earth. Only harsh fragments of rock, loose and sharp. 'I'm sorry.'

Indeed you should be, thought Jo.

'I thought we'd find a clump of bushes or trees where we could take cover and let the men pass us,' said Irina. 'But there's nothing—not here. Unless up on the bank above us. Could we get up there?'

'No way.' The bank rose steeply on their right. It had become a high wall of dry earth packed with gravel and broken ends of roots. 'We'll keep on going.'

'How far have we come?'

'A good third of the distance, I'd guess. Perhaps almost half.' From the hilltop above them Santa Maria's bell began to ring. The children didn't stay long: we'd have found ourselves in a very lonely little chapel, Jo realized. She glanced back at Irina. 'Perhaps your decision wasn't such a bad one after all. Hear that?' The little bell tolled gently. For thee and me, thought Jo. But she smiled, said encouragingly, 'Just take it slowly. It's safe enough if we are careful. Keep close to the bank. Don't look to the left. Irina!' Irina's eyes were hypnotized by the precipice. 'Don't look at the edge! Don't look down!' That was old Bob speaking, all right, bless his one-track mind.

Jo relaxed as Irina obeyed her, and turned carefully to lead once more.

The bell was still ringing, fading into the silence of the surrounding hills. There was a nearer sound, too; and harsher. Jo listened to the sharp clatter of falling stones. Her face tightened. Irina had been right. The men were following. 'Let's get around this bend.' The path curved to the right, and perhaps down there they'd find some place to clamber up the bank: it couldn't go on rising steeply for ever. Or could it? 'But no wild hurry,' she warned, as much for her own benefit as for Irina's. The impulse to slip and slide was strong. That's what the men were doing. 'Fools, utter fools,' she said. 'Just listen to them.' Or perhaps, she thought, we shouldn't. They were coming too close. 'They'll have to slow down soon. This stretch of path is a real brute. Oh, heavens——'

'Then let's not think about it.'

'How do I do that?' Jo asked, balancing herself in time from an unexpected slip. To her amazement she heard Irina laugh. 'What's so funny?'

'That bottle you've been carrying all this way in your left hand.'

'What about the handbag you've got strung around your shoulder?' Jo countered, but she began to smile. The silly little interchange had eased the tightened nerve ends. Her mind stopped its mad whirl into paralysing fear. We laugh that we may not weep, she thought, as she led Irina safely round the bulge of the high bank, and reached a broader stretch of path. Here the ground was less treacherous. It felt secure enough under her feet to let her raise her eyes to see what lay ahead. Nothing. The path had completely vanished, swallowed up in a massive landslide.

Irina came to stand beside her. They stared, unbelieving. The hillside before them had fallen away, perhaps last spring, perhaps the year before. What did it matter? thought Jo hopelessly.

There was nothing left for any foothold, just a huge spill of smashed stones spreading down into the ravine below.

Jo regained her breath. 'Let's move closer to the bank. They won't catch sight of us until they come round the curve.' And the men were almost there. 'You know, all I can feel is anger.

227

It's strange, but that's all I feel. Anger.' She faced uphill, waiting for that first glimpse of the hunters.

Irina nodded, her eyes watchful as she freed the strap of her handbag from its tight hold on her shoulder and gripped it in her hand. From the path above them, just around the curve of the bank, there was a heavy crash. Jo said quietly, 'Someone took a spill.' The next moment they were staring at a man, fallen on his face, who came slithering down on a toboggan of gravel and loose stones. Braking desperately with the heels of his hands and the toes of his shoes, he managed to stop the slide before it emptied him into the abyss. It was Jan. And the other? He must have fallen too, but he was out of sight. 'Keep back,' Irina said to Jo. 'I'm the one they want.'

She stepped out from the bank, watching the man as he began raising himself on his knees. I'm too slow, Irina thought as she took her first careful steps up the slope: he will be on his feet before I can reach him. And he will have a gun. Where is it? Still in his belt, or in some pocket? That's the hand I must aim for. 'Go back!' she told Jo. Jo said nothing, just kept following.

Jan was standing erect now, but not too certain of his balance. His feet sank and slipped among the layers of loose pebbles, which he had carried along with him in his fall and were now piled into a soft mound around his ankles and legs. He was a tall man, strong, and his weight did not help. 'There!' he was calling out, pointing at Irina, 'there!' She heard another voice, sharp with anger. Jan answered with a furious shout, and Milan the dark-haired one, came into view. He stopped abruptly, stared down the path, then at the two girls who faced Jan.

'No closer!' Jo warned Irina. She was only eight feet away from Jan, even less. But Irina took two more careful steps, stopping short of the heavy pile-up of loose stones and gravel. Oh no, thought Jo in anguish: he could make a lunge for Irina; he's watching her, he's getting ready.

'Behind you!' Milan yelled. 'The gun is behind you!' Jan's eyes were fixed on Irina.

'And this?' Irina asked. She held up the handbag. He reached to grab her. 'Take it!' she cried, and hurled it at his face.

His arms went up instinctively to ward off the blow. His

228

movement was too rapid, too abrupt, and his foothold uncertain. He tottered; he might have regained his balance except that Milan was shouting again and he was half turning to try to find the revolver that lay on the stones a short distance behind him. The loose surface under his feet shifted and slipped over the soft shoulder of the path, began spilling into the precipice. He made a wild effort to jump free from the small avalanche that trapped his ankles, swept him along in its sudden rush. He landed heavily on the shoulder. It crumbled, and he plunged over the side. The handbag fell with him, jolted around in the stream of stones that rattled over the edge and clattered downwards. A long, long fall.

Irina stood very still. Jo gripped her arm, pulled her back to the bank, felt her begin to tremble. 'Stay there,' Jo said, 'and hold on!' Her own legs were weak. For a moment, she had thought the whole path was going to break away. She steadied herself. At least her mind was still functioning. Remarkable how cool and detached it had become: all the ifs and buts and maybes were over, and there was nothing but certainty left. The men had not been simply following Irina. They had come to kill, and one of them had died trying to do just that. Everything was silent now, as if the hillside were holding its breath.

Milan had not moved. He was still staring at the crumbled edge where Jan had vanished without even a cry. He was standing uphill from them, no more than twenty feet away, where the path curved round the bank. But that was all the advantage he had; he was in the middle of a stretch of sharp loose stones. He had at least ten steps to take before he left that rough bed and reached the more solid ground—bare rock that had been swept clean of pebbles—where Jo stood.

Milan's eyes shifted, staring now at the revolver. It lay halfway between Jo and himself, on the last fringe of loose fragments. He tried a few steps, felt them slip, halted.

He is calculating something, Jo thought as she started carefully towards him with the empty wine bottle grasped now in her right hand; but so am I. The revolver has a silencer, all ready for some quiet work—and that was the way it should have been; no loud noises to attract attention, everything neat and tidy and unnoticed. He'd still prefer it that way. What about his own gun? Surely he has one—yes, he's drawing it now; and no silencer that I can see. He has decided the revolver isn't worth the risk of starting another small landslide. Or will he still try for it? He is inching forward. Cautious, and not so sure of himself as he usually is when he is waving that little pistol around. He can't watch his footing, either, not with his eyes on me. A small slip there—enough to make him switch his gun to his left hand, grab a tree root to steady himself. But I'm too close to Jan's revolver; and that he can't allow. He's raising his left arm, and I'm so near him he can't miss. How is my aim?

With all her strength, Jo threw the bottle, caught him on the chest. His arm jerked, the bullet went high. She made a desperate reach for the revolver, heard a second shot. I'm dead, she thought. But nothing hit her, not even a splinter of rock. She lifted her head from the bed of stones on which she had fallen. The second shot hadn't come from Milan. He had swerved round to look up the path behind him. He fired at some new target, but his left hand was unsure, his feet slipping, his body twisted back against the bank as he still held on to that root.

'Drop the gun!' a man's voice called out. 'Drop it!'

I can't move, thought Jo. I have the revolver in my hand, and I can't move. She could feel the loose stones stir uneasily beneath her. Someone reached her, caught her arm. Irina was saying, 'Slowly, Jo. It's all right. Slowly.' She got to her feet, Irina steadying her, pulling her on to safer ground. 'I *told* you to stay back!' Jo said sharply. And then, she was weeping.

You didn't stay back, either, Irina thought, as her eyes watched the path again. 'David is up there,' she said quietly. That had been his voice, but the bank hid him from view. 'He's coming,' she told Jo, as she listened to David's footsteps, still a little distance away. And then she saw that Milan hadn't dropped his gun. He had backed a step, using the curve of the bank as protection, his shoulders drawn against it, his head turned uphill as he waited. He had changed his pistol from left to right hand. Now he was pointing it slowly.

Irina pulled the revolver out of Jo's grasp, raised it waveringly as she moved forward. 'Yes,' she called out, 'drop your gun. If he doesn't shoot you, I will.'

Milan's head swerved round towards her voice. Angry eyes, incredulous, stared down at her for a split second. Instinctively she dodged close to the bank as he took a quick shot. It missed.

He had to sidestep out on to the path, to fire from a surer angle.

This time David aimed for the man and caught him on the shoulder. Milan staggered, his feet out of control. David saw him pitch forward on to his knees, his gun flying in a wide arc out over the precipice.

David made his way down to the curve, came round it as fast as he could—cursing and swearing at each slip of stones. This wasn't a path. At this point it was a scree. But at least he could put the Beretta back into his pocket, use his hands to grip and balance.

Milan was still on his knees. He was at the very edge of the path. He was not moving. He just knelt there, holding his wounded arm as if to silence its pain, staring down at the chasm beside him.

The hell with him, thought David, and then saw Irina. Irina and Jo. Both together. Both safe. Safe. A few more steps and he was beside them. He took Irina in his arms, hugged her violently. Then he looked at Jo (dried tearstains on her white cheeks?) and hugged her too.

He said, 'Let's get back to the car. Can you manage it?'

Irina nodded. David kissed her, hugged her again, kissed her once more.

'What about him?' Jo was looking at Milan.

'We'll leave him to explain to the police. Come on—come on——' he urged. 'Jo, you first. Then Irina. I'll be behind you.'

'Police?'

'Someone must have heard those shots. I just want us to get clear before anyone starts asking questions.' He picked up a forty-five, complete with silencer, that lay near Irina's feet. Thank God Milan didn't fire at me with that, he thought.

Jo said, 'That was Jan's.'

'Where is he?' David looked sharply along the path and, only now, saw its final end, abrupt, terrifying. God, he thought again, and looked at the two girls.

'*Sotto!*' said Jo, and gestured to the precipice. She was recovering. She even smiled at her grim joke.

David tested the revolver's safety catch, found it was already in place, and threw the gun where Jo's arm pointed.

Irina said, 'It didn't work, anyway. It wouldn't shoot. I——'

'Was the safety catch off?' Jo asked.

David said, 'Get moving, both of you. Talk later.'

231

They didn't look back. They rounded the curve, taking it with the utmost care. After that, the trail seemed almost easy. They reached the high field. The little church watched them pass through the long soft grass and start down the steps towards the meadow.

'Is that the bell?' asked Jo, listening to a shiver of sound, a gentle murmur that seemed to hang in the air for a brief moment. 'There it is again! Who is——'

'Keep moving,' David told her. 'It's just the late-afternoon breeze playing around it.'

'Bells talk to themselves?'

'Keep moving, Jo.' He shook his head. Women, he decided, were incredible.

They came on to the meadow, a peaceful place with empty tables and spreading shadows. Irina's weight was leaning hard on David's arm, as if she had got this far only by sheer will-power. Jo also was beginning to sag in spite of herself.

'Don't relax. Not yet,' he told her.

'Couldn't we lie down on that beautiful grass? Just five minutes?' she pleaded.

'You'd be asleep in three.' He started towards the Mercedes. He had parked it beside the Ford. (Don't think of the way you swung in here, he reminded himself, or what you felt when you saw no sign of them—only that empty car and a white Fiat.) The transfer of luggage would be no problem. But the Ford itself certainly was. 'What do we do with it?' he asked Jo, nodding towards her car, knowing exactly what he wanted done but hesitant about suggesting it.

'Leave it. It can be picked up later.'

'And no questions asked?' To save time, he began jamming the baggage into a back corner of the Mercedes. Irina was already in her seat, her head drooping, her eyes closed.

'Oh yes,' Jo said slowly, 'there's always that.' She sighed. 'I had better drive it out.' She hesitated. 'I suppose.' She waited for him to say they could leave the Ford exactly where it was.

'That's a good idea. But only drive for a mile. I'll pick you up at the side of the highway.' He found Jo's handbag in the Ford too, and gave it to her. She took it, as though it had been the most natural thing to leave her handbag lying around in an unlocked car. The keys were even in the ignition. There must have been a bad moment of panic, a mad flight, he thought, and tried not to imagine the scene.

'Driving north?' Jo asked slowly.

'That's the way to the border.'

'Just making sure.' She sounded apologetic. 'Funny, isn't it? My mind is going all fuzzy.' Up on the hillside—well, I never did so much cool thinking in my whole life. 'Funny,' she repeated as she got into the Ford.

Would she manage it? David watched her back out, and leave. Then he got into the Mercedes and followed. Irina's eyes opened. She was not asleep after all. 'Couldn't find your handbag,' he told her. He was really worried. 'Did you drop it? Where?' I can't go back up that damned trail.

'It went over the cliff with Jan.'

God in heaven, he thought. Had Jan got that close to her?

'I've got my passport,' she told him, noticing the expression on his face. 'It's in here.' She touched a pocket of her coat. 'But there's something else—I've been trying to think how to tell you—oh, David!'

'What?'

She lifted up his map, opened it, and said, 'Tarasp——'

'I know,' he said.

'It was an accident. I was angry and I had a pencil in my hand and I pointed at the name and the car went round a curve and I lurched and——'

'Yes, yes,' he said. 'Stop thinking about it, Irina.' That's a good one, he thought, considering how I can't stop thinking about it myself.

'But they will be in Tarasp to meet us.'

'Perhaps. Perhaps not. It depends on how much time we can make. Or how complicated it is for them to get there.' He kept his voice reassuring. And it worked.

Irina relaxed. She let her head drop back against the seat. 'Yes,' she said, as she saw Jo standing by the Ford at the side of the highway, 'they have their problems too. They seem so invincible. And yet——' She closed her eyes. She said softly, 'It was Alois who chose that handbag for me. It was his, in a way.'

David pulled up ahead of the Ford. Jo had released a valve in a rear tyre. It was settling slowly. 'Need a lift?' David asked with a grin, as she attempted a small run towards him. She settled for a walk, and not too fast either.

At that moment, an approaching car slowed up. Three men. David's heart missed a definite beat. Then, as the car halted beside him, he saw one police uniform. The other two were civilians—country style, with black waistcoats and silver buttons and small peaked hats.

'Have you been here long?' the policeman called over. He was young and brisk.

'Just arrived,' said David. He began to explain about giving a lift to this lady in distress (Jo was now standing by the Mercedes) but his Italian tipped over into French, and he ended in frustration.

The policeman looked at Jo, and stepped out on to the road. But it was only to salute her and ask, in a gentler fashion, how long she had been here.

'Not too long. I had trouble with my car, so I stopped. This gentleman will take me to the nearest garage.'

'Ah, the lady speaks Italian!' the policeman said with relief. 'Did the lady hear any shots from the hill behind us?'

'Yes,' said Jo. 'Probably hunters.'

'Not on *that* hill.' The policeman's handsome dark eyes were grave. 'It is a place of pilgrimage.'

'I could have been mistaken. I was a little distance away. And there are so many hills.'

The farmers jumped into the discussion. *This* hill, they insisted, it was this hill. They knew where shots came from. Besides, it was on Santa Maria's picnic meadow that Tommaso reported he had met two men—disagreeable types—one carrying a handgun of some kind. Tommaso was sure of that. He had seen it just as the two men were about to take the path to Santa Maria. Yes, he had seen a pistol. Tommaso had good eyes.

David listened to the rapid flood of Italian, and caught one word out of three. This could go on forever, he thought, and leaned over to open the rear door for Jo as a delicate hint.

Jo pulled it wide, put one foot inside, gave the policeman a warm smile. 'Where is the nearest service station?' she asked. She listened to his instructions, said 'Thank you so much,' and got into the car.

A crisp salute, a wave of Jo's hand, and David was driving

off. Once they were out of sight, he put on speed. 'And who the devil is Tommaso?' he asked.

But Jo had collapsed in her corner of the back seat, and Irina was drifting off into real sleep. All we'll ever know, he thought, is that Tommaso had good eyes.

Jo said, 'Just give me fifteen minutes, David. I'll spell you then. You've been driving all day, and——' Her voice merged into silence.

He let them both sleep until the Italian frontier post was almost in sight. Passage through it was painless. Then the Swiss border with its small formalities; and that too was behind them. There was still plenty of daylight, an hour at least, possibly more, and Tarasp less than thirty miles south.

Chapter Twenty-one

WALTER KRIEGER stepped on to good Swiss earth a few minutes after six o'clock and paused briefly to watch the light plane that had brought him from Bolzano. It was still bob-bobbing its way, this time into the wind to take off for the flight back to its own nest. But it had got him here; and that was something he wouldn't have bet on fifteen minutes ago, when they were skirting the massive peaks that marked the Italian-Swiss frontier. Next time he had to make a journey between agonized ridges, he'd hire himself a nice compact jet —like that one over there, at the side of the airfield—and no more vintage two-seater jobs. He gave an amused glance at the little plane as it rose and headed away from the broad green valley back towards the tormented shapes of sheer rock. Well, he thought, if hummingbirds can make twice-yearly flights between Brazil and New England, who am I to doubt we could make it to Samaden?

His attention switched back to the small jet. It had completed its landing as his plane was approaching the Samaden airport; now it was drawn neatly out of the way. There were still two crew members standing beside it. On guard? He studied the plane for a moment, and his frown deepened. Then he continued his way towards the formalities: passport and papers and general proof of innocence. They wouldn't take long. His legal residence was in Switzerland, and his firm in Vevey was practically a national institution. Besides, he used this small airport for occasional weekends at St Moritz. He wasn't exactly a stranger. All of which were little drops of oil to help the machinery of officialdom turn smoothly. He was not disappointed. He had no luggage (his bag was still in Merano, he hadn't even gone up to his room once he had picked up Dave's message) and that hastened the process.

There was only one delay. The car, complete with driver—he had radioed ahead for them—had not yet arrived. 'It should be here any moment, Herr Krieger,' said the man in charge of passengers' predicaments. 'There is a village festival today. Processions make traffic—well, uncertain. You understand?'

Krieger nodded. He consoled himself with the fact that Samaden was on the highway that led north, straight to Tarasp. Thirty-three miles. . . . With luck he could be there in half an hour. With luck, and no more processions or Saturday slow-ups.

The man glanced at Krieger's bandaged hands. 'I can see why you requested a driver with the car,' he said sympathetically.

'Nothing serious. Just slight burns.' Nothing to what it could have been, Krieger thought, and certainly nothing compared with what had been intended. He looked at the man's quiet, strictly Swiss-movement face, and wondered what would happen to it if he was to say, 'Back in Merano, in a peaceful courtyard behind a reputable hotel, the door of my car was fixed so that when I got in and closed it, the driver's seat would blow up. But a couple of ten-year-olds came wandering around, opened the door just to find out what the inside of a big American car looked like, and then saw me approaching, and slammed the door shut. Yes, that did it. How was that for a send-off? As for the boys—no damage to one: a partly burned jacket on the other. The flames didn't get full hold, could be soon beaten out. So he was left with only a scare, and I with some skin off my hands. And a problem. How to get out of Merano? Solution: a twenty-mile ride by taxi to the Bolzano airport.' But Krieger refrained. Instead, he looked at the bandages, thoroughly soaked in good old bicarbonate of soda (courtesy of the hotel kitchen), and said, 'The damnable thing is that I can't fill my pipe.'

The man lost some of his worry about the delay. The American was taking it well—not like those others who had arrived just before him. 'I'm truly sorry about this inconvenience.'

'Not your fault. I just chose the wrong time to get here. By the way, what's a Russian-built plane doing in Samaden? Don't tell me they are now jet-setting here for a week-end in St Moritz!'

237

The Swiss laughed. 'Just a short visit.' He dropped his voice. 'They aren't Russians. Czechs. Three Czechs and one American.'

'You don't say.' Krieger was casual.

'From Innsbruck, I understand.'

Krieger was all innocent astonishment. 'I'd have thought Prague more likely.'

'I believe the flight originated there.'

'Ah, they just stopped briefly at Innsbruck?' Odd, distinctly odd, thought Krieger. He looked around him. The place was almost empty. Most week-enders had arrived either yesterday or this morning. 'They seem to have left. They must have been luckier with their transportation than I was.'

'No, no. They are still waiting. For two cars. Nothing to do with us, of course. We didn't make the arrangements.' (But that didn't keep them from blaming me, as if I were responsible for a traffic jam.)

'Two cars?' Krieger was amused. 'They travel in style. Where are they now?'

'In a waiting room.' The Swiss was unable to repress a small grin. 'Quite by themselves.'

'Diplomats, possibly. Who else would be so discreet and retiring?'

'Yes, indeed,' said the man, something of a diplomat himself. So far I'll talk, his polite smile seemed to say, but no farther.

'Well,' Krieger said, 'I think I'll step outside and try a little willpower on my car—hurry it up. Or have you the telephone number of the garage? We might jog them a little.'

The Swiss gave him its number, and then had second thoughts. 'But your car is on its way. I'm sure of that. There's really no need to call.' And it's possibly my brother-in-law who is driving, he worried. 'It might just complicate——'

'Of course,' Krieger agreed. 'I don't want to get the driver into any trouble.'

'It really is not his fault. Believe me, Herr Krieger.'

'I do, I do.' Krieger gave a preoccupied smile, and moved towards the front entrance. His mind was giving him no rest: it jumped from one guess to another. Cut it out, he told himself. Innsbruck, plus an American, doesn't necessarily mean that Mark Bohn was instructed to get off the train on his way to

238

Munich, just so that a new team of Hrádek's experts from Prague could pick him up there and bring him along. Why should they? Because they think we still trust him? Because he's their pet Trojan horse? Cut it out, he told himself once more: why the hell would Hrádek's boys be coming to this part of the world, anyway? They didn't know anything about Tarasp. Switzerland, yes—if Bohn had added up his observations correctly. But Tarasp? No. That was something else again.

Yet Krieger still couldn't persuade himself; not fully. The question mark at the back of his mind was too big and bold, an instinctive doubt that cold calm reason could not answer. When his car arrived a minute later, he told its driver to wait; he had forgotten something.

The driver was philosophic. All that rush for nothing, he thought as he watched his passenger step out of sight. Then he drew the car farther along the kerb to leave plenty of space for two new arrivals: high-powered jobs, these were, and not a local hire at that. The chauffeurs were not known to him either. Stolid-looking men, but—at this moment—rattled. One of them was running inside to look for his clients. What was all the hurry? 'Take it easy, *du Kerl*; you'll live longer,' Krieger's driver called out. He shook his head, pulled out a tattered German paperback, and found the dog-ear that marked his place in chapter eleven of *The Oregon Trail*. How was that fight around the wagon train going to end?

The four men left the waiting room, with the chauffeur leading the way to the two cars. He was full of explanations. 'That's enough!' Jiri Hrádek said. 'Keep moving.' He was dressed in quiet dark grey, unobtrusive; but he was tall, straight-backed, and carried himself well, and nothing could disguise a certain authority in his manner. The Swiss, watching him leave with his two subordinates on either side, considered him a handsome man—strong features, carefully brushed dark hair, a healthy colour in his tanned cheeks—not like the other Czechs who had arrived with him, big potato faces. But they were neat enough in their dress and in their movements. The American who walked closely behind them was a mess by contrast, his hair ridiculous, his jacket wrinkled.

The Swiss looked away before they'd notice his interest, but he had the strange feeling that the American wasn't altogether a happy member of the tight little group. Then the sharp Swiss eyes saw the other American, back again, standing by the telephones, his head averted from the hall. If it hadn't been for the bandaged hands, the Swiss thought, I'd never have noticed him. He must have slipped in by a side door while I was watching the main entrance for his car to arrive. 'Mr Krieger!' he called in English. 'No need to telephone. Your car is outside.'

Krieger appeared not to hear, but his hand gave up the painful pretence of dialling. He stood very still, as if he were listening to the receiver cradled between shoulder and chin. God, he was praying, make this look good, and Mark Bohn deaf, and my Swiss friend dumb. But the man was calling out again, 'Mr Krieger!' He sounded nearer, as though he were hurrying in this direction. Then his footsteps stopped. Krieger dared not risk a backward glance. He could move out by the side door, and make it to the car. But that would give Tarasp no advance warning. Desperately he dialled, and managed it too. All he had to say was one word, 'Firetrap!' and Hugh McCulloch would take action.

But he didn't even get the chance to speak. There was a light footstep behind him, a hand pressed hard against the back of his neck, a deep sting. And then a sagging of his knees. He tried to yell out, and couldn't. He half turned as he began to slip. He saw his helpful Swiss, now with his back to him, engaged in conversation by one of the Czechs. He looked up at the other, who had caught him and lowered him to the ground. No sound. No sound at all. The receiver dangled, a distant voice came through, 'Who's there? Who's there?' Krieger's eyes closed.

The Czech replaced the receiver, stepped briskly over to the Swiss, tapped his shoulder. 'There is a man over by the telephone who seems to be ill.'

'What?' The Swiss whirled round, stared at Krieger lying motionless.

'I think you'd better call an ambulance,' the Czech said. 'Perhaps a small heart attack?' He watched the horrified Swiss run towards Krieger, calling out to two girls at the desk and the young man chatting with them. 'No one noticed,' he remarked with amusement as he began walking with his colleague to the door. Hrádek and his American were already on their way out.

'Very neat,' his friend agreed. And I didn't do such a bad job of distracting that Swiss dolt, either. All you had to do was to pour on the thanks for their kindness and efficiency, and you'd get them listening every time. 'No trouble at all.'

The pair reached the sidewalk, stopped briefly at Hrádek's car. Mark Bohn was already inside it, grey-faced and silent.

'Did he speak on the telephone?' Jiri Hrádek asked.

'He hadn't time.'

With a nod, Hrádek got into the car. It moved off at once. A good operation, not a moment wasted since he had halted at the sound of Krieger's name and sent Vaclav and Pavel to attend to the problem. They worked well together, needed little direction. In a way, he thought, this was a test run for tonight.

He looked over his shoulder. Vaclav and Pavel were already following in the second car. He relaxed completely. 'You know,' he said, smiling, 'we could have missed him. He was out of sight from us. Clever fellow, Krieger.'

Bohn said nothing.

Hrádek went on, 'I have a theory. I think it proved itself this evening.'

Still Bohn said nothing.

'I have a theory that it is the small unexpected things that are the most dangerous traps for a clever agent. He can cope with plans and counterplans, but a friendly voice calling out his name——' Hrádek shrugged his shoulders, laughed. Then he looked at Bohn. 'Get rid of that tense face,' he said abruptly.

'Krieger saw me.'

'You are travelling with three fellow journalists, all on their way to verify the fact that Jaromir Kusak is being restrained, against his will, from returning to his own country. That's your angle, Bohn. And we'll make it stick.'

Yes, thought Bohn, but how do I explain Tarasp? Of course I can say that I learned about it from Irina. That might hold, if Irina were out of earshot. 'There are just too many complications,' he said haltingly. Deeper and deeper; I didn't bargain for all this.

'There always are.'

'What if Krieger——'

241

'Forget Krieger. He is out of the picture.'

'Dead?' Bohn's stare was wild.

'Don't be ridiculous. A man dead in a small Swiss airport? There would be an investigation. Police, questions, suspicions, detentions. No, no. I intend to use that airfield tonight, without any of these embarrassments to hinder our leaving.'

'Do I go back with you?' That point had not been cleared up, and it troubled Bohn.

You can go to hell, thought Jiri Hrádek. He said, 'How about a weekend at St Moritz? You'll have your usual skilful news reports to write. I've got five papers lined up for them. Don't worry, your by-line won't be attached—not until the story is widely accepted and distributed round the world. Then you can take a bow, write your book, become the expert on the Jaromir Kusak affair. And you are, aren't you?'

That's to get my mind off Krieger, Bohn thought. 'How long will Krieger be unconscious?' I don't want to face him again. He's tough opposition, won't believe a word of my explanations.

'Long enough to suit us. Stop worrying about him, Bohn. He is definitely incapacitated.'

'And the others at Tarasp—will they be incapacitated too?' Bohn demanded. 'I want no part in it, Jiri. That's not my business.'

'Of course not. All you do is talk your way into Kusak's house. Pavel and Vaclav and their chauffeur will do the rest.'

'But I'll be there. I'll be linked up with——'

'Not if you are quick on your feet. I'll be nearby, waiting for you.'

That's right, thought Bohn, you'll be waiting, safely hidden in a dark car. 'Stupid of me,' he said. 'I forgot. You prefer remote control.'

'Don't you?'

Bohn managed a smile and eased his voice. 'But no violence, Jiri. That was your promise. I only agreed to make this journey if there was——'

'Of course. No violence.' Bohn's euphemism amused Hrádek. Violence, to Bohn, seemed only to mean murder. What did he think the attack on Krieger was? An act of nonviolence? 'We haven't many to deal with. McCulloch will be there, no doubt; and David Mennery. He must have arrived by this time—he

242

left Merano in mid-afternoon. Alone.' And he should never have been allowed to leave. A lost opportunity. Ludvik had slipped up badly on that Red Lion incident; he hadn't even known Mennery was there with Krieger until it was too late. 'What kind of man is this Mennery?'

But Bohn was still following his own startled thoughts. 'He left Merano alone? Without Irina? I don't believe it. You've been getting some inaccurate information, Jiri.'

There was a deep silence. Hrádek looked out at the small river flowing steadily down the valley along which they were travelling. 'I do not get inaccurate information,' he said. 'And why don't you believe it?'

He knows something about Irina and Dave, Bohn thought, but I'm not going to be the one who enlightens him further. Bearers of bad news have a tendency to get their heads chopped off. 'Well—Irina doesn't drive a car. Naturally, I thought she would keep travelling with Dave.'

'Naturally?' the word was emphasized.

'Just an assumption,' Bohn said hastily. 'I'll make another one: Jo Corelli is driving her to Tarasp. What's your estimated time for their arrival?'

Hrádek was still gazing at the narrow flow of water. 'So that's the River Inn,' he said. 'A small stream now but extremely ambitious. From here, it flows through Austria, edges Germany, and almost reaches Czechoslovakia. But at Passau its perseverance gives out, and it is swallowed up by the Danube. It reminds me of some people I've known.' Hrádek looked at Bohn.

Bohn ignored that. 'When do you expect Irina and Jo to arrive?' he persisted.

'I don't.'

'What?'

'They have been delayed.'

'How?'

'Nothing serious. A handbag missing. And a passport. Slight difficulty at the frontier—just enough to keep them from appearing while we are in the middle of negotiations with Kusak. We thought it better that way.'

Bohn relaxed, 'Much easier,' he agreed. 'So one of your men turned bag snatcher?'

Hrádek wasn't amused.

243

'A neat job,' Bohn tried. 'Just as well to make sure of Papa Kusak's diaries.' Hrádek still had no comment. 'You know,' Bohn went on, 'I've had a delightful thought. We aren't going to see Dave Mennery in Tarasp, after all.'

'Why not?'

'Irina would be waiting at the frontier for him with her new set of troubles. He's there with her right now.'

'Is he?' There was the suspicion of a smile on Hrádek's lips.

'You bet he is. The minute he saw them stopped at the——'

'He crossed the border before they reached it.'

Bohn shook his head. Hrádek certainly had been supplied with information all through the jet's flight from Innsbruck—there were even a telephone and a radio in this car—but the report on Dave did not make sense. 'I don't believe it. Dave wouldn't leave Irina behind in Merano.'

Hrádek turned away, kept looking out of the window. 'Tell me about Mennery and my wife.'

Bohn's eyebrows went up. 'Wife?' Divorced, surely; but tactfully Bohn avoided all mention of that. He was still trapped. 'Nothing,' he said, floundering for a safe reply, 'nothing of any importance. That is,' he added carefully as Hrádek's face swerved round to look at him, 'nothing that is connected with the business in hand.'

'I see,' Hrádek said, and was silent again.

He knows, thought Bohn. Just as well that I didn't give him a blank denial. And what are Dave and Irina to me, compared with Jiri's past favours—or future rewards? Jiri remembers his friends. And he's on the way up. Another few weeks, and he could be at the top.

Suddenly, to Bohn's relief, Hrádek came out of his black mood. 'I was reading a guidebook on the flight to Innsbruck,' he said, pleasant and genial once more. 'Did you know there are two Tarasps?'

Bohn stared at him, could only shake his head. That was a real shocker—if true.

'There is one near this highway—a village, apparently with a spa and a golf course. There is another, with quite a different approach, on the hill above it: it seems to be very small, just a castle and a few houses. Which is it?'

'The one marked on Dave's map.'

'And that was?'

'Beside the highway. I told you——'

'Show me.' Hrádek had unfolded his own map.

Bohn took it. 'This isn't the same map,' he objected. But he did find one Tarasp, near the highway. 'That's it.' He pointed. As for the other Tarasp, it was a blur. He couldn't read the name without holding the bloody map up to his nose. He peered hard, feeling ridiculous, and at last deciphered its thin tiny print. 'It's called Tarasp-Fontana,' he said. 'Not fair, Jiri, not fair.'

'It is still Tarasp, and that is what it is called in most guide-books. Fontana is the next hamlet, I suppose. People around here like to hyphenate their place names. You didn't see any Tarasp-Fontana marked on Mennery's map?'

'I couldn't have. I didn't have the time for any close work. What I saw was one word in normal print. Tarasp.'

'Then that settles it.' Hrádek folded the map, dropped it within easy reach. He added, half-jokingly, 'And you had better be right.'

Bohn let that go. Hrádek knew he was right. Bohn would never have reported Tarasp in the first place if he hadn't been quite certain. His information had always been reliable, and Hrádek knew that too. Why else had Hrádek acted with such incredible speed? There was no doubt, the man was a political genius; his powers of planning and organizing were brilliant. Dazing. In a few years, Bohn thought, there will be fifty books written about him, and a thousand articles, and I will lead the field. My book will be the best, too. With my contact, I can't miss. He sat back and let himself be enjoyably dazed as they approached Tarasp and Jiri Hrádek began giving com-plicated but accurate directions to their driver. Jiri, thought Bohn with amusement, had really read that guidebook. He was now making the signal to stop. They were nicely off the highway, no nuisance to other traffic.

Pavel's car drew up behind them and he came hurrying forward with the latest bulletins. Bohn tried to follow the rush of Czech words, get some meaning into what had been happen-ing. And there seemed to be plenty. Pavel must have been kept busy during his drive to Tarasp: he had been in constant com-munication with various places. In particular, a service station on this side of the frontier, a roadside café farther west, and a camping ground after the highway had turned south. They had given him the exact time when a green Mercedes, Vienna registration, had travelled past them at high speed—no complete identification, but the numbers of the licence plate were correct. At the camping ground Stefan had begun following. He had stopped twice very briefly to radio Pavel. Stefan's last report, ten minutes ago, was that the Mercedes was now approaching the town of Scuol. There had been no other report since.

'Separate!' Hrádek told Pavel. 'Draw well ahead of us. Give no hint that we are together. Once you are round that first curve, stop. Keep in touch by radio. And tell Stefan that further reports come to this car direct.' Pavel obeyed at a run.

Hrádek broke into English again as he turned to Bohn. 'We'll stay here, on the south edge of Tarasp. No need to move until we've got the Mercedes traced to Kusak's house. And it could be there any minute. Scuol is just ten kilometres to the north of us.'

Six miles. . . . 'That's cutting it pretty fine,' said Bohn. Sunset was approaching.

'We aren't. He is.'

'Dave?' But Dave had been travelling fast: *no complete identification*, Pavel had reported. What the devil did that mean, anyway? Identification of the driver? Possibly. Hrádek had accepted it as that—it was in line with his firm belief that Mennery was alone. And I'm not going to argue about that again, Bohn reflected. Especially when Hrádek has some new problem on his mind.

'Who else?' Hrádek asked irritably. 'He is late. What delayed him? He should have been here almost an hour ago.'

'Saturday traffic,' suggested Bohn.

'He managed that well, once he was across the frontier.' The delay, thought Hrádek, came before he reached Switzerland. What had caused it?

'Weren't you having him followed all the way?'

'No,' Hrádek said shortly. Ludvik had failed all along the line. Mennery had left that Merano garage before there had been a man available to pick up his trail. Ludvik had been too busy with Krieger's car. And all he had to show for it was Krieger's bandaged hands. 'There was no need. We had Stefan waiting where it was most necessary.' As for Ludvik—well, we shall deal with him later.

'Who's Stefan? How did he get into the picture?'

'I put him there.'

'I wasn't being curious,' Bohn protested. 'Just slightly astounded.' And he was. 'You're amazing, Jiri.'

Hrádek relaxed into a smile. 'Stefan reached Merano this morning. Early this afternoon I sent him into Switzerland. He prepared the ground, as it were, made sure some friendly eyes were alerted. Now, he is following the Mercedes. To its destination.' Hrádek glanced at his watch. 'We should be hearing from him any minute.'

'And then?' Some of Bohn's nervousness returned.

'He stays near Kusak's house, instructs us how to reach there. We wait. Until the first signs of dusk, when there is enough light left to find the house easily. When it is dark, we move in.' He paused. 'Simple. Surprise is always the winning factor.'

Move in . . . Bohn didn't like the sound of that phrase. Yet he might as well face the unpleasant truth: it would take some tough persuasion to get Jaromir Kusak into a car and headed for the airport. He stared bleakly at the road ahead, now disappearing in a curve, blotted out by thick trees. His lips were dry. He should never have come, he ought to have refused. But how? Not possible, not without losing everything: his past stripped bare, exposed by subtle leaks to the American press; his future—no, he couldn't even think about that. 'And after we move in,' he said, 'what happens?'

Hrádek looked at him as if he were a two-year-old child. 'Whatever it takes,' he said softly. 'I did not come here to fail.' Then, as he watched Bohn's face, he added impatiently, 'You have your own job to think about. Don't worry about us. Not your department, as you keep reminding——'

At that moment, his radio signalled, and Hrádek's attention switched to Stefan's urgent voice. He lowered the volume for his ears alone, said 'Speak clearly. Yes, that's better.' He listened in silence until the report was over. 'Take that road! Yes, immediately. Before the light fades. And keep out of sight until we get there.'

Something wrong? Bohn wondered. But Hrádek still remained cool and efficient as he instructed the driver to start up and get moving. Almost in the same breath he was sending revised orders to Pavel and Vaclav. Once that was over, and their car was taking the curves and twists on a highway that had narrowed, seemed swallowed up by close hillsides and thick woods as the river plunged deeper into the valley, Hrádek turned to Bohn. His control slipped for a few seconds. He poured out a stream of violent Czech curses that paralysed Bohn into complete silence.

Then Hrádek's control came back. 'Stefan lost the Mercedes on one of the curves in this damnable highway. He kept on going till he had almost reached Pavel's car. It was then he knew that the Mercedes must have crossed the river a little way back, and taken a side road on its right bank.' Stefan had also reported a new item of information: at least two people in the car, possibly three. Reinforcements, of course. Well, thought Hrádek, we can handle them. With Stefan and our two drivers, there will be six of us. Six and a half, counting Bohn.

'Has he sighted the Mercedes again?' Bohn asked. Dusk would soon be here. By night a dark-green car would be hard to see.

'No.'

'Then we'll never be able to find Kusak.' And all this nightmare for nothing, Bohn thought, all these endless hours I've been stretched on the rack.

'We'll find him. The side road is short. It leads uphill. To that other Tarasp.'

Bohn's face was drained of colour.

'The one with the castle. Remember?' Jiri Hrádek's eyes were as hard as his voice.

248

Chapter Twenty-two

DAVID drew a quiet breath of relief once they reached the highway to Tarasp. He had taken a short cut down from the Swiss border, with a stretch full of hairpin bends that had produced a marked silence in the Mercedes. Now there was only a steady ascent along the left bank of the Inn, flowing to meet them, and he could start concentrating on the next problem. One damned worry after another, he thought. He said, 'Jo, you're beautiful enough. Give me some help with this map.' He tossed it over to the back seat.

'You're doing fine. Right highway, right direction,' Jo said. She went on brushing her hair to get some life back into it. Irina had already finished combing hers. Their faces and hands had been cleaned of dust and streaks; they looked presentable once more. 'Better get rid of that raincoat, Irina. It's a mess. I'll lend you a cardigan. We can't have you meeting your father like a——'

'Damn it,' David burst out, 'check the map, Jo!'

'Tarasp lies south—on this highway. You can't miss it.' But she dropped the hairbrush back into her suitcase. Never argue with a tired man, she thought, especially when he's hungry. Food, that's what we need; and hot baths; and some clothes that aren't beginning to look straight out of a thrift shop. She opened the map, saw Tarasp at once. 'Marked?' She was incredulous. 'Wasn't that——'

'My fault,' said Irina.

'An accident,' David said. 'What do you see, Jo? Any side road leading out of Tarasp?'

'Nothing.'

'Are you sure?' His voice was sharp. 'Krieger talked about an Upper Tarasp. That means two of them.' Sharing a hilltop with a castle, Krieger had said of the village. But a castle might not be visible until it was too late for David to make the right turn-off. He wanted no delay, no backing and searching.

'I see only one Tarasp, and that's near the highway.' Jo reached into her suitcase. 'I have a Swiss map—it may give more detail.' She spread it out. 'Dave, can't you ease up—just for a moment? This small print is really——' She broke off, concentrating more surely as their speed slackened. 'Oh my, this *is* complicated.'

'Tell me.' David was resigned to the inevitable. He ought to have guessed that Krieger would never choose an assignation point that was easy to find: no village bang on a straightforward highway for Krieger.

Jo said, 'How far are we from Scuol? Don't you love those names?'

'We'll reach it in ten minutes or less.' David was watching a motorcycle that had almost caught up with them when they suddenly slowed down, and now had fallen back a little. It was a high-powered job that had been behind them for several miles. A Swiss cowboy, he had thought, and expected the machine to zoom past them any moment. But it hadn't. Given up the challenge? He wondered, and kept an eye on it.

'Okay,' said Jo, head bent over the map, finger firmly on their route. 'Pass through Scuol. Keep going for one mile. Turn left and cross the river to reach its right bank. You are then on a small road for Vulpera.' Oh, these wonderful names, she thought. 'After that, turn right. The road divides and you take the left fork. Travel uphill for about two miles. And there you are. Tarasp. In small print.'

'With a castle?'

Jo looked again, saw the significant triangular dot put in by a careful map-maker. 'Yes.' And then, as David didn't answer but only put on speed, she asked, 'Shall I repeat all that?'

'No. Bless you, Jo. Clear as crystal.' David saw the motorcycle again. It too had speeded up.

'Now may I brush my hair?'

'No, keep watching the road signs. We'll check them together.'

'Careful, aren't you?' But she moved well over to the left side of the back seat to give herself a clear view of the river and its bridge.

'Sometimes.' David glanced at Irina. 'Hello, darling,' he

said softly. 'All right?' And now, he thought, there is one last problem to be solved, the most important of all. Yet he knew it had been solved for him already, and not according to his will or choice. What else could be done? He watched the motorcycle, and slackened speed. It eased off too, and had to pull in behind a large bus.

'Why slow up here?' Jo wanted to know. She looked out of the rear window, drew back instantly as she remembered David's instructions. Low profile, heads down, he had told them; slump, go to sleep again, but don't help anyone notice you.

'Just keeping a steady pace.' And that was what he wanted now. Get that bastard accustomed to this speed, David thought.

Irina said in alarm, 'Is there a car following us?'

'No car.' He didn't mention the bike. There was too much anxiety breaking through her apparent calm.

'Scuol,' Jo announced. 'Irina, put on the cardigan. *Please!*' She held it out.

With a smile, Irina refused it. 'I need this raincoat.' She patted its pockets, felt the reassuring touch of the small notebooks. David had noticed the movement of her hands. 'Yes,' she told him, 'both are safe.' She saw his surprise, and then amusement.

He shook his head, began to laugh. Then his eyes were on the road again.

'Well, that's a good sound,' said Jo. David hadn't even cracked one small smile all this journey, not even when he had wakened them at the first frontier post by telling them to yank off those damned wigs and keep their passport photos credible.

'David,' Irina began, 'I've made my decision. Is that what had been worrying you?' But he didn't answer. A bad moment to talk, Irina decided as she watched his face. She lapsed into silence.

David's full attention was on the highway. They were leaving Scuol now, and the motorcyclist had dropped back as if he felt that, at this rate of travel, he risked being discovered. The man was still in sight, though. But not for long, you son of a bitch, David told him silently. The road ahead was beginning to twist like a snake. On one side, thick trees and closely crowding hills; on the other, a fast flow of water in a deepening gorge.

Now—once round the next curve—was the time for a burst of speed. 'Hold on!' he warned.

'The bridge——' Jo called out. 'Don't forget the turn-off!'

He hadn't. He slowed enough to make a safe left over a high viaduct, and they crossed the gorge. He checked quickly: the motorcycle hadn't yet rounded that curve. He turned right. And now they were in a densely wooded area, completely hidden from the highway on the opposite bank. 'Next turn is uphill—at the left fork?' He sounded almost cheerful.

'Yes,' Jo said. 'And what was that all about?' He seemed not to hear her. 'Shut up, he explained,' she said lightly. An old joke, and not mine, but still better than none, she thought. What's troubling him? He's on the left fork, there are only two miles to go, he has got his girl, and he ought to be jubilant. Or is someone following us? Jo looked back in alarm. Nothing except a narrow country road, climbing between banks of wild flowers, winding its way up a hillside. On her right, green fields sloping down to the valley and a highway lost from sight; on her left, a rise of crags and rocks and Alpine bumps covered with grass. Peace, she thought, and a magnificent sunset coming up, soft white clouds nicely arranged for the very best effect. The mountains pleased her too, encircling but not too near, as if they had decided to let this hill have a breathing space all around it. She had had enough of mountains towering above her, in these last two days. But in the distance they made beautiful patterns against a sky of fading blue.

David reached out for Irina's hand. 'We'll soon be there. One last mile.' And then? But he knew what had to be done. His lips tightened. He looked abruptly away.

Irina leaned up to kiss his cheek. 'Darling,' she said softly, 'don't worry. Please don't. I'm staying with you. My father will listen to me, I know he will. Just give me some time to talk with him alone, tell him—oh, he will listen, I know.' She released David's hand to let him manœuvre past two children, three goats, and a small dog. 'All he wants to see is that I am safe, and free. All he needs to know is that I'm happy.' She laughed and waved to the children. 'And he will meet you, talk with you. It won't be difficult. Just a little time to let him——'

'Instant castle!' Jo exclaimed, and pointed uphill to her left. Incredible, she thought, that anything standing so proudly on its own green eminence should have been invisible until this moment.

The Mercedes took its final curve, passed the castle's unpretentious gates, and drew up beside a fountain crowned with a small shrine and red geraniums. They were in a little square —if he could call it that, David thought—with a few houses drawing back discreetly to face the castle above them.

'Uninhabited?' Jo asked. 'Or are they at supper, all two hundred of them?' Not many more could live on this flat-topped hill. 'Irina, look at those decorated walls—and the woodwork—these recessed windows—just look at them, will you? Pure Engadine.'

David had been studying the one street he could see ahead of him. It was edged by more Engadine houses, close-packed, large and solid, whitewashed, brown-timbered, three storeys high. Many were decorated with carefully painted designs, some emphasizing a window or doorway, others brightening a free patch of wall. He was looking for the pattern that Krieger had described, and wondering if he could risk the bulk of a car along that narrow little street without scraping off a part of the village. But he didn't have to search. Two men came out of a house near the corner of street and square, stood at its second-storey door for a moment, and then came down a broad flight of stone steps to ground level. One was in uniform. The other was a civilian, tall, fairish hair turning white and thin. He was smiling broadly, waving. It was Hugh McCulloch, a much happier man than when David had last seen him, on a transatlantic flight to Amsterdam.

'Which house?' Jo asked David as he switched off the ignition and secured the brakes. 'I hope it's the one with the dog in the window.' She pointed to the house overlooking the fountain.

Irina saw it and laughed. 'Look, David! One large dog, on a window sill, lying beside a pot of geraniums.'

But David was already out of the car, saying, 'Come on, both of you!' There was not a minute to lose, he kept reminding himself.

Irina heard the urgency in his voice. She came running around the car, her hand outstretched for his. 'Something wrong?' She halted abruptly as she noticed two men— strangers—who stood at the foot of the steps.

'No.' He couldn't tell her. (She would resist: five, maybe ten minutes, spent in pleading, in tears and useless argument that would tear his heart to pieces.) He only said, 'You've reached your friends.'

She caught him around his shoulders, hugging him tightly. 'We are here and we are safe, thank God, thank God. Oh, David——' She reached up and kissed him. He took her in his arms, held her close. The hell with a lost minute, or McCulloch and his uniformed friend, David thought, and he gave Irina one long last kiss.

Then hand in hand, Irina laughing and talking excitedly they walked across the little square.

Couldn't be better, McCulloch thought as he mastered his astonishment. He glanced at Colonel Thomon standing beside him. What price that kidnap story now? But, as a diplomat turned lawyer, McCulloch did not make any attempt to influence or lead this most important witness. He couldn't resist looking back at the doorway to the house, to see if Ernst Weber had come out to see the arrival too. Yes, he was standing on the top steps, discreetly in the background, watching everything with his trained journalist's eyes. Better and better, thought McCulloch, and reached out to give a warm handshake to David. 'And Irina,' he said to the girl—fair hair, blue eyes, a sweet smile in a lovely face—'welcome. You have no idea how welcome. Your father is waiting inside. We insisted he stay out of sight. Hello there, Jo—glad to see you!'

'How soon can Kusak——' began David, but McCulloch shook his head warningly and said, 'First let me introduce you all to Colonel Thomon, who has made a special journey here to ensure that there are no irregularities.' What's this—an immigration examination on a hilltop? David wondered; but McCulloch was having his way. Colonel Thomon was saluting, first Irina, then Jo; and then he shook David's hand. He studied their faces, pretended he didn't notice their clothes.

'We've been here for almost two hours,' McCulloch was saying. 'Colonel Thomon was about to leave. He has a few questions he would like to have answered.' And so would I, loud and clear.

The colonel nodded. 'Shall I speak in English?' he asked Irina. 'Or French, or German?'

'English.'

'I'll be very brief. Did you leave Czechoslovakia of your own free will?'

'Yes,' said Irina in surprise.

'No one forced you to come here?' The colonel looked at David and then at Jo.

'No one. They helped me escape.' And why should he ask that? Irina wondered. Then she remembered the newspaper story that Jo had mentioned in Merano. 'I was *not* kidnapped. My friends met me in Vienna and got me safely here.'

'Why did you come?'

'To meet my father, Jaromir Kusak.'

'And you too,' the colonel prompted helpfully, 'would like to ask for asylum in Switzerland.'

Irina hesitated. 'I——'

'Yes,' said David urgently, 'that's exactly right.' He glanced pointedly at his watch and then at the road that had brought them to Tarasp: he hoped the colonel would get the message.

'No further questions,' said the colonel with a smile for Irina.

But his eyes, studying David again, were curious.

'Irina—get indoors and out of sight,' David insisted.

'And you too.' She caught hold of his hand again.

'Later,' he said. He kissed her hand, tried to push her towards the steps. He turned in desperation to Jo. 'Get her inside, for God's sake.'

Jo paused to say to the colonel, 'There was an attempt on her life today.'

'By whom?' The colonel was no longer smiling.

'Two murderers who are wanted by the Vienna police. Czechs. Jiri Hrádek's men.'

The colonel knew the name. 'Are they still following you?'

'Not those two. But there are others—I think——' She glanced at David; yes, there were others. 'Come on, Irina, let's see if we can get up those steps. They aren't as bad as the ones we climbed today with Jan and Milan behind us.'

'Yes, go!' said McCulloch in alarm.

'Were we followed here?' Irina was asking. She was still watching David.

'Why else did David drive like a maniac?' Jo told her sharply.

With no more delay Irina climbed the steps, stopped halfway, turned and looked back. David waved her on. She reached the door, and it closed.

'How soon,' began David all over again, 'can Kusak leave here with Irina? In five minutes? Ten? No more. Believe me. No more. And where is your car?' he asked McCulloch. 'They know mine.'

'In that barn over there. The colonel came by helicopter, of course.'

'Helicopter? Where is it?'

'Down on the meadows.'

'East or west of this hill?'

'East.'

'Then they won't see it.' David was thinking out loud. 'West is towards the highway.' He verified that with an angry stare at the setting sun. 'How do you reach the helicopter?'

'Just one minute, Dave,' said McCulloch, looking anxiously at the colonel.

'A motorcycle followed us through Scuol. I dodged it at the bridge. But he'll be back, looking for that turn-off. He'll find it. He'll be here——'

'One man.' McCulloch relaxed a little.

'And others to follow,' said David. 'Reinforcements—they've been bringing in reinforcements all day. Why stop now?'

The colonel moved briskly towards the steps. 'You had better come too,' he told McCulloch. 'You can explain to the girl more easily than I can. She may be——' He shrugged. He looked back at David. 'I'm sorry we can't take you with us. The helicopter is limited.'

'I have to wait for Krieger,' David said to McCulloch, who was still hesitating. 'Have you heard from him?'

'Not yet.'

'Get going, Hugh. Tell Irina—tell her we'll work something out. Once it's safe.' David watched McCulloch run up the steps, stop for a moment to speak to a dark-haired man who had been an unobtrusive part of the background for the last few minutes.

'Not at all,' the stranger called after McCulloch. 'Glad you persuaded me to come along. It has been most enlightening.' Then, coming down the steps towards David, 'I am Ernst Weber,' he said, and put out his hand. 'Journalist. From Geneva.'

256

David shook hands. 'I thought Kusak avoided all reporters.'

'As a rule, yes. But this was a rather special day. You agree?' Weber's sympathetic brown eyes studied the exhausted face of the American. 'Have you a jacket in your car? You will need it in this evening air. It is always cold in the mountains.' He himself was well prepared in a camel-hair coat. 'And I think it is better to get away from this house.'

David nodded. Halfway across the square, he halted to look back.

No sign of Irina or Kusak; no colonel, no McCulloch.

'They will not use that door,' said Weber. 'They will make a less public exit. And after that, a path down to the east meadows. They may already be on their way. If I know the colonel, he got them moving at once. Here—I think you should have some of this.'

He handed David a flask of brandy.

'What is he? Immigration?'

Weber laughed. 'No. Intelligence of some kind. He is always decidedly vague about it. I have never been able to pin him down.'

'But why——' David gave up. I'm just too tired to puzzle this out, he thought. He drank some brandy.

From behind came Jo's voice. 'Wait for us!' They turned to see her coming down the steps, with a young man in uniform leading the way.

'A captain,' said Weber, 'one of the colonel's bright boys.' Then he laughed again: he was enjoying himself enormously. 'So he got bumped too. Is that the right word? He has been playing watchdog over Kusak. Now, I suppose, his appearance means that Kusak is no longer in the house. You see, our government feels a great responsibility for Jaromir Kusak. They keep a very friendly eye upon him. Oh yes, they know where he lives—at least, two or three men do.'

'Do you?' David was reviving.

'I do not even know who these two or three men are.'

'Never a leak?'

'Ah—your Washington specialty? No. Lack of discretion is not one of our vices.'

'I drink to Switzerland,' said David, wondering if he was not already a little drunk.

'May I too?' asked Jo.

'Just one swallow,' Weber said. 'This cool air doubles the effect.' The nameless captain agreed with a small smile.

'Why did you stay on?' David asked Jo, half-angrily.

'I think we should all leave now,' said the captain. 'Mr McCulloch gave me the keys of his car. I shall do the driving. Where do you want to go?'

'Samaden would suit me. That is where I came in.' Weber smiled. 'Just pull some rank, captain, and we shall find a plane. That is the nice thing about travelling with the military: everything is arranged. And I really do think,' he told Jo, 'that you need a good night's rest—away from here.'

'I'm waiting for Walter Krieger,' said Jo. She looked down at her scuffed shoes, at the tear in Irina's blue coat, at the earth stains that wouldn't rub off. Her right elbow ached; and her knees were bruised. 'Don't worry about me. I'm fine. I always look like this.'

'I'm staying too,' David said. He watched the two Swiss draw aside for a quiet conference.

'Idiots they think we are,' said Jo. 'Perhaps we are, at that. But—' she looked anxiously at David—'Krieger may be here any moment. We can't have him chasing in here to find nobody.'

Or the wrong people, David thought. He nodded to reassure Jo, kept his eyes fixed on the sky to the east. There was still some light, but dusk was approaching. And then he saw it—the helicopter swinging up into view, tilting forward, stationary for a minute before it swerved into flight. She's safe, he was thinking. She's safe.

The captain was beside him again. 'There is a motor bicycle coming up the hill. Listen!'

The helicopter was still in sight, a small black midge against a far background of darkening peaks.

'Listen!' the captain repeated.

David's attention focused on him slowly.

'It's the motor bicycle,' said Weber. 'You were right. It followed you. But a little too late, I think.' David looked back at the eastern valley. The helicopter was gone.

Jo was watching him. She turned away, searched in the car for her cardigan, wrapped it round her shoulders. 'I've got that news clipping somewhere,' she said, continuing her search. 'Have you seen it, Dave? A wild story about a kidnapping.

258

Irina,' and she spoke the name deliberately, 'Irina was kidnapped by some nasty Americans playing their dirty tricks on poor old Jiri Hrádek.' That had the right effect.

'News report?' David asked, swinging round to face her. 'Let me have it, Jo.'

'Can't find it,' she said cheerfully. 'But that was the gist of it.'

'Do not worry,' Weber assured them both. 'It will not live long. I have heard and seen enough to end that rumour before it even reaches half growth.'

'You know,' said Jo, 'you're the most valuable man we have around here. I think you should leave right away. I'd like to read your column tomorrow.'

Weber smiled. 'Not a column,' he said mildly. 'A page.'

'Oh my, we have a blockbuster on our side.' And then Jo said, 'It has stopped. It was almost here and it stopped.'

It was true. The motorcycle had halted on the last curve. In the deepening dusk it could be seen only as a distant shadow.

'What is he waiting for?' Weber asked.

'The others,' said David.

Chapter Twenty-three

SEEMINGLY ENDLESS, a minute passed. The motorcyclist stared up through the dusk at four figures grouped beside a car. He couldn't identify them at this distance, but the car was the right size and shape, and dark in colour. It was standing in front of the house that faced this road. So that was the place. He turned, wheeled his cycle back round the curve, drawing close to the steep bank.

'Was he the one who followed you?' the captain asked David, as the cyclist vanished.

'Couldn't see him clearly.' Which meant that the rider hadn't been able to see them clearly either.

'Has he left? Completely?' asked Weber. 'Perhaps he was someone who lost his direction. Perhaps he found himself in the wrong village.'

Like hell he did, thought David. 'And I suppose he is now walking all the way downhill?'

'He may have had trouble with his battery,' the captain suggested. 'You notice he came up without any headlight.'

'I noticed,' David said curtly. Just then the street lamps came on behind him, two of them high under the gables of nearby houses to illuminate some of this area. Now the man could certainly see them, if he were to take a few steps out from the curve of the bank. 'Keep back, Jo—out of sight!' He motioned to the captain and Weber. 'You too.' Jo and Weber heard the urgency in his voice, and moved closer to the shelter of the car. The captain stood his ground, his hands clasped behind his back, his eyes looking down a road that had become a black ribbon. 'What about you?' the captain asked.

'They expect to see me.'

'Ah—but not Miss Corelli?'

'No,' said Jo. 'Definitely not.' For a moment her mind

flashed back to Santa Maria. She shivered, and noticed that Weber's curiosity was no longer concealed. 'Where are all the people? Why aren't they taking an evening stroll round the village?' She glanced angrily at the house behind her. 'Not even a dog to be seen.' As in the other houses, a few windows had lighted up as dusk had thickened, and been immediately shuttered tight. In fact, all shutters had been closed. Nothing but patches of heavy dark wood stared back at her from white walls.

The captain said, 'They have been out in their fields all day. Why should they go walking at night?'

'Oh,' said Jo, 'and will they still sleep soundly if any shooting starts?' But by that time it could be too late for Dave and me.

Weber looked hard at her. 'You are joking, surely.'

'That's right. I'm joking.' But she shivered again. She drew the cardigan sleeves around her throat.

'They had better not try that kind of thing,' Weber told her. 'There is not a house in this village—or any other village in Switzerland—where you will not find a rifle stored, along with a uniform. We are all in the reserve army, you understand.'

'You too?'

Weber nodded. Her astonishment pleased him. 'It is a matter of enforcing our—neutrality.'

I hope, thought Jo, you can enforce it right here. But first you'll have to stop searching for reasonable excuses for everything that happens: we aren't dealing with reason, dear man. Not tonight. 'There's a car now!' she said, and stared like the rest of them towards the dark road.

'It is about halfway up the hill, I think,' the captain said to David.

'They are using a lot of car.'

'They would, of course, have to go into first gear.'

'Yes. Even so——' David tried to gauge the volume of sound. 'More than one car?'

'That can be. Yes, two possibly.'

David said, 'You know, I'd like to draw them right into this square, and see who they are.'

'So should I,' the captain agreed.

'Then I think you should step away from me. If they catch sight of a uniform——'

'They will still be forced to come up into the square. There is no place for a car to turn on that road. And there is very little turning room here either.'

'I know. But as a matter of tactics——'

'Ah yes. A slight surprise?' The captain smiled as he glanced in Jo's direction. 'That is better than any shooting. Mr Weber, please go with Miss Corelli behind the shelter of the car. Keep down your heads.' He himself turned towards the barn at the other end of the square, but only walked a few yards. 'This will be very well,' the captain said. He was now blocked from the view of any car until it actually came up into the village.

A stubborn man, thought David, and was glad of it. And the size of this small piece of ground was another bit of comfort. This wasn't a hit-and-run kind of place. Manœuvring space for any car was at a minimum, and not helped by the Mercedes; or the well, which was substantial enough—a combination of trough and fountain. So they've come to trap us, thought David. What would they try? He thrust his hand into his pocket, kept it there, his fingers gripping the Beretta as he saw the first sweep of headlights. 'Two cars,' he reported to the captain. They halted, engines still running. 'Talking now with the motorcyclist, I think.'

The talk was brief. The cars moved again, headlights dimming, and then stopped almost at the entrance to the square. Someone must be directing them, David decided: they are too well co-ordinated.

Suddenly, all the headlights switched off. Black on black, David thought; I can see nothing. They are so near me—fifteen, twenty yards away, not much more; but all I can do is stand and wait and stare at shadows. Then he heard the stumble of a footstep as someone got out of the rear car. A man came walking out of the darkness, stepped into the outer edge of light. It was Mark Bohn.

'Hey there,' Bohn said with a broad smile, as he made straight for David. 'You know, you shouldn't have been in such a hurry at Brixen. If you had just waited for me to put that call through to Munich, you could have given me a lift all the way. The Munich assignment is postponed—no need for me to be there until next weekend. So here I am.' Friendly, conversational, that was Bohn. The only nervous thing about him was the way he kept his eyes on David's face.

David said nothing.

'Why not?' Bohn rushed on. 'This is too good a story to pass up. Besides, there have been developments. Yes, quite serious ones, Dave. Have you had time to see a newspaper today? I read a couple at Brixen. There is a report—not a rumour—that Irina was kidnapped.'

'Oh, for God's sake——' said David in disgust. 'You know damned well——'

'There was one fact I didn't know. And you didn't know, either. Washington is behind this whole thing. Krieger is their agent. Irina's so-called escape could be a political kidnapping. And that's what people are reading about, right now. We'd better start investigating thoroughly, you and I, try to clear ourselves. We've been used, manipulated. And that's one thing I don't take from anyone.'

David restrained a comment.

'Irina knows more than she told you. You might get the truth out of her. Krieger will deny everything, of course, but Irina will listen to you. Won't she?'

Get rid of Bohn before you blow your stack, David told himself. His hand tightened around the gun in his pocket. 'She is not here.'

'She's late, is she?' Bohn didn't seem too surprised. 'Oh well —it's a difficult journey. Even at the end of it, down by that fork, we almost missed the hill road.' Bohn shook his head, remembering that error: more minutes lost, with Hrádek counting every one of them in silent rage. 'Yes, a difficult journey.'

'We?' asked David pointedly.

Bohn's voice quickened again. 'I brought another journalist with me, an old friend, reliable. He jumped at the chance to come—this kidnap report has got us all by the ears. And two of his news-service buddies tagged along—but he vouches for them, so they're all right.' Bohn paused for further inspiration. His variant on Hrádek's story would get him off the hook if Pavel and Vaclav started any rough stuff: they were strangers to him, taken on trust. 'I thought it was a good idea to have them around, David. We need an extra witness or two, to verify what we uncover.'

'And where did you find all these helpful friends?'

'Oh, come on, David—you know the marvels of the telephone, don't you?'

263

'One call from Brixen, and you all gathered where?'

'Met them in Innsbruck.' Bohn caught himself. 'All very simple—just routine for any correspondent. You get a hot tip, you grab your overnight bag, and you're on the first plane available.' Bohn was still watching David. 'What's wrong? What's at the back of your mind?' Then he found an answer that amused him. 'I bet you're wondering how I knew about Tarasp. That was simple enough too. Irina dropped the magic word. It slipped out and I snatched it. And why not? You might have told me yourself,' he added, slightly hurt and showing it. 'Oh, let's forget it. Where is Kusak?'

'How about your friends? Aren't they going to join you?' David's face was tight with anger. It had been with a considerable effort that he had managed to keep talking. They had some plan, no doubt about that. But what?

'Oh, they'll be all right where they are—until I've seen Kusak, and explained to him who, why, and what. I don't want to scare the old boy by descending on him unprepared. But this is one time he has got to give up some of his damned privacy. Otherwise you're in deep trouble, David. You're the chief accessory to a kidnapping. If that story can't be killed——'

'Oh, this is too much,' Jo said, and she began walking round the car with Weber beside her.

Bohn's head swerved towards the voice. He kept staring. Then he turned on David. 'You lied.' He pointed to the house behind the Mercedes. 'Irina is there. With her father.' He recovered himself, noted David's expression, and eased his voice. 'Of course—just a matter of supercaution. But with me, Dave? Come on, let's join the family reunion. It's damned chilly out here. Don't worry—I won't stay any longer than it takes to ask three sharp questions. I'm planning to have dinner in St Moritz tonight.'

'You can leave right now. Kusak has gone. Irina with him. And that was not the house.'

'I don't believe you,' said Bohn. 'What's the idea, Dave? What's——'

Weber interposed. 'Mr Mennery is telling you the truth. Mr Kusak and his daughter left some time ago—with a friendly escort. There has been no kidnapping of any kind.'

'And who's this?' Bohn demanded. 'Just who——' But as he looked more closely at the stranger's face, his question faded.

'I am Ernst Weber of the *Geneva Gazette*. I am also a correspondent of several newspapers—in London, Paris, and Rome. But I think you know all that. We met in Prague. Two years ago?' Weber waited. There was no answer: not one word, not one comment from that extremely facile tongue. Weber half smiled. 'You were correct about only one thing, Mr Bohn. It is damned chilly out here. So why do you not leave, as suggested?'

Bohn rallied. 'There seems little point in staying.' He gathered together some of his dignity and most of his assurance. 'Dave—we can talk about this later—right?'

'Clear out!' David's voice rose in fury. 'All of you—clear out!' He took a step forward.

Bohn backed away. Then he turned to walk to the car. And for the first time he saw a uniformed man who had stood watching and listening; quite motionless, completely silent. Bohn's pace increased. He reached the beginning of the road, almost broke into a run.

David kept watch, his hand still gripping the pistol in his pocket. The dark road swallowed Bohn up, leaving only the sound of his footsteps. They passed the first car, kept on going for several seconds. Then, abruptly, they stopped. A car door closed. Complete silence.

It was broken by a yell from somewhere overhead. David's attention switched to the house behind him. He half turned, looked up at a window with its shutters flung open and an angry woman leaning out. He couldn't understand one word; it was a language he had never heard before, but the meaning of her shaking fist was clear. Then David looked back at the two cars. The captain would have to take care of this protest. He did. He stepped forward, replied, and silenced the woman effectively. Or perhaps it was the uniform that reassured her. There was peace in the square again.

The captain walked over to stand beside David, and gazed down the dark road. 'They are taking their time.' He didn't approve of it, either.

'The second car—that's the important one. That's where Bohn is making his report.'

'Perhaps they do not accept it.' That would account for the delay. 'They may believe Jaromir Kusak and his daughter are still here.'

'Irina was never expected to arrive,' David reminded him.

'That makes a difficult situation,' the captain answered. He was younger than David, tall, well proportioned, neat and capable; at this moment he looked twenty years older. 'If they believe Miss Kusak never arrived, they may also believe her father is still waiting for her.'

'I think not. Bohn saw Jo quite clearly. And she is proof that Irina did get here. The living proof,' said David grimly. We beat them at Santa Maria, he told himself. *That overpassing, this also may.*

'But the delay——'

'Cancelling one set of plans, improvising something else?' David suggested.

'Then the two cars must be in close communication.'

'Someone is in control. That's for sure.'

'The second car, you think?'

'Yes.'

'Which side of that car did Bohn take?'

'He went down the left side of the road.'

'Then he entered the car's right-hand door.'

'It sounded like that.'

'You have good ears.'

'That's my job,' David said, and he had a sudden impulse to laugh. 'I'm a music critic.'

The captain drew something out of his pocket. 'Only a cigarette lighter,' he told David, and smiled. 'Not a pistol.' Lightly, he tapped David's pocket. 'And I'm glad you did not use yours. What kind is it?'

'An automatic. A Beretta.'

'A simple solution, I agree. But of a type that always brings too many complications, usually unpleasant.' The captain smiled again, very briefly. 'Do not use that automatic. We shall manage.' He was walking to the centre of the square. 'The minute they start moving up the hill, get behind your car. Weber——'

Like hell I will, thought David. But he drew his right hand out of his pocket.

Weber, at the captain's voice, looked round. He was still standing beside Jo. 'Yes, Captain Golay—what can I do?'

'Get the girl out of this square.'

Weber took Jo's hand. 'Captain's orders.'

266

'No.' Jo looked at the house behind her. Three windows were now unshuttered, with dark figures pressed against the glass. Its front door was open, too, and a man stood there half-concealed, with an army coat drawn over his shoulders. She saw a gleam of metal in his hand. 'More captain's orders?'

'The man, yes. But those upstairs—just curiosity.' Weber had felt more than a touch of it himself, as he watched David and Captain Golay in close conversation. He had missed that, damn it, because of this girl; but how could he have left her, cold and miserable, practically out on her feet? 'Please,' he urged her.

'I've *got* to stay. Bohn's friends must see me too. Or else they won't believe him, and——' She stared at the road as the cars roared into sight. 'David—look out!'

The lead car missed him, dodged the Mercedes by a few feet, made a frantic left turn to avoid a crash against a wall; the second car followed it exactly. And the men inside them had seen more than Jo in that split second: a house with shutters open, figures at the windows; a man at the doorway, rifle in hand. There was a shriek of brakes as the two cars pulled up abruptly, one almost on top of the other. The first car had just saved itself from smashing into the stone staircase.

The captain moved with incredible speed. He had reached the second car, taken its left side, rapped sharply on its window, gestured for it to be lowered, even before David could join him. The two men in the back had been badly jolted by the sudden stop. Bohn was one of them; he was heaped in the far corner, and shouting as he struggled up, 'I *told* you I saw a policeman. I *told* you there must be others. I *told* you——'

The man in the left-hand seat said, 'Stop it! Stop it!' He turned to face the captain, lowered the window with a finger on the electric control. 'What do you want?' he asked in German. He looked more closely at the uniform.

'I thought someone might have been injured.'

The man's voice became less truculent. 'Nothing, nothing. A small shake-up.'

'I understand you lost your way coming to Tarasp. Perhaps I could help you make sure of your direction when you leave.' Captain Golay had a small map ready in his hand; he extended it as he leaned on the car door. 'Much too dark to see,' he said. 'You need this.' He flicked on his cigarette lighter. Flicked again. It didn't flare.

Sharply, the man turned his head aside. 'We have maps.'

And who is he? David wondered. Someone, certainly, who doesn't want the captain to have a clear view of his face. Too bad the lighter hadn't worked, but a neat try. Curiously, David kept staring at the head firmly turned aside and held there.

'Very good.' The captain was as equable as ever. Then his voice changed. 'Drive out!' He stood back, signalled the chauffeur to reverse, gave an authoritative sign when to stop. Now he took charge of the first car, backed it up slightly, eased it round the corner of the steps, and urged it on with a go-and-keep-on-going wave of his arm. It went partly round the square, stopped. The captain swore under his breath, signalled to it again. It stayed where it was.

'No!' Bohn had caught Hrádek's arm as he raised the transmitter for his final instructions. 'For God's sake, Jiri—risk everything? And for what?'

'This matter is my own.'

'Will Prague listen to that?'

Hrádek shook off Bohn's hand. But the warning had taken hold. The failure here was bitter, but if it spread to Prague—disaster. His hesitation ended. 'Drive!' he told the man at the wheel. And then he said to Pavel, 'The plan is cancelled. Follow me out. No delays.' Hrádek laid the transmitter aside. He sat well back, his face averted from the two men who kept watching his car as it moved towards the road.

'That's Weber—the journalist,' Bohn said in alarm, pointing to a solitary figure at one side of the square. They had passed close to where he had stationed himself.

'He did not see me.'

'He tried.'

'What does he matter?' Hrádek asked impatiently. 'Before his report can be published I shall be back in Prague.' With a sound alibi, already prepared, for this Saturday afternoon. Can Bohn really be so naïve as to imagine I have not planned an alibi in advance? 'Your Swiss journalist will be the joke of the newsrooms.' Hrádek glanced over his shoulder to make sure that Pavel and Vaclav were following dutifully. They were. 'Hurry!' he told his driver. 'Get moving!' He drew back into his corner, head bent, eyes half-shut, arms folded. But his rigid jaw and tightened lips were signs that he was far from sleep.

'You are well out of that,' Bohn tried. There was no answer. Bohn fell silent. He had enough brooding to do of his own. At least Dave Mennery had not been forced into Pavel's car, to be dealt with later. But it had been a damned close thing. Dave, thought Bohn, will never know how much he owes to me.

Behind them Tarasp had vanished. Only its bitter memory lingered in the car.

Chapter Twenty-four

DAVID kept watching the road, listening to the two cars' steady descent. Their sound lessened, diminished at last into nothing. Complete silence.

'They have gone,' he told Jo, who had come to stand beside him. He couldn't believe it.

'Can we be sure?' Jo asked.

'Yes,' said Captain Golay. He was jotting down some figures in a notebook.

'I don't know,' said David. His nerves had tightened, his tensions had mounted; and suddenly—nothing. 'They meant business. They came in here looking for trouble. And then—and then they just left. Why?'

Weber grinned. 'We had a deterrent.' He pointed to the man who now stood in front of his doorway, well in view; so was the rifle held ready. 'Captain Golay, I think you can dismiss your troops.'

Golay completed the last digits on the cars' licence plates, and put his notebook away. He called over to the man. They both shared a laugh. The man added a sentence of his own, moved into his house, closed the door. Upstairs the shutters were closing, too.

Captain Golay was still smiling broadly. 'I told him our visitors would not return. His description of them cannot be translated—' he glanced at Jo '—but I think we would all agree with it.' He noticed her strained face. 'Believe me, Miss Corelli, the danger is over.'

Jo tried to cover her despondency. 'They'll come back. Perhaps not here. But——'

'No, no. I think we can make an end to this threat. Perhaps we have already made it tonight. Mr Weber—did you recognize the man?'

'I had only a glimpse of his face. He turned his head away. For a moment I thought I had seen that profile before—when I visited Prague two years ago. But it could not be. Impossible.'

'It could not be Jiri Hrádek?' Golay asked.

'Hrádek?' David and Jo had spoken the name together.

Weber said, 'Then it *was* Hrádek?' His astonishment gave way to jubilation. 'And you actually recognized him. We are in business, captain.'

'I recognized him from a photograph I have seen. The likeness was exact.'

Weber's smile faded. 'Not sufficient. You will need my corroboration of what you saw. And I cannot give it to you. I did not see the man closely enough to swear that he was Jiri Hrádek.'

'This,' said Golay, 'is all the proof that Colonel Thomon will need.' He drew out his lighter, held it up briefly before slipping it back into his pocket.

David said, 'A camera—infra-red film——' He began to smile. Krieger, he suddenly thought, ought to have seen that little gadget at work. The captain's performance would have delighted him. Krieger. David's smile vanished. Krieger should have been here—by this time—surely. . . .

'Now,' said Golay, 'I have some messages to send. After that I can drive you out of here. I could take you as far as Zurich.'

'Oh no!' Jo said softly.

'Samaden,' said Weber, 'would be better. It is only a short journey. I think that is what Miss Corelli wants.'

Miss Corelli, decided Jo, wants no journey at all. She glanced at David, but he was preoccupied with his own thoughts.

'We do not use Samaden tonight.' The captain was firm about that. He had several good reasons, but he kept them to himself. Bohn had let the name of St Moritz slip out. It was a mistake often made by adept liars when they were fabricating an explanation: they invariably added some provable fact to bolster their fictions. *Dinner at St Moritz.* Yes, that was where Bohn intended to be seen tonight. His mention of Innsbruck was interesting too: he must have been there, must have felt his journey to Innsbruck could be easily traced; and so, out came a little fragment of truth. But what he hadn't realized— another mistake often made by liars—was that one fact can

271

lead to another. So now, we know that Hrádek's plane touched down in Innsbruck. We can trace its flight pattern into Switzerland. 'Samaden,' Golay explained, 'will soon be under close surveillance. We do not want to complicate matters.' Nor, he was thinking, do we want to have you come face to face with any of Hrádek's rear-guard. Hrádek was bound to leave at least one of his men behind as an observer. 'Decide where you are going tonight,' Golay said, backing away. 'Let me know before you leave.' There was a friendly salute for Jo, and he hurried off.

'Well?' asked Weber.

'Don't worry about us,' David said. 'We can stay here overnight.' It was the last thing he wanted, but Jo wasn't fit to travel. And there was Krieger too. 'Krieger said he had booked a couple of rooms—some place——' David looked around vaguely. God, he was tired; but even so, he would travel anywhere just to lose sight of that house. He stared at it now, and saw Captain Golay running up its flight of steps. The house where Irina had walked out of his life.

Weber was saying with relief, 'Well, that is fortunate. The inn has not many rooms. Let me show you the way.' He took Jo's arm to hurry her. 'It is not far—just beyond the house that Mr Krieger borrowed for tonight's meeting.'

'But where is Krieger?' Jo asked. 'Dave, what happened to Krieger?'

'Nothing.' Weber smiled. 'He will arrive and be angry that he missed all the excitement. Please—there is no purpose in standing here. Mr Krieger knows where the inn is.'

Jo began walking. Nothing could happen to Krieger, she kept telling herself; not to Krieger. But why hadn't Dave answered her? He was staring down that road as if he hoped to see the Chrysler zooming up there any minute. 'Dave——' she called back to him.

'He is coming,' Weber said, and urged her on. David was following slowly, his head turned away from the house. Jo had an impulse to call out, 'Please—don't worry. Irina will be all right. You'll see.' No, she decided, don't mention Irina's name; not at this moment.

David passed the house, a heavy wall rising at the side of the stone stairs, blotting them from sight. He wished they could blank out the last picture he had of Irina, standing on these same steps, halfway, hesitating, looking round at him for reassurance. Is this right, is this what you want? she had seemed to ask. And he had answered with a smile and a wave that had sent her on her way. Tomorrow, or the next day, he could let himself think about her. Tonight the wound was still raw.

He started up the short rough road, trying not to believe that life kept repeating its pattern, that once again Irina and he were separated; and there would be no third chance. Another thought slid into his mind, took hold. You made the choice this time. You. This was not Vienna sixteen years ago, when there had been no choice at all, and nothing he could fight. Then there had only been unseen forces, beyond reach, powerful enough to twist a man's life against his will. But he was not helpless now. He knew what was against him, what he could expect. And that way, he could fight. At least, he would make a damned hard try. Jiri Hrádek. . . . There stood the real threat to Irina's future. Not her father, not duty or sentiment. Jiri Hrádek.

Weber was waiting for him at the door of the inn, a house like most of the others in the village except for a few lights and its small sign. 'Miss Corelli has gone upstairs. Oh, not permanently. She wanted to—freshen up, I think the expression was—before supper.' Weber was smiling as he thought of Jo. 'A remarkable girl. Quite attractive too. Don't you think?'

'Wait till you see her freshened up,' David told him. 'She'll knock your eye out.'

Weber laughed. 'Only one eye?' Another American idiom for his collection. But, more important, Mennery seemed to be recovering. Not completely. Just enough to let the dismal prospect of a wordless supper, steeped in heavy gloom, seem more remote. A man could share his joys around, thought Weber, but never his troubles. He clapped David's shoulder lightly. 'Let us move inside and have a drink. I think we can allow ourselves a little celebration. After all, we have won the battle of Tarasp.' He pointed to the castle on its hill above them, looming like a white ghost against the night sky. 'It never looked down on a stranger skirmish in all its eight hundred years.'

David halted. 'Is that your lead story on Hrádek?' he asked with a touch of bitterness.

'No,' Weber said patiently. He lowered his voice. 'I shall write about Irina Kusak's safe escape from Czechoslovakia, and it will be published immediately. The story on Hrádek comes later, once his political enemies have dealt with him. They will. And soon.'

'But how will they know——'

'Let Colonel Thomon and his superiors attend to that.'

'Hrádek would never have risked leaving Prague unless he could produce a good cover story.'

'Oh, he will try that, I am sure. A brief hunting trip in the Tatras, or an afternoon's fishing, with two companions who will swear that every word is true. But his alibi will crumble to pieces.'

'It will take more than a couple of photographs to shake it.'

'I think,' Weber said very softly, 'you are forgetting the source of these photographs. We Swiss do not fabricate international incidents.'

'Sorry. My mistake.' He relaxed a little.

'And are you forgetting Captain Golay's preoccupation with Samaden? It is the nearest airport to Tarasp. Hrádek's plane must be waiting somewhere close at hand. Don't you think?'

David could almost smile. *Under surveillance*, the captain had said. Arrivals and departures recorded; photographs of men boarding the jet. There would be a heavy use of cigarette lighters and other neat devices tonight. 'That may nail Hrádek,' he said. He added, 'As far as the Swiss are concerned.'

'As far as others are concerned, too,' Weber insisted. 'The men who head the regime in Czechoslovakia do not tolerate any power-play except their own. Hrádek is neo-Stalinist; he is also a strong nationalist. Russia does not trust that combination—not in a satellite country. And the Czechs who are now in command follow that line. Hrádek has been very clever: he has never opposed them openly. But secretly? I think he has made his own plans, and I cannot be the only Hrádek watcher who has these suspicions. He is close to the top, as it is. But a man who reaches out for the highest peak, and loosens his grip, has a long way to fall.'

'He is just clever enough to fall on to a ledge, and wait there until he can boost himself up again.' Perhaps, thought David, exhausted, despondent, he may even climb off that ledge before Kusak's book can be published. 'And he has friends. He would not have risked today's wild action unless he was sure of them. If he feels he is beginning to slip, he won't wait to fall. He will give the signal. They will seize control.'

'The Czechs in power will think of that too. They will move, and with all speed. Hrádek will be eliminated within a week.'

David looked at him sharply, but Weber was serious.

'Perhaps even sooner,' Weber said. 'His enemies will not lose any time. That is one certainty.'

A certainty? If Weber had only been able to talk with Irina about Hrádek, he might not be so sure. 'All right,' David said. 'So Hrádek is faced with tonight's photographs and sees his alibi destroyed. What then? He will plead necessity, and add a touch of sentiment.' David could almost hear Hrádek's smooth defence: Irina, his wife until a month ago, had to be stopped from leaving Czechoslovakia. Harmful propaganda for the State, apart from his own deep feelings about her desertion. Tarasp was his last chance to find her—and Jaromir Kusak—and bring them both back to Prague. A desperate journey, Hrádek would admit, but its secrecy protected the State's image. And so on and so on and so on, David thought wearily.

Weber was shaking his head. 'Sentiment? There is little room for that in power politics. His enemies would laugh——'

'And he would seem more foolish; therefore less dangerous. He might gain the time he needs to——'

'You actually believe he could extricate himself?' Weber was incredulous. 'But I assure you, my dear fellow, the present regime in Czechoslovakia will not tolerate tonight's——'

'What they need is a real scare, hard evidence of——' Of a past conspiracy against them. They would call it treason. 'Yes,' David said slowly, putting the brief thought of Kusak's notes right out of his mind, 'that would have jolted them right into action.'

'The photographs will be evidence enough.' Weber was slightly hurt that they should be questioned. But tired men were always querulous, he reminded himself. He looked pointedly at the inn door.

'Let's have that drink,' David said, and made an effort to cross the worn threshold into the warmth of four stout walls.

Chapter Twenty-five

DAVID SLEPT for fourteen hours. He awoke in a strange room with a window looking out at mountains he didn't recognize. Where the hell am I? he wondered. And then he remembered.

He got up, glanced at his watch. It must have stopped just before midnight, he thought at first, but it was still ticking away. Apart from a tightness across his shoulders, a slight stiffness in his back, he felt fine.

Then he became aware of voices, a lot of voices blending together, a mingling of talk. He crossed over to the window.

Below, there were half a dozen tables, filling rapidly, set out on a small grass-covered terrace that ended in a long drop to green fields, a placid valley sweeping out until it reached a wall of enormous mountains. He was on the eastern edge of the village, and the valley below him must have been where the helicopter took off last night. He stared at it for a full minute.

'Dave!' The voice was distant, but it was Jo's. She raised an arm to catch his attention.

She was sitting with Weber at the far end of the terrace. There was a third chair beside them, tilted forward against their table. Jo pointed to it, waved a come-quick signal. He got the message. He needed no second invitation to hurry.

He shaved, showered, and dressed as rapidly as possible. A complete change of clothes was no trouble, either. Thanks to Weber's efficiency, his bag and raincoat had been brought up to the inn last night along with Jo's suitcase, and the car itself had been garaged—or stabled?—to give more elbowroom in the village square. Just as well, judging by the Sunday visitors beginning to crowd the tables on the terrace. There must have been news, he kept thinking. Good or bad, there must be news by this time.

*   *   *

David climbed a short steep path and reached the terrace, now totally filled with hungry tourists who were paying more attention to their plates than to the superb view. Jo and Weber made a handsome picture of their own. She was back to her chic elegance once more. White sweater, white pants. 'You look good this morning,' he said as he reached the table. But there was a fine-drawn quality about her face, as if she were still near breaking point. Weber was completely relaxed. Today he was wearing a light gaberdine suit, immaculate shirt, a restrained tie. His manner was as smooth and unperturbed as his face.

David sat down, tried to appear nonchalant, braced himself inwardly. 'Heard anything?'

'There are various messages,' Weber said. 'But I do think it is much too public here to discuss names and places. Let us have something to eat, and then——'

'No,' David insisted. 'We'll keep our voices down.'

'And everyone is too busy with his veal cutlet,' Jo said, glancing around the other tables. She was trying to recapture some of her old gaiety, but it was a poor effort.

'Bad news?' asked David.

'Mostly good.' Weber had pulled out several small pieces of paper from his pocket. 'I have the messages here—just as they came in this morning.'

'Oh, for heaven's sake,' Jo said, 'give him the news about Irina first. The rest can wait until he orders breakfast. She's safe, Dave, she's safe.'

'Here is her message.' Weber selected a slip of paper, handed it to David. *All my love always wait for me darling.*

Weber said, 'It came along with this one from McCulloch. He is back in Geneva.' He gave it to David. *All is well. Destination safely reached. No difficulties. Hope to see you soonest possible. Congratulations and sincere thanks. Hugh.*

Weber passed over a third message. 'This came along with the other two. They were all dated yesterday midnight, but of course they were telephoned from McCulloch's Geneva office early this morning.'

So by midnight, Irina had been safe. Where? David wondered. He looked at the message. It was brief and unsigned, as Irina's had been. It read: *I am in your debt. Someday I hope we may meet.*

'I thought,' Weber said, a combination of tact and curiosity, 'it might be from Kusak himself. Is it?'

'Yes. We have never met.' David kept his face well in control. *May meet.* Not *will meet.* The difference troubled him. Kusak was being indefinite. That was what David had feared. And yet it was to be expected. Kusak wanted Irina kept hidden. He was afraid for her safety: Hrádek, of course; the permanent threat. David took a deep breath. Well, it was up to Captain Golay and his colonel now.

'Dave—let's order,' Jo said. 'You didn't eat much last night.'

'Nor did you.' A bowl of soup was all that Jo had managed to swallow.

'But I had breakfast almost four hours ago.'

'Toast and coffee, or just coffee?' He smiled for her, and eased some of her worry away. But there was still a strange sadness in her eyes. 'What's the other message, Weber?'

'It will keep until you've eaten,' said Jo.

Weber had put the remaining scrap of paper into his pocket, and trapped a waitress. 'Breakfast or lunch?'

'I begin the day with breakfast,' David said. 'Make it solid. Eggs, ham, sausages, the works.'

'Ah, London style. I rather liked that, I remember.' Weber gave David's order, in triplicate. 'We keep it simple, and then we have it promptly. Very fine panorama, don't you think? That is the Swiss National Forest—over there! Those mountains——'

'Let's have the bad news,' David said. 'Is it from Krieger, or from Captain Golay?'

'Not from Krieger. It's about Krieger,' Weber said. 'Shall I tell it, or do you want to read my French? I noted it down as McCulloch called me at breakfast. That was after I had received the other——'

'Yes, yes. What about Krieger? Tell.'

Jo said, 'They nearly killed him.' She turned her face away.

'But he *is* alive,' said Weber. 'And he is a strong man. He will recover. In a day or two he can leave hospital.'

'In Merano?' So he never got my message, David thought. He put out his hand and grasped Jo's. It was cold and rigid.

'In Samaden,' Weber said. 'That was where he was attacked. At the airport.'

'How?'

'An injection in the back of his neck. A drug was used that can be deadly—if it is not treated in time with the correct anti-toxin. The problem, you see, is that the patient may not recover consciousness enough to talk, or he does not even know what has happened to him, and so the doctors are given no help. He simply seems to have had a severe heart seizure. But Krieger managed to recover consciousness *and* to tell what happened.' Weber paused, shaking his head. 'Then it was only a matter of the right treatment being given.'

Jo said, her voice strangled, 'It always is. But will the right treatment be given to Hrádek? Oh, why didn't you shoot him through the head last night, when you had the chance?' She tried to pull her hand away.

Both men stared at her. David's answer was to keep his grasp on her hand. Weber said, 'That is for someone else to do. And perhaps sooner than you think. Captain Golay——' Weber hesitated.

'You've heard from him?' David asked sharply.

'I had a telephone call only an hour ago. He simply wanted to reassure us that everything is developing very nicely. A neat double meaning, don't you think?'

David nodded. Any comment he could make might seem a bit rough. *Developing very nicely.* Diplomatic phrasing, but that was not enough. When the hell were the photographs of Hrádek being sent to Prague? When was that stiff protest to be made by the Swiss? That was what counted: the when of it all.

Weber noticed David's noncommittal silence but he ignored it and went on talking about Captain Golay in his quiet and deliberate way. 'There was also reference made to some documents that had just come into Kusak's possession.'

'The notebooks? What about them?'

Weber frowned, both puzzled and interested. 'Notebooks?'

'What about them?' David repeated.

'Jaromir Kusak has agreed to have a copy made of certain pages, so that they can be relayed to Prague.'

David recovered from the shock: incredulity gave way to stunned relief; and then anxiety returned. 'When?'

'Immediately.' So that is what has been troubling my friend here, thought Weber. He did not think we were moving quickly enough. 'It will be handled most delicately, of course: a part of our dossier on Hrádek, perhaps, which we will lodge along with a most serious complaint.'

'Immediately?' David insisted.

'The complaint will follow—it takes a little time to word. But the initial evidence, and the Kusak material, are already on their way.' Weber smiled. 'Speed, after all, is essential. You agree?'

David nodded again, but this time there was an answering smile in his eyes.

'I'm not really following this,' Jo tried.

David didn't even hear her. 'But who persuaded Kusak? Was it McCulloch?' Someone must have twisted the old boy's arm, got him to take action and at once.

'It was the daughter, I believe.'

'Irina?' David's sudden jubilation was transparent.

'At least,' said Weber, 'it was she who insisted that Captain Golay let you know about this new development.' He studied the American's face. 'Does it solve some problem?' he hinted gently, angling for a little clarification.

'Yes,' was all that David said.

'It makes sense to you?'

'It makes good sense.' Wonderful, wonderful sense. He felt like catching Jo round her waist and waltzing her across the terrace.

'Not to me,' Jo said. Her words were clipped. 'Notebooks, developments——'

'Later, Jo, later.' First let me get my thoughts straight. I never even dared hope for this news about Kusak.

'What is there to be so excited about?' Jo was angry. 'Hrádek is still alive, and Walter Krieger is lying helpless——'

'Now, now,' Weber broke in placatingly, 'not helpless. He is being most helpful. The fact that he is lying in a hospital bed proves that he was criminally attacked at Samaden airport. That assault verifies the actual time of Hrádek's presence at the airport yesterday evening. Hrádek was there, at that place, at that minute, and neither he nor any of his men can manage to deny it. Krieger has identified all their photographs.'

David said, 'Krieger—yes, trust Krieger to supply the finishing touch.' He checked his laughter: Jo was still too worried. 'Yes, Krieger really clinched it,' he told her.

'And what good is that? Hrádek is now outside Swiss jurisdiction. He is back in Czechoslovakia, plotting and planning and thinking of vengeance. He will, too.'

'Hrádek is finished, Jo.'

She said nothing, just kept watching his eyes.

'We managed it, Jo.' His voice had the true ring of confidence. 'We can stop thinking about Hrádek.'

She was almost persuaded. 'Hrádek has friends. Don't forget them, Dave. Because they won't forget us.'

'Cancel them too.' A few pages from Jaromir Kusak's notebooks had made sure of that. 'There is no more threat to any of us.'

'You really believe——' Jo hesitated. She was torn between doubt and hope.

'Yes.'

'And so does your friend Mr Krieger,' Weber said. 'I think this small item proves it.' He began fishing in his pockets for McCulloch's report.

Jo said slowly, 'You seem so sure, Dave. Have we really managed it?'

'Yes. You and I and Krieger and Irina. Above all, Irina.'

Weber had found the scrap of paper he was looking for, but his attention was caught by David's words. He didn't interrupt.

He waited, McCulloch's report in his hand: it could keep.

David was saying, 'Irina took the biggest risk, brought out two notebooks from Czechoslovakia, and doubled the danger to herself right then. They contained highly sensitive information, disastrous to Hrádek. He must have known or feared that such material could exist. When he learned that Irina had managed to bring it out of the country, he went into action. She was no longer a pawn in his game of tracking down her father. She became a prime target, someone who had to be destroyed along with the information she carried. She knew this could happen when she took the notebooks with her. If she had wanted to play safe, she would have left them behind.'

Weber said, 'And when did Hrádek learn that she had them?'

'Yesterday. Around noon.'

'But how?'

'From a telephone call made in Brixen by Mark Bohn.'

'Oh?'

David sidetracked the question by one of his own.

'What's that you've got in your hand, Weber? Another surprise?'

'No, no. Nothing important. Just a few words from Mr Krieger—a message he sent to McCulloch's office in Geneva. I think you will find it reassuring, Miss Corelli. Now, let me see——' His eyes searched through his tight script. 'Yes, here it is. *We have met the enemy, and they are ours.*' Weber began shredding the piece of paper. 'That's all,' he said. 'He has quite a turn of phrase, your Mr Krieger.'

'It's a quotation, isn't it?' asked Jo. She had recovered her smile. She might still be a tired girl, but she could smile. 'I know. Nelson said it.'

David shook his head.

'Then it's John Paul Jones.'

'Perry.'

'I knew it was someone nautical. It has that definite ring. Are you sure it wasn't Nelson? He's so quotable.'

'Kiss me, Hardy,' David said, and set Jo laughing. Her hand was no longer clenched tight, though it was still too cold. He released it gently as the waitress arrived. 'You'll need both of them for the ham and eggs. Eat them, will you?'

Jo nodded. 'Damn the calories! Full speed ahead!'

David caught Weber's astounded eye.

'Yes,' he agreed with him. 'We are possibly a little crazy at this moment.'

'Relief, of course. I understand.'

Either this, thought David, or tears.

Extraordinary people. Weber stopped watching them, and concentrated on his food. They were talking now about leaving Tarasp once they had eaten, and going to see Krieger. After what they had been through last night, really extraordinary. As for their journey here from Vienna—he had still to find out about that. It must have been much more than a long drive west. Jo, this morning, had been charming but vague. 'Dave will tell you about it,' she had said. Would he? Weber pushed his plate aside. 'I shall be leaving here too. I must be back in Geneva by this afternoon. Would you give me a lift as far as Samaden?'

'You do the driving, and it's a bargain,' David said.

'And after you see Mr Krieger, where are you going?'

Jo said, 'I'll fly to Zurich and get a plane for Rome. A few days there, and I'll be able to face a fashion show again. What about you, Dave?'

'I'll call in at Geneva.'

Ah yes, she thought, Geneva and Hugh McCulloch and talk about Irina. She poured herself one last cup of coffee and fell silent. Weber lit a cigar. David was looking at the valley below them. His thoughts were farther away than the mountains.